WALTZ IN THE WILDERNESS

CHAPARRAL HEARTS

KATHLEEN DENLY

Kristen,
I hope you enjoy this story!
Kathleen Denly

WILD HEART
BOOKS

The characters and events in this fictional work are the product of the author's imagination. Any resemblance to actual people, living or dead, is coincidental.

Unless otherwise indicated, all Scripture quotations are taken from the Holy Bible, Kings James Version.

Cover design by: Carpe Librum Book Design

ISBN-10: 1-942265-15-8

ISBN-13: 978-1-942265-15-3

To God who loves us more than we can comprehend and to my husband, for whom there are not enough words to express my gratitude and love.

Trust in the Lord with all thine heart; and lean not
unto thine own understanding.
In all thy ways acknowledge him, and he shall direct
thy paths.

— PROVERBS 3:5-6

ACKNOWLEDGMENTS

It is a myth that the writer's journey is a solitary one. Left to my own devices, this novel would be an embarrassing ramble of words no reader should be forced to slog through. That it is not, is owed to many people.

First, to my husband who never let me give up on my calling and stood by me through all the craziness that comes with trying to start a writing career while homeschooling four young children. His willingness to do more than his share of the household chores, attempt to keep our rowdies to a dull roar while I typed in the other room, help me act out action scenes (complete with cardboard knives), remind me to get my behind in the chair when distractions sang their siren song, and let me soak his shirt with tears when I was convinced I just couldn't juggle it all—his sacrifice and support are what made this novel possible. He is my real-life hero and the inspiration (on some level) for each of my fictional heroes.

I can't forget to thank my children who've knocked on my door five times in the space of twenty minutes (completely ignoring the *Writer at Work* sign), bickered loud enough to be heard through the walls and fried my laptop in a puddle of spilled water. They've also listened to me read aloud chapter-after-chapter, fetched me food when I've forgotten to eat because I was burning up the keyboard, and celebrated successes with me.

I have to thank my Super Beta Reader Squad. These women have been with me from the beginning and seen more iterations of this novel than I ever planned to write. Their tireless support, honest feedback, and ceaseless prayers as I climbed the mountains and sank into the valleys of this unpredictable writing journey have been a gift from God.

My sincerest gratitude to my first editor, Karen Ball, who set her own health issues aside and went above and beyond to help me meet my writing deadlines. Not only is she a true professional who knew exactly how to help me polish my manuscript while still keeping it *my* story, she is a true example of a woman striving to glorify God. God has used her on more than one occasion to touch my heart and I am blessed to know her.

My humble thanks to Misty Beller, my publisher, for taking a chance on this new author. Her patience and understanding helped make this path to publication as painless as possible. Also, I thank the staff at Wild Heart Publications for working so hard to get this novel into readers' hands.

I also want to thank my Kathleen's Readers' Club members, my Armchair Adventure Krew, and my Advance Readers who have supported me and cheered me on. Your enthusiasm and encouragement mean more than I can say.

Last, but most important of all, I thank God for this calling He has placed on my heart, the people He has put in my life to help me along the way, and the unending grace and love He shows me each and every day.

CHAPTER 1

"*N*o!"

The scream pierced Eli, ripping her from sleep. Cramming a fist in her mouth, she muffled her sobs. The voice that used to sing her nursery rhymes, pray for her, hum her to sleep. She couldn't hear it. Now it only came to her in echoes of that ghastly scream, tearing through her mind, shredding her heart.

No more. She clamped her hands over her ears, squeezed her eyes against the blackness.

Dark images forced their way in. Shovels of dirt falling onto that dear, beautiful face, skin pale with death, smile gone forever. Loving eyes shuttered. Arms that once comforted her now crossed over a faded blue bodice as the grave was filled in. Pa, her rock, crumpled on the ground. Inconsolable.

Stop! Don't think about it!

She sat up. Crawled from the tent. Cold night air slapped her cheeks. She hugged herself, rocking.

1

Her eyes sought the heavens, the weight of His gaze suffocating her. "Make it stop. Please. I'm sorry."

The pockmarked moon stared at her through the trees. *And the cow jumped over the moon.* The familiar tune crushed her heart.

A frosty breeze cut through her shirt. She shivered and ducked back inside.

Pa's snores continued. She curled onto her thin blanket, wrapping the end over herself.

Of course God wouldn't answer. It didn't matter.

Eli wouldn't fail again.

She forced her eyes shut. One of them needed to be thinking clearly come dawn. And it wouldn't be Pa.

~

*T*hey were going to starve to death, if they didn't freeze to death first. Sure, they had beans for dinner, but Eli'd had to trade her spare shirt for them—the one she'd been wearing beneath her everyday shirt to keep the early-October frost from biting her skin. She shivered beside the fire. Not much left to trade for supper, but then, there wasn't another miner in these diggings that had grub to spare even if she had something worth trading.

She studied each bean, careful not to burn a one. Her hollow stomach cramped as the sweet smell of the simmering meal mixed with the scent of wood smoke filling the air.

A pinch of rosemary would have added flavor. Would Mama have been disappointed Eli'd traded the last of their herbs for Pa's new coat? She shook her head. If Eli couldn't coax Pa from the creek, the least she could do was keep his shoulders warm. Mama would have understood.

A shift in the cold wind blew soot into Eli's eyes as she lifted the pan from the fire. Brushing a grimy strand of hair from her face and blinking away the sting, she turned her back to the smoke and stirred the beans.

Time to get Pa.

She walked to where he squatted in the icy mountain creek.

He wouldn't be happy she'd traded the spare shirt. He'd wanted it to hide her blossoming womanhood. Of course, he'd have to notice the shirt was gone first.

Standing beside the babbling water, she toed off her boots before yanking her tattered socks off. After stuffing them into a boot, she pulled up her trousers and, with a bracing breath, waded into the chilling water.

"Here, Pa."

She held the spoon out handle first, but he shrugged her away. Afternoon sunlight bounced off his thin, greasy hair—brown like hers, but darkened by muck. His dirt-encrusted brown eyes continued squinting into the swirling pan of water. The gentle rotation of his wrists never ceased.

"Come on, Pa. You gotta eat."

He cleared his throat and spat to the side opposite where she stood, never taking his eyes from the water. "I'm fine. You eat."

Eli lifted the spoon higher. "But, Pa—"

"I'll eat later." He shifted in the calf-deep water so that her worried stare landed squarely between his broad shoulder blades.

Her fingers tightened around the spoon as she planted her fist on her hip. The rocks shifted beneath her feet. "That's what you said this morning."

"I'm busy, Eli. Now hush and leave me be."

She stood there a moment longer, taking in the sight of him. That tall, too-thin frame draped in the now too-large, thread-bare shirt. She'd mended that thing more times than she could count. The trousers he kept up with a rope at his waist needed mending in the right knee, but she doubted the fabric could endure another stitching. She peered down at her own trousers.

3

The worn threads of the cuffs drifted and tugged with the current.

She frowned at the beans cooling in the pan. A body shouldn't have to choose between clothes and food. But miners upstream caught any fish in the creek, and hunting around here was pointless. All the digging, rattling, and mining commotion scared the game away.

She'd tried to coax Pa to leave their claim long enough to hunt elsewhere to no avail.

Mama could've convinced him.

Mama isn't here. Eli straightened her shoulders. "Pa, this is the last—"

"Hey, Eli!" The familiar voice cut her off.

She turned in time to see a small rock sail toward her head and managed to duck it, but the move upset her balance. She tipped backward.

The beans!

Contorting herself to right her balance without spilling their dinner, she wobbled back and forth as stones rocked beneath her. She shifted her footing, but the sloped face of a large, moss-covered rock hastened her descent. Holding the pan aloft as she fell backward, her body tilted sideways and she overcorrected—

Sending the beans spilling down her shirt and into the creek.

For a moment she sat still, the chill of the icy mountain runoff failing to cool her blood as gales of boyish laughter drifted toward her from the bank. She erupted from the creek, wielding her now-empty pan above her head. "Morgan Channing, I'm gonna have your hide for this!"

She sloshed three full steps to the edge of the creek before she froze.

The eleven-year-old had stopped laughing and was staring at her, mouth hanging open, eyes wide. "Y-you...! Y-you're a...a..."

Eli followed his gaze to her chest, where a few beans still

clung to her drenched, oversized shirt. She dropped the pan and covered herself. Oh, how brainless of her! Would Pa send her away?

"Here now, boy!" Pa jumped to stand between Eli and Morgan. "What're you doing? Thought you was supposed to be a friend. Did your pa send you over here? You trying to drive us out by starvation?"

Eli peeked around Pa. Morgan snapped to at Pa's suggestion that he and his pa were trying to steal their claim. Men had been killed over such suspicions.

Pa was thinner than Job's turkey now, but he still loomed over most men. His presence never failed to intimidate. He patted the ever-present Colt Walker at his waist.

"No! No, sir, Big Jim! I swear!" Morgan backed away, hands raised. "I was just funnin'. I didn't mean to make ya lose your fixin's, I swear it. Please, you gotta believe me. I'm sorry, sir."

"Oh yeah?" Pa scratched his bearded chin, making a show of considering Morgan's words. "And how am I supposed to know you're telling the truth?"

"I-I..." Morgan's eyes drifted downward and then shot back up again. "I'll bring ya my own fixin's to make up for it!"

Eli opened her mouth to protest, but it was no use.

The boy was already racing away. "Back in a jiffy!"

"Pa!" She swatted at his back, and he turned to face her. "We can't take his food!"

"We can and we will, *Son.* He's done us wrong, and it's only right that he should make amends."

"But—"

"And we needed to distract him from what he saw." He lifted an eyebrow, and she blushed. "Now get in that tent and out of sight before he gets back."

Snapping her mouth shut, Eli ducked into their tent, grateful for the one luxury they'd managed to keep since coming to the fields. She'd sold off everything else they owned, piece-by-piece, animal after animal, as the months turned into a year and all the gold those blowhard trappers and hornswoggling newspapers promised Pa had failed to appear. They hadn't even found enough to keep their bellies full and their bodies clothed.

She secured the flap and picked at her clinging clothes. Oh, for another set to change into. At least the tent blocked the breeze. She gathered the hem of her shirt and wrung it. Water streamed, trailing a muddy path across the dirt floor until it disappeared beneath the canvas wall.

She was wringing the hem of her trousers when Morgan returned, still apologizing. Pa gave him a brusque thanks mixed with a warning that it not happen again before sending him back to his camp.

Morgan's hurried footsteps faded away as the crunch of dirt beneath boots grew louder. Pa's quiet voice drifted through the flap. "You decent?"

She crossed her arms over her chest and tucked her chin. How could she have been so careless? "Yes, Pa." The words came out just louder than a whisper.

He lifted the flap and crawled inside like a three-legged dog, balancing a plate of beans in his right hand. "Here." He plunked it on the ground before her.

Her stomach rumbled, but she just stared at the plate. "You need to eat too, Pa. You haven't eaten all day." Had he eaten yesterday? She didn't think so.

When they'd first left Oregon for the gold fields, Pa's excitement gave her hope that he was healing, but the months of hard labor for little reward had worn him down. His enduring drive to succeed used to be comforting. Then, it grew to an obsession. If Pa sent her away because of what had happened with Morgan, who would remind Pa to eat?

His silence grew long and she lifted her head. He stared at her—no, *saw* her—in a way he hadn't seen her in months.

"Pa?"

His eyes pinched at the corners. He cleared his throat. "Eat. I'll be fine. I got work to do." He crawled toward the flap.

She leaned forward to follow, but he held up his hand. "You just stay here. Understand? It won't take me long to get our things together, so by the time you're done with those beans, we ought to be ready to go."

"Go?" It had taken weeks of pleading to convince Pa to bring her along to California instead of leaving her with neighbors in Oregon. He kept saying he wouldn't bring a female around so many lonely men.

"My Pa made that mistake," he told her during one of their many discussions. "My sister came with us when we went to Georgia. He thought we could keep her safe." Something had flickered in Pa's eyes. "He was wrong."

He never said more than that, but it was clear he wasn't changing his mind. Not until Eli dressed as a boy. Somehow, that made the difference.

But now…

She straightened. "You're not taking me back to Oregon, Pa. I won't stay there. You need me."

"Too late to make it, anyway." He turned away. "Snow's coming."

She grabbed his shoulder. "Then where are we going?"

He shook her hand off and glared at her. "How long you think it will take for Morgan to get over that scare I gave him and remember what he saw?" She opened her mouth, but he kept talking. "And when he does, how long you think it'll take him to go blabbin' the news all over these hills?"

"But…" She wanted to argue that Morgan could be trusted, but Pa was right. Secrets ate Morgan alive. It was only a matter of time before everyone around knew her secret.

"We've got to get before that happens." His gaze darted away. "Get someplace far away."

~

*T*hree days later, Eli rubbed her arms as Pa stepped up to the front door of the grand two-story house. She shivered and wiped the rain from her face. "Pa, are you sure this is the right one?"

He grunted and knocked on the elegant wood door.

As they waited, Eli took in the fancy carvings, delicate trim work, and second-story balcony decorating the front. She lifted a brow. Uncle Henry had set out west before her birth, so she'd never met him and Pa almost never spoke of him. What little Pa shared about his brother revealed they had once been close friends. Still...

Nothing Pa shared even *hinted* at Uncle Henry having the means to afford a home as grand as the one before them.

"Did Uncle Henry strike it rich?"

Pa shrugged without moving his gaze from the door.

Why did Pa never mention that Uncle Henry was in California? And that he lived as close as San Francisco? Three days ago, the slightest breeze could have felled her when Pa suggested they see if his younger brother would put them up for the winter.

Eli shifted from foot to foot. She glanced at Pa, still staring at the door. Come spring, they'd return to the cold, muddy fields in search of a new claim. It would be nice to spend the winter somewhere warm, but she didn't relish the idea of spending so much time with the kind of people who would own a house like this. When was the last time she held a sliver of soap? The dousing she'd given herself earlier this morning would have to do.

At last, a dark-skinned man in a long black waistcoat answered the door. "Yes?"

"I'm Jim Brooks, here to see my brother, Henry Davidson."

Eli looked at Pa. "Why's he got a different last name than you?"

Pa squinted at her. "Same ma, different pas. My ma married Henry's pa after my pa died when I was eight."

"So he's your half brother?"

Pa nodded as the servant motioned for them to enter, and Eli followed Pa out of the rain. Their wet boots squeaked on the sleek wood floor. A narrow table stood flush against the wall, topped with an expensive vase filled with dried flowers. A fancy mirror hung above it. Warmth radiated from an open doorway.

Why hadn't Pa suggested they visit his brother *last* winter?

A tall, dark-haired man wearing spectacles emerged from a doorway down the hall and hurried toward them.

"Jim!"

"Henry." Pa nodded. "I hope we're welcome."

Eli blinked at Pa. Why wouldn't they be welcome?

"Don't be ridiculous." Uncle Henry grinned as he pulled Pa into a tight hug.

Pa returned his brother's embrace before stepping back.

They stared at one another a moment before Henry took Pa's shoulders. "It's been too long, brother. Tell me, how are you?"

"Well, actually..."

Uncle Henry's gaze swung to Eli.

He offered his hand. "Oh, do forgive me. I'm Henry Davidson. Welcome to my home."

Eli accepted Uncle Henry's hand. "I—"

"This is Eliza, Henry."

Had someone come in behind them? Eli turned to see whom Pa was speaking of.

"My daughter."

Oh. Of course. It was so long since she'd heard her full name she'd almost forgotten it.

Uncle Henry's mouth rounded as he released her hand.

"Your…daughter?" He stared at her, eyes wide.

She drug her fingers through her chopped curls. So her hair was short and she was wearing trousers. So what? Did he have to stare like she'd just sprouted wings and flown about the hall?

He finally blinked. "Eliza?"

A click sounded down the hall. All three turned toward the noise as the most beautiful woman Eli had ever seen emerged from a dark room. She looked to have stepped straight off the fashion-plate pages the miners sometimes carried around in their pockets to stare at when they were lonely. The woman's rich brown silk dress glided across the floor as if her feet floated somewhere above the carpet. Blond hair hung in perfect ringlets on either side of her pale face. Her pink lips curled in a smile.

But it didn't quite reach her brilliant blue eyes.

The woman scrutinized Eli and Pa in a head-to-toe glance so swift Eli almost missed it. The tiniest lift of her chin said they'd been found wanting.

Eli scowled.

The woman paused beside Uncle Henry, laying a hand on his shoulder. "Henry dear, I can handle this."

Uncle Henry opened his mouth, but the woman had already spun to face Eli and Pa.

"I'm sorry. There seems to have been some misunderstanding with The Society. We are fully staffed." The woman lifted a hand toward the door, signaling they should leave.

Pa frowned. "But—"

"I'm terribly sorry for your inconvenience, but truthfully, were we in need of services, I'm afraid you would not do." The woman stepped around them toward the front door.

Eli clenched her fists. This wasn't the first time they'd been treated rudely, but she'd be hanged if she was going to stand here and take it from this slicked-up ninny. "We—"

"While we are sympathetic to your plight, we must insist on a certain level of personal cleanliness and pride in appearance."

"Why, you...!" Eli stepped forward, ready to plant a sockdollager on the ninny's smeller, but Pa caught her shoulders.

"Cecilia." Uncle Henry's face had grown redder with the woman's every word.

She raised her free hand to silence him. "Don't worry, darling. I'm sure they understand and there are plenty of positions with lower standards to which The Society can refer them."

Uncle Henry needed to bat Cecilia's hand away as Pa would have Ma's. Instead, he sucked in a deep breath, clamped his lips together, and squeezed his eyes shut.

Cecelia opened the door and poked her head outside, checking both directions before swinging it wide. "Now go, please, before someone sees you."

Uncle Henry's eyes flew open. "*Cecilia!*"

Cecilia jumped. She stared at him with wide eyes and a gaping, thankfully silent, mouth.

Eli pressed her lips against a cheer.

Uncle Henry spoke through his teeth. "Shut the door." He waited for the woman to comply. "Cecilia, this is my brother, Jim, and his daughter, Eliza."

Cecilia gasped. "Your..."

Eli sneered as the color drained from the ninny's cheeks.

Uncle Henry ran a hand down his face. "Jim, Eliza, this is my usually charming wife, Cecilia. I do hope you'll stay for supper and allow us the opportunity to make amends for this...misunderstanding."

Pa kept hold of Eli's shoulder as he accepted his brother's proffered hand. "Of course."

Eli forced her pinched lips to curl upward. Dinner, fine. She'd never turn down free food. But as soon as she could, she'd convince Pa to escape this snooty home. And she just might shove haughty Cecilia into the mud on her way out.

"Thank you." Uncle Henry smiled at Pa, then narrowed his

eyes at Cecilia. "They've had a long journey. Please instruct Martha to prepare rooms for them. I'm sure they would like to rest before joining us for supper."

"Yes, of course. You must be freezing in those wet clothes." Now all stiff smiles and open arms, Cecilia ushered them into a nearby room, which had carved furniture and a blazing hearth. "Come, you can warm yourselves by the fire while I fetch Martha to prepare your rooms." She hesitated, one fine brow arching. "I'll have her heat water for baths as well."

~

*E*li leaned back and rubbed her full belly through the soft, brown fabric of the maid's dress that she'd been blackmailed into wearing.

Two hours ago, she'd emerged from her bath to find someone had stolen her clothes. A pile of women's garments sat in their place. Eli shouted for Pa. Instead of fetching her clothes, he gave her a choice—wear the dress or go hungry. So she'd tugged the impractical thing over her head. But left the under-garments where they lay. The ninny might choose to suffocate herself with corsets and petticoats, but Eli wanted to be ready to run if the need arose.

A satisfying belch burst from her mouth and she had to admit—the meal was worth the sacrifice.

Her gaze settled on Cecilia's empty chair. Too bad the ninny had claimed a headache and disappeared. Her reaction might have been fun.

Uncle Henry pushed his chair back from the table and stood. "Shall we move to the drawing room, then?"

Eliza's eyelids tugged downward, but she forced them open.

Pa set his napkin on the table. "Did Amanda send you Pa's Bible when he passed?"

Uncle Henry quirked a brow as Pa stood. "Yes. Along with a

crateful of other things our sister thought I might like. Why do you ask?"

"It's in your study, I suppose."

Eliza eyed the door the servant had disappeared through. The kitchen must be that way.

Uncle Henry clapped his hands together. "Would you like to see it?"

Had she spoken her thoughts aloud? No. He was looking at Pa.

Pa faced the hallway. "You get to bed, Eliza." Without a glance in her direction, he strode from the room, Uncle Henry trailing behind.

Eliza blew a strand of hair from her face. As much as she'd love to find the kitchen and see what else the cook had stored, her eyelids insisted on slamming shut. After a moment, she forced them open and pushed herself to stand.

Instead of going to the room Cecilia had assigned her, she went to Pa's. They needed to discuss his acceptance of Uncle Henry's invitation for them to stay "as long as they liked." Putting up with the ninny, the dress, and all the Davidsons' daft ways of doing things for a single evening was one thing. What sort of halfwit needed to be escorted from one room to another? And what was with all those forks? But she was clean and her belly was full. It was time to find their clothes and vamoose. Eli flopped onto the fancy bed. Her fingers rubbed the soft blanket and she shifted. The puffy pillow crimped her neck. She yanked it out. Much better.

Across the room, strings dangled from the edges of the curtains. How silly was that? Most folks worked hard to keep the strings in their things from showing. Here they added them on purpose. She closed her eyes, shutting out the fancy nonsense.

∾

*E*liza bolted upright. What was that sound? And when had she fallen asleep?

"Eli!" Pa shut the door behind him. "What're you doing here?"

"What did you mean when you told Uncle Henry we'd stay here? I don't want to stay here. I want to go."

Pa stepped back and crossed his arms. "Go where?"

She threw her hands up. "I don't know. But not here with that snooty woman and creepy servants and...and..." She picked at the mattress. "Can we just go now? Please? We'll find a place. We always do."

His arched brow spoke volumes. "You want to go now? Sneak out in the middle of the night?"

"We can leave a note. They won't care anyway. Probably be glad to see the back of us."

Pa sighed. "Your mama must be rolling in her grave, the mess I've made of raising you."

Her gut cramped as the air rushed from her lungs. Why would he say that? She'd been trying so hard. Surely Mama wouldn't be ashamed of her. Would she? Tears stung her eyes. "Pa?"

His expression softened. He stepped forward and opened his arms. "I'm sorry, Eliza."

She scooted onto her knees on the bed and leaned into his bony embrace. His long arms didn't hold the strength they had when she was younger, but the comfort was there all the same.

He kissed the top of her head. "I'm so sorry."

She wanted to tell him it was all right, that she understood. The words stuck in her throat. She waited for him to explain his hurtful words about Mama, but he just held her. For a long time, they said nothing.

"All right. We can stay the night. Morning is soon enough to leave." She waited, but Pa didn't answer. "We can stay for breakfast, too. That way you can say good-bye real proper, and we'll have full bellies before we set out."

Still, Pa said nothing.

Her mouth grew dry, and she held him tighter. It wasn't like him to stay upset with her. Her full belly threatened to empty itself. She struggled to breathe. Was she such a disappointment?

At last, he whispered, "She loved you so much." He stroked her hair with one hand, still hugging her close with his other arm. He smelled of the lemon and spice fragrance he'd donned after his bath. When was the last time he'd worn cologne?

Not since Mama.

She slumped against him. No wonder he was so upset. All this fancy stuff...Mama had enjoyed it, too—though they never had as much as the Davidsons. Eli had almost forgotten how Mama always smelled of roses—even on the trail west. Being in this house must be reminding him of his promise to build Mama her own fancy home in Oregon. Of how they'd lost her before he could keep his promise. She squeezed her eyes shut. "I know, Pa. I'm so sorry."

"Don't say that. It's not your fault. Ain't none of this ever been your fault." He pulled back to wipe tears from his face. "It's mine."

He'd said this hundreds of times, but it wasn't true. She squeezed him again. "I love you, Pa."

"Love you, too, Angel." His voice broke, and silent sobs shook his shoulders.

Being around Uncle Henry must be bringing back strong memories. He hadn't cried this hard in years. Why hadn't Pa and Uncle Henry kept in better touch?

After a few minutes, she pried his arms loose and stood. "All right." Taking him by the shoulders, she eased him down onto his bed. "You go on to sleep now."

He nodded as the tears continued to fall.

She snagged the blanket from the foot of the bed and draped it over him.

He caught her hand. "Everything will be all right. You'll see."

She tipped her lips up and gave his hand a squeeze. "All right, Pa. Good night." She walked out, shutting the door behind her.

~

er mouth moved but her lips wouldn't open. She couldn't scream.

Eli bolted upright in bed, her breath coming in short spurts. Familiar pain sliced through her, her foolishness replaying in her mind. *No! It's over. Stop thinking about it!* When would the nightmares end? Shoulders tight, her fingers gripped smooth linens. Linens?

Her eyes popped open.

Heavy drapery pulled tight over a window cloaked the room in darkness. The flicker of a candle set on the mantle gave the only light. She widened her eyes to search the dim room, took in the fancy wallpaper and elegant furnishings...

This wasn't their cabin in Oregon. Where was she? How had she gotten here?

She tilted her head to one side and then the other. Aches and pains, her steady companions for months, were dulled by a good night's rest in a soft bed. She rubbed her belly. Full.

Like the growing spark of a wood fire, the memories came to her. She was in her uncle's house in San Francisco.

A groan escaped her.

She scrambled from the bed. Was it morning yet? She peeked through the curtains. Bright dawn sunshine spilled over the muddy streets below, causing her to squint. Good. One more meal and they'd be gone.

Spotting her men's clothes folded in a neat pile on a small table, Eli dressed and gathered her few belongings.

She paused before the mirror. Her men's clothes were clean now, thanks to one of the maids, but still so raggedy and stained it was difficult to tell the difference—aside from the lack of smell. What would it be like to wear something as fine as the fancied-up, blue plaid dress Cecilia wore to supper?

She snorted and spun away. The simple brown dress had been bad enough, tickling her legs all through dinner. Thank heavens she'd refused the corset and petticoats. Even the night-dress Cecilia loaned her had bunched around her knees until she sprang from the bed and changed back into her long under-wear. Silly frills.

Maybe the clothes were what made these women so unpleasant. *Thank you, Lord, that I don't have to worry about such nonsense.* She snapped her carpetbag shut, tightened the rope on her trousers, then combed her fingers through her hair.

Knock. Knock.

Must be Pa come to fetch me for breakfast. She snatched her bag, slung it over her shoulder, and strode across the room. She pulled open the door with a grin. "All ready to go, P—"

Her grin fell to a scowl.

A frowning maid stood before her.

"Oh." Eli frowned back at the woman. "What? Am I late for breakfast? Where's Pa?" Eli craned her neck to see past the maid down the hall. Empty.

The door to Pa's room stood open.

The maid wouldn't meet Eli's questioning look. Instead, the woman's gaze skittered about the room behind Eli. "Mr. Davidson asked me to fetch you. He wishes to speak with you before the meal is served."

Eli blinked. "What for?"

Finally, their gazes met. The maid's eyes were watery. Why was she so upset?

Shoving past the maid, Eli rushed down the hall. "Pa!" She

glanced into his room. He wasn't there. She stormed downstairs to the dining room. "Pa!"

Uncle Henry sat alone at the dining table sipping his coffee. He saw Eli and set his cup in its saucer. Why did he look so sad?

She whirled from the room, brushing past Cecilia. Uncle Henry called after her, but she raced back upstairs to Pa's room. The bed was made. No fire. She shoved her fingers into the ashes. Cold. She scanned the room. Not an item was out of place. She yanked open the wardrobe.

Empty.

Running into the hallway, she collided with Uncle Henry. He grasped her shoulders. She twisted away, sprinting down the hall.

"Pa!" She darted from door to door, flinging them open. Pa wasn't in any of the chambers. He wasn't in the parlor. He wasn't in the kitchen. She burst out the back door and crossed the yard to the stables. He wasn't with the horses.

"Pa!" Her throat clogged and she fought tears as she sank to the ground. What had he said last night? *I'm sorry...Everything will be all right. You'll see.*

Shivers snaked through her body. He'd been saying good-bye.

Oh, Pa! How could you?

Uncle Henry strode toward her. She stood, and he took hold of her shoulders. "Listen to me. Look at me."

She closed her eyes. Where would Pa have gone? Back to the claim? No. She'd seen him sign over his rights. To town then, to find work for the winter. But where?

Uncle Henry locked his arms around her and dragged her toward the house.

"No!" She wrestled to break free, but he proved stronger than he appeared. "I have to find Pa." He'd forget to eat, to bathe. He needed her.

Uncle Henry turned her to face him. "Jim is gone. He left last night. He's been gone for hours."

She froze. Her gaze snapped to his. "Last night?" She couldn't breathe.

"Yes."

A strangled cry ripped from her throat, and she felt herself falling. There were shouts, then hands. She was lifted. Her eyes closed as a moan escaped her soul.

Pa was gone.

And she'd never find him.

CHAPTER 2

*D*aniel thanked the postman and stepped away from the window. Tapping the single envelope against his palm, he strode past the long line of men who, like him, had been waiting hours for news from home. He scanned their weary faces. Perhaps they'd find more success than he. Not that he wasn't grateful for Mother's letter. Of course he was. But why had Alice still not written?

His employer's carriage drew to a stop across the yard. What were the Davidsons doing here? Didn't the rich families on their street have their mail delivered? A young woman vaulted from the carriage's confines, nearly bowling over the manservant opening the door.

Miss Brooks.

Daniel's gaze followed her striking figure as she wove her way toward the ladies' line. Whose letter was she so eager to receive that she could not await its delivery? A distant suitor, perhaps? He knew nothing about his employer's niece other than the fact that her beautiful brown curls distracted him from church service far too often. She always sat in the pew three rows in front of him, beside her aunt and uncle.

He tried to recall Alice's sweet face framed in pale blonde hair, but all he could summon was a blurry image.

He'd made the right decision yesterday.

He prayed that Mr. Davidson would understand.

Of course, he had the evening to get through first. *Lord, guide my words.*

~

*E*liza dashed past several groups of men discussing the latest news from the newly arrived, two-month-old papers. Three of the men were engaged in a heated debate, waving their papers in the air. She dodged an arm, just missing being struck.

A gentleman stood at the end of the long line leading from the ladies' window. She cleared her throat. The man peered over his shoulder. "Oh, excuse me, miss." He tipped his hat. "Please"— he stepped to the side and gestured for her to go before him —"ladies first."

She nodded her thanks. This was one of the few circum-stances in which she found benefit to the nonsensical rules of social conduct that Cecilia promoted so ardently. Stepping forward, Eliza leaned to the side and craned her neck to count the number of women ahead of her. Twenty-three. With a harrumph, she settled back into place and waited for the line to begin moving.

A moment later, Uncle Henry joined her. He gave her elbow a squeeze. "I could ask for you, you know."

She shook her head but let a smile soften her refusal.

He had made the same offer every two weeks since she

insisted on coming to the post office three months ago. She'd had enough of waiting for Pa's letters to arrive at the house.

Cecilia repeatedly told her that men were too busy to write letters to their children. "It was an anomaly that he wrote to you at all."

Cecilia was wrong. Pa loved Eliza and wouldn't stop writing to her without reason.

With each arrival of the mail steamer, she expected a bundle of letters and an apology from the postmaster explaining how they'd been set off at the wrong port or some such mix-up. Perhaps today would be the day they admitted their error.

Henry waved down a newsboy and procured one copy of the *New York Herald* and one of the *New York Tribune*. He handed her the *Tribune* and they both read as they waited.

Two hours later, the windows had finally opened and the line was creeping forward. She leaned sideways. How many women were still in front of her?

The conversation between two men walking past caught her ear, distracting her from her count.

"Another one died of cholera." One man, his nose buried in a paper, sighed.

His companion grunted and rustled his own paper. "Better than this one what died of gunshot, I reckon."

"Least the shot's quick."

"Not always. Remember Virgil..." The men's conversation faded beyond her hearing as they continued on their way.

Please, God, don't let that be it. She took a deep breath. She would not cry. *That can't be the reason.*

Uncle Henry squeezed her elbow, drawing her watery gaze to his face. "None of that now." He patted her shoulder as they stepped forward in the line. "Your pa is one of the toughest men I know. He's probably just up in a mountain somewhere afraid to leave his claim unattended."

She blinked until her vision cleared. "His last letter said he was working on a dike in San Diego."

"It said he was going to *inquire* about working on a dike in San Diego." He squinted at her. "That doesn't mean he got the job or that he didn't get distracted once he was down there."

"But what if—"

Henry held up his free hand. "No."

Eliza pulled her elbow free and pivoted to face him, lifting her chin for the too-familiar battle. "If he's hurt or sick, he needs me."

"He's a grown man, Eliza. He knows how to care for himself."

Uncle Henry still resents Pa for stealing Mama's heart away from him. That's why he doesn't want me to go after Pa.

Eliza pushed away the nasty thought. It took her weeks after Pa left to get the reason for the brothers' estrangement out of her uncle. He claimed to be over the hurt, but if that were so, wouldn't he be more concerned? "He—"

"Eliza, I said no." His voice rose. "Whether you like it or not, a young woman has no business traipsing around the wilderness unescorted." He glanced around. Several curious faces looked their way. He continued in a much lower voice. "This is one instance in which your aunt is correct. It is neither safe nor decent for you to go searching for your father alone, and I simply cannot be away from my businesses at this time. Perhaps in another month or two, but not now. And I don't want to hear another word about it."

She swallowed her retort. She was being unfair. His businesses *were* struggling. They were far less profitable than they'd been before this recent decline.

The woman in front of her stepped away from the window. At last. Eliza gave the clerk her name and tucked the newspaper under her arm as the man proceeded to search for a letter addressed to her. Several minutes passed before he returned to the window.

"I'm sorry, miss. I have no letters addressed to that name."

"Try Eli Brooks."

The clerk looked as if he'd sucked a lemon. "I have, miss. I do remember you."

She gritted her teeth. "Well, look again."

"Eliza," Henry whispered.

"Yes, miss." The clerk searched for another moment before returning with a stony expression. "I'm sorry, miss."

"That's not possible. You must not be looking in the right place. Here"—Eliza reached into her reticule and retrieved Pa's last letter—"look at his handwriting again. Perhaps that will help."

The man didn't even glance at the letter. "I'm sorry, miss. There are no letters addressed to either an Eliza Brooks or an Eli Brooks. There are no letters addressed to simply Eliza. There are no unaddressed letters that match the handwriting on the letter that you have shown me every two weeks for the past three months. And no, you may not come in and look for yourself." As he spoke, the clerk's voice grew louder until a clearing throat interrupted him.

The postmaster took the clerk's place at the window. "Good day, Miss Brooks. I'm so glad to see you. I wanted you to know that, per our discussion two weeks ago, I did give special attention to searching each and every letter that came in for any hint that it might have been written by your father for delivery to you. Unfortunately, as my clerk has already informed you, I was unsuccessful in my search."

A wind gust cast one of Eliza's curls into her face. She swatted it away.

The smile on the postmaster's face didn't hide the steel in his eyes. "However, I will be pleased to continue my search as the day continues and, should a letter of such description come to my attention, I will deliver it myself posthaste to the address that you so generously provided for me upon our last meeting. I appreciate your understanding our need to keep the lines moving at this time in deference to our other applicants." He gestured to the women waiting behind her. "I do thank you for stopping by and, if I do not see you sooner, I will look forward to speaking with you upon the arrival of the next mail steamer."

She opened her mouth to protest, but Henry snatched her elbow and tugged her from the window.

"Thank you, sir," Henry spoke over his shoulder as he steered her away.

Eliza yanked free and spun toward the window. Another woman blocked it. Eliza turned to Henry, hands on her hips. "Why did you do that?"

"To avoid the scene you caused last time, of course. Do not mistake my defending you to your aunt as approval of your behavior. I do not enjoy your scenes any more than she does." He glanced around them. "Ah. Here is Frank. I asked him to return for you once he had delivered Cecilia. I have other business to attend, but he'll see you home."

~

What has happened to Pa? Eliza rapped the folded newspaper against her palm as she counted the months since the arrival of Pa's last letter. *Four.*

She stepped into the entryway of Uncle Henry's home and pulled the cord that would ring a bell in the kitchen, letting the housekeeper know she'd returned. She set the *New York Herald* on the side table before untying her bonnet. With the felt brim clutched in her hands, she squeezed her eyes shut as the newspapers' horrors swarmed her mind. *Died of cholera. Died of fever. Died of pistol shot wound to the abdomen. Drowned. Stabbed. Lynched.*

With effort, Eliza closed her mind to the possibilities. Pa was alive.

Please, Lord. Keep Pa safe. Amen.

Opening her eyes, she lifted her chin to inspect her appearance in the framed mirror on the wall. Two wavy, brown hairs were loose. She should have been more careful removing her bonnet. Tucking the stray hairs back into her bun, she eyed the curls on either side of her face. Satisfied that they'd not been disheveled by the strong breezes at the wharf, she left her bonnet on the side table and proceeded down the hall. Where had Amelia got to? She ought to have come to the foyer by now.

Ah. There she was.

The Davidsons' latest housekeeper was entering the dining room with a precarious armload of dishes, glassware, and silverware. A sheen of sweat glistened on her forehead.

"Amelia Murphy!" Eliza hurried to relieve the woman of the rattling glassware. "What have I instructed you about setting the table?"

"Not to carry too much at once, miss." Amelia's round cheeks flushed as she shifted the delicate dinner plates in her short arms. She bent her right arm to swipe at several red hairs sticking to her sweaty forehead. "But the missus asked me to prepare a full-course meal, and I'm run off me feet as it is."

"She—"

"Oh!" Amelia's large green eyes widened and her jaw sagged, jiggling her second chin. "The pie!" She dropped her load of plates and silverware onto the table with a terrible crash and dashed out of the room.

Pursing her lips, Eliza marched to the table, set down the glassware, and lifted a plate to inspect it for cracks. If Amelia had broken one it would be the third this month.

Why did Cecilia tolerate the woman's distracted nature, never mind her complete inability to remember the simplest of instructions from one day to the next? After the second cracked plate, Eliza had argued for Amelia's dismissal, but Cecilia would not hear it. She reminded Eliza that Amelia was their fifth housekeeper this year, and she refused to dismiss another one for "failing to live up to Eliza's exacting standards."

Eliza snorted as she set down one plate and picked up the next.

Cecilia had claimed it was unfair to the women they'd employed to expect such perfection, but Eliza couldn't help that the women sent to them by the San Francisco Ladies' Protection and Relief Society had all been incompetent layabouts.

She winced as she picked up another plate and ran her fingers across its smooth surface. All right, so *layabout* was an exaggeration. With the downturn in her uncle's business, the family relied on two servants to accomplish the tasks once performed by a staff of six. Still, shouldn't a housekeeper perform her duties with efficiency and attention to detail? Eliza wasn't asking them to do anything she herself couldn't do. And that was just it, wasn't it?

Eliza drew a deep breath and blew it out.

"Looking for more to complain about?"

Eliza whirled toward the hall as Cecilia glided through the doorway. "She was carrying too much again and let it all crash onto the table. I'm checking whether she's cracked anything."

"Too much, too little." Cecilia tisked as she approached the table. "These women can never do anything right in your eyes. What would you have me do? Turn them all out and leave the tasks to you?"

"I'd do a better job and save Uncle the money he spends replacing dishware broken by careless hands."

Cecilia laughed. "Utterly unsuitable. As much as you eschew the position, you are a gentleman's niece and are expected to behave as such." She lifted a glass and appeared to inspect it. "Besides, where would Mrs. Murphy go?"

Eliza stifled a snort. As if that were Cecilia's true concern and not the risk of offending her friends at The Society.

Cecilia set down one glass and lifted another. "These women turn to The Society for aid because their sons and husbands have gone off to the mines and left them to fend for themselves. The last time we let a housekeeper go, Mrs. Swenson reminded me that we have far more women in need than positions available these days. I would think you, of all people, would be a little more understanding of their situation."

Eliza's fingers squeaked across the plate's surface. Of course she understood. Too well. It was Cecilia who didn't understand. Amelia and the other housekeepers were a daily reminder of exactly what Eliza understood—she'd been abandoned.

No. Eliza wasn't like them. Pa hadn't left her in the streets. He brought her to Uncle Henry because he thought staying here and learning to be a lady was what Mama would have wanted. It didn't matter that he was wrong. His intentions had been pure and loving and she would do anything to reunite with him. If he had ever stayed in one place long enough over these past four years, she'd have found a way to join him long before his letters stopped.

But these women. Most of them knew exactly where their men were, yet not one of these women had the courage to go after their men—to find them and make them listen.

What was it that made a man think it was necessary to abandon the women in his life? California was crawling with men who'd left their families behind—if not in San Francisco, then somewhere back east. Didn't they love their wives, mothers, and daughters? Didn't they understand they were needed far more than any gold they might—

Was that a chip in the surface?

Eliza tilted the plate to catch the light. Just a water spot. With a sigh, she huffed on its surface and used the fabric of her skirt to wipe it away. Having satisfied herself that none of the plates were cracked and all were spot-free, she placed them about the table. Seeing that her uncle enjoyed a pleasant meal at the end of each work day was one of the small ways she'd found to repay his kindness. He should be able to rely on his wife and housekeeper to oversee the task, but as usua—

Wait. She counted again. *Four dinner plates.* She sighed. Amelia had miscounted. She stepped toward the kitchen with the extra plate.

"If you're headed to the kitchen"—Cecilia's voice trailed after her—"please remind Mrs. Murphy that we have a guest joining us for supper this evening."

Eliza's hand froze on the kitchen doorknob. She counted to ten before turning. "I thought we understood one another."

Cecilia didn't glance up from her inspection of the place settings. "Whatever do you mean?"

Eliza waved the extra plate. "I thought you had given up your endeavors to marry me off. I thought you understood, after Mr. Anders practically ran from your last supper disaster." She sliced her empty hand through the air in an imitation of Mr. Anders's hasty departure. "The man who will accept me as I am doesn't exist."

Cecilia opened her mouth, but Eliza held up a finger as she returned to the table. "And before you say it, I am not interested in changing." She thumped the plate onto the table.

Cecilia's cold gaze lifted to Eliza's. "Are you quite through?"

What could she say that she hadn't already said in a prior conversation? She shrugged.

"Good." Cecilia folded her hands.

Eliza inwardly cringed. How many times had her aunt admonished her not to gesture when speaking? She'd forgotten again.

"First, I should like to remind you that this is my home and that you are here out of the kindness of my heart."

Eliza sucked in her lips. *More like the kindness of Uncle Henry's heart.*

Cecilia had been so determined to turn Eliza into a lady. A determination that disappeared after Eliza's uncensored tongue humiliated her at a Society fundraising event last year. Cecilia was so incensed, she tried to get Henry to kick Eliza out. Blessedly, Henry had held firm in his refusal.

"Second, although I do endeavor to take your preferences into consideration whenever possible, as a guest in this house, you have no say in whom we choose to invite to dinner. Should you find yourself unable to refrain from improper behavior, such as you have done on too many occasions in the past"—the knuckles on Cecilia's hands whitened—"you are welcome to excuse yourself politely and retire to your room."

~

JUNE 1853 (7 MONTHS BEFORE)
ROXBURY, MASSACHUSETTS

*A*lice Stevens tossed another crumpled letter into the fire. It was no use. How could she find the correct words when she didn't know what she wanted to say?

She stood and paced the confines of her chamber. Her foot tangled in a heap of crumpled silk. With a huff, she scooped her younger sister's nightdress from the floor and tossed it onto their unmade bed. Surveying the chaos, she rubbed her forehead. Three days until their new maid arrived. Yanking the nightdress from the bed, she dropped it back to the floor. A few flicks and tugs had the bed to rights. She folded Caroline's nightdress and returned it to the wardrobe.

Her friends would be horrified to learn the depths her family sank to each time a maid couldn't hold her tongue about her father's indiscretions. Though many of her acquaintances were not of a class to employ a lady's maid, they expected more of her family, given Father's lineage. Yet there was a limit to how many of Father's dalliances her mother's substantial dowry could cover. The money was running out. The servants murmured in the halls. Soon, there would be whispers in parlors and ballrooms across the city.

Alice *must* marry.

She stalked back to the small table she employed as a desk. Daniel simply *had* to return and fulfill his promises. He was the only man she trusted to do so. She had hoped...but no. Shaking her head, she took a seat and lifted her pen.

My dearest Daniel,

I sincerely apologize for the delay in my response to your lovely letters. While I have enjoyed reading of your continued success in California, I must confess—

Shouting rose from the first floor. Alice stood and hurried down the hall.

Her brother's voice carried up the stairs. "That money was not yours to spend, you greedy oaf!"

"Watch how you speak to your father, boy."

After a year away, the first thing Richard did was start an argument with Father?

"I haven't been a boy for a long time, thanks to you. That money was mine!"

Did Richard have to shout so? The neighbors might hear.

A maid poked her head from the guest chamber, her ear cocked to the scene below.

Heat flushed Alice's body. Richard had little more sense of propriety and discretion than Father.

"Balderdash! I haven't the time for this. When I return, you'd better have come to your senses."

She rushed down the stairs in time to see the front door slam behind Father.

Richard spun from the closed door and stormed into the

parlor.

She followed him.

He stopped in front of Mother, who, as usual, sat wet-faced and weary upon the settee. Richard pointed toward the door. "I have not spent the past several months slaving as a sawyer so that that oaf could waste the money I sent you on fripperies for his—"

"Richard!" Alice kept her voice to a harsh whisper. "Lower your voice. Do you want the servants to hear you?"

"I do not care."

"Well, you ought." Alice crossed her arms. "Last week we had to let go our lady's maid and our dairymaid after I caught them in the barn gossiping about Father. One can only imagine what they've been saying about town. I—"

Richard splayed his arms toward Mother. "Which is exactly why you must allow me to take you away from here. Let me take you to California, where you'll be safe from the humiliation and pain he causes you. The mining companies are said to pay an excellent wage." Richard dropped to one knee and took Mother's hand. "I'd be able to support us. You've read what Daniel says about the growth there. San Francisco is becoming a real city with houses as grand as we have here. Why will you not consider it?"

Alice rolled her eyes. "You cannot be serious. Besides, Mother's leaving would only confirm any rumors tha—"

"Heaven forbid." He covered his mouth, widening his eyes.

"Hush, children." Mother's soft command silenced them. She turned to Richard. "As a man with your lineage, you can afford to be less concerned with such things. However, I have your sisters' futures to consider—"

"As you've said for years." Richard splayed his hands. "But they are settled now, even Caroline is engaged."

"They are not yet married. Which reminds me—" she pinned narrowed eyes on Alice—"Have you completed your letter?"

CHAPTER 3

*A*s Daniel approached his employer's four-story home that evening, he glanced up and his steps faltered in the middle of the street. Miss Brooks stood on the second-floor balcony, bathed in the golden rays of the setting sun. Her expression as she stared out to sea held such intense longing that a strange desire grew deep within him to fulfill whatever it was she yearned for.

Lord, I don't know what it is she wants, but won't you please grant her peace?

Pulling his gaze from Miss Brooks, he continued his approach to the house and knocked.

The Davidsons' manservant opened the door and led him upstairs to the drawing room, where he announced Daniel's arrival.

As Mr. and Mrs. Davidson greeted him, Miss Brooks entered from the balcony. The last rays of the sun followed her in, adding a soft glow to her rich brown curls.

Mr. Davidson smiled at Daniel, then at his niece. "Miss Brooks, allow me to make you acquainted with Mr. Clarke." He gestured to the crown molding that had been Daniel's bane for several days as he struggled to coerce the stubborn oak to yield the intricate leaves and flowers Mrs. Davidson requested. "Mr. Clarke is the talented carpenter responsible for the fine home in which you now stand, and he oversees my projects in Happy Valley."

Mr. Davidson lifted his hand toward Miss Brooks. "Mr. Clarke, my niece, Miss Brooks, who has been staying with us these three years past."

Miss Brooks gave a little curtsy. "I am glad to meet you, Mr. Clarke."

Daniel bowed. "The pleasure is mine, Miss Brooks." He tilted his head toward the balcony. "A beautiful sunset this evening, is it not?"

Dimples appeared in Miss Brooks's cheeks. "It is indeed, and the balcony that you so finely constructed affords me a perfect view of it."

"Are you not also responsible for our exquisite drawing room set, Mr. Clarke?" Mrs. Davidson indicated the two sofas, two armchairs, and four side chairs, all upholstered in a light-blue silk to match the drapery, and the ornately carved round-table topped with white marble. It had taken him the better part of a year to create the set.

"I am, ma'am."

"I thought as much." Her lips curved upward. "This is Miss Brooks's favorite set in all the house. She spends half her day here and is forever exclaiming about its beauty and comfort."

A pink tinge appeared on Miss Brooks's cheeks and her lower lip tucked in. Although flattered by Mrs. Davidson's claims, he doubted their verity. "And you, Mrs. Davidson? How do you spend your day?"

Miss Brooks chose that moment to turn and retrieve a book from an end table.

Daniel spent the next several minutes conversing with the Davidsons while their niece all but buried her nose in the book. Though her aunt tried multiple times to draw Miss Brooks into their conversation, the beauty proved adept at succinct answers that allowed her to return to reading. His finger drummed his thigh. Her beauty disguised an ugly self-centeredness.

At last, the Davidsons' manservant returned to announce that dinner was ready. Daniel offered his arm to Mrs. Davidson, but she stepped away.

"Oh, you don't need to escort me, Mr. Clarke." She minced across the room to take her husband's arm. "I have my husband, you see. It is Miss Brooks who requires an escort."

Daniel's cheeks warmed as his hostess all but dragged her husband in the direction of the dining room.

Swallowing his embarrassment, Daniel offered his arm to Miss Brooks, who'd finally set aside her book.

Her blazing eyes caused him to withdraw.

"Miss Brooks?" He offered his arm again, but she did not take it. She did not even look at him. Was she offended he hadn't offered to escort her first? Offering to escort Mrs. Davidson was the proper thing to do. Etiquette dictated that he should escort his hostess and that Henry should escort Miss Brooks. "What's wr—"

She strode from the room.

~

*H*eat scorched Eliza's face as she marched to the dining room. Were she a teakettle, she'd be whistling. For the first time in more than three years, Cecilia had broken propriety by insisting that Mr. Clarke escort Eliza. Left him no choice, in fact, but to offer Eliza his arm.

Cecilia must be getting desperate. Eliza squared her shoulders as she entered the dining room. Her aunt had underestimated her.

When Eliza entered alone, Cecilia's mouth gaped, then snapped shut. Eliza smothered a laugh and waited beside her chair for Mr. Clarke, who had followed her. He performed his duty of assisting her to be seated before seating himself across from her.

Her aunt's composure returned, blue eyes glinting.

Eliza lifted her chin, holding Cecilia's gaze until Uncle Henry began to say grace.

At the close of grace, Frank entered the room with a plate of oysters in their half-shells. Had her instructions for their neat arrangement been followed? Eliza strained her neck for a better view. Their points were together at the center of the plate, where fresh lemon slices accented the dish. She relaxed. Perfect.

Henry accepted his oysters and then addressed Mr. Clarke.

Eliza peered at Cecilia's newest candidate through her lashes. At least he was young. Mr. Anders was fifteen years her senior if not more, whereas Mr. Clarke appeared to be near her age. His hygiene was an improvement as well. Mr. Anders reeked of the oil he used to slick over his thinning blonde hair, and he allowed his whiskers to grow unchecked in the way that was popular among the miners. She shuddered.

Mr. Clarke's curly, dark hair was thick and trimmed. His face was freshly shaven, and when he laughed at Henry's quotation of the newspaper humorist, Squibob, dimples dented his cheeks.

Mr. Anders smiled only when being complimented. He never laughed.

In short, Mr. Clarke appeared different in every way from the older, well-established gentlemen Cecilia had invited to dine nearly every week for the past six months. Did Cecilia think this change would make Eliza more amenable to her machinations?

Eliza jerked her glass from the table, sloshing a drop of elderberry wine over the rim. She wanted to explain to Cecilia in no uncertain terms that if and when she married, it would be when she was ready and not because her aunt wanted her gone. However, antagonizing Cecilia was foolishness when Eliza did not know how long it might take to set her plans in motion. Until then, she was dependent upon her uncle's generosity to keep and house her. The savings she needed to execute her plan would be greatly reduced were she to find herself with the expense of room and board in San Francisco.

Eliza bit her lip. Respectable lodging might not even be offered to her should her uncle choose to put her out without a reference.

Cecilia inspected her oysters before addressing their guest. "Have you spent any time mining, Mr. Clarke?"

"But of course, ma'am." Daniel returned his glass to the table. "When I first arrived in '49, I headed straight for the rivers with everyone else. Unlike most, however, I was soon blessed and thus decided to quit while I was ahead."

"Did you indeed, sir?" Henry's brows lifted. "I have not heard this tale before. Tell me, how did you find your fortune?"

Frank served the baked salmon as Mr. Clarke enthralled her uncle with what must be a more entertaining variation on the true facts of his discovery. To hear his tale, one would think finding gold were as easy as bending to retrieve a dropped kerchief. She stabbed a piece of salmon. Years of her own back-breaking labor belied the rosy picture their guest painted of a miner's life.

Frank served the roast beef followed by the salad as the conversation drifted to the writings of Charles Dickens.

"I declare, *Pickwick Papers* is by far the funniest book I've ever read." Uncle Henry set down his fork. "And my favorite. Though, I've not yet had the opportunity to read his latest... Oh, what is its title?" Henry rubbed the side of his face, his eyes narrowed.

Eliza speared another mound of lettuce. *"Bleak House."*

Henry beamed at Eliza. "Yes! *Bleak House!* That's the one."

"Pickwick Papers is amusing, I'll grant you"—Mr. Clarke cocked his head—"but I find *Oliver Twist* to be more moving, and so I find I like it rather better."

Mr. Clarke shifted toward her. "What about you, Miss Brooks? Are you a fan of Dickens?"

Her mouth fell open. None of their other guests had shown interest in her opinion. Was he truly interested or merely feeling guilty for leaving her out of the conversation?

Cecilia took advantage of Eliza's hesitation. "Oh, indeed! Eliza is a great reader and is Mr. Dickens's greatest fan." Then without taking a breath, her aunt ventured into the topic Eliza dreaded. "Such a shared interest must be a rare find in such a beautiful young woman. Do you not agree, Mr. Clarke? Many women are prevented from such extensive reading by the necessary attentions to their appearance, but Eliza's beauty is so natural, she has all the time in the world to pursue other passions."

Mr. Clarke's smile tightened as his gaze bounced from Cecilia to Eliza. He shifted in his seat.

Eliza opened her mouth to reassure him she had no interest in him, then hesitated. He was displeased by the prospect of being matched with her. Her mouth snapped shut. Did he think her unattractive? Why should she care? Her spine straightened as Cecilia continued.

"Henry has a copy of *Hard Times.* I am certain if you ask her, Eliza will grace us with a reading when we retire to the drawing room."

Mr. Clarke cocked an eye at Eliza.

She ducked her head and fiddled with the fabric of her skirt, waiting for him to speak—to make clear his disinterest in her. Seconds ticked by in silence.

What was he thinking?

~

*D*aniel's shoulders sagged. He'd been too slow in bringing the conversation round to the news of his departure and betrothal. *Lord, help me.* Mrs. Davidson could not have been more obvious. Why hadn't he foreseen this possibility and made his announcement sooner? The moment he entered the drawing room, he should have declared his plans and been done with the matter. He could have avoided this entire debacle.

It was on the tip of his tongue to decline Mrs. Davidson's suggestion, when his gaze connected with Eliza's. An unmistakable flash of hurt flickered in her eyes before she lowered her head again, her cheeks rosy. His situation demanded a blatant rejection. Still...

No. He would not injure her further. He forced his lips upward. "It would be an honor."

Miss Brooks's head jerked up, her eyes bulging. Far from soothed, the woman was angry. Oh, what a mess. He must make himself clear before the situation grew worse.

CHAPTER 4

*D*aniel opened his mouth to speak.

"Wonderful!" Mrs. Davidson beamed at him. "And here is dessert. I do hope you like apple pie, Mr. Clarke. Our cook has used the last of our dried apples in preparing it."

The Davidsons' manservant placed a plate with a slice of warm pie before him. The fragrance of cinnamon and apples filled his nose, causing his mouth to water.

"As it happens, Mrs. Davidson, apple pie is one of my favorite desserts as it reminds me of my mother—"

"How truly amazing!"

Again, the woman forestalled him from raising the issue of his departure.

"Why, apple pie is Eliza's favorite dessert as well." Mrs. Davidson beamed at him. "The two of you have so much in common. We shall have to invite you to dine with us again soon."

"Oh, what utter nonsense!" Miss Brooks jerked back her chair and stood.

Daniel sprang to his feet.

"Oh, *do* sit down, Mr. Clarke." She waved at him. "You've

done quite enough, I think, to encourage my aunt's ridiculous scheming."

"I beg your pardon?" He drew himself to his full height. He'd done nothing to deserve such treatment. How dare she speak to him in such a manner?

Mr. Davidson stood. "Eliza!"

She lifted her hands toward her uncle. "I'm sorry, Uncle Henry, but I am at my end with Cecilia's humiliating attempts to marry me off. Am I so very horrid to live with?" Eliza jabbed her finger at Daniel. "And for you to encourage her!" She raised her arms before lowering her hands to rest on her hips. "Well, I'm sorry, Mr. Clarke, but I am not interested in marrying you simply because society has determined that I am of marriageable age and my guardian has no more wish of my presence."

"Then we are agreed, Miss Brooks, for neither am I interested in marrying you."

At his near shout, Eliza dropped her hands and stepped back, eyes wide.

That was too harsh. He lowered his voice, though he could not gentle it. "I am, in fact, already betrothed to Miss Alice Stevens of Roxbury, Massachus—"

"*Truly,* Cecilia!" Eliza glared at her aunt. "This is a new low, even for you. To invite a promised man—"

Mr. Davidson cleared his throat. "*I* invited, Mr. Clarke, Eliza."

Eliza whirled toward her uncle. "What?"

Daniel swallowed a groan.

Eliza's wide eyes blinked at him over flushed cheeks and lips pressed tight. Her shoulders slumped.

He ran a hand through his hair then straightened his shoulders. "Sir, it was my intention, after we completed our meal, to announce my planned departure for the Atlantic States on the steamship *Virginia* in less than two weeks' time."

Mr. Davidson scratched his chin. "I see—"

41

"The *Virginia!*" Mrs. Davidson's over-bright smile implored him to allow her a change of subject. "Why Captain Swenson has charge of that ship. His wife is a dear friend, though I am sorry to say she plans to leave us soon to return to her family in New York. Have you had the pleasure of making her acquaintance during your time here?"

He'd distressed his hostess. How had he allowed his temper to take such control of him?

Miss Brooks slipped into her seat, drawing his attention. Her dark lashes hid downcast eyes.

Daniel took a deep breath. *Lord, forgive my hasty temper. Help me to be as patient with others as You are with me.* His peace renewed, he returned to his seat and Mr. Davidson followed suit.

Daniel sank his fork into the pie, cutting off a bite-sized piece. "I have not had the pleasure of meeting Mrs. Swenson."

"Oh, that is a shame, for she is the kindest lady you will ever meet and has been such a help with our Ladies' Protection and Relief Society. I do not know how we shall get on without her."

For the next half hour, Mrs. Davidson extolled the many virtues of the apparently saint-worthy Mrs. Swenson and chattered on about the various activities of the Ladies' Protection and Relief Society. By the time the pie was gone, so was Daniel's sense of peace—eaten away by the palpable tension still lingering in the room.

An ache grew in his head.

At last, Mrs. Davidson invited Miss Brooks to follow her to the drawing room for coffee and suggested that the gentlemen soon join them for continued conversation.

Daniel pushed back his chair. "My sincerest apologies, ma'am. My day's work has left me more fatigued than I would like and I find I must excuse myself earlier than I had hoped." He stood. "Mr. Davidson, it has been an honor to know you and to be in your employ. Please excuse my early departure. I have a long day's work tomorrow."

"Certainly, Mr. Clarke. I understand." Mr. Davidson walked past Daniel. "Please allow me to escort you to the door."

In the front hall, Mr. Davidson rubbed the back of his neck. "Please accept my apologies for my niece's behavior this evening. She lost her mother at an early age and her father..." He spread his arms with a shrug. "Well, I'm afraid her upbringing was somewhat lacking. My Cecilia is trying to fill the gaps, but my young niece does not always appreciate her efforts."

"Apology accepted, of course. After all, we cannot choose our relations, and family can be complicated."

Mr. Davidson exhaled. "Yes. Exactly. I'm glad you understand." He rubbed his cheek. "So you depart with the *Virginia*, then?"

"I do, sir."

Mr. Davidson frowned. "You've been the only reliable carpenter I've worked with in this city. Too many men wandering off to the fields at a moment's notice. Had the evening gone as planned, it was my intention to offer you a raise to stay on to help build a new shop on some property I've purchased near the waterfront. Are you certain I can't talk you into staying another month at least? I could offer you as much as sixteen dollars."

Daniel steeled himself against Mr. Davidson's hopeful gaze and generous offer.

"My fiancée is anxiously awaiting my return, sir." *I hope.* No, of course she was. There was any number of explanations for—

"Well, you sail in very fine hands, then." Mr. Davidson adjusted his spectacles. "Captain Swenson has transported a great deal of my goods, and I've sailed with him on more than one occasion myself. There was one squall, I recall, when I was certain we would perish and I would never see my dear wife again, but Captain Swenson brought us all through safely. He'll do the same for you, I'm sure."

"Glad to hear it, sir." He didn't mention that he'd heard mixed reports of Captain Swenson.

Mr. Davidson extended his hand. "I'll see you in the valley next week to check on our progress?"

"Yes, sir." Daniel accepted his hand. "The work should be nearly complete by then."

"Good."

"Good evening, sir." Daniel turned to leave and caught sight of Miss Brooks peering into the hallway. She'd been eavesdropping. He flicked his gaze upward. Miss Brooks was one of the most puzzling women he'd ever met.

The Davidson's manservant opened the door.

Daniel pressed his lips in a mild grimace. Thank heaven he was not obliged to figure her out.

CHAPTER 5

*S*lipping into the parlor, Eliza sucked in a breath. She counted down from ten as the front door closed behind Mr. Clarke and Uncle Henry returned to the dining room. How could her uncle have said such awful things? Her upbringing had been...well, that didn't matter. Uncle Henry ought not to speak so. And to a virtual stranger. She snorted. *"Cecilia's efforts,"* indeed. Efforts to see her married and out of their house, more like. Not that Eliza wished to stay where she wasn't wanted.

The *Virginia* was scheduled to sail in two weeks. Energy surged through her. This was it! The opportunity she'd been praying for.

She scurried to the kitchen and out the back door to find Frank, the Davidsons' old manservant, a former slave. He accompanied her uncle on his business errands and spent hours at the wharfs helping check on shipments. Next to Eliza, no one knew more about Uncle Henry's business contacts.

He was in the tack room rubbing oil into a harness and looked up as she entered. "Hello, Miz Brooks. Ain't you s'posed to be dazzlin' that young man what come to dinner?" His twinkling eyes teased her.

"Oh, never mind that. He's gone anyway." She made a face at him. "What do you know about the *Virginia?*"

"The ship?"

"And Captain Swenson."

"Well, let's see." He continued rubbing the harness, but his eyes grew unfocused as he cocked his head to the side. "Captain Swenson, now, I know your Uncle thinks real highly of him. Been sailin' on his ship least two times as I can remember."

Eliza tapped her foot. "Yes, but where does it go? Does it set in at San Diego?"

He paused his rubbing and cocked his eye at her. "Why you be wantin' to know, Miz Brooks?"

Gah! She shouldn't have asked about San Diego. Frank may be an uneducated man, but he was no one's fool. "Mr. Clarke, our guest this evening, is planning to board the *Virginia* in two weeks' time. I thought perhaps if it set in at San Diego, I might trouble him to deliver a letter for me."

"He a letter carrier?"

"Well, no, but I've about lost faith in the postal service. You know that."

He nodded and resumed rubbing the leather. For several seconds he said nothing more. Had he forgotten her question? She didn't dare ask it again.

He added oil to his cloth. "Seems to me it does stop at San Diego."

She struggled to keep her expression calm as he glanced at her, then back down to his work.

"Awful small little place. Stank, too, is what your Uncle said once to a man he met at the wharf. Man was thinkin' to buy some land down there. Talk of a railroad, I think."

Would Frank *ever* stop talking? She needed to be alone. To think. To plan.

"But your uncle, he said not to. Said the man oughta stay right here and invest in this here growin' city. Said his money'd be safer here." Frank paused to add more oil to his cloth.

"Thank you, Frank. That's all I needed." Turning, she rushed toward the door. "I don't want to keep you from your work. Good night!"

She scurried across the courtyard, then yanked open the door to the house and dashed through the kitchen. Ignoring Amelia's startled cry, she scampered up the stairs and into her room.

Pa's last letter came from San Diego. She read and reread it for any hint as to why he stopped writing, but it spoke only of his hope in finding employment with a Lieutenant Derby—the officer rumored to be in charge of a new dike being built on the local river.

She paced her room as plans formed in her mind. Uncle Henry would not approve. He would want her to wait, but she was through with being patient.

It was time to take matters into her own hands.

~

*T*en days later, Eliza sat in the drawing room listening to the mantel clock tick as she poked her needle through the fabric in the frame before her. She pulled the thread through as the slosh of pouring water and the scuffing of feet moving about the dirt yard below drifted in through the open window. Amelia was busy preparing the water for laundry—a task that would keep her occupied out back for the rest of the day. Before Uncle Henry and Frank left early this morning, to check on a construction project across town, she overheard her uncle inform Cecilia that they would not be back until supper.

This was her chance.

If Cecilia ever retired for her afternoon nap.

She peeked at her aunt. The woman wasn't watching her. Eliza checked the clock from the corner of her eye. Cecilia should have retired ten minutes ago. Restraining the urge to growl, Eliza jabbed her needle through the fabric and pulled it through to the back of her piece.

The heat of the afternoon sun warmed her neck. She shifted. Her foot jiggled and her hands grew damp with sweat. The needle slipped from her fingers. Releasing her growl, she fetched the needle from the floor.

Cecilia didn't look up from her needlepoint, but shook her head. She didn't approve of emotive vocalization.

Eliza sneered at the fabric as she jabbed it with her needle.

She silently counted to ten, then made a show of leaning forward to squint at the clock on the mantel. "Oh my."

Cecilia paused in her stitching. "What is it?"

Eliza placed a hand at her back and stretched while pretending to yawn. "I am getting so tired and sore from sitting so long. I believe I'll go rest a while." She set her sewing aside and focused on the clock. "Why, don't you usually take your rest at this time?"

Cecilia regarded the clock. "Well, yes, now that you mention it. I suppose my eyes are growing a bit tired." Her aunt set her needlepoint down and rose from her chair.

Eliza resisted the urge to cheer.

"I suppose I should rest now." Cecilia smoothed her skirts.

Eliza forced herself to stroll out of the room and up to her chamber, her aunt at her heels. She turned to give Cecilia a sleepy smile, then she stepped into her room and shut the door. Leaning against it, she listened until her aunt's door closed with a click.

Her body tingled. She wanted to pace as she waited for her aunt's unladylike snoring to begin, but her aunt would hear the creaking boards. Eliza threw herself on the bed instead. Thinking of her daring plan, she rubbed the embroidered hem of the pillowcase between her fingers. Her aunt would be horrified if she knew.

Eliza smothered a giggle with her pillow.

The image of her uncle's brows pressed over his spectacles floated through her mind. She sobered. He wouldn't approve either. He'd worry about her. She bit her lip. So many things might go wrong. But they wouldn't. They couldn't. She sucked in a deep breath, then let it out slowly. She'd write Uncle Henry a letter. He'd be fine.

What would it be like to sail on a large ship at sea instead of the small boats that had carried her up and down the rivers of the gold fields? The image of Mr. Clarke seated across from her at supper flashed in her mind. How many people could a ship like the *Virginia* carry? She sniffed. It didn't matter. A carpenter like Mr. Clarke would secure passage in the lower cabins, or perhaps even steerage. As a guest of the captain's wife, she'd be expected to dine with them and likely wouldn't see Mr. Clarke for the whole of her journey. Not that that mattered at all.

Soft rumbling from her aunt's room caught her attention. It paused. Then it came again, louder.

At last! Eliza slipped off the bed.

She crept to her chamber door and eased it open. Peering into the hall, she didn't see Amelia. Cecilia's snoring continued. She slipped out and tiptoed downstairs, careful to avoid the boards that creaked the loudest.

Amelia entered the hallway, and Eliza froze. The mound of soiled linens Amelia carried in her basket came to her forehead. Her face tilted to the opposite side of the heap, Amelia disappeared into the kitchen.

Eliza exhaled and hurried to the front door.

Turning the knob, she took one more scan of the empty hallway as she pulled open the door, and stepped out into the sunshine. She scurried up the hill to Montgomery Street, chin tucked and praying no one would notice her.

The Swenson house was one block away from the Davidson home. At this time of day, the men from this neighborhood were at the wharves or at their businesses, and the women were reading or resting like her aunt. She prayed Mrs. Swenson was not asleep.

Turning left at Montgomery, she continued along the alternating planks and stairs that formed the sidewalks of that street.

"Ahoy there!"

A man swayed on the opposite sidewalk.

The drunkard stumbled as his foot missed the edge of the planks and sank into the muddy street. Unfazed, he called out lurid suggestions even as he tugged his foot free of the mud. He lost his shoe in the process. She ignored the man and hastened her step. *Please, Lord, keep him on his side of the street.*

When the Swenson home came into view, Eliza nibbled her lower lip. She must gain admittance, secure Mrs. Swenson's promise of help, and return to the Davidson home before Cecilia awoke.

The pickled man's shouts grew louder.

She glanced back.

He had regained his shoe, crossed to her side of the street, and was gaining on her.

She lifted her skirts and broke into a jog. The man yelled for her to stop. She looked back. He was still pursuing her. She slammed into something hard. Male arms clamped around her. She fought to pull free, but her strength was no match for his.

"Easy, miss. I mean you no harm."

It was Captain Swenson. She'd met him once before, and his long, glossy black ponytail, well-groomed beard, large build, and towering height made him a difficult man to forget.

His head pulled back. "Miss Brooks." He searched the road behind her. "Is something wrong? Where is your manservant?"

She checked over her shoulder. The drunkard had reversed direction and was hurrying away. She stared up at the captain, who still held her. An uncomfortable feeling slid through her. "I believe it is safe to release me now."

"Oh. Right." He dropped his arms.

She stepped back to a proper distance. What was it he had asked? Oh. The manservant. She waved away his concern. "He's with Mr. Davidson and thus unavailable to escort me." She squared her shoulders. "But I have a matter of some urgency that I must discuss with your wife."

Captain Swenson's chin lowered. "Oh, my dear, I am so sorry to have to tell you after you've made such an effort in getting here, but Mrs. Swenson is unwell and has taken to her bed for the rest of the day."

Oh no! Her shoulders slumped. What was she to do now?

"Is there anything I may do to be of assistance? Deliver your message, perhaps?"

Eliza hesitated. She'd counted on speaking to Mrs. Swenson. The captain's heart might not sway in her favor, but what choice did she have? It had taken her ten days to find this opportunity to sneak away from the house, and according to the advertisement in the paper, the *Virginia* would be leaving the day after tomorrow. If Mrs. Swenson boarded that ship without her, Eliza would miss her chance of having a chaperone to escort her to the port of San Diego.

She considered the captain's concerned expression. Perhaps he *would* help her.

Uncle Henry would be angry when he found out. He'd feel betrayed. Her gut twisted. What kind of niece repaid her uncle's kind generosity with deception and disobedience?

She pictured the *Virginia* waiting at the wharf. She'd prayed for Pa multiple times a day, every day for months, and still there had been no word. The image of him lying ill in a bed somewhere, calling for her, flashed in her mind. She pressed her lips together. She was done waiting.

"Miss Brooks?"

"Is it true Mrs. Swenson plans to leave with the *Virginia* when it departs in two days?"

The captain's bushy eyebrows rose again. "Who told you she was leaving?"

"Mrs. Davidson said your wife planned to return to your family. Is it true?"

"She is planning to return to her family, yes. It seems the...material comforts here do not suit her." He rubbed his nose. "She misses the States with its paved streets and interminable social events."

She missed life in the east? More people, more rules, more social events. No, thank you. Mrs. Swenson could keep her paved streets. Eliza would bathe in mud if it meant she could live as she pleased. "Do you anticipate that her current illness will affect her plans?"

"No, it is merely a severe headache. I'm sure she shall be well by tomorrow, but if you pardon me, Miss Brooks, I'm uncertain how this affects you in such a way as to prompt your coming here with such urgency." He tilted his head and squinted at her. "Surely, a farewell visit might have waited until your manservant was able to escort you."

Eliza took a deep breath and straightened to her fullest height. Still, her eyes came no higher than his shoulders. She lifted her chin. This was it. If she failed to convince the captain, all would be lost. "I have not come for a farewell visit, sir." Best to stick as close to the truth as possible. "I've come to ask if I might join her in her journey. Partway that is."

His head tilted.

"It's my pa. He's in San Diego"—she placed her fist on her chest—"and he needs me, but the Davidsons are unable to leave their business to escort me. It is my hope that your wife will agree to be my chaperone. Will you please ask her for me?"

"Your father has written, requesting your presence? Why does he not fetch you himself?"

"He is not well, which is the reason for my grave urgency." It must be true or he would have written her these last months. She widened her eyes. "Please, sir, will you give your wife my message?"

The captain rubbed his beard, then smoothed the front of his frock coat. "I have no need to. I know already what my kind wife's answer would be. Yes, of course, she will be happy to assist you."

Eliza's breath caught and she touched her throat. "Are you quite certain, sir?"

"Miss Brooks, you have met my wife, have you not?"

Eliza chuckled. He was correct. Mrs. Davidson had not over-stated Mrs. Swenson's kindness when describing her to Mr. Clarke.

"Then, it's settled. Now, I'm off to tend to some business, but may I first escort you home?" The captain offered her his arm.

She mustn't be seen returning to the house with him. She kept her smile in place as she backed away. "Thank you, Captain, but I wouldn't wish to further delay you from your business. You've already been so gracious and kind. I cannot thank you enough. I shall see you in two days."

She spun and hastened her steps. She did not slow until she reached the corner of Alta Street. When she peered over her shoulder, the captain was gone.

∾

*E*liza angled her book to better catch the afternoon sunshine streaming through the parlor window. She would miss her uncle's book collection. She swung her legs over one side of Cecilia's favorite chair and arched her back until her hair brushed the floor on the opposite side. My, but it was wonderful escaping her corset, even for an hour.

She checked the clock on the mantel. Cecilia should return

from the Ladies' Protection and Relief Society meeting soon. They were planning a ball to benefit the Society's causes. Perhaps they'd run late. Those ninnies did love their decorations.

Five minutes later, Cecilia glided into the room. "It will be the absolute event of the season!" She walked straight to the chord on the wall and gave it a pull, summoning Amelia. "We shall need new gowns, of course."

"What?" Eliza jumped to her feet. She couldn't allow Cecilia to spend more of Uncle Henry's money on a silly gown Eliza wouldn't even be around to wear. "I've not worn my pink dress but once. I'm certain that will do."

"Nonsense! Did you not hear me?" She spoke every word of her next sentence slowly, as if Eliza were a simpleton. "The event of the season."

Amelia appeared in the doorway, huffing and puffing, her skin flushed.

"Eliza and I have urgent need to visit the store. Please tell Frank to ready the carriage and have him make haste."

"Yes, ma'am." Amelia trundled away.

Eliza threw up her hands. "Why such haste?"

"The store has received a new shipment this morning. I am determined we should arrive before the other ladies so that we might select the best possible fabrics for our new dresses."

Davidson & Co. already overflowed with unsold merchandise, thanks to the recent economic downturn. Eliza had argued against ordering more fabric, but Uncle Henry continued to place orders to please his wife.

Eliza flopped into her usual chair. "You aim to arrive before Mrs. Prichard."

"Do sit like a lady, Eliza." Cecilia paced closer. "I see you've removed your corset again."

Eliza straightened. Her lazy afternoon was over.

"And yes, certainly before Mrs. Prichard." Cecilia patted her curls. "And why not? The uppity woman won't have a stitch to complain about this time. Your dress will be perfect for this event." She narrowed her eyes. "Absolutely perfect."

Eliza flinched. She had made last-minute adjustments to the scratchy sleeves of her ball gown prior to the last ball—adjustments that gained the notice of blabber-mouthed Mrs. Prichard, who made it her duty to bring it to the attention of everyone in attendance. Mortified, Cecilia sent Eliza home. And gave Eliza a serious tongue-lashing the next morning.

Eliza stood. "But I haven't the time for shopping." She strode toward the door. Perhaps Uncle Henry had finished writing his letters. If not, she would find something to keep her busy in his study until Cecilia gave up this idea of going shopping. "There is so much here that needs my attention. I—"

"Nonsense. Go and put your corset on. Make yourself presentable. We must leave as soon as possible."

❧

*E*liza held the door for her aunt to enter the store.

Cecilia made a beeline for the new bolts of fabric at the back. She pulled a rich blue silk from the shelf. "Oh, but this is lovely."

Eliza's lips parted. It had exquisite white flowers running its length in wide stripes. Her fingers twitched with the urge to touch the fabric. Was it as smooth as it appeared?

"Well?" Cecilia lifted the bolt. "I know you have an opinion. You always do."

Eliza shrugged. "I still think my pink dress will do."

One delicate brow lifted on her aunt's face. She set the blue silk on the table beside her and turned her back to Eliza before pulling two more bolts from the shelf.

Eliza ran her fingers over the silky blue fabric. Heavenly.

After some vocal debate with herself, Cecilia settled on the rich blue silk for Eliza and a rosy pink silk for herself. She was giving the final orders to Henry's clerk when the door opened, revealing Mrs. Swenson.

Eliza sidled toward a shelf large enough to hide behind.

Mrs. Swenson's gaze met hers.

Too late.

The large woman bustled across the store.

"Mrs. Davidson, Miss Brooks. What a delightful surprise." She beamed at them as Eliza's muscles twitched to flee. How was she going to keep the woman from mentioning Eliza's departure? Cecilia was sure to ask about Mrs. Swenson's trip, and of course the kind woman would express her pleasure in having Eliza's company for part of the journey. Oh, this was a disaster!

"Surprise, indeed." Cecilia's eyes twinkled. "You know exactly why we're here. But why are you?"

Mrs. Swenson chortled. "I never could resist new fabrics, ball or no. And have you picked yours out already?" She eyed the bolts of pink and blue that the clerk was setting at the back for delivery to the Davidsons' home.

"We have." Cecilia clasped her hands together. "But tell me, how are your plans…"

The door opened again.

Three members of the Ladies' Protection and Relief Society hurried toward them. Mrs. Prichard was the shortest among them. The small corner of the store holding the fabric display began to fill as the women, having dispensed with their greetings, focused on the task at hand.

Mrs. Prichard maneuvered herself between Eliza and Cecilia and inspected a pale blue bolt resembling the fabric of Eliza's previous gown. "I do hope the ladies will take particular care with their ensembles for this event. It's so important to The Society. It would be a shame if we did not place our best foot forward. After all, what do we ladies have if not our reputation?"

Eliza peered over Mrs. Prichard's head at Cecilia. Not a hint of irritation showed in her aunt's serene expression. *How does she do that?* Eliza forced herself to sound as relaxed as her aunt appeared. "Since we have completed our purchases, shouldn't we go and give these ladies more room to do their shopping?"

Cecilia clasped her hands together. "It might be best."

ale morning sunlight spilled across the writing desk as Eliza's pen moved across the page.

Dear Uncle Henry,
By the time you read this letter, I will be aboard the Virginia *on my way to San Diego. Please do not worry...*

No, she couldn't write that. Of course he would worry.

Balling up her third sheet of paper, Eliza sighed and leaned back in her chair. What should she write? Perhaps she should start with her gratitude for his kindness and generosity.

She leaned forward.

Dear Uncle Henry,
I cannot begin to thank you for the kindness and generosity
you have shown me these past three years. I know that I have
not always been the easiest person to live with. I am sorry for
any embarrassment or...

What good was it to apologize for hurting him when her plans would feel like a betrayal?

She crumpled the paper and tossed it with the others in the bin.

What choice had he left her? He would not consent to her travel, and she could not remain one day longer without knowing what had become of Pa.

She pulled another sheet from the stack and began again.

Several drafts later, the clock chimed the advancing hour. Her hand jerked, leaving an ugly smear on the page. She blew it dry, wrote one final sentence, and signed her name. It would have to do.

The *Virginia* would depart in little more than two hours. If she didn't pack now, she would not make it to the wharf in time.

She dragged the carpetbag from its hiding place beneath her bed and pried it open. In its confines she placed the practical garments she'd had made to suit her work around the house. The fancy dresses and impractical shoes Cecilia had forced on her remained in the closet. After adding a sturdy pair of boots, two of her favorite books, and a few sundries, her bag was bulging. Last, she retrieved Mama's cherished Bible and Pa's letters. She hesitated, clutching the leather Bible in one hand, the crumpled letters in the other. *I'll find him, Ma.* After adding them to the bag, she pressed down on the contents and squeezed the closure shut. *There. All packed.* She checked the clock. Thirty minutes had passed.

She lifted her bag and peeked into the hallway. Empty. She crept down the stairs, peering around each corner as she went.

Cecilia's voice floated into the hallway from the drawing room, where she was giving Amelia instructions.

The kitchen was vacant. Eliza dashed to the corner and withdrew the last three bottles of wine from their crate. The packing straw was removed next. She crammed her bag into the now-empty container. The sides of the bag scraped against the rough wood, snagging the fabric. She cringed. At least there was room on top. Grabbing handfuls of the straw, Eliza filled the box until her bag was concealed. She moved the wine to a shelf in the corner. *Please, let no one notice them.*

She paced back to the crate.

Amelia trundled into the kitchen.

"Oh!" Eliza jumped.

"Didn't mean to scare you. What are you doin' in here?" Amelia glanced at the sink where a handful of dishes awaited cleansing. "I've just come to do those." She dashed toward the sink. "The misses had extra instructions for me this mornin'."

"Of course."

Amelia began scrubbing a pot, her back to Eliza.

Eliza wiped bits of straw from her damp palms. "Do you know where Frank is?"

"Out back feedin' the horses."

"Thank you."

Eliza hurried out.

Frank was in the yard, brushing a horse. "Good morning, Frank."

"Mornin', Miz Brooks." He paused his strokes. "What can I do for you?"

"I need you to take me to the wharf."

He wiped his sleeve across his sweaty forehead. "Just you?"

"Yes." Eliza fiddled with the fabric of her skirt. She hated lying to Frank. "Mr. Davidson planned to give the last of our wine to Captain Swenson and his wife as a farewell gift. But he's gone off without it this morning, and the *Virginia* departs in an hour." She held her breath.

"I'd be happy to deliver the wine for you, Miz Brooks. No need to rush yourself."

Eliza's hands tightened on the folds of her skirt. "Mrs. Swenson has been ill these last few days and I haven't had a chance to say farewell. When I saw the wine, I realized this was my chance to do so."

"That don't give us much time."

"No, it doesn't." She wrung her hands. "We'd better hurry."

Frank set down the brush and headed for the carriage house.

Eliza returned inside for the crate.

Amelia still scrubbed at the sink. "Did you find him, miss?"

"Yes, thank you."

As Eliza lifted the crate and turned toward the door, Cecilia entered the kitchen.

"Where are you going?"

Taking a deep breath, Eliza stepped to the side. *Please don't let her notice the bottles.* "Uncle Henry's forgotten this." She shifted the crate. "He meant to give it to Captain Swenson this morning. I've asked Frank to take me to the wharf before the ship sails so that I might deliver it for him."

"Well, I don't see why Frank cannot deliver it himself, but so long as you are going to town, I'll come along. We'll stop in and visit Mrs. Woods after we drop off the gift." She turned toward the hall. "I'll only be a moment."

"But the ship…" Her protest fell on her aunt's departing back.

～

*E*liza scooted to the end of the bench as the carriage pulled to a stop by the wharf.

Cecilia laid a staying hand on hers.

"What's truly in the crate, Eliza?"

Eliza froze. Squawking seagulls and calling sailors filled the moment it took for her to respond. "What do you mean?"

"I saw the wine on the shelf in the kitchen. You aren't as clever as you think." Cecilia watched Frank lift the crate from the wagon. "What are you hiding?"

Eliza's mind whirled with a myriad of excuses. None would do. What did it matter? She'd be gone in a matter of minutes. Why not tell the truth?

"I'm leaving."

Cecilia drew back. "Leaving?"

"For San Diego. I'm going to find Pa."

Cecilia's nostrils flared. "But you can't go! Not without an escort. Not without your Uncle. Think of the scandal!"

"I have arranged for Mrs. Swenson to be my escort and the captain has assured me I will be safe aboard his ship."

"Mrs. Swenson? But she never said." Blond tendrils blew into Cecilia's face, and she twisted her head, dislodging them. "She is going to Massachusetts, not to San Diego."

"True. I will disembark in San Diego and she will continue on."

"But who will be with you in San Diego?"

"I'll have Pa, of course."

"You don't know that. You don't even know that your father is still in San Diego."

"He's there. And I will find him."

"No. This is not acceptable. Don't you understand what this sort of scandal will do to your Uncle's reputation? If you go now..." Cecilia studied Eliza. "Are you determined to do this? To travel on your own?"

Eliza gave a firm nod.

Cecilia pressed her lips together. "Then you must never come back."

"Wh-What?"

"If you do this, you must promise never to return. If you do, you will cause even greater damage to your uncle's reputation than with your departure. Is that any way to show your gratitude for everything we've done for you?"

Eliza had no burning desire to return to this pretentious, mud-splattered town, yet she would miss her uncle. And it would pain him never to see her again. Yet there was truth in what her aunt said. Eliza's actions would cause scandal—something her uncle's business could ill afford right now.

"Promise me." Cecilia seized Eliza's wrist. "The moment

your foot hits that wharf, there is no turning back. I will have your word."

Eliza swallowed. She could turn back—wait for her uncle to escort her. No. She'd already waited too long. If Pa was sick or injured... She had to find him. Now. "I promise, I will never return. You have my word." *Please let Uncle Henry forgive me.*

Cecilia released her. "Good. Thank you."

Frank assisted Eliza from the wagon. His lips pursed and he shook his head. Grimacing, she pulled the letter from her pocket. "I wrote a letter—" She held it out to Frank, but Cecilia snatched it from her hand.

"I'll take that."

"It's for Uncle Henry."

Cecilia's lips curled upward. "Of course, and I'll see that he gets it. Run along now. You don't want to miss your ship." Cecilia flicked her fingers in a shooing motion.

Eliza's shoulders drooped as she stepped from the wagon. Frank bent over the crate at his feet and brushed the straw aside. He handed the carpetbag to her.

"Thank you, Frank." She gave him a quick hug. "I'm sorry," she whispered before pulling away.

Tears glistened in the man's eyes. "You take care, Miss Brooks." He climbed into the driver's seat.

"Safe journey!" Cecilia waved.

Carpetbag in hand, Eliza straightened her shoulders and started down the wharf. Behind her, Frank clicked to the horses. She turned back. As the wagon pulled away, her letter fluttered from Cecilia's hand. Eliza rushed to capture the missive. A breeze carried it beyond the planks of the wharf and dropped it onto the dark waves below.

The paper floated for a few seconds, then sank from sight.

CHAPTER 6

*D*aniel stood on the deck of the *Virginia* and looked over the city where he'd spent the past four and a half years. The most miserable, exhilarating, tedious, and rewarding years of his life. In all likelihood, he would never see the place again. Would he miss it? His gaze skimmed past the tangle of masts to the lines of streets and buildings beyond. Not likely. He didn't harbor the bitter animosity of those who'd lost their fortunes and good health in this bustling, mud-clogged boomtown. And yet, neither did the place evoke a sense of home or belonging for him the way it did for those like the Davidsons, who'd set down firm roots and spent their days working to improve their burgeoning city in every way possible.

Daniel shook his head. Home must still be the place he'd left in Massachusetts, where his family and his fiancée would welcome him with open arms.

He pulled his mother's latest letter from his pocket and reread it. His father's health had improved. His elder brother, Benjamin, had taken on more responsibilities in the family carpentry business. Mother was excited about Benjamin's plans to build his own home on the family land but declined to go into detail. She wrote that Benjamin wished to share them in his own letter.

Rubbing his jaw, he reread the words. He'd never received a letter from his brother.

He continued down the page. As with her last two letters, his mother did not mention Alice except to write that she was still away on the trip she'd taken with Richard to visit a mutual acquaintance. Richard was the youngest and least settled of Alice's three elder brothers. Daniel didn't think they were close, yet Richard and Alice had been gone for months. Might this trip explain Alice's silence? No. Alice could have mailed a letter from anywhere she might have gone. Unlike in California, every town on the east coast enjoyed mail service.

He skimmed his mother's letter again. No matter how many times he read it, he found no answer to the questions that plagued him. Pride had kept him from mentioning to his mother the cessation of Alice's communication. Yet, if something had changed—if Alice had given any indication of a change in her affection for him—his mother would have told him. Wouldn't she?

"Look where you're goin'!" A man was being jostled in the frenzied activity on the wharves.

Along the wide platform, passengers of every class scurried to and fro. Hired draymen weaved their horses and carts around bags of mail and piles of luggage in a hurry to unload their cargo, collect their payment, and return to carry another load. Hoping for a fare, cabmen swooped in on passengers disembarking the ferries. Stores built on pilings along either side were doing a brisk business. A stench of rotting fish mixed with salty sea air drifted to him from the boats off Fisherman's Wharf.

The crew of the *Virginia* loaded crate after crate of cargo into the ship's hold. Despite their brisk pace, there was still a mountain of items to be loaded. How could they be ready to leave port at noon, as scheduled?

As the crew continued their strenuous work, a swish of blue skirts near the gangway caught Daniel's attention. A lady in a blue bonnet attempted to board, but a swaggering youth stepped into her path, blocking her way. The lout! Daniel stepped toward the gangway opening, then stopped. Captain Swenson himself was hurrying toward the woman. With a sweep of his arm, the captain brushed the offender aside. He relieved the lady of her large carpetbag and waved for her to precede him.

With one foot on the narrow board leading to the top deck, the lady paused to stare up at the ship. Daniel's breath caught.

Miss Brooks!

Daniel searched the wharf for the Davidsons but found no sign of them—no sign of anyone who gave the appearance of accompanying Eliza. He frowned. A woman traveling alone was vulnerable to all kinds of evil. What were the Davidsons thinking to permit Eliza to take such a risk?

As Eliza stepped aboard the *Virginia*, Daniel walked toward her. He must convince her to delay her journey until such time as the Davidsons or some other appropriate chaperone might accompany her.

～

*E*liza stepped aboard the *Virginia* and turned to face the captain who boarded after her. "Thank you for your assistance, Captain Swenson. That man was discourteously persistent."

"My pleasure, Miss Brooks. I'm sorry you had to deal with such a fellow at all."

She scanned the top deck for the captain's wife. Instead of the kind woman, she spotted Mr. Clarke striding in their direction, glowering. Eliza pretended not to see him and continued her search of the deck. Mrs. Swenson was not in sight.

She turned back to the captain. "Is Mrs. Swenson below?"

"I'm sorry to tell you, Mrs. Swenson has been delayed, but if you'll come with me, I'll show you to your cabin where you may wait, safe from any further unwanted attentions." He offered her his arm, and she accepted it. She restrained herself from peeking at Mr. Clarke as the captain led her to a steep set of stairs that led below deck.

Eliza followed Captain Swenson through an elegant dining saloon to a narrow corridor.

At the end of the corridor, he opened a cabin door and stepped aside.

"Here you are."

She walked into a modest room equipped with two beds, one above the other, on the left. To the right, a small bench was attached to the wall. At the rear of the room stood a tiny table with a washbasin and pitcher. The space between the beds and the bench was so narrow that it pressed against the sides of her full skirt. She could not take four complete steps from the door without running into the table. Still, her accommodations were far superior to that of the other passengers. On her own, she would not have been able to justify the expense of more than a steerage passage. As Mrs. Swenson's companion, she had been permitted to upgrade her ticket to first class at no extra cost. She turned to thank the captain for his generosity.

He had entered the room behind her.

"Oh!" As he leaned toward her, he seemed to fill the room. She took a step back. "I...uh..." He stood so close.

"There you go." His breath tickled her cheek as he leaned toward her and set her carpetbag on the lower bed. The next moment, he stepped backward out of the room.

She released a breath.

He pinched the brim of his hat. "If you will excuse me, Miss Brooks, I've work to do before we shove off."

Eliza's cheeks warmed as the captain strode away. He had been depositing her bag. Of course. How silly of her to have been nervous. Taking a deep breath, she gave herself a gentle shake to erase the last hint of lingering nerves. She unsnapped her carpetbag and began setting her new living quarters to rights.

~

*E*liza inspected the room. Had she forgotten anything? Her writing utensils were on the table. Why had she entrusted Cecilia with Uncle Henry's letter? She would need to write a new one, but she couldn't stomach the task now. Her bonnet hung on a hook in the ship's wall. Mama's Bible sat atop her pillow. Eliza's nightdress was laid out beneath the blanket on her bed. She'd emptied and reorganized her carpetbag to assure the best access to the items she would need during her brief stay on board. She patted the clasp. Everything was in order. With nothing else to do, she withdrew her copy of *Woman in the Nineteenth Century*, sat on the bench, and began to read.

A while later, Eliza checked her pocket watch. Five minutes till noon and still no sign of Mrs. Swenson. After closing her book and setting it on the table, Eliza went to the door and pulled it open. As she stepped into the corridor, a steward rounded the corner. The oil wall lamps flickered, casting shadows across the walls.

"Afternoon, miss." The steward stopped to bow.

"Good afternoon. I wonder if you can tell me whether Mrs. Swenson is now on board."

"I'm sorry. I have not seen her."

What could be keeping her?

"I've been busy below dealing with a disturbance among those in the..." The steward shuddered. "The lower births. I'm now here to check on the cabins. Is yours satisfactory, miss? Is there anything you need?"

"My cabin is lovely. Thank you." Eliza paused. "Would you please inform me when Mrs. Swenson has arrived?"

"Of course. Although, I should warn you. When she has sailed with the captain in the past, she has always been the last aboard and the first to disembark. And once aboard, she spends her time up top." He leaned toward her and whispered. "They say she doesn't enjoy sailing!"

The man's scandalized expression threatened her composure. She covered her mouth.

She'd met many who were less than enthusiastic about their voyages to San Francisco. After hearing their tales, she had her own reservations regarding the journey before her. Her steps on the *Virginia* that day had been her first aboard a seafaring vessel. God willing, the stomach that had held steady during her voyages on much smaller, river-bound ships would remain as calm and unflustered once they were in the open waters of the Pacific.

She thanked the steward for his information, handed him a coin, and repeated her request to be informed of Mrs. Swenson's arrival.

"I shall inform you the moment she steps aboard, miss." After a bow, the steward continued checking each cabin in her corridor—all of which appeared to be empty—before he exited toward the dining room.

Eliza returned to her seat and her reading.

A few minutes later, there was a knock on her door. *At last.* She set aside her book and hurried to open the door.

The same steward stood in the corridor.

She searched the hall behind him. Empty. "Is Mrs. Swenson up top?"

"No, miss. But I thought you would like to know that the ship's departure will be delayed an hour or more due to the mail not being ready yet. I think it likely Mrs. Swenson will wait for the mail to arrive before boarding."

Eliza thanked the steward and returned, once more, to her reading.

After several chapters, her concentration gave out. She read the same paragraph twice with no memory of what she had read. She closed the book with a sigh. Stretching to return the book to her bag, Eliza fell from her chair as the ship moved beneath her. She placed a steadying hand on the bar connecting the two beds and managed to right herself. As she absorbed the strange sensation of the large vessel swaying beneath her, the truth hit her like a plank to the chest.

They had departed!

CHAPTER 7

Once above, Eliza scoured the *Virginia* for Mrs. Swenson but could not spy her among the growing crowd of passengers. Captain Swenson stood near the stern of the ship, giving orders to one of his crew. She marched across the gently swaying deck.

Never interrupt a man while he's working.

The memory of Cecilia's chiding stopped Eliza in her tracks a few feet short of the captain. She sidled into his line of sight, then waited for him to finish his instructions. Her foot tapped the smooth decking.

A moment later, the captain dismissed his crewman. He stepped toward her. "Miss Brooks, I was just coming in search of you."

"We've set off." Eliza pointed to the passing masts of ships still at anchor. "Please tell me your wife is aboard."

"I'm so sorry, Miss Brooks." The captain placed a hand on her shoulder. "As you know, my wife was ill."

"I thought it was a headache."

"That's how it started, yes." He clasped his hands behind him. "At the time I spoke with you, I had every confidence that she would recover in time to join you on this journey. However, there were some other...complications. I received word at the last possible moment that, in light of her illness, my wife had decided to put off her journey until such time as she is recovered."

Heat warming her face, she splayed her arms. "Why did you not inform me immediately?"

"I have been quite busy with my duties as captain." He scowled at her. "I had not the liberty to seek you out until this moment."

Eliza lowered her arms, still clenching her jaw. "You could have sent the steward, or—"

"Every member of my crew has been busy preparing for this journey, or did you think the *Virginia* sailed herself?"

"Of course not. Forgive me." She cringed and fiddled with her fingers behind her back. The captain had been nothing but kind to her. It wasn't his fault his wife had changed her plans at the last minute. He must be as disappointed as Eliza that his wife was not aboard. She quit fiddling. "Of course you were busy. I am simply distressed, as I am now without a proper chaperone. Are there any other ladies aboard with whom I might spend my time?"

The captain's expression softened. "I'm afraid not. The only other ladies aboard are... Well, let's say they aren't the sort your aunt and uncle would approve to keep you company. But do not be distressed, my dear Miss Brooks. There've been many female passengers aboard my ship without a chaperone before, and not a one has come to any harm." He grinned. "With your own impeccable behavior and, if I may say, myself as your captain, I am certain your journey shall end as safely as theirs. Never fear."

Physical safety was well and good, but what about her reputation? Eliza opened her mouth to protest, but a crewman called for the captain.

The captain's head swiveled toward the shout. "Please excuse me." He gave a slight bow and hurried off.

The lightless Alcatraz lighthouse caught her eye as the ship sailed past it. The shadow of its windows reflected the gloom Mrs. Swenson's absence cast on her journey. What was she to do? Despite her promise to Cecilia, she had hoped her reputation might be preserved. That she might one day return without bringing scandal upon her uncle.

Her vision blurred. Why must her attempts to protect those she loved always hurt another? She turned toward the rail to hide her teary eyes from the other passengers.

Mr. Clarke blocked her path.

~

She's going to cry. Daniel's breath caught.

He took a step toward her, but she moved around him.

"Wait." He caught her arm.

She glared through unshed tears. "Unhand me, sir."

He released her at once. What was he thinking? "Of course. I'm sorry. I only want to help."

Her lips trembled. "You heard?"

He should have walked away when he realized the private nature of her conversation with the captain, but he found himself unable to move. She had been counting on the captain's wife to act as her chaperone. Yet Mrs. Swenson was not aboard, and the captain displayed little concern. "I'm sorry."

She shuffled past him to lean against the rail, staring across the bay. He joined her. A single tear trailed down her cheek. Clearly, more than Mrs. Swenson's absence troubled her. What had happened to this strong woman that could cause such pain? The inappropriate urge to draw her into a comforting embrace had him leaning toward her. He handed her his kerchief instead.

She sniffed, wiped the tear away, and returned his kerchief. Straightening, she smoothed the wrinkles in her bodice and cleared her throat. "Thank you, Mr. Clarke, but there is nothing to be done. The ship has sailed." Her mouth tipped at the corner, her eyes still sad. "Literally."

With her soft pink lips, rose-tinged cheeks, and doleful brown eyes framed by long, dark lashes, she was...beautiful. And vulnerable. She ought to be at home with the Davidsons where she was safe and cared for, not standing alone on a ship filled with men of every class. He surveyed the deck. Several passengers were darting glances her way. A few were outright staring, as if she were a pie in the baker's window and they hadn't eaten in a month of Sundays.

He caught one man's eye and glared until the audacious lout turned away. Heat grew within him as he turned back to Eliza. "You should not be here alone."

She blinked. "I..." She placed her hands on her hips. "I have no choice."

Don't say it. This is the wrong approach. "Why did you not wait for your chaperone when you learned she was not aboard?" There had to have been some way she could have avoided placing herself in such a vulnerable position. "Why did you not arrange to meet Mrs. Swenson at her home so that you could travel together to the ship?"

Eliza's lips grew thin, then moved without sound. Then her voice came through clenched teeth. "The captain assured me his wife would be on board. I expected that she would be here when I arrived, but she was not. Are you suggesting I would have stood better waiting on the wharf, Mr. Clarke?"

Ah. So she knew he'd witnessed the scene with the impudent young man.

Daniel sighed. "No. Of course not." He rubbed the back of his neck. How had he gotten here? He had intended to offer her his protection during their journey, not to criticize her decisions. What was it about this woman that got him so turned around? He took a deep breath. "I only meant that it isn't safe for a—" He caught himself. Confessing he found her beautiful could give the wrong impression in light of the offer he intended to make.

"A what, Mr. Clarke?" She raised an eyebrow at him.

He held his hands up. "What I meant—"

She cut him off with a wave of her hand. "Forget it. I don't care to know what you meant." She gave a hasty curtsy. "If you'll excuse me."

∼

*E*liza paced the tiny confines of her cabin. Two steps forward, turn, two steps back, turn, and repeat. It was hardly satisfying, but she could not make herself be still. *Of all the impudent, arrogant... Arrrrgh!* She kicked the wall. Thank goodness Mr. Clarke would be in steerage the rest of their journey. He should have been there this afternoon. The stewards must have been too busy with departure activities to notice and shoo him below.

The worst part was that he was right. If she'd met Mrs. Swenson at the captain's home as Mr. Clarke suggested, she would have found out right away that her chaperone was too ill to accompany her. She could have...what? What would she have done? Returned to the Davidsons' home to continue waiting? She jammed her hands beneath her arms. No. She couldn't have done that.

She pulled Mama's Bible from her bag and stroked its leather cover. "I'm sorry." Her chin dropped. She had promised Mama she would take care of Pa in Mama's stead. She'd never counted on him leaving her behind.

She slid off the bench to kneel beside the bed and repeat her now-regular prayer. "Dear Lord, please watch over Pa. Keep him safe until I can reach him. Help me to find him soon. Amen." Just four more days and she'd be in San Diego.

~

*T*hat evening, Eliza exited her cabin and walked the corridor toward the upper dining saloon. The odors of wet, musty wood, burning oil, and boiled potatoes grew stronger as she entered the room. As elegantly decorated as any hotel Eliza had seen in San Francisco, the saloon was a long, narrow space in the middle of the ship. It was lined on either side with short corridors that led to first-class cabins. The soft glow of the oil lamps shone down on the upholstered sofas lining the outer walls as well as the long tables and chairs occupying the center of the room.

A few heads turned her way and the men stood. Eliza paused. As men comprised the majority of the passengers, it felt as if the entire room had stood for her. She fought the urge to duck her chin.

The captain beckoned her from beside his chair at the head of the first table. "I have a seat for you here, Miss Brooks." He moved to stand beside the chair at his right and, when she was seated, pushed her in before returning to his seat.

There was a rumble and scraping of chairs as the rest of the men returned to their seats.

"Thank you."

"My pleasure." He lifted a hand toward the opposite end of the saloon. "Ah. I see the last of our guests have arrived." Two men entered from a far corridor. As soon as they were seated, the captain lowered his head.

"O Almighty Lord, Who alone controls the skies and the raging sea. Preserve us, Your servants, from the dangers of this sea, that we may continue in thankful remembrance of Thy mercies, to praise and glorify Thy holy name. We thank Thee

75

for this, Thy bounty and grace. In Thy holy name, through Jesus Christ our Lord. Amen."

She lifted her head and stared at the captain. His prayer had been delivered with the same volume and authority the preacher used in his Sunday sermons.

The captain shook out his napkin and set it on his lap. "Not to worry, now."

He must have read her expression as dismay.

"I've got it all under control, but if I didn't add in that bit asking for protection...well, after dinner, some of this lot"—he gestured toward the other passengers—"might accuse me of arrogance, and complain that by failing to ask protection, I've somehow angered God and doomed our ship." He shrugged. "Now they've nothing to complain about and will leave me be, but you have nothing to worry about, my dear."

My dear? Cecilia would be offended by such impertinence.

He patted her hand.

An unpleasant sensation slithered through her. With a small smile, she withdrew her hand and hid it in her lap. As she tried to compile an appropriate response, the steward appeared at her side with a platter of boiled potatoes.

She nodded her acceptance.

As the steward served her, another member of the crew approached the captain and they conversed, saving her from responding to his outlandish remarks. *Thank you, Lord.*

She chewed a bite of potato as she surveyed her companions. There were about twenty men seated with her at the first table. Those seated nearest her were dressed in the finest manner of the latest fashion. The fashions of the guests near the end of the table—though all perfectly acceptable—were not quite so fine.

She was the lone female at the first table. Her chewing faltered.

Beyond the elderly gentleman seated across from her was the second table. Her gaze collided with that of Mr. Clarke, who faced her from his seat on its far side. She blinked. How could he afford a first-class ticket with a carpenter's wages? She had not taken him for one of those fools who wasted their money living beyond their means. She must have been wrong.

He smiled and dipped his chin.

She appraised the second table as having the same number of guests. These guests were dressed in a similar level of fashion, suggesting they were each other's equals. Near the end, there were three ladies seated among them.

No. Not ladies.

These women were dressed in bright shades of red, orange, and purple. Their bodices were opulently decorated, their necks enshrined with shimmering jewels. As the women guffawed and conversed loudly with the men beside them, it was clear how they had come by the money to purchase their first-class tickets. The clerk who sold them their tickets must not have realized what they were. Or else, he hadn't cared.

One of the women glanced up and caught her staring. Eliza averted her gaze.

The captain was watching her.

A bit of potato clung to his dark beard. Should she tell him? Cecilia wouldn't. Ordinarily, she wouldn't give two figs for what Cecilia thought, but now that Eliza was traveling unescorted, it seemed wise to keep as close to the behavior of a lady as she could manage.

He smiled at her. The potato in his beard spread. "Enjoying your potatoes?"

She paused with the last forkful halfway to her mouth and swallowed a laugh. "Yes."

He leaned toward her. "Are you really?"

She hid her annoyance as she returned her last bite to the plate. "They are surprisingly tasty."

"Surprisingly?" He drew back. "Did you not expect such elegant cuisine aboard our ship?"

Eliza opened her mouth to apologize for her low expectations, but swallowed her words. There was a twinkle in his eyes. He was teasing her. She exhaled.

He winked at her!

She tensed. Did anyone notice his impertinence? She appraised the others, but all were either engaged in conversation or focused on their meal.

All except Daniel.

His gaze met hers, flicked to the captain, then returned to hers with a raised brow.

She schooled her expression not to reveal her embarrassment and turned to the captain. She whispered, "Captain Swenson, please!"

He chuckled and winked again before digging into the beef that had been placed before him.

She scraped at the meat on her plate. He could *not* be flirting with her. It simply was not possible. She'd heard scandalous stories of captains at sea, but who could be unfaithful to a woman as kind as Mrs. Swenson? Was he one of those who believed winking was harmless? Perhaps she was overreacting. Maybe the captain was overwhelmed with relief to be out to sea once more and was letting his joviality overcome his good sense. Yes. That must be it. Therefore, her best recourse would be to ignore him until he'd had sufficient time to adjust and return to his normal self. She stabbed a large piece and shoved it into her mouth. Cecilia's rules be hanged. She would keep her focus on her plate for the remainder of the meal.

A few moments later, the captain coughed, but she pretended not to hear.

He cleared his throat and coughed again.

The gentlemen across from her enquired whether he was well.

Eliza concentrated on cutting her beef into the smallest

possible pieces and slipping them into her mouth. Cecilia would be proud of that, at least.

Having assured the other man of his good health, the captain waved his fork at her plate. "You seem to be enjoying your beef."

Shoving several small pieces into her mouth at once, she focused on her plate. "Mmm."

He set his cutlery down and inched his hand across the table. She dropped her own cutlery with a clatter and shoved her hands into her lap.

Swiveling away, she caught the attention of the middle-aged, golden-haired gentlemen to her right. "What did you think of Sausalito?" The *Virginia* had anchored there that afternoon while their casks were refilled with fresh water.

"Well, I had seen it once before, you know, in '49. I was surprised…" The man went on to describe the changes he'd noted between their current voyage and his previous one. Eliza feigned fascination with the topic, adding the proper encouragements where needed to keep him talking about his travels at sea.

A few minutes later, as dessert was being served, something nudged her foot.

She glimpsed the edge of the captain's boot pressed against her own. Jerking her foot away, Eliza jumped to her feet, drawing the attention of everyone in the room. The previous low hum of conversation came to a halt as the men surged to their feet. One man was nudged into compliance by the man beside him.

Her cheeks warmed. "Please, excuse me." She mumbled and gave a little curtsy. "I am feeling unwell." She spun toward her room.

The captain stepped into her path. "Allow me to escort you, Miss Brooks." He offered his arm.

She gritted her teeth but kept her expression neutral. "Thank you, Captain, but it's a short walk. I'm sure I can manage."

"Please, I insist." He took her hand and placed it on his arm. "After all"—he raised his voice—"as captain it is my duty to ensure the safety of the passengers."

All eyes were on her.

Why was Mr. Clarke glaring? Oh, what did it matter? He seemed always put out by her. Even when she'd done nothing wrong.

She dipped her chin and the captain led her the few steps to her corridor, around the corner, and to her cabin door.

"Thank you, sir. Good night."

"You're not still upset with me, are you?"

"I…" Was he apologizing for his behavior at dinner, or referring to his wife's unexpected absence?

"Because I truly am sorry, my dear." The ship swayed a little and he braced himself with a hand on her cabin door. "Forgive me?" His gray eyes appeared anything but repentant as he placed his other hand on the door beside her head.

Eliza shrank against the wood. "Of course." If telling him he was forgiven would get him to leave, she was happy to do it. She even mustered a smile for good measure. "You're forgiven."

"I'm glad." His breath rushed across her face as he leaned forward.

She inhaled the unpleasant aroma of his digesting meal.

"You see, I've made it my personal mission to see to it that you have an enjoyable stay aboard my ship." Shifting his weight, he drew a calloused finger down the side of her face, pausing at her chin.

She gasped and fumbled for the doorknob.

A commotion in the dining saloon caused the captain to turn his head. He leaned back to see around the corner toward the noise, lifting his remaining hand from her door.

Eliza twisted the knob and stepped backward into her cabin. "Good night!" She slammed the door in his face.

CHAPTER 8

*B*utterflies rioted in Eliza's stomach as she approached the dining saloon for breakfast the next morning. After writing a second letter to Uncle Henry and giving it to the steward to post, she'd lain awake for hours last night. How had she been so foolish as to judge the captain by his wife's virtues?

No, Uncle Henry had thought him a fine captain as well. He must be unaware of the blackguard's true nature.

She rubbed her arms. What had she gotten herself into? As captain on this ship, there was no one to stop his unwelcome advances.

Mr. Clarke's visage flashed in her mind, but he could not interfere with a captain on his own ship. She thrust her shoulders back. Besides, she didn't need his help. She'd survived more than a year in the gold fields. Not to mention, fending off the advances of any number of men who'd attempted to maneuver her into the shadowed corners of San Francisco's ballrooms. She could handle Captain Swenson now that she knew his true character. A shiver tickled her spine, but she lifted her chin.

If only she could contrive a reason to excuse herself from sitting beside him at meals.

She'd considered remaining in her cabin for the rest of the trip, but he might seek her out there. His supposed concern for her health would have been sufficient excuse, should anyone have discovered him outside her door. She shuddered.

Sometime during her restless night, she'd realized that Mrs. Swenson was likely ignorant of Eliza's request for a chaperone. No wonder the kind woman had not said a word when they met in Uncle Henry's shop. Eliza shook her head. What a naïve fool she'd been.

She entered the dining saloon. The captain's chair was empty.

Thank You, Lord. She rocked up on her toes to see beyond the shoulders of the passengers still standing. Mr. Clarke sat in the same seat as the evening before, too busy conversing with the man beside him to notice her. She continued surveying the room. There was an unoccupied seat farther down the table. She took a step in that direction.

"Here you are, Miss Brooks." The gentlemen she'd conversed with the evening before held the seat near the captain's chair for her.

Smothering a groan, she forced her lips upward as she sank into the seat.

"I trust you slept well?"

Eliza nodded. "And you?"

"Tolerably, I suppose. I've yet to grow accustomed to the incessant movement of this beast, but it is one of the concessions one must make for travel by sea. Far better a little swaying than the dangers of overland travel, I'd say."

"Have you experienced such dangers?"

"Let me tell you..." With that, the gentleman was off and running with wild tales of encounters with natives, harrowing river crossings, and long dreary days of endless walking. He'd launched into a gruesome tale of passing a wagon train stricken with cholera when the steward appeared beside the captain's chair and caught everyone's attention.

"The captain has asked me to extend his sincerest apologies for not joining you all this morning." Though he spoke to everyone, the steward's attention lingered on Eliza. "He is quite sorry, but an urgent matter of business has come up that he must deal with while we are anchored here at Monterey."

Had anyone else noticed the steward's unusual focus on her? She cast a look about the room. More than a few passengers scrutinized her. Including Mr. Clarke.

She cringed.

Even in his absence, the captain managed to cast suspicion on her reputation. She smoothed the napkin in her lap. Perhaps if she pretended all was well, their suspicions would seem unfounded and disappear.

❧

*D*aniel lifted a hand to block the midafternoon sunlight bouncing off the deck. A large crowd stood near the bow of the ship. People leaned over the rail, pointing to something in the waves below.

What had caught their attention? He wandered closer. The excited conversation grew more distinct.

"Look at them jump!"

"What are they?"

"Dolphins."

"They're beautiful."

Daniel tipped his head to another passenger hurrying toward the commotion. The first time he'd seen the creatures had been one of the few joys on his trip to San Francisco. It would be fun to watch them play again. If he could find an opening at the rail.

Eliza. She stood dead center in the crowd, leaning against the rail, facing the water. He stiffened. Was she oblivious to the men surrounding her? Did she not feel herself pressed arm to arm on either side by men who'd surely seen plenty of dolphins?

The man to her right leaned close, pointing toward the water. His full beard brushed Eliza's cheek as she turned to squint at the waves. Heat grew in Daniel's chest. He pushed his way through the throng to reach her side, ignoring the protests his jostling created.

His hand shot out to pull her away from the rail, away from these men, but he stopped before taking her arm. She didn't respond well the last time he touched her. Dropping his hand, he cleared his throat. "Miss Brooks?"

She didn't respond.

He raised his voice. "Miss Brooks?"

She lifted her head and craned her neck toward his voice. Seeing him, she frowned and returned to watching the dolphins.

The muscles in his neck tightened. He tapped her on the shoulder. "Miss Brooks, may I have a word?"

She heaved a sigh and faced him. "Yes, Mr. Clarke?"

The man to her right stepped forward with crossed arms, a wide stance, and a glare aimed straight at Daniel. "This man bothering you, miss?"

Eliza placed a gloved hand on the man's arm.

It took all Daniel's control to not pry it off.

"No. No, he's not. It's fine, truly." She smiled. "Thank you so much for your assistance. I never would have spotted that little one without your help."

The man's stance softened, but he didn't budge.

She patted the man's arm again. "I promise, I'll let you know if I need anything."

The man gave Daniel one more glare before stepping aside.

Daniel surveyed the group. The dolphins had been abandoned. Every man in the group was now watching him.

He offered Eliza his arm. "Would you take a walk with me?"

Her lips pinched.

She's going to refuse. "There is something of importance I would like to discuss with you"—he paused to look pointedly at their audience—"in private."

Her head swiveled left and right.

The men watched, obviously waiting on her response.

Her gaze moved to the rail and lingered there.

The man beside her ogled her bosom.

Daniel suppressed the urge to drag her away.

She turned back to Daniel. "Can't it wait?"

"I'm afraid not."

With another heavy sigh, Eliza accepted his arm and stepped away from the rail.

Daniel led her across the deck to a vacant section on the opposite side of the paddlewheel. He paused by the rail. How could he express his concern without offending her?

Eliza withdrew her hand. The cold sea breeze gusted up his cuff to chill the place she had kept warm.

"Well?" She crossed her arms. "What was so urgent it couldn't wait till the dolphins had gone?"

Daniel opened his mouth, then hesitated. She would not respond well if he chastised her for allowing herself to be surrounded by men. He pressed his lips together. Had she always had this habit of walking blindly into situations in which she was vulnerable?

If Daniel had not deliberately tripped the poor steward last night during supper, there was no telling when the captain would have returned to the dining saloon or what damage might have been done to Eliza's reputation. As it was, the captain's extended absence had caused whispers and furtive glances toward her corridor. What *had* the captain been doing?

Daniel dismissed the insinuating question. It was absurd. But then, how well did he know Miss Brooks? Could this be why she was so opposed to her aunt's attempts at finding her a match? But no, she'd been expecting Mrs. Swenson to escort her. Surely she wouldn't...would she? He scowled as images of the captain's arms around Eliza invaded his mind.

Eliza snorted and walked away from him.

Daniel hurried to stand in front of her. "Tell me, what transpired when the captain escorted you to your cabin."

She drew up short. "I beg your pardon?"

"He was delayed in returning to the table."

"How *dare* you!" She swung to slap him, but he blocked her arm.

Her face grew pink and her shoulders pulled back, fists at her sides.

He would not back down. If he was to appoint himself her guardian for this voyage, he must know what sort of woman she truly was. The idea that she was any other than the lady he took her to be churned his stomach. His heart ached, begging him to relent. Surely she was innocent. Still, he did not truly know this woman before him, however beautiful she may be.

"I have made no accusation." He gentled his tone. "I am simply asking a question."

"A question?" She clamped a hand on her hip. "Would you ask your mother that question?"

He narrowed his eyes. "Will you answer?"

She narrowed hers in return.

Searching the depths of her brown irises, he found no guilt. Beyond the simmering anger lurked hurt. His question had injured her. A woman of questionable character would not have been so wounded by his doubts. He smiled, then caught himself and arranged his features into a more sober expression. "I retract the question, Miss Brooks, with my sincerest apologies."

She tilted her head.

He held his hands out. "Will you forgive me?"

She hesitated. Then gave a curt nod.

"Thank you." He exhaled, then widened his stance. His primary goal had not yet been accomplished. "Miss Brooks, might I ask a favor?"

"You wish to ask a favor of *me*?" She stared at him as if he'd grown a second head. As well she should, given the circumstances. Still, he plowed ahead.

"As you are traveling unescorted"—she crossed her arms and he raised his hands to show he had no intention of rehashing that topic—"and I am the only person aboard with whom you have a prior acquaintance—aside from the captain, of course—I find myself preoccupied with your safety."

"Do you?" Her tone dripped with sarcasm.

"I do. With that in mind, would you do me the honor of giving a bit more forethought to your actions? That way, you might avoid finding yourself in situations like the one from which I have just extracted you."

"From which you have just…" Eliza stepped away and peered around the sidewheel toward the bow of the ship, then turned back to face him. Her pink lips pressed into a line as she considered him.

She did not immediately refuse his request. He exhaled. She was going to be reasonable.

After several moments, her expression relaxed and she folded her hands in front of her. "Please do accept my apologies, Mr. Clarke, for being so thoughtless of your concerns. I am sorry my actions have caused you such distress. In the future, I will be sure to consult with you prior to taking any course of action."

So saying, she spun on her heel, marched to the stairway, and disappeared below deck.

~

*E*liza sauntered down the corridor. Dinner had been a pleasant affair with the continued vacancy of the captain's chair. He must still be occupied with whatever had kept them at anchor for so long.

Her step faltered as she entered the dining saloon.

The captain stood from his seat at the head of the table, followed by the rest of the men.

Straightening, she continued to the place he indicated, at his right

Every muscle in her body tense, she didn't dare close her eyes as he prayed, lest he reach for her again.

At the close of grace, the elderly gentlemen seated across from her engaged the captain in a discussion of the sea creatures spotted from the bow that afternoon.

Thank you, Lord.

She finished her roasted apples and ate half her hot collops before the gentleman to her right shifted toward her.

"The sun was quite pleasant today, was it not? A nice change from the chilly days of winter, I must say. And the wind was neither too weak nor too strong, I think."

Eliza liked the man, despite his being rather dull—and the bit of apple stuck between his teeth. "Do you suppose it will continue as well for the whole of our trip?"

"Well, I don't know about that, but I should think it will continue for the rest of the night."

"Indeed?"

"Goodness, yes. What's more, I think we should take advantage of it." He turned to gain the captain's attention. "How about it, captain?"

Captain Swenson turned from his conversation with the elderly man. "How about what, Mr. Gray?"

"How about a dance?"

Eliza stared at her dinner companion. A dance? How were

they to have a dance when there were no other ladies present? Were the women from the second table to be included? Did he plan to recruit the married women from steerage for this entertainment?

"A splendid idea!" The captain stared at Eliza as he continued. "I cannot think of a more pleasant way to spend the evening."

~

*A*s soon as supper was completed, the guests all rose and drifted toward the stairs. The captain offered his arm to Eliza. She took it, forcing a smile.

Once the first-class passengers were all above deck, the other men, seeing there would not be enough ladies to go around, persuaded the captain to send stewards to fetch the second- and steerage-class passengers. Soon the deck was swarming with passengers, and the musicians were taking their place.

As the captain swung her to stand before him in preparation to dance, Eliza looked past him.

Mr. Clarke stared at her from a few feet away. He leaned back against the rail, outside the group of passengers paired together on the impromptu dance floor. As usual, he was frowning.

As the musicians tuned their instruments, the captain announced that the first dance would be a quadrille. The dancers took their cue to form the necessary squares. Several men paired together for want of female partners.

A small boy from steerage stood beside his mother. He waved at Eliza and she waved back.

The music began and she forced her attention back to the captain standing beside her.

As soon as the quadrille came to an end, the musicians began what sounded to be a polka, but the captain waved at them to stop. "No, no. Give us a rest, now. Let us have a waltz so that we might catch our breath."

Oh, no. A waltz among so many men? Oh, why hadn't she prepared an excuse?

A few of the men paired with other men protested but were ignored. The impromptu band switched to a slower tune.

She seized the folds of her skirt. What should she do?

Mr. Gray stepped closer, as if to request her next dance. The captain moved in, taking her hand and placing his right hand on the small of her back. The would-be dance partner retreated.

"Please excuse me, sir. I am not familiar with this dance." Eliza tried to step out of the captain's arms, but he held her in place.

No. Her mouth was like cotton. Should she cause a scene? *Mr. Clarke!* Her gaze found his.

He straightened away from the rail.

"Do not worry, my dear." Captain Swenson's low tones drew her attention as his leer slithered down her body before returning to her face. "I will teach you all you need to know."

Eliza pulled again at the hand he squeezed. "I beg you would excuse me, sir. I am fatigued."

The musician's completed their introduction.

The captain's bruising grip tightened on her hand as he pushed her back to begin the dance. A hand landed on his shoulder.

Mr. Clarke's glare would set the sails ablaze. "Sir—"

"Sail ho!"

Everyone but the two men before her turned toward the faint white of a ship's sails some distance beyond the bow, a speck in the deepening twilight.

Captain Swenson aimed a narrow glare at Mr. Clarke and released Eliza, then stalked toward the bow.

Mr. Clarke snatched her hand and led her against the flow of passengers following the captain. Where the captain's hand had been rough, cold, and bruising, Mr. Clarke's hand, though also rough, was warm and strong, yet gentle. His hold provided an odd comfort. However vexing he may be, his intentions had always been honorable.

When they reached the top of the stairs, he released her hand. "Miss Brooks, I have no wish to cause you further offense, but—"

She held up her hand, her mouth tipping up on one side. "But you feel it would be better if I were to retire, now?"

His shoulders relaxed. "I do."

"For once, we agree, Mr. Clarke. Good night." She gave a small curtsy and dashed down the stairs.

CHAPTER 9

*E*liza checked her watch. Too early for breakfast, but she could still catch the sunrise. Surely the captain would still be abed at such an early hour. She craved a few minutes of solitude to enjoy the beauty of a new day.

The ship's mild heave and sway of the last two days had changed in the night to an unsteadying dip and roll. She tottered through the empty dining saloon toward the stairs. Thank heavens for the rail.

Strong winds pushed the hair from her face as she emerged on deck. The sky was gray with the coming dawn, but the sun still slept below the horizon. Ropes rubbed, sails slapped, and waves crashed against the hull. Still, there was something serene about the ship as she shuffled across its slick surface.

Heavy air dampened her cheeks. A gust of wind threatened to steal her bonnet so she clamped a hand to the back of her head, keeping the cover in place. The ship rolled, sending her off balance, and she tumbled to the wet floor.

Pushing up with her gloved hands, she scanned the deck. Had anyone witnessed her fall? No other passengers were above deck. The crew were too engaged in adjusting the sails to take notice of her. Thank goodness.

What was the proper term for what they were doing with the sails? They'd been calling out all sorts of commands to one another during their voyage, but she understood little of what it all meant.

The dampness of the deck penetrated her gloves. She had better return to standing before her backside grew damp as well.

Pulling her feet beneath her, she attempted to rise. Her heel slipped and she fell again. Twice more she tried and failed to gain her feet. She growled. Could she crawl toward that rail? Her skirts would get in the way, but perhaps if she—

An open hand appeared over her shoulder.

She craned her neck to look behind her.

"Good morning, Miss Brooks." Mr. Clarke's lips were pressed together. Silent laughter shook his shoulders.

What sort of gentleman laughed at a lady in distress? Then again, she must appear ridiculous, slipping and scrambling on the deck.

Taking his hand, she joined his laughter as he hauled her to her feet.

He placed a steadying hand on her arm, and warmth spread from the point of his touch. Once she was steady, he released her arm, keeping her hand. He led her across the deck to a rail, and released her.

She shivered as she gripped the handrail.

"You're cold." He removed his coat and set it on her shoulders. "Shall I escort you to the stairs?"

"I want to see the sunrise."

"I'm afraid there won't be much to see this morning." He gestured to where large gray clouds were moving to block the sun peeking over the horizon.

"Oh, no."

"I think a storm is brewing." His mouth opened, then snapped closed. His lips parted two more times, but shut again without uttering a sound. He stared at her as if waiting for some response.

He hadn't asked a question. What was she supposed to say? *"I think a storm is brewing."* Like the light of dawn she'd been hoping to witness, understanding grew.

She bit her lip. Clouds now completely blocked the rising sun. Another passenger appeared at the top of the stairs and, after a quick glance at the sky, disappeared below deck. She sighed. He was right. She would be safer below.

She forced a smile. "Would you be so kind as to escort me to the stairs, Mr. Clarke?"

He beamed at her and extended his arm. "It would be my pleasure, Miss Brooks."

∽

At the base of the stairs, Eliza blinked. The dining saloon was crowded. The approaching storm must have woken everyone early. Most frowned as they lounged in chairs or on the sofas lining either side of the saloon. Some appeared green around the gills.

The captain stood as she entered. "Miss Brooks, good morning." His narrowed eyes darted between her and Mr. Clarke, glinting. The other men rose as well.

Eliza's neck warmed as she drew her hand from Mr. Clarke's arm and grabbed the rail. Her lips pressed together. Why should she feel guilty? Mr. Clarke had been nothing but a gentleman. He was engaged, for goodness sake. She had done nothing wrong.

She lifted her chin and strode toward her chair.

A sudden drop of the floor sent her falling against the now-slanted wall.

Another gentleman toppled against her, knocking her bonnet askew. "Beg your pardon, miss!" He scrambled away from her.

The ship righted itself for a moment before dropping and rising again. Eliza's bonnet ribbon threatened to strangle her.

Rain drummed the deck overhead. Roaring thunder filled the saloon. The captain sprinted to the stairs, shouting orders as he disappeared above deck, slamming the hatch behind him.

Passengers scrambled to their cabins. One man's digested supper spread itself across the floor. The stench filled the enclosed space.

Eliza placed a hand over her mouth. *Please don't let me be sick.* With her other hand, she clutched the nearest sofa.

Wind howled through the ship as the saloon continued to heave and sway.

A severe tilt pulled her from the wall. She crashed against the table. Dishes shattered on the floor. The table didn't budge. *It must be bolted down.* Chairs scraped and tumbled across the room.

The ship rolled in the opposite direction, tugging her toward the sofa.

An arm wrapped around her waist. Locked her in place.

She craned her neck. Mr. Clarke held her.

He pressed her back against his chest, her bonnet crushed between them. "We can do this."

Together, they staggered through the saloon, pausing at the peak of each tilt to grab the nearest table's edge. After what seemed an eternity, they made it to her corridor.

"Which is yours?" His breath warmed her ear against the chill of the storm.

She pointed to her cabin door.

He led her down the passageway and threw open her door. Shoving her inside, he kept hold of her arm. She steadied herself with the doorframe, and he released her. The ship tossed him against the opposite wall.

She gasped.

He waved aside her concern. "I'm all right. Shut your door and get to your berth. Wait there until the storm passes."

The ship sent him forward again. He clasped her doorframe to keep from plowing into her, clinging to it through another roll of the ship. He panted, his face inches from hers.

A dining chair slid into her corridor, smashing against the wall behind him.

She yanked at the ribbon on her bonnet. "What about you?"

"I'll do the same. Now shut your door." He let go, allowing the ship's sway to pull him through the corridor.

≈

July 1853 (6 months before)
Roxbury, Massachusetts

*A*lice tugged at a fingertip on her right glove as the landau bumped up the lane toward the Clarke home. Beside her, Mother nodded encouragingly to Richard who sat across from them, prattling on about his adventures as a sawyer. But Alice couldn't bring herself to focus on his stories.

Sweltering in the humidity and midsummer sun, she shifted on the bench, her unseeing gaze directed at the passing landscape. Her future mother-in-law would surely ask about the letters Alice had received from Daniel since their last visit. If Alice lied and said she had not received a letter, Mrs. Clarke would worry that something ill had befallen her son. If she answered that she had, Mrs. Clarke would expect Alice to share the letters as she had done previously. But Daniel's patience had grown thin, his letters full of questions she wasn't ready to answer. She could not share them.

And then there was Benjamin.

How would Daniel's brother behave this evening? Since their return from the Summer Ball, he'd refused to escort her to any functions—in direct opposition to Daniel's standing request. Benjamin had even avoided her at church.

Had he written to Daniel? No. If Daniel knew, he'd have mentioned it in his letters. Or stopped writing altogether. Neither had Benjamin said anything to his parents, judging by this evening's invitation to supper.

The twisted glove pinched her finger. She pulled it free. Would she have a chance to speak with Benjamin? Or had he manufactured an excuse to be absent?

Richard plucked the loose glove from her hand, a wicked grin splitting his face.

"Give it back." She reached for the pilfered accessory, but he held it beyond her reach.

"I cannot. As a gentleman, it is my duty to rescue anything in distress, and this"—he jiggled the mangled glove—"poor thing is certainly in distress."

She shoved her open palm at him. "Oh, stop being ridiculous and return my glove at once." Out the window, a lone figure hurried off the porch of the farmhouse. Her breath caught. *Benjamin.* He disappeared into the Clarke's woodshop. "We've nearly arrived. Do not make a fool of me."

"How could I, when you've already done such a splendid job of it yourself?"

She glared at him.

Mother rolled her eyes, an indulgent smile tugging at her lips. "Richard, your sister is correct. We *are* nearly arrived, so do quit tormenting her. For my sake."

"Of course, Mother. Just as soon as she says the magic words."

Alice coughed. "Of all the—"

Richard sing-songed, "Say it."

97

"I will not."

"Tsk-tsk. Do you want your glove back or not?"

Alice turned to Mother for help.

Amusement sparkled in Mother's eyes as she shrugged.

If Caroline were here instead of spending the evening in the home of her future in-laws, she'd make Richard return Alice's glove. She was better at handling Richard's vexing moods.

Alice huffed. "Richard Stevens is the best brother on the face of this earth and any woman would be lucky to marry him. I am forever humbled to live in his shadow."

Richard's mischievous grin stretched from ear to ear. He tossed the glove toward Alice. "There. Was that so hard?"

Catching the glove midair, she stuck her tongue at him. "You're an odious pig."

He bowed. "I do my best."

The carriage came to a halt and Richard flung the door open, leaping out with a laugh. "We're here!"

As Alice stepped from the carriage, Mrs. Clarke came onto the porch. "You've come!" She hurried down the steps to embrace first Mother, then Alice.

Richard scooped Mrs. Clarke into a scandalous bear hug and swung her in circles until she begged to be put down.

She wiped away tears of laughter. "Oh, Richard, you are a dear. You always know how to make me laugh." She patted her graying brown hair. "I'm sorry Caroline wasn't able to join us, but I'm glad the three of you are here. Come, let's go inside. The men are almost finished for the day and will join us shortly."

Alice followed her hostess up the stairs. "Will your whole family be joining us this evening?"

Mrs. Clarke gave her an odd look. "Except for Daniel, of course."

Alice's cheeks warmed. "Obviously." So Benjamin hadn't made an excuse.

"Speaking of Daniel"—Mrs. Clark's eyes lit—"I've just

finished reading his most recent letter. How many letters have you had from him since we last spoke?"

Alice swallowed. "Oh, a few."

"And?"

"I'm afraid I've forgotten them at home."

"Oh dear." Mrs. Clarke sighed. "I suppose you'll bring them next time, yes?"

"Of course."

CHAPTER 10

January 1854 (Present Day)
California Coast

*C*rash!

Eliza jerked awake. She rose on one elbow. *Something's different.* The ship's lurching and swaying was restrained.

Metal groaned, reverberating through the ship. Wood cracked all around.

Boots thundered on the boards above. Men shouted.

She clutched the blankets. What was going on?

"All passengers on deck! All passengers on deck!"

She leaped from her berth and snatch up her carpetbag. Thank heavens she'd returned Mama's Bible to it the night before. She yanked open the door and ran down the corridor. Joining the throng of passengers rushing through the saloon toward the stairs, she craned her neck. Where was Mr. Clarke? She didn't see him in the crowd. He must already be on deck.

Terrified voices rose above the din.

"We've struck a reef!"

"We're going to die!"

"Nonsense. Captain Swenson has it all in hand."

The crush of people mashed Eliza against the wall at the base of the stairs. She struggled to breathe. The handrail pressed into her abdomen. Mr. Gray pushed passed her. His eyes bulged in his flushed face. Someone shoved Eliza into his wake. She must climb or be trampled.

On deck, she was pushed aside as more passengers spewed from below. She froze on the rocking surface, clutching her bag. Swinging lanterns sliced through the gray of a waning night. Hundreds of people roamed the ship, like an army of ants whose hill had been trampled. She couldn't breathe. Couldn't think. People were pushing. Shoving. Yelling for their loved ones. Children were crying. A dog ran about barking at every- one. Smoke belched from the hatch where steerage passengers spilled onto the deck. Everyone was drenched by the pouring rain.

Her bodice clung like a second skin. Her skirts grew heavy. Shivering, she hugged her bag to her chest. *I'm going to die. I'll never see Pa again.*

Her knees gave way.

Before she hit the deck, strong fingers wrapped around her upper arms, pulled her to her feet.

"There you are!"

The captain had found her.

~

*C*rash!

Daniel jumped from his berth. They had struck something. He burst from his cabin. He must find Eliza and get her to safety.

He struggled against the tide of fleeing passengers to reach her door.

It was ajar, the room empty.

His breath left in a whoosh. Where was she?

He raced back to the dining saloon. She should be easy to spot among so many men. No sign there of her bonnet, nor her soft brown curls. She must already be above.

It seemed an eternity before he emerged on deck. He scanned the panicked passengers. *There!* Miss Brooks was being hauled away by the captain.

Daniel chased them. A terrified child cut across his path, and Daniel halted short of colliding with the boy. The child crashed into the open arms of his mother.

Daniel turned back toward Eliza.

She was gone.

～

*E*liza grabbed the slick rail. Over the side, a lifeboat dangled, nearly filled by first-class passengers and two crewman at the oars.

The captain scooped her up.

"What are you doing?" She pushed at his shoulders.

He swung her over the rail and deposited her into the boat. The three fancy ladies blubbered beside her. A man on the bench in front of her shivered in his nightclothes. Now full, the lifeboat descended toward the heavy surf. Eliza pulled one hand from her bag to clutch the side.

She stared up at the captain. He shouted orders at someone on deck and dashed away.

Mr. Clarke appeared in his place. Rain-drenched, breathing hard, he stared down at her.

Would she ever see him again? *Please, God, don't let him die.*

～

*H*e was too late. Daniel raked a hand through his wet hair as Eliza's dinghy lowered toward the raging sea. Would she be safe?

Beside her boat, another was being filled. A well-dressed man tried to push his way in with women and children from steerage. A crewman shoved the man, who fell against Daniel before righting himself. The man swung at the crewman. He missed and pulled back for another go. Daniel grabbed the man's arms.

A large wave crashed against the ship. One of the crewmen lowering Eliza's dinghy lost his footing. The rope flew through the crewman's hands. The boat's bow lowered faster than its stern.

Daniel shoved away the man he'd been restraining and snatched at the rope. *Too late.*

Eliza and her fellow passengers screamed as they plunged into the sea.

Their dinghy broke loose, crashing into the waves beside them.

Daniel set a foot on the rail and launched himself into the roaring waves.

CHAPTER 11

*E*liza smacked face-first into the thrashing ocean. Her mouth and nose filled as she went under. She fought her way toward the surface. Breaking free, she spewed water.

She sucked air, once, twice. A wave washed over her, pulling her down.

Resurfacing, she gasped. Kicked against her cumbersome skirts. Her bag pulled like an anvil, growing heavier by the second. She struggled to keep her face above the water.

A second lifeboat lowered from the ship. People all around her screamed and flailed.

Waves rushed her toward the ship. *I'm going to crash against it!* The waves changed course. She was surging away. Out to sea!

Her legs screamed. Her arms were on fire. She couldn't keep afloat much longer. The capsized lifeboat floated to and fro in the surging waves, but not close enough. She couldn't reach it.

Another wave brought the elderly gentlemen near her. Wild-eyed, he grabbed her shoulders. Climbed her like a ladder. Sent her plummeting beneath the surface.

A scream formed, but she didn't dare open her mouth. Summoning all her strength, she shoved her bag at his legs.

Clawed at his grip with her free hand. Her lungs burned. She couldn't shake him loose.

God, help! I'm going to di—!

She was free! A strong arm slid around her chest and a hand yanked her bag from her grasp, releasing it to its watery grave. Someone dragged her to the surface, where she gulped air. Blinked her eyes.

Mr. Clarke was behind her, holding her.

She opened her mouth to thank him, but another wave slapped her face, choking her.

He dragged her through the waves.

She flailed her legs a few times to propel them. Succeeded only in kicking him. Gave up and wrapped her empty hands around the strong arm holding her.

Her chest ached from more than her near drowning. *It's all gone.* Everything she owned, at the bottom of the sea. *That doesn't matter right now.* All that mattered was getting out of this water.

The small lifeboat, now somehow upright and fast filling with sodden passengers, was a beacon of hope. Seconds, minutes, years passed before they reached it. Two men already aboard grabbed her hands and pulled from above as Mr. Clarke pushed from below. More than once, he sank himself with the effort. At last, she tumbled into the small vessel, too weak to do anything but look toward her rescuer.

Mr. Clarke swam away.

~

*D*aniel stroked through the water, away from the dinghy. *Thank You.* It was all the time he had to express his gratitude for Eliza's safety, for strong swimming skills, and for the carpentry work that kept his arms strong.

Lord, help me. He swam to where another woman struggled

105

to stay afloat. He hooked his arm around her. Fought the waves back to the dinghy. He shoved her aboard with the help of those already in the boat.

Again and again, he found people in the waves and dragged them to safety. His whole body trembled and his lungs ached as he shoved a fifth passenger into the boat. The man's foot slipped on the boat's edge, kicking the side of Daniel's head.

Stars blurred Daniel's vision as he sank beneath the water.

A hand reached out. Grabbed his arm. Stopped his helpless decent. It tugged but didn't pull him up.

The stars faded. Stabbing pain refocused his brain. He kicked toward the surface.

Breaking through, he sucked in air.

Eliza's wide eyes met his. "You're too heavy. I can't lift you."

CHAPTER 12

*E*liza craned her neck toward those in the lifeboat. "Help me!"

Two men reached around her and hauled Daniel aboard. He huddled on the boat's bottom, shaking.

She collapsed to the bench beside him. Panic had stretched moments into years as she struggled to pull him from the water. Her heart still pounded against her ribs, but her breathing eased now that he sat at her feet. Alive. She closed her eyes. *Thank you, Lord.*

Water in the bottom of the boat sloshed against her ankles and his backside. She should pull him from the puddle to the bench beside her. Her body quivered. She didn't have the energy.

Beside her, one of the fancy women clung to the side of the lifeboat, wailing. She yelled for her friends. No reply came. No bright colors flashed among the waves.

All the ship's lifeboats were in the water now. Many were halfway toward a long, skinny strip of land Eliza could see jutting from a larger strip of land to the north, about a half-mile away. A few boats, like hers, continued to fight the waves, their passengers still searching for survivors.

When at last their boat was full, the men rowed toward shore. The fancy woman became hysterical. "Don't leave 'em!" She clutched at the jewels dripping from her neck. "You can't leave 'em! They'll drown!" She lunged as if to jump overboard, tilting the boat.

The man behind Eliza jerked the woman back to her bench. "Crazy woman! Want us all to drown?"

"I'm sorry. I—" The woman broke down.

Long minutes passed as the men fought the stormy sea with no apparent progress.

The man across from Eliza pointed at the floor. "We're sinking!"

He was right. Water seeped through a half-inch hole in the wood. Already, there were five or six inches of water in the boat's bottom. Eliza ripped a large strip from her soaked petticoats and jammed it into the hole. It wouldn't keep all the water out. It didn't need to. It just needed to slow the leak enough to get them to shore.

Another man pressed his boot on the makeshift patch, keeping it in place.

"N-n-nice work." Mr. Clarke smiled at her.

She stared at his dripping face. Her fingers flexed, still sore from gripping the carpetbag handles. He'd tossed her last connection to Mama like a piece of garbage.

It couldn't be helped.

He didn't even try.

You're alive.

But Mama's gone and Pa's gone. Mr. Clarke threw them away.

Not them. Their things.

The only things of theirs I had. And Mr. Clarke let them sink to the bottom of the ocean. For what?

To save your life.

She scowled and turned away from him. As if doing so could stop her warring thoughts.

~

*D*aniel's head dropped to his hands. He rubbed his temples. The woman had scowled at him. Scowled at him for complimenting her! She was, without a doubt, the most exasperating woman God had ever created.

Their boat did not progress toward the closest land—which appeared to be an island of some sort. Instead, the sailors manning the oars of their little boat insisted upon heading toward a thin strip of shallow land they called Ballast Point. Several passengers expressed bafflement and aggravation with this decision. Daniel was too weary to care. So long as he wasn't required to row, they could take him to Mexico.

When they drew near the strip, a few men jumped into the shallow water and hauled their dinghy onto the rocky shore.

Once the boat was beached, Daniel forced his wobbly legs beneath him and rose, intending to assist Eliza. But while he was still finding his balance, Eliza clambered over the side of the boat and set off across the rocks at a march.

Fine.

He offered his hand to the other woman in the boat.

"Thank you." She accepted his assistance and stepped out.

He followed her out of the shallow water and saw her settled a safe distance from the slapping waves.

He swiped the rain from his face. What had the *Virginia* struck that held her captive in the churning blue ocean?

Several yards down the strip, the captain conferred with his crew. Many passengers gathered around them. Daniel trudged toward them.

Bits of conversation carried on the wind.

"...we strike a reef?"

"...Zuniga Shoal. The sand..."

"...be saved?"

"That's the Playa." A sailor motioned toward a sparse group of buildings near where they were meant to have anchored. "'Bout four miles more to town."

"It'll be a miserable walk in this weather."

"What should we..." A strong gust of wind stole the rest of the man's sentence.

Daniel caught the last of the captain's words as he joined the group.

"...take count of who's here. See who's missing before we risk heading back in this storm. Are there any injured?"

A member of the crew stepped forward. "A few, sir, but none's too serious."

Daniel had forgotten to check whether Eliza was injured. She hadn't appeared so when she marched off. Still, he ought to find her and make certain she was well. He shivered. In any case, they needed to find shelter and warmth. He searched the group around the captain. Eliza wasn't there. He walked a few steps away.

There.

She was hurrying along the rocky point toward the main peninsula.

Where is she going?

~

*E*liza's foot slipped on the wet rock. She righted herself. Another few steps and the rocks gave way to a narrow sandy beach. The odd sensation of swaying continued to plague her. Why wouldn't it stop?

A little more than a mile ahead were four rough structures situated a short distance from the water's edge. As the crewmembers were rowing, one had said these were hide houses—storage buildings for the small town's biggest export—cowhides. Near the hide houses were supposed to be a store and a hotel of sorts. Beyond that was the road that led to town.

She would find it. She couldn't stop now. Not here.

She had read that the small town of San Diego was located four miles away from its port, which was a great inconvenience for sailors and merchants who disliked having to venture so far from their ships. At the moment, four miles sounded like a splendid distance. If she never saw another drop of salt water again, it would be too soon.

She shivered as a strong breeze drove rain against her dress. Wrapping her arms around herself, she rubbed her shoulders as she trudged along the wet sand. The calmer waters of the bay lapped the shore to her right. She turned her head left, blocking them from view. It didn't stop their whooshing from filling her ears.

The remembered screams of men, women, and children fleeing the crippled ship hounded her with every slap of water. The taste of iron filled her mouth. She quit gnawing her inner lip.

Had the other fancy ladies found their way to a different lifeboat or were they lost to the sea?

A sob pressed its way up her throat. She swallowed it down.

How many others had failed to reach safety?

Her lungs grew tight. She wheezed in wet, salty air.

Had the small boy who'd danced with his mother survived?

What about his mother?

Mama. Her legs wobbled—and she fell to her hands and knees in the wet sand. Her stomach churned and lurched upward. She fought and failed to keep its contents within.

Oh, Mama. I miss you.

If only Mama were here to hold her.

CHAPTER 13

*E*liza's down!

Daniel rushed forward, but when she began retching, he halted a discreet distance behind her. She probably took in too much seawater when she was tossed from the boat and nearly drowned by that crazed old man. *I should have gotten to her faster.*

Her heaving stopped and she eased back on her heels.

He closed the distance between them. "I'm sorry I don't have a kerchief to offer you."

She accepted his hand, and he pulled her to her feet. "Thank you."

They strolled away from the offensive odor.

He clasped his hands behind his back. "Are you well?"

Hugging herself as she shivered, she tilted her head and raised a brow.

What a foolish thing to ask. Of course she wasn't well. "That is…I meant to ask, 'Are you injured in any way?'"

She looked down as if to check herself. "I don't believe so."

His shoulders relaxed. "Where are you going?"

She raised her chin and wiped at the rivulets of rain running down her forehead. "To town."

"That's not the town. San Diego is another four miles beyond that."

Her lips pressed together—a sign he was learning did not bode well for him.

"Thank you kindly for your information. However I am well aware that those sorry-looking hide houses do not constitute the town of San Diego."

"Are you planning to walk there?" He wiped the rain from his face. "In this weather?"

"What else?" She placed a hand on her hip.

He gaped at her. He had saved her life. She had saved his. Were they truly arguing once more? The ridiculousness of it rumbled deep within him before bursting forth unchecked.

Her face grew red, but hysterical mirth had overcome him. He could not stop laughing. His stomach cramped and he doubled over. Why was he so amused?

She spun away.

Still bent, he grasped her arm. "Wait." He gasped between laughs. "Wait." He said again as his self-control returned and he straightened. "I'm sorry."

She crossed her arms.

"Truly I am." At last, he managed a sober expression. "I don't know what came over me. Please forgive me."

Her expression softened. "Of course, you're forgiven." She uncrossed her arms and exhaled. "But will you forgive me? You saved my life, and the moment we were ashore, I left you without so much as a hint of gratitude. I don't know what came over me. I'm so sorry."

He smiled. "You forget that you saved my life as well. Of course you are forgiven."

"Thank you."

"May I ask you a question?"

She cocked her head to the side.

"Why did you scowl at me? In the dingy?"

"Oh." Her cheeks flushed again as her chin dipped down. "I'm sorry about that. I wasn't really scowling at *you* as much as I was thinking of the things I'd lost. They were special."

Shivers shook her body. She needed a barrier against the cold. Should he offer his coat? No. It was as soaked as she. "I'm sorry."

"It couldn't be helped." Her gaze darted past him, then returned to him. "I truly am grateful for your rescue, but I must go now."

He looked over his shoulder. The rest of the survivors meandered down the beach toward them, led by Captain Swenson. He turned back to Eliza. She was already walking away. "I understand your wish to avoid the captain, but I'm certain he will be far too busy determining the fate of his ship to cause you any further trouble."

She continued down the beach. "I'm not leaving on account of the captain."

"Then why?" His voice rose to carry over the increasing distance. "I'm certain the captain will arrange accommodations for his passengers until a new ship arrives."

"Fortunately"—she sidestepped a pile of kelp—"I haven't the need to wait for a new ship."

He jogged to catch up with her. "What do you mean? How do you intend to reach...?" What *was* her destination? The base of his throat tightened. Did she not intend to disembark in Boston when he did? Even if she did. What then? He'd likely never see her again. Heaviness slowed his steps. He shook himself. Beyond that of his self-appointed role as her protector during their journey, he had no connection to Eliza. It was right that they should part ways at journey's end.

She swiped damp tendrils from her face. "I am at my destination. Or very soon will be. San Diego is as far as I ever intended to go."

"San Diego?" He drew his head back. "What purpose can you possibly have in coming here?"

"My pa is here."

He tripped over a clump of kelp and barely stopped himself from falling face-first into the sand. "Your father is here? And he sent for you?"

She increased her pace.

He hurried to catch up.

They passed the first of the hide houses, a foul stench wafting toward him on the winds of the storm.

Suspicion seeded his mind. "Miss Brooks? Your father did send for you, did he not?"

He tried to catch her eye.

She stared at the sand.

He frowned. "Is he expecting your visit?"

Eliza's head rotated away from him.

He stopped. Taking her arm, he forced her to face him. "Tell me that you know where he's staying."

She lifted her chin. "I will find him." Her eyes sparked, but behind the challenge was a flicker of something else. That haunting pain he'd glimpsed their first day on the ship.

"You will...?" He rubbed the back of his neck. "Do you at least know someone here with whom you may stay until you do?"

She squeezed the folds of her damp skirts.

He swallowed the urge to yell and shake her.

Releasing her arm, he paced in front of a hotel with a sign nailed across the door, painted in both English and Spanish that marked it as closed. At least only the vacant stare of its boarded windows served as witness to his frustration.

She had traveled all this way alone, to an obscure little town where she knew no one. Had no idea where her father might be.

If that weren't enough, she'd lost everything she had in the wreck and was set on walking miles to town alone. Through the pouring rain in a dress that was soaked and torn.

The woman had more temerity than many men he knew.

For goodness sake, had she no respect for the sanctity of her own life?

He walked past the clearly empty hotel and store to stare out at the bay. What was he to do? There would be another ship come within a day or two to take the enervated passengers onward to Panama.

He needed to be on that ship. Alice was waiting for him. Yet, how could he leave Eliza in such a situation?

He couldn't.

He must locate her father before the next ship departed. Eliza was right. They mustn't waste time waiting at the Playa. They must proceed at once to San Diego and procure themselves rooms so that he might begin his search.

Daniel turned toward Eliza. Except, she wasn't there. She had continued down the flat, muddy road leading toward town. With a last glance toward the group of passengers just arriving at the first hide house, he ran to catch up with her.

~

*W*hen Eliza and Daniel were about a mile from their destination, the rain finally ceased its downpour and the strong wind tempered to a slight breeze. The change was of little benefit. A chill had settled deep in her bones. She ached with every quaking step.

Oh, to sink into a hot bath!

As they approached the town, pale morning sunlight broke through the clouds illuminating a barren, muddy plaza surrounded by a dozen or so brown and white adobe buildings, along with a handful of clapboard structures. An empty flagstaff stood tall in the center, its flag presumably removed for the duration of the storm—much like the town's citizens, who were nowhere to be seen.

This was San Diego?

Entering the plaza, they came first upon a grog shop that— owing to the earliness of the hour—was blessedly closed. No ribald songs or pickled men's shouts disrupted the post-storm quiet as she and Daniel passed. A long, white adobe building sported *Commercial Restaurant* in red paint over the door.

For the first time since she'd set foot on land, Eliza's steps faltered. Should she inquire about a meal? No. She would enjoy it more after resting. *Thank you, Lord, that I kept my money pouch in my petticoat pocket.* The coins patted her leg with every step.

Two buildings past the restaurant, a sign read, *The Exchange Hotel.*

At last. Her feet were aching.

Mr. Clarke hastened to knock.

A minute later, a gentleman opened the door. "Why, you're soaked through! Come in, come in." He ushered them into the front room, where a blazing fire filled the hearth.

Eliza held her shaking hands toward the flames.

Mr. Clarke stood beside her. "Please forgive our appearance. Our ship is wrecked and we've walked here from the Playa."

Their host called for another man, whom he dispatched with instructions to hurry to the Playa and bring back more passengers. Once the man had gone, the gentleman faced Mr. Clarke and Eliza.

"Please forgive me for not introducing myself. I am George Tebbetts, welcome to my hotel." He gave a small bow.

"A pleasure to meet you, Mr. Tebbetts. I am Mr. Clarke, and this is Miss Brooks."

He looked back and forth between them. "You are not married?"

Mr. Clarke cleared his throat. "No, sir, merely acquaintances who happen to have been traveling aboard the same ship."

"I see." Mr. Tebbetts walked toward the door and motioned for them to follow. "Come. I will show you to your rooms."

Mr. Clarke cleared his throat. "Thank you, sir, but one room is all we require."

"I *beg* your pardon?" Eliza turned on Mr. Clarke.

"For you!" He held his hands up, palms out. "The room is for you. I—"

"Where do you plan to sleep?" Eliza's hand met her hip. "If you believe that because you saved my life—"

"Of course not." He stepped back. "I meant to say that although I *will* need a room later tonight, I have not the time to sleep at the moment, as I intend to commence inquiring about"—he mouthed the last two words—"your father."

She wanted to respond, but she and Daniel were making a scene. Mr. Tebbetts shifted beside the door.

Eliza took a step closer to Mr. Clarke and whispered, "You're going to look for Pa?"

He nodded.

This man's generosity was astounding. She eyed his wet clothes.

"Don't you need to change?"

"I'm afraid I have nothing to change into. My things are still aboard the ship."

He was right, of course. They should have found a store before coming to the hostelry.

Mr. Clarke wrung rainwater from his coat sleeves into the fire. Drops sizzled on the hearth. He glanced at Mr. Tebbetts. "Would it be possible to have a warm bath sent to Miss Brooks's room, sir?"

"Of course."

Rain glistened on the window overlooking the plaza as the

sun rose. The thought of a bath was enticing, but... "If you're going to look for Pa, I should come with you."

"No, please stay and rest."

"He's my pa, and you're as tired as I."

"I am fine. I will find a store, obtain a fresh change of clothes, and begin the inquiries. I promise to return the moment I've learned something."

Mr. Tebbetts stepped toward them and focused on Eliza. "I apologize for overhearing, but did you say you're looking for your father?"

She leaned forward. Might he know Pa? "Yes, his name is Jim Brooks. He's a thin man, over six feet tall and has dark brown hair like mine. He last wrote that he hoped to find work here with Lieutenant Derby."

Mr. Tebbetts scratched behind his ear. "I'm sorry. I don't recognize the name. I heard Lieutenant Derby was using Indians. Still, you might try asking him. Perhaps he's spoken to your father and can be of some help. " Mr. Tebbetts pointed south. "Derby's renting a house from Don Bandini. It's a short walk from here. A white, two-story, wood house. You can't miss it."

Eliza spun toward the front door, only to have Mr. Clarke step in her path.

"I'll go. You stay here and rest. I'll return as soon as I know anything."

She hesitated. She *was* exhausted. But Pa was so close.

Mr. Tebbetts stepped toward the stairs, his hand inviting her to follow. "I'm sure my wife will be happy to wash your clothes for you while you bathe, miss."

She sighed. A warm bath, clean clothes, and a good rest did sound splendid. Mr. Clarke *had* proved himself trustworthy. He could handle the inquiry.

For now.

≈

*A*fter a stop at the general store, where he purchased and changed into a new set of clothes, Daniel set out for Lieutenant Derby's home. With Tebbett's description and directions, it didn't take long to find the place. Unfortunately, the lieutenant wasn't there and Mrs. Derby expressed uncertainty as to when her husband would return. She invited Daniel to wait, but he politely declined.

Less than an hour after leaving Eliza at the Exchange, he reentered the plaza. Where should he try next?

At the opposite end, the man Tebbetts had sent to the Playa earlier was pulling up with a wagon full of passengers. They stopped in front of the Exchange, and the passengers piled out of the wagon before shuffling into the hotel.

Daniel strode across the plaza to ask the driver whether he'd learned anything about the *Virginia*.

"They say she broke a shaft in the storm and her engine gave out trying to make it to port." The man shook his head. "Cracked her hull on the Zuniga Shoal. Not sure they'll be able to save her."

"I see." He would have to see if he could save his trunk, which was still aboard. He couldn't afford to lose the carpentry tools his father had gifted him before his journey west. "What of the cargo aboard?"

"The Goliah's out there now with the *Virginia* crew trying to save what they can."

Daniel drew in a sigh. Time to get back to the Playa and secure his trunk.

CHAPTER 14

a rap on her door pulled Eliza from slumber. She struggled through the thick fog of sleep toward coherent thought. She pried one eyelid open. Where was she? A rough blanket scratched her skin. She was undressed. In the hotel. The storm. The shipwreck. Everything she cherished lost to the bottom of the ocean. Her vision blurred. She curled into a ball, closing her eyes.

Another knock at the door drew her head up.

Sniffing back tears, she pinched the thick blanket around herself and shuffled to the door. "Yes?"

A man's muffled voice responded. "Sorry to disturb you, miss. Mr. Clarke said to inform you that he's gone to the Playa to fetch his belongings but that he'd return when he was through."

"Thank you." She shuffled back to sit on the edge of the bed. The light peeking between the curtains was brighter than when she'd fallen asleep. How long had she slept? She peeled back a tiny corner of the curtain and checked the sky. She must have slept around three hours. The sun was halfway to its peak. She let the fabric drop.

So Mr. Clarke had gone to fetch his belongings? How nice for him that he had belongings to fetch.

She winced.

That was unkind and unfair. Mr. Clarke had been trying to help when he took her carpetbag away and let it sink to the bottom of the ocean. It wasn't his fault she lost Mama's Bible and Pa's letters. If Mr. Clarke hadn't taken that bag from her, she would have lost her life as well.

She held her breath against the sob pressing its way up her throat. The walls in this hotel were thin. She could hear a child crying in the next room. She would not humiliate herself by crying where everyone could hear. She was a grown woman. They were only things. She lifted her chin. There was no time for tears. She had a job to do.

It was time to find Pa.

She sprung from the bed, then stopped. Her clothes were gone. Being washed by Mrs. Tebbetts. With a sigh, she fell back to bed. The child's crying continued. Closing her eyes, she prayed for the Lord to comfort the child.

Then she covered her ears with the blanket.

She would *not* cry.

~

*D*aniel hopped off as the wagon pulled to a stop in front of the Exchange. Afternoon sun had warmed the wood of his trunk during the trip back to town. Thankfully, the same Zuniga Shoal which the *Virginia* crashed onto also prevented the ship from sinking and Daniel's trunk had been spared the fate of Eliza's carpetbag. He lowered it to the ground before paying the hired driver. As the wagon pulled away, Daniel opened the hotel door. He lifted his trunk and turned to carry it inside.

Eliza blocked the doorway.

She wore a new dress. The rich brown color complemented her complexion. Her thick brown hair—which had been in a dreadful state when last he saw her—was arranged in its usual tidy bun and curls. She appeared wholly refreshed.

Yet she was not smiling.

"I see you've retrieved your belongings. Have you also spoken with Lieutenant Derby?"

He shifted the heavy trunk. Her tone held strong skepticism. Didn't she trust him? He stepped closer. "If you would be so kind as to step aside? This trunk is rather heavy."

"Oh." She stepped out of the doorway, and he walked past her into the hotel.

After speaking with Mr. Tebbetts about the storage of his trunk, Daniel placed it in the area indicated and walked back to the front door.

Stepping outside, he found Eliza still waiting for him.

He squinted against the sun. "Nice dress."

"Thank you. Mrs. Tebbetts was kind enough to fetch this from the store for me to wear while my other clothes are drying." She crossed her arms. "You haven't answered my question."

He sighed. "He was not at home."

Her hands moved to her hips. "Did you inquire as to where he'd gone?"

"Of course." Did she think him a simpleton? "His wife thought he might have gone to see a friend at a local ranch, but was uncertain as to when he planned to return."

"Oh." Her arms fell to her sides, and she was quiet for a moment. "Well, thank you for your efforts. My rest was quite refreshing and I am now prepared to make inquiries on my own." She gave a small curtsy and turned to go.

"Miss Brooks."

She looked over her shoulder. "Yes?"

"It would be my pleasure to continue the inquiries on your behalf."

She pivoted away. "Thank you, but that's not necessary. I'm quite capable of conducting them myself."

He caught her shoulder and walked around to face her.

"I have no doubt of your capabilities. You are a strong, intelligent woman." He ran his thumbs beneath the lapel of his coat. "Which is why I'm sure you'll agree that it would not be wise to make it widely known that you're here alone and have no family close by to protect you. Which is what you making the inquiries would do. Even coming with me to inquire will lead to questions that I think would be best avoided."

She opened her mouth, then closed it. "I suppose you do make a valid point. But…" She considered the hotel, brow furrowed. "I can't stay in that room a minute longer. There's a crying child in the next room, and I…"

Tears filled her eyes, softening his heart.

She blinked them away and straightened her shoulders. "I must have something to do."

He surveyed the area for inspiration. His gaze landed on the Commercial Restaurant two doors down. "Have you eaten?"

She shook her head.

"Then you've missed breakfast *and* dinner. You must be famished. Why don't you allow me to escort you to the restaurant?" He offered his arm and she accepted it. "While you eat, I will continue my inquiries around town." Ordinarily, he wouldn't suggest a lady dine alone in public, but it seemed the better of his current options.

Besides, how much trouble could even Miss Brooks get into while dining?

She cocked her head at him. "But you *will* fetch me the moment you find Pa."

"Absolutely."

"Oh, and you should probably start with the doctor's office."

"Is your Pa ill?" She might have mentioned that. He would have made the doctor's office his first stop.

"I don't know, but it would explain why his letters stopped."

Her father stopped writing to her? "How long ago?"

Her forehead wrinkled. "What?"

"How long ago did he stop writing?"

"What does it matter?" She pulled her hand away. "On second thought, I think I will come with you. If Pa's ill—"

"Oh no." He snatched her hand, held it to his arm, and strode toward the restaurant. "I told you, we need to protect your reputation. I'll do the inquiring. If anyone tries to speak to you —asks you about your purpose in town—just tell them about the shipwreck. There's no reason to share that you're looking for your Pa. I'll speak with the proprietress and any other patrons as soon as I settle you at a table, so you don't have to worry about whether they know anything. The less you say, the easier it will be to protect your reputation. If they don't know anything, I'll start asking at the other businesses in town. I promise to fetch you as soon as I find him—and if he's ill, I'll run."

❦

Having finished her meal, Eliza thanked the proprietress and stood to leave. Daniel had returned only long enough to inform her that he'd spoken with the town's doctor, but the man had never heard of Jim.

She stepped outside with a sigh. *Where are you, Pa?*

The cool breeze running across the plaza caressed her cheeks. Twilight softened the rough edges of the town, giving it an almost romantic feel. It was so peaceful here compared to San Francisco. Few people wandered about, and most who did she recognized as passengers from the ship.

Across the way, a small boy exited a store, sucking on a

candy. The same boy she'd seen during the dance. *He's alive!* His mother followed close behind him, her shoulders drooped. *And so is she!* They crossed the plaza and disappeared into the Exchange.

Oh no. His must have been the crying she'd heard earlier. She hadn't asked Mr. Clarke if he knew whether any of the passengers succumbed to the sea or if all were saved. She hadn't wanted to know. But there was no father with the young boy and his weary mother. She blinked back tears. Had the boy lost his father? Or was his crying just a result of the terror they'd all experienced?

A small brown-and-black bird fluttered past. It pecked at something on the ground a few feet away from her before flying off again.

A burst of nearby laughter broke the quiet. Two men approached the two-story building beside the Exchange. A large sign on the building advertised that the offices of the *Herald* were located on its second floor.

"Derby, you didn't!" One of the men grinned at the man next to him.

Derby! The lieutenant Pa came to talk to! Eliza hurried toward them.

"Oh, but I did."

Chuckling, the first man bid Derby farewell and disappeared into the building.

Lieutenant Derby turned to leave.

"Wait! Lieutenant Derby!" She must not miss this opportunity.

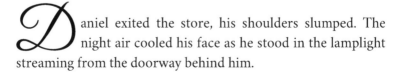

*D*aniel exited the store, his shoulders slumped. The night air cooled his face as he stood in the lamplight streaming from the doorway behind him.

The shopkeeper closed the door a moment later.

Daniel waited for his vision to adjust. After the doctor, he'd stopped by the *San Diego Herald*'s offices, with no luck. Then he visited each hotel, inquired at every store, and still came up empty. No one remembered Eliza's father, nor recalled seeing anyone who resembled him. The last store owner had recommended Daniel try asking at the grog shop. Daniel tended to avoid such places, but the suggestion made sense.

Eliza must be anxious for news by now. He walked across the plaza to the restaurant and stepped inside, scanning the small space.

Eliza wasn't there.

He spoke with the proprietress, who told him Eliza had left the restaurant more than an hour before.

He bolted outside, then stopped. Why was he so worried? She must have returned to the Exchange.

Despite his rational thoughts, his feet sped toward the hotel. He encountered Mrs. Tebbetts in the front room.

"You're the young man who came in with Miss Brooks, aren't you?"

"Yes, ma'am."

"Would you please let Miss Brooks know that her clothes have dried? I've just left them in her room."

She wasn't there?

He darted back outside and scanned the plaza. No sign of her. He hurried toward the south, then froze. What if she'd gone north or east or west? Which way should he search first? He whipped his head in every direction, scanning the dark for clues.

Eliza, where have you gone?

CHAPTER 15

*E*liza hurled a small stone into the moonlit river. The tiny splash sounded harsh in the quiet night. She hurled another. And another. Tears streamed down her face. She threw her fists in the air. *Why?*

Lieutenant Derby had been gracious and kind, but he had known nothing. Pa had never spoken with him. Pa's interest in working for Derby had been her only lead. She would never be able to find Pa and convince him to go back to Oregon with her. She'd come here for nothing. She'd suffered the captain's impertinence for nothing. Nearly drowned for nothing. Lost everything that was precious to her for nothing.

It was all for nothing. Nothing. Nothing. Nothing.

She swiped at her tears as a roar ripped from her throat. Bending, she gathered another handful of stones and hurled them one at a time as far as she could up the river.

Footsteps crunched the dirt behind her. She whirled about, stone in hand, her arm poised to attack.

"Whoa!" Mr. Clarke raised his hands to protect his face. "It's me. It's just me, Miss Brooks."

She lowered her arm. Let the rest of her stones fall to the ground.

"What are you doing out here?" His voice was gentle. Even tender. "I've been searching for you everywhere. Are you all right?"

She nodded as she rubbed the dirt from her hands. "I'm sorry. I intended to return before you came looking for me. I guess I lost track of time and I just..." She cleared her throat. "I spoke with Lieutenant Derby. He doesn't know where Pa is. Never..." Despite her best efforts, her last words emerged in a warbled whisper. "Never even spoke with him."

"I'm so sorry." Mr. Clarke lifted his hand toward her, then lowered it. "We should head back to the hotel. It isn't safe out here."

She started toward town.

He fell in step beside her. "I spoke with the proprietors at each of the hotels and stores in town. No one has heard of or seen your father. I'm sorry."

She kicked a rock in their path. "There must be somewhere, someone else to ask."

"The owner of the last store recommended that I inquire at the grog shop."

"The grog shop?" She frowned. Too many men entered such establishments for "just a drop" and didn't come out till dawn, far worse for the wear.

"It does seem a likely place to find information."

She said nothing, giving him a sidelong glance.

"I do not plan to imbibe spirits, if that is what worries you."

She lifted one brow.

"You have my word."

Her shoulders relaxed. Mr. Clarke was a man of honor. "All right. I'll wait for you in the plaza."

∾

"*N*o!" The word burst from Daniel's lips. He would not allow her to wait outside in the dark. "This may be a small town, but it is still far from safe for a lady to be standing alone outside after dark—even if Captain Swenson *is* holed up in the abandoned hotel at the Playa with the rest of his crew."

"Nonsense." She waved a dismissive hand. "I'll wait near the entrance. If anything should happen, I'll simply call for you."

He halted. "Absolutely not."

Her steps didn't even slow. "Why ever not?"

She couldn't be that naïve. She must not be thinking clearly. He hastened to catch up. "Have you any idea what your reputation will be if you are seen standing outside a grog shop at night?"

Her eyes widened.

"As it is, your reputation is in danger. We should not be here alone after dark." He stopped a few yards short of the entrance to the plaza. "I think it best if I'm not seen in your company as you enter town. I'll wait and watch from here. Go directly to the hotel and do not stop or acknowledge anyone."

"But—"

"Go!"

She pressed her lips together and her eyes narrowed. But—miracle of miracles—she went.

CHAPTER 16

*A*s Daniel entered the small, one-room, adobe building, his nose was assaulted by the scents of liquor, bread, leather, exotic spices and other aromas he couldn't identify. The source of the smells—an amazing array of goods for sale—lined the walls in barrels, open crates, and shelving.

In the center of the room, a handful of men sat around tables enjoying drinks. Daniel asked permission to join one of the tables and was welcomed to do so. To set the men at ease, he ordered a drink. He sipped it slowly as the men grilled him on everything from his experience in the mining fields to the grounding of the *Virginia* on the Zuniga Shoal. Many of the men at the table spoke both Spanish and English. Thanks to his time mining, Daniel could say *si, eso es mio,* and *yo no hablo español.* But that was the extent of his Spanish. It made sense that these men were fluent. This town had been part of Mexico until the war less than a decade before.

After a while, the conversation slowed and Daniel sensed the men preparing to depart. He cleared his throat and leaned back in his chair. Keeping his tone casual, he repeated the same lines he'd said all afternoon. "Actually, I'm looking for the father of a

131

friend of mine, name of Jim Brooks. He wrote that he was in these parts sometime last year, but my friend hasn't heard from him recently. I promised I'd do my best to locate him while I was here. Any of you gents know him?"

The men shook their heads, then several of them took another draw from their mugs.

Daniel tapped his finger against his thigh. All this time wasted. How would he tell Eliza?

The man who'd introduced himself as Farley set down his mug. "Brooks, ya say?" He rubbed his chin, squinting his eyes.

"Yes, Jim Brooks. He's a tall man. Be hard to forget."

Farley grinned. "Why sure I remember Big Jim!" He faced the man across from him, who'd introduced himself as Oris. "Don't you remember? He got all het up on account of them two Indians we strung up for murdering. Wanted us to wait on a judge. 'Member that?" The man laughed as though it were a great joke.

The ale soured in Daniel's stomach.

"Oh sure," said Oris. "Big Jim. Haven't seen him around lately, though."

"No." Farley rubbed his chin again. "Think he mentioned something about maybe heading to Frisco last I saw him, though he hadn't quite made up his mind. Was missing some gal, I think he said."

"When was this?" Daniel held his breath.

"Weren't too long after the hanging. Almost a year ago, I'd say." He took a swig of his drink as the other man agreed.

"Sure, it was right about the time of the big fiesta."

Daniel's heart sank as the man went on to describe the horse races that had occurred during the fiesta. It didn't take a year to reach San Francisco no matter how one went. Jim hadn't made it there, or he would have been to visit Eliza. Wouldn't he?

When the racing story was finished, there was a lull in the

conversation till Oris spoke again. "Didn't Big Jim say something about visiting that hunter friend of his, first?"

"Oh, right." Farley scratched the back of his head. "Thought his friend might be up in the mountains near the river's head. Said he might try to find him before he went north."

Daniel leaned forward. "Are you certain?"

"Pretty near."

That would be enough for Eliza. She'd run off into the mountains, facing who-knew-what dangers. Meanwhile, Daniel would be on a ship to Boston. There would be no one to protect her. He'd promised to share any information he uncovered. But how could he tell her this?

~

*E*liza paced the confines of her hotel room. The little boy was crying again. Eliza had removed her bonnet but could not make herself prepare for bed. What had Mr. Clarke learned in the grog shop? He'd been in there for ages.

Returning to the window, she pulled back the curtain to peer into the darkened plaza below. She squeezed the rough fabric. Someone was approaching from the direction of the grog shop. She rushed downstairs.

She threw open the front door and dashed outside, colliding with a male body. Except, it wasn't Mr. Clarke. It was the steward from the ship.

"Miss Brooks!"

"I apologize, sir. Are you all right?" She stepped back, but he followed.

He leaned close. "I knew you'd find me." Whiskey laced his rotten breath.

"Pardon?" She shuffled back and bumped into the wall of the hotel.

He stepped closer and pinched a strand of her hair, twisting it between his fingers. "They all do, once the captain's through with them."

What was he talking about? She sidled left.

He dropped the strand and grabbed her waist with both hands.

"Sir!"

He pulled her toward him, his lips pursed.

She shoved at his hands, leaning away from him. "Unhand me this instant!"

"Don't play coy with me." He snarled as his fingers dug into her sides. "I know what you are, despite your prim clothes." His right hand left her side to capture her flailing wrist. "I know what you want, now he's cast you aside and left you to fend for yourself."

"Let me go!" She shoved at him with her free hand, but he was surprisingly strong for such a skinny man.

He yanked her body against his and tried to kiss her. She pushed his chin up, curling her fingers to scratch him. At the same time, she jerked her knee upward—where it would hurt.

"*Ah!*" He released her and hunched over. Stepping back, he touched his chin and his fingers came away spotted with blood. "You...!"

He lunged for her, but an arm snaked around his neck. "Don't you *touch* her!"

"Mr. Clarke!" *Oh thank heavens!* He held the steward at bay.

Mr. Clarke's eyes met hers. "Are you—"

The steward elbowed him in the stomach and twisted away. He punched Mr. Clarke, then took off down the street. In seconds, the scoundrel rounded a corner and was gone.

She rushed to Mr. Clarke, who was rubbing his jaw. "Are you all right?"

"I'm fine." He straightened his coat. "What are you doing out here? We agreed it would be safer for you inside."

"Yes, but I couldn't wait to ask and when I saw..." She

glanced to where the steward had disappeared, then at Mr. Clarke. "What did you learn from the men in the grog shop?"

He brushed dirt from his trousers. "Nothing."

Her breath whooshed from her lungs. "Nothing?" How could no one know where Pa had gone? "Did you not ask them about Pa?"

Mr. Clarke squared his shoulders. "Of course. They simply do not know where your father is." He stepped closer to her. "I'm sorry, Miss Brooks. Truly I am, but I think it best if you give up this quest."

"Give up?" She stepped back, her heel catching on a rock, causing her to fall against the wall.

He caught her arms, steadying her. The steward's closeness had terrified her, repulsed her. Mr. Clarke's closeness...her gaze caught on his lips. There was nothing repulsive about him.

"Just for now, so you come east with me. I can protect you during the journey, and—"

What was he saying? She squeezed her eyes shut as the warmth of his hands penetrated her sleeves.

"I'm certain my family would welcome you once we arrive in Roxbury, which is on the outskirts of Boston. My brother is moving into his own home and Mother has already been complaining how empty her house will be. Your coming will be a blessing."

Her eyes flew open. He wanted her to leave California?

"You can stay with them and send letters back here asking about your father. It is a much safer plan than remaining here and continuing this fruitless search on your own."

She held her hand up. "You want me to abandon Pa?"

He held his palms up. "You're not abandoning him. He's not here."

"He could be." *What if he isn't?* She had no idea where Pa was and when Mr. Clarke left, she would be on her own. The prospect hadn't sounded so intimidating when she'd left San

Francisco. Now, her knees trembled. She clenched her jaw against the tears that filled her eyes. "He *is* here." She hated the telltale warble of her voice. *He must be.*

Mr. Clarke's face softened. "Miss Brooks." He wiped a tear from her cheek with his thumb. His touch sent something warm pinging through her as his fingers spread to encompass her cheek. His compassionate gaze held hers. Her breath caught.

A long moment passed.

The scuffing of boots grew louder, interrupting the charged silence.

～

*D*aniel dropped his hand. What just happened? When he'd touched her...what *was* that? He shook his head. Was that Farley jogging toward them? *Oh, no.*

Daniel had to stop him before he noticed Eliza. He stepped into Farley's path. "Farley, I'm glad you're here. Let's head back. I'm feeling thirsty again."

Farley craned his neck to peer behind Daniel. "You didn't say nothing about a pretty lady friend."

Daniel set a hand on Farley's shoulder, urging him to turn back toward the grog shop. "Listen, let's not talk where our voices might disturb those resting." He waved his free hand to the upper windows of the Exchange.

Farley didn't budge. He stared at Eliza another moment before looking at Daniel. "I been thinking. You might be a sight better off heading into them hills if you have a map to show you the way."

Eliza stepped forward, a crease between her brows as she studied Daniel. "Why would you go to the mountains? You'll miss your ship." Her brows lifted and she faced Farley. "Has there been a discovery?"

"Gold? In these mountains!" Farley guffawed. "Not likely." He gave Eliza another lengthy appraisal.

Daniel squeezed Farley's shoulder.

"Uh, right." Farley dragged his gaze back toward Daniel. "So, about that map. I was thinking I might be persuaded to draw you up a real fine one for the right price."

Daniel nudged Farley away from Eliza. "Thank you, but I'm not—"

Farley leaned forward. "I could have it ready for you first thing tomorrow." He winced. "By noon, that is. First thing tomorrow by noon."

Maybe if Daniel agreed to pay Farley for the map, the man would leave. "Yes, fine. Thank you. Will a dollar, do?"

"A dollar will do fine."

"Good. Right then. Shall we say noon at the grog shop?"

"You got it." Farley shook Daniel's hand and turned away.

Eliza stepped forward. "Just a moment, sir."

Daniel's back tightened.

"Where will this map be leading Mr. Clarke?"

"Why the mountains, of course. Where Big Jim said he might find his friend."

Daniel didn't dare turn around. But then, he didn't need to. His memory showed him the fury that would be on Eliza's face —a fierce glare through narrowed eyes over pressed lips.

Farley blanched before mumbling his good nights and hurrying off down the plaza. The troublemaking coward disappeared around a corner.

Daniel straightened his shoulders and took a deep breath before turning to face Eliza.

He froze.

Her lips *were* pressed, but they trembled. She wasn't glaring at him. Her eyes were wide. And they shimmered.

He was the worst kind of no-account. "I—"

She raised a hand. "Big Jim? You know where Pa is and you lied to me?" She clasped her elbows. "Why?"

"I didn't...I don't..." What could he say? It had seemed so clear. Wandering into the mountains on a wild goose chase was something only a fool would do. He didn't have time for foolishness. The men at the grog shop said another ship would arrive to take the *Virginia*'s passengers first thing in the morning. He needed to leave with the ship. But he couldn't leave Eliza here defenseless. His best choice—his only choice—was to withhold the information until she was safely aboard the ship with him. The deception had been for her own good.

Hadn't it?

CHAPTER 17

*E*liza slammed the hotel room door behind her, fell back against it, and slumped to the floor. She stared into the darkness. Her shallow breathing echoing in the stark room.

Minutes passed.

She drew a deep breath.

Mr. Clarke had betrayed her. Heat grew in her chest, spreading outward until her whole body burned. She jumped to her feet. She needed to hit or kick something. Nothing in the room satisfied as a target. She clenched her fists as her gaze darted about. She needed to *do* something. Her gaze landed on her new carpetbag. She crossed the room in three sharp strides and placed the bag on her bed beside her clean laundry.

She was a fool.

After snatching her chemise, she shook out its wrinkles.

For three years she'd kept everyone at a distance. Only Uncle Henry had earned the slightest amount of trust after months of demonstrating his dependability.

She folded the garment and added it to her bag. She did the same with her drawers and petticoats.

Yet after a few days in Mr. Clarke's company, she had allowed herself to trust him.

She rolled her tattered stockings and stuffed them inside.

Had she not promised herself she would never again risk such betrayal?

She shook out her dress and folded it.

Her own pa had deceived and abandoned her. Why had she believed she could rely on Mr. Clarke?

After cramming her dress inside the bag, she shut it with a snap.

She turned to survey the room. A small table sat near the door. She grabbed its edge. It emitted loud scrapes and groans as she dragged it to a more practical location near the window, where sunlight could illuminate its surface during the day.

Her shoulders slumped.

With both the bed and the table next to the window, the room appeared lopsided.

Grabbing the bedframe, she dragged it, which emitted still louder scrapes and groans, in the opposite direction. She shoved it against the far wall.

Her head throbbed.

Now the bed's length was too great to fit its new space without blocking the swing of the door.

She'd made things worse. Again.

Her breaths shortened.

She fell onto the mattress. She had nothing. No one.

Loud, deep moans pushed their way out of her. She buried her face in the pillow. She threaded her fingers through her hair, clutching at her scalp, and screamed into the mattress. Her stomach cramped. Her lungs burned. Her whole body curled in on itself, shaking. Sob after sob wracked her body as the depth of her losses sliced through her.

*D*aniel stood outside Eliza's room as she grieved.

He'd followed her inside the hotel, hoping for a chance to explain, but as he approached her door, the high-pitched scraping of furniture being dragged across a wood floor stopped him in his tracks. When the scraping stopped, he raised his hand to knock.

Then she'd started crying.

The sounds of her anguish anchored him in place. He should have told her. He'd convinced himself the deception was for her good, but the disgusting truth was that he'd wanted her on that ship so that *he* wouldn't have to worry—wouldn't feel guilty for leaving her. What had made him think he had the right to try to control her life? She had the right to make her own decisions, the same as he did. The question now was, when the ship sailed in the morning, could he leave her behind?

He bowed his head. *Lord, please show me what to do.*

"As we have opportunity, let us do good to everyone." His father's favorite verse. How was Daniel to do good to everyone? If he remained to help Eliza, he would be causing dear, sweet, patient Alice to wait still longer for his return. If he left with the ship to return to Alice, he would leave Eliza alone and unprotected.

He trudged to his room. He needed his Bible.

~

*A*fter a long while, Eliza ran out of tears. She lay on the bed, still curled, staring at the wall. The cold seeped into her bones and she shivered. Then stirred herself enough to shift her weight off the scratchy blanket and pull it over her.

Enough moping. What were her options?

She could return to San Francisco, risking what she now understood were the very real dangers of traveling alone. Beg her aunt and uncle to take her back, or else find work...somewhere, along with a family willing to let her a room. All at the expense of her uncle's reputation.

Or she could accept Mr. Clarke's unorthodox offer to escort her to Roxbury. Throw herself upon the mercy of his parents until she could find a suitable place to work and live. Despite his deception, she believed his offer sincere.

Or she could stay here. Travel alone to the mountains and face any number of dangers that she was ill-equipped to handle.

God, grant me the wisdom and the strength to do what's right. She waited, but no whispering voice offered guidance—which was how Mama had described the voice of God.

A voice Eliza had never heard.

Outside her window, the moon ambled through the night sky as she mulled over the possibilities. Though she tried, she could not find peace in either returning to San Francisco or continuing to Roxbury. Yet traveling into the mountains alone, was foolish. Did they have bears in San Diego? There would be storms this time of year. How much snow did the mountains here get? How would she defend herself if she encountered another man like the steward?

Her eyelids drooped low. Her mind grew still. She drifted into sleep.

CHAPTER 18

*E*liza's eyes popped open. *Men travel alone into the mountains every day.*

She sat up with a start. Why hadn't she thought of that before? Throwing the blanket aside, she stood and smoothed the wrinkles from her sleep-pressed dress. Since she had not removed her boots the night before, fixing her hair and pinning her bonnet in place were all that were required before she left. The door would not fully open with the bed in the way, but it swung wide enough for her to pass through.

She would fix that later.

Stepping out of the hotel into the sun-drenched plaza, she squinted against the brightness but didn't slow. She crossed the plaza to a mercantile that displayed ready-made clothes and other sundries in the window.

The clerk hurried toward her. "What a delightful surprise, Miss Brooks. I thought you'd left us with the rest of the passengers this morning."

Everyone seemed to know her name and her business in this sleepy town. Eliza drew back. "Have they gone?"

"Yes, miss. Nearly two hours ago, I hear."

So, Mr. Clarke was gone. Eliza struggled to maintain a calm appearance. The light of morning had brought a clearness of mind. While Mr. Clarke's act of deception was deplorable, his intentions were likely to protect her in the same high-handed way he'd been using since leaving San Francisco.

The clerk's brows pinched. "You weren't meant to be with them, were you, miss?"

"Oh no." She forced herself to smile and wave a dismissive hand. Before he could quiz her further, she asked him to show her the pre-made clothes display.

She selected a men's shirt and trousers, along with an over-large Panama hat that would help hide her long hair. A length of muslin would bind the rest of her feminine tells. To that, she added a length of rope for use as a belt.

As he wrapped her purchases, the clerk cocked his head and examined her. "If the gentlemen for whom you intend these clothes has any trouble with the fit, please send him over and we'll be happy to assist him with any necessary corrections."

Eliza recognized the implied question and replied the same way she had in her youth. "Thank you, sir, I will inform him of your kind offer."

"Will the gentleman be needing anything else, miss?"

Pausing to consider, Eliza scuffed her boot on the wood flooring. *Boots!* Her bitty women's boots would be a dead give-away. She needed men's boots to complete the disguise.

∽

*H*is feet planted wide in the sand, Daniel waved to the passengers on the *S.S. Golden Gate* as they steamed out of the bay.

He tipped his face to soak in the morning sun, his steps light as he returned to town.

He had informed the captain that he would not continue to

Boston at this time. He also gave the captain letters to deliver to his parents and his fiancée.

His parents would be disappointed by his delayed return. Alice? When she read that he was about to spend several days alone in the wilderness with an unmarried woman...she would be livid. Understandably so. What he was doing went against so much that his parents had taught him about propriety...

He drew a deep breath.

After hours of reading his Bible and begging God for a way out of this situation—one that wouldn't hurt Alice or leave Eliza vulnerable—the truth had slipped into his heart with an inexplicable surety.

Forced to choose between Eliza's safety and what society deemed proper, he must choose Eliza's safety. He prayed Alice would come to understand and accept his decision, but regardless, he could not ignore his conviction to do what was right in God's eyes. He would deal with the consequences of his choices when he returned home.

For now, he left it in God's hands.

$\sim$

*E*liza peered down at the men's shirt, trousers, and boots she wore. She had no mirror in the room to tell her, but she suspected the strips of fabric restricting her bosom beneath the baggy garments were not concealing her curves as well as she would like. Had Pa been right? Had she grown too womanly to pass as a man?

She jerked at the cuff of her sleeve. Tugged at the shirt creating a drooping fullness above the rope belt. She shook out her hands. In a moment she would step out of her room and reveal her new self. If she were recognized as a woman dressed in men's clothing, her reputation would be destroyed. She would be vulnerable to every kind of slander and lurid comment. There would be no going back.

She straightened her spine and squared her shoulders. It wasn't as if she had a better option. Her reputation would be scarcely less damaged and her vulnerability far greater were she to traverse the countryside as a woman.

She jammed the Panama hat low on her head, shoved her hair into it, and snatched up her carpetbag. She reached for the doorknob and paused. Her shoulders were too straight. She relaxed her posture into the slouch more common of the miners. Adding a touch of heft to her step as well, she exited her room, pulling the door shut behind her.

CHAPTER 19

*E*liza stopped cold in the hallway, staring at the man standing before her.

"Mr. Clarke! You're still here." Why was her face spreading with a silly smile?

Mr. Clarke stood still as a tree stump at the top of the stairs. His gaze moved from her face down to her men's boots and back up again.

Oh! She'd forgotten how she was dressed.

Resisting the urge to flee to the safety of her room, she lifted a brow as his gaze traveled down again, lingering on her legs. "Do I pass?"

"Pass?" He blinked and looked at her face. *"What* are you wearing?"

"Pass as a man." She planted a hand on her hip. "If you didn't know me, would you recognize me as a woman?" She swiveled to show him the full ensemble.

Mr. Clarke's gaze started to lower, but he spun away and spoke to the wall. "Miss Brooks, there is no chance anyone could ever mistake you for a man—whatever you chose to wear."

She released the breath she'd been holding.

Mr. Clarke cleared his throat, still staring at the wall. "Miss Brooks, will you please change into something...more appropriate?"

Her cheeks flamed and she whirled around. She yanked open the door to her room, stepped inside and shut it behind her.

It only took moments for her to strip the men's clothes from her body and dress in the more restrictive garments of a woman. Her cheeks hurt from grinning.

Mr. Clarke had *not* left with the ship! What could this mean?

She folded the men's clothes and pressed them into her carpetbag—pressing her lips down as well. She would not get her hopes up. That he hadn't left with the others did not mean he intended to help her. Getting excited would only serve to distract her when the truth was revealed. She needed to focus on the task at hand.

She gathered her things, then went downstairs, where she found Mr. Clarke chatting with Mr. Tebbetts by the fire in the front room.

Mr. Tebbetts smiled at her as she set her bag by the door. "Good morning, Miss Brooks."

"Good morning, Mr. Tebbetts."

"I trust you've enjoyed your stay with us and will tell all your friends in San Francisco of our fine accommodations."

"Of course." She had no one to write to aside from her Uncle —and she could not imagine him leaving his business long enough to take a trip to San Diego—but she would tell him nevertheless.

"Thank you. I understand you're to catch the clipper bound for San Francisco this afternoon. Have you had word of your father, then? Is he not here but up north?"

Eliza blinked. What was he talking about?

"Speaking of our departure"—Mr. Clarke took Eliza's elbow

—"you must excuse us, for there is much to accomplish before we leave." He strode to the door, Eliza in tow, giving her no chance to refuse. At the front door, he lifted her carpetbag and held it out to her.

Mr. Clarke was up to something. Best to wait until they were outside to find out what.

～

Daniel led Eliza toward the center of the plaza before pivoting to face her. But, as usual, the woman spoke before he could.

"I thought you were an honorable man, but it seems telling lies comes naturally to you."

He ran a hand over his face. "I did not lie to Mr. Tebbetts. When you didn't leave with the other passengers, he made an assumption, which I refrained from correcting. I'll explain my reason for this in a moment. But first, please allow me to apologize for deceiving you last evening. I deeply regret my actions. It was very unlike me and I have no excuse for it. I hope that you'll find it in your heart to forgive me."

As expected, she crossed her arms without comment.

"As you see, I too, remained behind this morning. I've decided that, if you are determined to venture into the mountains in search of your father, it is my duty to accompany you and keep you safe."

"Wh—"

"That said"—he raised a hand for patience—"it will not do your reputation any favors to announce our plans. I've decided we shall allow people to believe that I'm planning to escort you to your ship before continuing my trip into the mountains alone, as Mr. Tebbetts appears to have assumed." He tapped his finger against the side of his thigh. "Despite what my actions of late may lead you to believe, I deplore deception and I refuse to lie. However, I am attempting to avoid the *appearance* of evil where you and I know none truly exists. I recognize it's far from a perfect plan—there's still a good chance rumors will flow—but it's the best plan I can devise under the circumstances."

He paused to ascertain her reaction, but her expression was inscrutable.

She tilted her head to the side. "What of your fiancée? Won't she object to your plans?"

"Undoubtedly. But as you once told me, 'That ship has sailed. Literally.'" He shrugged. "I sent a letter of explanation with this morning's ship and hope to win Miss Stevens's forgiveness when I finally return to Roxbury. Meanwhile, I will fulfill my duty here and leave the consequences in the Lord's hands."

"I see." She was quiet for several moments as she studied him. Then her eyes sparkled and a gentle smile lifted her cheeks. "Thank you. You've proved yourself a generous and kind man. With the notable exception of last evening's deception—for which you have repented—you've been in every way my unexpected benefactor. Please do not think me insensible of it. Of course, you're forgiven, and I sincerely thank you for your assistance in finding my pa."

Of all the reactions he'd expected, this reasoned and kind response hadn't even entered his mind. Daniel tossed his head back and laughed. "You are an incredible woman. You repeatedly have my head over the smallest of unintended offenses, but when I've done something truly deplorable and worthy of a tongue lashing, you graciously forgive."

Eliza frowned for a moment, then her lips trembled and she burst out laughing as well. "Well, Mr. Clarke, what now?"

"You have all your things in that bag?" He nodded to the carpetbag at her feet.

She bent and lifted it from the ground. "All my personal

things, yes, but I still need to stop by the store for food, blankets, a tinderbox, and other sundries I'll need for the journey."

"Good. Make a list and I'll make those purchases for you, to avoid any questions. I've already told Tebbetts that I intend to travel overland, so my making the purchases shouldn't draw any attention."

She scrunched her lips together. "I'll need to come with you to pay." She stuck her hand into her skirt and coins jingled.

He firmed his mouth. "Don't worry about the cost. Just make me a list. I'll pay for what we need."

She drew her hand from her pocket. "You wouldn't need anything if you'd boarded that ship this morning. You remained to help me. It's only right that I should pay for our supplies."

What she said made sense, but he would not give in. He didn't know what amount of money she carried in that pocket of hers, but he could guess it wasn't much. And it would have to last her a long while. Especially if, as he suspected, they could not find her father. "Still, I'm afraid I can't allow you to come."

He winced the moment the words left his mouth. Had he truly just suggested she needed his permission? What was it about her that had him speaking first and thinking second?

$\approx$

AUGUST 1853 (5 MONTHS BEFORE)
ROXBURY, MASSACHUSETTS

*T*he slamming of the front door rattled the walls, waking Alice from a deep sleep. She opened her eyes but could tell no difference with the curtains drawn, blocking even the starlight from their chamber.

Her younger sister, Caroline, rolled in the bed beside her. "What's that?"

Alice sat up, listening.

Father's clumsy movements downstairs and the timber of his rumbling voice disturbed the silence of their home.

She frowned. "Father's home." Lying back down, she closed her eyes, ready for sleep to reclaim her.

Sharp, unfamiliar feminine laughter sent a chill down her spine. *Not again.*

Whipping back the blanket, Alice stood and yanked her dressing gown from the wall.

"Oh, don't, Alice." Caroline's whine was muffled by her pillow. "You'll make it worse."

Alice trailed her fingers along the wood bed frame as she crossed the pitch-black room. She found the smooth doorknob and flung the door wide. She strode down the lightless hall to the top of the stairs.

In the entryway below, flickering sconces illuminated a scantily clad woman clinging to Father like a leech.

Get out! Alice bit her tongue to keep the shout from escaping. She listened for any sign that the servants had been disturbed. The hallway was quiet. For now.

Lifting her chin, she crept down the stairs.

Father tilted to one side.

"There you go again, luv." Another cackle echoed off the painted wood floors. "I told you we ought t'have stayed at Moira's. I'll not be able to lift you if you fall here."

"Nonsense." Father's slurred words were blessedly low in volume. "Wasn't any brandy. I've best bottle here." He stumbled toward his study.

Alice stepped in front of them, focusing her fury on the stranger threatening their home. She kept her voice low, but firm. "Vacate this house at once."

"Why, you—"

The rest of the woman's response was cut short by the slap of Father's hand across Alice's face. Alice stumbled backward, gasping.

He'd struck her! Father had struck her.

Again.

Her back met the wall. She slid to the floor, legs too shaky to hold her upright.

"Hey!" Heavy steps pounded down the stairs. Richard flew forward, his punch knocking Father against the wall.

The stranger screamed.

Father swung at Richard.

Richard ducked and landed another blow to Father's face.

Father landed a jab in Richard's gut.

Their fists continued swinging—landing and missing in turns.

"No! Father, *don't!* Richard, *stop!*" Tears streamed down Alice's face. What was happening? Father hadn't struck any of them in months. This was her fault. She ought to have listened to Caroline, pretended she couldn't hear them.

"Abner!" Mother dashed down the stairs. "Richard, what are you *doing?* Stop!"

Alice turned in time to see Richard land a hard blow to Father's temple.

Father slumped to the ground.

Mother screamed. "He's dead! You've killed him!" She rushed past Alice, but Richard blocked her from reaching Father.

"He's not dead, Mother. Only unconscious." Richard panted as he pointed to their Father's chest. "See. He breathes."

Mother ducked beneath Richard's outstretched arm. Kneeling beside Father, she shook him. "Abner! Abner, wake up." She glowered over her shoulder at Richard. "How *could* you?" Her attention switched to their butler, who'd appeared at the base of the stairs. "Fetch the doctor, Morris."

"Yes, ma'am."

Caroline joined them, passing the butler as he left. "What happ— Oh! Richard, your face!" Her gaze shifted to the floor. "What's happened to Father?"

The rest of their staff now hovered near the top of the stairs in various states of dress. Their candles flickered light across the upper hall. How long had they been standing there? Two of the maids exchanged whispers, their worried eyes fixed on Alice.

Alice lifted her hand to her stinging cheek. Was there a mark?

"Alice, you're hurt." Caroline's voice drew Mother's attention.

Mother's hand fluttered at her throat. "What happened to you?"

"Father struck her." Richard knelt in front of Alice. He held her chin with his fingertips. "Are you all right?"

"He *struck* you?" Mother leaned away. "He wouldn't. He promised—"

"See for yourself." Richard lifted Alice's chin to give their mother a clear view of her cheek.

Mother closed her eyes. "I—"

Father's moan cut off whatever Mother intended to say.

Mother smoothed her husband's hair. "Abner, dearest, wake up. Speak to me."

"Lucy."

Mother jerked back.

The strange woman dropped to her knees beside Father, taking the hand Mother had dropped. "I'm here."

Alice jumped to her feet. She couldn't watch this. Fleeing up the stairs to her chamber, she grabbed the door to fling it shut.

A large hand stopped it mid-swing.

Richard entered, with Caroline on his heels. He strode to the wardrobe and jerked open the doors. He grabbed two bags from its base and tossed them onto the bed. "Pack your things, we're leaving."

Caroline pulled unmentionables from their cupboard and folded them into one of the bags.

Alice stared at her brother. "Where will we go?" Neither Spencer nor William, their two eldest brothers, owned homes of their own. And no other relative would take them in against Father's wishes.

Richard pulled dresses from the wardrobe and began cramming them into the other bag. "Mason Jefferson would marry Caroline this instant if it were possible. He's only postponed their wedding because Father insisted that he first finish his apprenticeship. We'll go to the Jeffersons' home tonight and convince Mason to marry Caroline first thing in the morning."

Alice rescued her garments from her brother's mangling. "That will cause a scandal. People will say Caroline is with child."

"I don't care." Caroline tossed a brush into her bag. "And Mason won't care either. I've hated waiting this long. Besides, the rumors will die when I don't have a babe in arms nine months from now."

What foolishness! "If you marry tomorrow, that is still a possibility. Hasn't Mother explained things to you?"

Caroline's fists crushed the stockings she was adding to her bag. "I am not a child, Alice."

"Fine." Alice turned back to Richard. "What about you and me?" She folded the dresses he'd crumpled and stacked them on the rumpled bed sheets. "These will not all fit. We'll need our trunks."

Richard sliced his hand through the air. "There's no time to fetch the trunks from the attic. Pack what you need for tonight. I'll return for the rest later. I want to be gone before Father recovers enough to come after us."

Alice considered her dresses. She couldn't choose one unless she knew where she and Richard were going and who might see them. "Return from where? You still haven't said where we're going."

"I have a friend who owes me a favor." Richard selected two

dresses for her and added them to the bag. He tossed petticoats, a corset, drawers, and stockings atop the dress. "What else do you require?"

A whiff of oranges tickled her nose, the sachet of dried rinds having spilled across the bed. "What friend?"

"No one you know. I met him while I was away."

"What makes you think a gentleman of such short acquaintance would take us in?" She lifted her chin. "I'll not be a charity case, Richard."

"He may not meet your definition of a gentleman, but he's fine enough and, as I said, he owes me a favor."

"What do you mean? What are the arrangements of his house? His circumstances? Surely he has family. Even you would not expect me to reside with one of the lower class. It would ruin my reputation."

His grin faded. "The man is happily married and treats his family well. I'm certain you'll be safe there. As to the quality of his home, I've not seen it, but we have little choice. You cannot stay here." He pinned her with his gaze. "I expect you to be kind and respectful."

She turned away. Richard didn't know this was not the first time Father had struck her—though each time still shocked her. She patted her tender cheek. The pain had already dulled. Once the alcohol left him, Father would repent of his actions and she'd be safe once more. A few days ensconced at home and the marks would fade, with no one the wiser.

But fleeing into the night to beg charity of a stranger? That was an overreaction destined to cause wagging tongues. In any case, she could never pack all that she would need in the few minutes Richard meant to give her. A trip such as this would require careful planning and preparation. "I *could* stay here. I—"

"Richard!" Father's infuriated voice accompanied heavy steps clomping up the stairs. "Alice!"

Mother's voice sounded near the top of the stairs. "Abner,

wait. You've been injured and need to rest. Wouldn't it be better to wait and speak with them in the morning when you'll feel better and can think more clearly?"

"M' thoughts are perf'ly clear. Get out m'way."

A scream. Then a series of receding thumps.

Richard spun toward the hall. "Keep packing. I'll check on Mother and keep Father away."

Alice trembled. *This isn't happening.*

CHAPTER 20

*E*liza mentally shut out Mr. Clarke as he dogged her steps, trying to convince her not to enter the store. She may be grateful for his protective presence, but she was not about to allow him to take control. He had deceived her once already. Yes, he had repented of that act, and Eliza had chosen to let go of her anger—after all, she certainly understood making a wrong choice with the right intentions—but she was no fool.

She would not provide him with another such opportunity to deceive her.

Entering the store with Mr. Clarke on her heels, she smiled at a clerk assisting another customer. She perused the shelves as she waited.

When the customer left, the clerk turned to Eliza. "Good morning, Miss Brooks. How lovely to see you again." His attention moved past her to Mr. Clarke. "Is this the gentleman you spoke of? Oh my, but I see why you've come. Those trousers will be far too short on a man of his stature. I'll be happy to exchange them for you, of course."

Mr. Clarke gave an odd cough behind her. It sounded suspiciously like a strangled laugh.

"Oh, no. This is not that gentleman, sir."

"No?" The clerk's brows raised in question.

She gestured toward Mr. Clarke, who stepped forward to stand beside her. "This is Mr. Clarke. He told me he's planning an overland trip, but is lacking certain supplies. Of course, I told him yours was the shop he must come to."

The clerk beamed. "How may I be of assistance, sir?"

When they had gathered everything they needed—with Eliza providing a "suggestion" here and there to Mr. Clarke—the clerk stepped behind the counter to tally their purchases.

Mr. Clarke's hand moved toward his pocket.

Oh, no, you don't! She reached into her own and withdrew a handful of money that felt to be about the amount she needed. When the clerk announced the total, she snatched Mr. Clarke's wrist below the surface of the counter, preventing him from withdrawing his money.

"Tell me"—she batted her lashes at the clerk—"how much is that coffee pot on the wall behind you?" The clerk turned to retrieve the item in question and Eliza plopped her money on the counter.

She released Mr. Clarke's arm.

He scowled.

The clerk turned back to them, coffee pot in hand. "It's…" He blinked at Mr. Clarke. "Is something amiss?"

Eliza beamed at the clerk. "On second thought, I'm not sure Mr. Clarke wants a coffee pot."

∾

*D*aniel gritted his teeth as they made arrangements to return later for their purchases. He held the door for Eliza to exit the store. She had outmaneuvered him. He would have had to make a scene in front of the clerk to stop her from paying—a scene they could not afford.

They needed to be as forgettable as possible.

Following her into the plaza, he stalked to a place far enough from the few others wandering about that they would not be overheard.

He pivoted to face her.

She grinned at him.

He couldn't help it. His frustration dissolved.

He rubbed a hand over his mouth to cover his smile. "Proud of yourself, are you?"

"Quite." She bounced on her toes.

He widened his stance. "Well, I need you to let me handle things this time."

Her smile disappeared.

He chuckled. "I need to negotiate the purchase of horses. Have you ever purchased a horse, Miss Brooks?"

"No." She heaved a sigh. "All right, but I'm coming along and you must promise to allow me to reimburse you afterward."

He grinned. "Of course."

She hadn't stipulated how soon afterward.

~

*B*y noon they had completed their purchase of the horses, and Eliza returned to the store while Mr. Clarke went to meet Farley outside the grog shop. They'd had an argument about whether she would accompany him to retrieve the map, but in the end she had conceded her presence would draw more questions from Farley, who wasn't the tight-lipped sort.

In the store, she posted another letter to her uncle and purchased some bread and preserves to add to the jerky, beans, and other provisions they'd purchased earlier.

She met Mr. Clarke near the edge of town where he stood waiting with their new horses. Her mare dipped her head and Eliza scratched her muzzle. "Did you get the map?"

"Right here." He patted his pocket.

"Good."

He assisted her into the saddle before mounting his gelding, and they started down the road, following it toward the Playa until they were certain no one was paying them any attention. Then they veered north toward the river and followed its sandy banks eastward.

"I think it worked." He steered his horse around a large bush and then back to walk beside her. "No one seemed to pay any undue attention to our departure."

"Good." She held out her hand. "May I see the map?"

"Certainly." He pulled a folded piece of paper from his pocket and set it in her palm. As she unfolded it, he said, "It's not much, but it's all we've got, so I'm hoping it's enough to get us where we need to go. Farley claimed it'd make more sense as we went along."

Their map was little more than a long squiggly line, labeled *rivr,* with a couple of branches coming off it. There were three rectangles that must represent buildings of some kind, and some open-ended triangles near the end of the river that probably indicated the mountains. Almost at the end of the squiggly line, amid the open-ended triangles, was an *X.*

She held the paper up so Mr. Clarke could see it and pointed to the *X.* "Is this where we're going?"

Mr. Clarke nodded. "Farley said that's where your father said his friend was supposed to be hunting." He squinted at her.

"I don't suppose I can talk you out of this? It's been several months since your father said he was going up there. Even if the map is accurate, there's no reason to believe he hasn't moved on."

She refolded the map but didn't hand it back to him. "I am determined, Mr. Clarke. However, if *you* have changed your mind..." She held her breath.

"No."

She exhaled.

He held his hand out for the map and she returned it. "I had to ask."

They rode in silence for a while. The hills surrounding them, and the valley through which they rode, appeared dry and consisted of chaparral browns and dull greens. The area beside the river, though, was lush with a variety of bright green plants and trees. It looked much like Oregon.

She pictured the small log cabin in Oregon, which the neighbors helped Pa build while she fetched water and cooked meals. In the winter, she rode through the snow to her neighbor's house for lessons in reading, writing, and arithmetic. All at Pa's insistence. The rest of the year, she and Pa were inseparable. They worked together, growing crops and raising animals. In the yard near the front door, she planted the cuttings Mama had carted all the way from Ohio. Eliza nursed those cuttings back to life till they grew full with the beautiful white-and-pink striped blooms Mama had so cherished.

Oh, to return to the only place that had ever felt like home!

Home.

Mr. Clarke was delaying his return home to accompany her into the mountains. She considered him as they rode. "What is your home like?"

"In Roxbury?"

"Yes."

"My parents live on a small farm. Well, I call it a farm, but it was my great-grandfather who worked the land. Now, my father's father, he built the workshop and was working as a carpenter when he met my grandmother. He taught my father, and as soon as we could hold a hammer, my father started training my brother and me. There was never any question what occupation I was to take. My father's talents are well known in Boston. He always has more work than he can handle. He's been asking me to come home for years." He shifted in the saddle. "He expects my return home will mean my return to the family business."

Eliza guided her horse around a tall bush. Mr. Clarke would be on his way home now if it weren't for her.

"In any case, there's the main house with four chambers. The woodshop, of course. We have a barn and a few other small buildings as well. And, like I told you before, my brother is almost finished building his own house on the property. So there's plenty of room for…guests." He cleared his throat. "Both my parents' folks live nearby, as well as a few uncles and aunts. They all come over for the holidays." He shrugged. "Christmas hasn't been the same since I came to California, that's for sure."

What would it be like to have such a large family to celebrate with? Pa had once received a letter from his married sister, whose husband had taken over the family farm in Ohio and ran it with the help of their eight children. And, of course, Eliza had Uncle Henry, but with the exception of her uncle, she'd never met any of her living relatives. She barely remembered her grandparents, who'd remained behind when Mama's yearn for adventure lured them west. "Your home sounds nice."

"It is."

For a few seconds, the only sounds were the rustling plants, babbling waters, and the clop of their horses' hooves.

Daniel steered his mount closer to her. "What about you? Where did you grow up?"

"Oregon, mostly. We moved there when I was seven to

homestead." She looked away, studying the ripples of the river. Her memories of that trip were hazy. Except for that one awful day, carved into her heart—

She shook the thought away. Most of her memories were of walking beside the wagon, first with Mama…

And later alone.

"Did your whole family travel west? You've never mentioned your mother."

Her breath hitched.

Sliding rocks. Cracking wood. Men shouting. Women screaming. A dog barking. "Eliza, no!"

She struggled to breathe past the lump clogging her throat. Turning away, she pretended fascination with the hills. It was a full minute before she could speak. "Mama's buried beside the trail." She swallowed. "There wasn't time for a ceremony. We couldn't even mark her grave, for fear it'd be disturbed."

"I'm so sorry." He leaned across and squeezed her arm. "I shouldn't have pried." The terrain forced them to separate again.

If Eliza dwelled on Mama's passing, the tears would return. Better to talk about after that.

"We were the first in our area to get our cabin built. It took four long, hard years, but we earned our certificate free and clear. Oh, and what beautiful land it is, the way the grass glistens after the rain, the musky scent of the pines, the soft trickling of the stream running through it, and the song of the meadowlark ringing across the field. You've never seen anything like it. God's handiwork is so clear up there."

"Sounds like you miss it."

"Oh, yes."

"Why'd you leave?"

She frowned. Pa had been obsessed with getting to California to claim his share of the gold. "Why'd *you* leave home?" She gave him a pointed look.

"You came to California for gold?"

"Pa did. I came along to take care of him."

"Shouldn't that be the other way around?"

"No." Her brows dipped down. "Pa needed me—*needs* me. If I'd been with him when he came to San Diego he wouldn't be…" What? In trouble? She didn't know that he *was* in trouble. *Or that he isn't.* "Well he wouldn't be missing, that's for sure."

"Mmm." Mr. Clarke's tone revealed doubts, but he didn't elaborate.

More time passed in silence.

Daniel adjusted his hat. "Do you think you'll ever go back to Oregon?"

"I'm going back as soon as I find Pa."

"You are?" His eyebrows lifted. "What about your father?"

She lifted a shoulder. "We'll go together."

"Have you talked to him about this?"

"I wrote to him about it." Not that he'd acknowledged her suggestion in his next letter. She shifted in her saddle. "What about you?"

"What about me?"

"You said your brother is building his own house. Surely you aren't planning to live in your parents' home once you're married?"

Daniel straightened in the saddle. "Actually, that's one of the reasons I've stayed so long in California. I have enough now for Alice and me to start our life together."

A life he was putting on hold for Eliza. "Alice is your fiancée?"

"Yes. Miss Alice Stevens."

Wait. What *was* Mr. Clarke's Christian name? She giggled.

Mr. Clarke stiffened. "You find my fiancée's name amusing?"

"No." She grinned at him. "Sorry, it's just that I realized that, after all this time, here we are riding through the wilderness and well…" She laughed again. "I don't even know your Christian name."

"Oh." He relaxed. "Daniel. Daniel Adam Clarke, at your service, Miss Brooks." He tipped his hat to her with a grin.

Daniel Adam Clarke. She liked it. It suited him. "Pleased to make your acquaintance, Daniel Adam Clarke." She dipped her head, then grinned back at him. "What do you say? Should we dispense with the formalities now? I would be pleased to have you call me Eliza."

"And you must call me Daniel." He returned his attention to the trail ahead of them. "Whoa!" He reined his horse to a halt and held his hand out to signal Eliza to stop. "Wait a minute."

Daniel dug the map out of his pocket. He unfolded it and lifted it to catch the light of the sun lowering behind them.

Beside him, Eliza leaned forward, squinting into the distance. "What is it?"

"Mission San Diego de Alcala. Or what once was." He waved a hand toward the distant rows of tents surrounding a large adobe structure. Men wandered the grounds, but Daniel wasn't near enough to make out their faces. What he could see, though, were their uniforms. "The cavalry has taken it over."

He pointed to the bend in the squiggly line on the map. "The river turns north ahead." In the northwest corner of the river's bend was a small rectangle indicating the mission. He considered the hills bordering the northern portion of the valley. "Let's head up these hills and come back to the river here." He pointed at a place on the map far beyond the mission. "With the tall scrub brush and the fading light, we should be able to pass unnoticed."

"Unnoticed?" Eliza's brows pinched together. "Shouldn't we ask the soldiers if Pa came through here?"

He'd considered it when Farley mentioned the outpost this morning, but it wasn't worth the risk. Would she agree? "From what I gathered, your father was only in town for a couple weeks. If he passed through the mission at all, it was nearly a year ago. The soldiers aren't likely to remember him. It's not worth the risk to your reputation."

She planted her hands on her hips. "But they might remember him."

Stubborn woman. He tilted his head and gave her a pointed look.

She threw up her hands. "Oh, all right. We'll go around this time." She lifted her chin.

"But if we don't find him in the mountains and have to come back this way, I am going to ask, whatever the consequences."

Of course, she would. He nudged his horse toward the hills. *Lord, please don't let it come to that.*

CHAPTER 21

A cold breeze sent a shiver through Eliza as she followed Daniel through the thick brush at the peak of the hill. The last vestiges of the sun's rays were gone, but the moon had yet to appear. Only twinkling stars lit their way.

Daniel pulled to a stop in a small clearing.

Would they camp here for the night? Her aching back begged for relief. Her backside was numb. She wiggled the toes in her boots and was rewarded with the sensation of pins and needles pricking her feet. Standing on them wouldn't be pleasant.

Daniel twisted to face her. "We should dismount and walk the horses to avoid injuring them. They aren't the youngest animals, and I'm not sure how well they can see in this thick brush without the moon."

She grimaced as he slid off his horse. Would her body support her?

She pressed a hand to her back and stretched before gingerly swinging her right leg around the back of the horse.

Daniel's hands circled her waist, and tingles trilled up her spine. He eased her to the ground. As she turned, his hands on her waist sparked a fluttering in her stomach.

Squelching the unwanted feelings, she focused on straightening her unsteady legs.

He tipped his head, catching her gaze. "Are you all right?"

She nodded and, now confident that her legs would support her, stepped away. "Just not used to riding horseback for so long."

"It won't be much longer now. I just want to get us a little farther from the mission to avoid encountering any patrolling soldiers." He returned to his horse. "You ride like a natural." Grabbing the reins, he lead the way through the brush on foot.

"We had horses in Oregon." She sighed as she stepped over a fallen branch. "But after we'd been working the mines for a while, I realized we needed the money more than the horses and I sold them. I haven't ridden since."

"I still can't believe your father took you to the mines with him."

Her shoulders sank. "You think Pa should have left me behind." Every one who had heard her story had said something similar. Why did Daniel have to agree with them? And why did she care? He'd be gone soon enough. His fiancée was waiting for him.

"No." He stopped and faced her. "You were his daughter. You deserved more than a childhood spent in the mines. He should have stayed in Oregon and raised you where it was safe and proper. From what you've described, it doesn't sound like he needed the money. Forgive my saying so, but your father was being greedy and selfish to drag you away from your home to chase after gold."

"He was not!" Her fingers tightened on the leather reins. How dare he say such things about Pa? "You don't even know him. You don't understand. He just..." She searched the black silhouettes of the plants surrounding them as if the answer lay hidden in the darkness. Why *had* Pa come to California?

Her fingers flew to her lips. It was true. Pa hadn't needed the gold.

But he *had* needed to come to California.

As happy as she'd been in Oregon, Pa never found peace there. Eliza's efforts to fill the void she'd caused never succeeded. Because no matter how little or how much they had, Pa always needed more.

Eliza shook her head. "You don't understand. Pa is a good man. He's just…lost."

And it's my fault.

~

*L*ess than an hour later they rejoined the river and, with the moon lighting their way, remounted their horses. Although used to the physical exertion of carpentry work, Daniel's body still ached from the hours of nonstop travel.

He twisted to check on Eliza. Her perfect posture was sagging and she shivered, but she appeared steady in her saddle and hadn't uttered one word of complaint. Considering her leisurely life with the Davidsons, it was a wonder she hadn't begged him to stop.

He faced forward, smiling. He'd known men with less tenacity.

They continued along the river for another two miles beside a long, disused and crumbling aqueduct. As they rode, the land on either side of the river rose to form a gorge. Daniel followed a narrow path that broke off from the river. It led to a terrace in the steep hill with a grouping of trees and shrubs. The plants sheltered them from the cold night winds.

He dismounted and assisted Eliza from her horse.

Taking the reins, he tethered the horses to a nearby tree with plenty of grasses beneath it. After tucking his gloves into the saddle bag, he withdrew a loaf of bread, a jar of preserves, and a small knife, that he handed to Eliza. "Will you slice the bread while I open the preserves?"

She removed her gloves. "Of course." She drew her kerchief from her pocket and spread it on the ground in place of a table.

They worked together to slice the bread and spread preserves on two slices. When they were finished, he stashed the leftovers in the satchel and waited for her to take a seat.

A moment passed and she remained standing.

He gestured toward the ground, indicating that she should sit.

Her chin dipped. "I, uh, think I'll stand."

He frowned. Just when he'd begun to think she wasn't as fastidious as she seemed, she turned up her nose at a little dirt. How had she survived the gold mines? "We'll be traveling for days. Do you intend to stand at every meal?"

"Well, I—"

"If you're concerned you'll soil your new dress..." He let his words trail off as he waved to the layer of dust and bits of plants coating the lower portion of her skirts.

"No, it isn't that. I..." She closed her eyes before continuing in a rush. "I'm not sure I'm capable of lowering myself gracefully."

He clamped his lips between his teeth to keep from laughing, but she peeked one eye open and must have noted his amusement because her other eye flew open and she glared at him.

She planted her free hand on her hip and winced. The muscle must be sore.

Laughter burst from his lips, his shoulders shaking.

"Oh, all right." Her tone was stiff, but a smile tugged at the corners of her lips. She held her hand out imperiously. "Quit laughing and help me down."

He took her hand—and the heat of their connection evaporated his mirth.

CHAPTER 22

*D*aniel shook his head as he stood on the sandy bank of the river, a slice of bread in one hand and canteens dangling from the other. What was happening to him? He'd never reacted to a woman's touch this way. It needed to stop. But how to make it stop?

He stared at his hand holding the canteen straps. Did the warmth linger? Or was he imagining it? *No.* He wouldn't dwell on the sensation. He needed to think rationally.

Touching caused the feeling. And holding her gaze. So he would avoid touching her. And looking at her.

With a harsh laugh, he scuffed his foot in the dirt. That was hardly practical, given the journey they were on. What was he to do? He shouldn't be having these feelings for her. It wasn't fair to Alice. Sweet Alice had been waiting three long years for his return. Yet even as he scolded himself, he wanted nothing more than to climb out of this gorge and take Eliza into his arms. To pull her close and…

Daniel sank to his knees in the sand. *Forgive me, Lord. Please, take these feelings from me. Help me to be a man of my word, the man I know you would have me be.*

He closed his eyes. *What am I doing here? Did You lead me to protect Eliza, or am I pursuing my own desires?*

A bolt of conviction straightened his spine. *I did* listen to the Lord. *He guided me on this path. Regardless of these unwelcome feelings, my intent is sincere.*

Lord, please help me remain true to the woman I love and am promised to.

Do you truly love Alice?

He frowned at the small, nagging voice in his head. *Of course I do.*

Her loving letters had kept him going through the long, lonely days and nights. Knowing she was waiting for him kept him away from the sinful temptations that claimed his companions. His anchor in a sea of change, her letters kept him tethered to home. Until they'd stopped.

Unlike Eliza, Daniel had reports from his mother to assure him of Alice's wellbeing. What must it be like for Eliza to not know whether her father still lived?

Daniel set the canteens in the dirt, balanced the slice of bread on top, and retrieved the letters from his pocket, where he'd stowed them before leaving his trunk in Mr. Tebbett's care. He opened his mother's letter first and reread it before returning it to his pocket.

Then he unfolded the worn pages of Alice's last letter.

April 25th, 1853

My darling Daniel,

I have the most exciting news! There is to be a Summer Ball! As usual, Benjamin has agreed to escort me in your absence. I would much rather be on your arm, as you know, but as I cannot have you, I am delighted to have your brother, at least. Mrs. Willaker has been hired to sew me a new gown exactly like the one...

Daniel skimmed over the details of her dress and speculations about who might escort whom to the ball.

Caroline, of course will be escorted by Mason Jefferson. He has finally proposed after all these years, and they have set their wedding date for the first of next May. You absolutely must return to me before then, my darling. People are already asking how I will feel to be the last of our family to marry. Though, of course, Richard is not yet married, but they do not count him. I do not worry about it, though. I know that you would not wish such humiliation on me, and therefore trust that you will return before then.

I have everything planned out for our wedding and my trousseau is complete, although I may need to make a few minor adjustments to keep up with the fashions. But that is merely a trifle. It is nothing compared to the joy of having you in my arms and calling you "husband," at last.

Do hurry home, my love.

Yours truly,

Alice

*D*aniel refolded the letter.

He had written her in reply, stating how glad he was that she had his brother to keep her company in his absence. He explained that business had slowed, so it would take him a little longer to reach the sum he had in mind. He didn't want to return without the confidence that they would have what they needed to begin their life together. He'd mailed his letter with the next ship, but received no reply.

When two more of his letters went without reply, questions picked at his mind. Had she found another man—one not so far away—who turned her affections? Several men of Daniel's acquaintance had received letters bearing such tidings.

He shook his head. No such letter had come for him and he would not think so poorly of Alice. Aside from the missing letters, she had given him no cause to doubt her loyalty. She must be angry with him for not returning. Perhaps she hoped her silence would convince him to return in haste.

He rubbed a hand down his face. Nine months was a long time for a person to remain angry. And silent. Was this a sample of how their marriage would be?

He kicked a stone. He'd planned that returning in time to purchase a house and have their own ceremony before her sister's wedding would smooth things over.

That was unlikely to happen now.

With a sigh, he tucked the worn paper into his pocket, then grabbed the bread and ate it in four large bites. He refilled the canteens before returning to the terrace.

Eliza sat on her bedroll.

He handed her her canteen before sitting down several feet away.

"Is everything all right?" She tilted her head. "You were down there for a while."

"Just thinking."

They lapsed into a companionable silence, sipping from their canteens. Then he retrieved his blanket and laid it a respectable distance away from hers, yet not so far that he wouldn't be alerted if she had any trouble in the night.

Eliza removed her bonnet and set it beside her blanket. She

lay down and wrapped herself in the rough wool with an exhausted moan. Her eyelids drifted shut.

He checked on the horses one more time before lying down, his back to Eliza.

Several quiet minutes passed with plants rustling in the breeze, water tumbling over rocks in the gorge below, and the occasional distant cry of a coyote piercing the night.

"Daniel?"

Her voice whispering his name touched a deep place within him he didn't want to examine. He rolled to face her.

Her eyes sparkled with the reflected light of the moon. "Thank you. I can't imagine being out here on my own."

Her quiet admission caught his breath. From the moment he'd met her, she'd been bent on proving she could do everything on her own, yet she'd just as good as admitted she needed him. *Thank you, Lord.* What better confirmation could he ask for? He drew a long breath, filling his lungs.

He was exactly where he belonged.

~

*E*liza was being shaken. There was a hand on her arm. She cracked an eye open. Daniel stood above her, silhouetted by the gray light of an approaching dawn.

"Sorry to wake you, but we need to get moving."

Closing her eye again, she released a long sigh. The aches of the previous day were compounded by a night of sleeping on the hard, lumpy ground. Every part of her was sore. *Pa.* She was doing this for Pa. With a groan, she silenced her mental whining and focused on the task at hand.

It didn't take long to eat breakfast and pack their things. They mounted up and rode down the narrow path into the gorge. Turning north, they continued to follow the river.

A few hours later, they came to the crumbling dam that had

once fed the old flume. Here, the gorge opened into a wide valley and they came to a small, shallow lake surrounded by trees. They took the opportunity to rest the horses and refill their canteens.

As the horses grazed, she and Daniel ambled along the lake's shore beneath the cottonwood, oak, and elderberry trees. Although some had lost their leaves, several of the trees retained enough greenery to cast shade onto their path.

"Look." Daniel pointed to a large, fierce-looking bird sitting in the branches. It had a curved, black bill and its white head and body glistened in the sunlight. Its dark brown wings matched the wide eye-stripe surrounding its large, yellow eyes. The regal creature took flight to soar high above the water. Then it swooped down, piercing the surface with its feet and coming back up with a fish wriggling in its talons.

"Smart bird." Daniel began wandering, seeming to search the ground for something.

"What are you doing?"

"You'll see."

A few minutes later, he returned with a long, thick branch in one hand and a worm in the other. He set the worm on a nearby rock and laid the stick beside it. After retrieving a string and a hook from his saddle bag, he tied the hook to the string and the string to the branch before sticking the worm with the hook. Then he cast the hook into the water.

She bit her lip. The knots he'd tied weren't very strong ones. She tapped her foot. Didn't he know he needed a curve or a short branch at the end of his stick to keep the string from coming loose?

∾

*D*aniel scanned the surface of the water. *There.* Tiny air bubbles floated to the surface a few feet to the left of where his string broke through the water. He maneuvered his bait closer.

Beside him, Eliza's hands landed on her hips.

Uh-oh.

He flicked a glance at her face.

She was biting her lip.

He sighed. How long could she keep her opinion to herself? *One, two....*

"You're going to lose your string and hook."

He hadn't even gotten to three. "Is that so?"

"You used the wrong knot."

"Uh-huh." The knot he'd used had served him well on many occasions, but it wasn't worth arguing over.

As he waited for a nibble on the line, she rooted through the bushes. After a few minutes, she popped up brandishing a long stick similar to his, but thicker. Her bonnet sat askew and a leaf clung to her hair near the nape of her neck.

"Here." She said as she tramped through the brush toward him, holding out the branch. "This is what you need. See the short branch at the end?"

He nodded, but his focus remained on the caught leaf. The soft curls restraining it beckoned him.

"That will keep your string from sliding off." She jiggled the stick at him, but he ignored it. Instead, he set aside his stick, stepped closer and reached for the leaf.

She sucked in a breath.

He froze and met her gaze.

Her eyes were round.

His hand drifted toward her cheek, but he caught himself before touching her. Snatching the leaf from her soft curls, he stepped back and spun toward the lake. *No looking. No touching. Remember?*

He plucked his stick from the ground.

"Daniel?"

Clearing his throat, he kept his focus on the lake. "Yes?"

"Don't you want this stick?"

"No, thanks."

"You're going to lose your string."

"I've caught plenty of fish with sticks like this one and haven't lost my string yet."

"You've been lucky."

Something tugged his line and he focused on catching the fish.

Eliza continued to expound on how he was doing it all wrong, but a few minutes later, he had a small trout dangling from his hook. He swung it in her direction.

She jumped back as droplets of water flew off the fish, spraying her skirts.

He grinned. What would she say now?

"Ooh." She waved both hands in mock celebration. "Yes, all right. You caught a small one and managed to keep your string. But if you happen to hook a bigger fish, you're going to lose it." Her hands returned to her hips.

The obstinate woman couldn't admit when she was wrong. He removed the trout from the hook, slid it onto a new string, and hung it from a nearby tree. "Your branch is too heavy."

"It most certainly is not." She waggled the branch like a scolding finger.

"All right." *Stubborn woman.* He marched to the horses and pulled a second string and hook from the saddle bag. *Let her learn the hard way. As usual.* He walked back and held it out to her. "Here. Do it your way."

When she held out her palm, he deposited the hook and string on it, then returned to the water's edge.

As she tied her knots, he recast his line and chuckled. "That club-of-a-stick has to weigh at least five pounds. I bet your arms give out in under a quarter hour."

She lifted her chin as she tossed her hook into the water. "And I bet you lose your string to the first big fish you hook."

"Loser does all the cooking and scrubbing for the rest of the day?"

"You're on."

CHAPTER 23

*T*wenty minutes later, a bead of sweat sat on her upper lip and her arms were shaking. Yet she continued to cling to her rod. The woman was tough, Daniel'd give her that.

He considered their string of half a dozen small fish—three of which she had caught. It was more than enough to feed them for the day. They ought to call off the bet. He wasn't going to catch a large fish. He opened his mouth to say as much when there was a strong tug on his line, jerking his attention back to the water.

A big one. At last.

Several minutes of coaxing and fighting later, he pulled in a trout the size of his forearm. And his string was still attached to his rod.

∾

*S*omething frigid and wet splat against Eliza's cheek. She gasped as her eyes flew open. More drops splattered her face as she sat up. It was raining!

Across from her, Daniel shot up from where he'd been sleeping. "Quick!" He wrapped his belongings in his bedroll and jerked his head toward the silhouette of a nearby tree, its darker shape barely visible in the black of night.

Eliza scrambled to her feet and threw her own belongings onto her bedroll. She grabbed up the corners of her blanket, creating a sack, and joined Daniel beneath the tree's thick branches. It protected them from the worst of the downpour, but as the rain continued, fat drops dripped from the sodden limbs.

She rubbed her arms. "We should have set up our tent."

He shrugged. "The clouds didn't appear heavy, and even if we had, this rain would blow right through the open sides."

To cut down on weight, she'd convinced Daniel to purchase a basic shelter kit—an oiled-canvas tarp, some rope, and two wooden poles. "I know how to rig it to block wind-blown rain."

He wiped raindrops from his forehead. "Good to know."

By the time the rain stopped, their outer clothes were soaked through. They took turns changing behind a bush before emptying their bedrolls and lying down to catch a few more hours of sleep. The sun was more than halfway to its zenith by the time they'd risen, eaten breakfast, packed their things, and resumed their journey. They ate dinner in the saddle and began their ascent into the mountains by mid-afternoon.

The wind picked up as the day wore on. The path narrowed as the vegetation thickened and the terrain grew more uneven. They rode single file, making conversation difficult.

A hint of sage came to her on a gust of wind. Now and then a bird's call sang above the crunch of their horse's hooves.

These mountains were neither as tall, nor as green, as those she'd climbed with Pa in the north, but still they appeared vast. Staring up at their peaks, and then twisting back to take in the valley through which they'd come, she was struck by the sheer size of this world God had created. She was tiny in comparison

—like an ant on the Great Prairies her family had crossed on their way to Oregon.

But she wasn't alone. Daniel rode tall in the saddle ahead of her. *Thank you, Lord, for sending him.*

As the sun dipped below the horizon, they found a clearing large enough for them to make camp above the river. After a quick supper, they laid out their bedrolls.

Eliza checked the sky for the first time since nightfall and gasped. The clouds that had blocked the moon and stars for the last two nights were gone. An expanse of sparkling glory danced in the heavens above her.

Daniel hastened to her side. "What is it?"

"The stars." She held her arms wide. "They're so beautiful."

He lifted his face toward the sky. "'When I consider thy heavens, the work of thy fingers, the moon and the stars, which thou hast ordained; What is man that thou art mindful of him? and the son of man, that thou visitest him? For thou hast made him a little lower than the angels, and hast crowned him with glory and honour.'"

Her brows rose.

He shrugged. "My mother made me memorize it before I left home. She was afraid wealth would change me and wanted me to remember where my true glory comes from."

"Your mother sounds wise." She ducked her chin, picking at the dirt under her nails. He'd be almost home if it weren't for Eliza. "She must miss you."

"Hey." His rough fingers cupped her chin and lifted her face. "It was my choice to stay and help you, and I know she'll understand when she receives my letter. She would never have wished me to leave you here alone."

Their gazes held and her belly fluttered.

He dropped his hand as if he'd been burned.

Taking a step away, he faced the sky. "I don't think we've seen stars like this since the ship."

She inspected his profile. Had he felt what she had? She spun on her heel and retreated to her bedroll. *He's engaged!* "Not since the night of the dance." She shuddered at the memory. "To think I nearly danced my first waltz with that..." She let her sentence trail off as she settled onto the blanket.

"Your *first* waltz?" He gaped at her. "Surely you were invited to the balls along with the Davidsons? How is it you have not yet danced a waltz?"

She bit her lip. *Thank you, Lord, for the gloom or he would see the heat searing my cheeks.* She fiddled with the cuff of her sleeve. "It's a long story."

"I'm not going anywhere."

She caught him wincing before he corrected himself.

"We've got plenty of time." He sat on his bedroll. "Tell me, please."

Should she? She'd never shared her dream with anyone else.

She took a deep breath. "You remember I told you Mama died on the way to Oregon?" She managed to say it without a warble in her voice. "One of my last memories of her is the night one of the married couples in our wagon train taught everyone the latest dance from Europe called the waltz." A small smile teased her lips. "It stirred some folks up. Some of our group threatened to leave the train because of it, but Mama and Pa didn't see a thing wrong with it."

She chuckled. "I remember Pa stepping on Mama's toes a few times. But by the end of the night, they were dancing as well as the couple that had taught them. They were happy and so in love, and I..." She hesitated. It hadn't lasted. Days later, Mama was dead. *No! Don't think about that right now.* She focused her mind's eye on the vision of Pa twirling Mama around in his arms. "Well, I promised myself that I wouldn't ever dance the waltz with someone unless we were as in love as Mama and Pa, but then the captain, well—"

"He didn't leave you a choice." Daniel scowled.

"No."

"What about the balls?"

"Oh…" She snickered. "Cecilia said I couldn't turn a man down without being rude, so at the start of every event I would check my dance card for when they were scheduled to play the waltz and made an excuse to leave the room before they began."

Daniel laughed. "Did your aunt never suspect?"

"Oh, I'm sure she figured it out after a while, but since the men never seemed the wiser, she let it slide."

"Those poor men." Daniel chuckled as he lay down. "What does your Pa say about such behavior? Does he approve?"

"I've never told him." Stretching out on her blanket, she shivered. Despite the cloudless day, the winds gushing through the gorge were chilling. They seemed to be rushing onward without her. Wrapping the blanket around her, she peered into the darkness.

Where are you Pa?

～

The next day, they continued their upward ascent and each turn revealed nothing but more of the same. Did this river never end? The slopes climbed ever closer to the sky. She fidgeted in her seat. How much longer till they reached another point on the map? When would they find Pa?

As the sun sank behind the western slopes, they reached a small creek feeding the river from the east.

"Daniel!" He stopped his horse and she rode up beside him. "Can I see the map?"

He handed it to her. "What is it?"

She unfolded it and held it tight against the wind. "The *X* isn't along the main river. See, it's on one of these side branches." She shifted the map so that the wind pressed it against her mare's neck. Eliza pointed to where the long squiggly line split into what resembled tree branches snaking over the little triangles that represented the mountains.

"What are those?" Daniel pointed to a tiny row of dots on the western edge of the squiggly line, where the branch with Pa's *X* broke off from the main squiggle that represented the river.

"I don't know, but..." The map flapped in the wind and she smoothed it back down to run her finger along the main squiggle as she traced their route thus far. "Here's where it turned north by the mission, and here's where it turned north this morning." She pointed to the creek trickling into the river beside them. "That must be the creek."

"I don't know." Daniel scrunched his lips and his mouth tilted to one side as he studied the map. "Everything else on this map has connected with something we've seen so far, but I don't see anything here that could be what he was showing us with these dots."

Eliza scanned the area and her lips pressed together. He was right. There wasn't anything in sight that might be what Farley had meant to indicate with the dots. *But this must be the creek he meant.*

Daniel pointed to the map. "There are two lines coming off the main line after that last bend. The *X* is on the second one."

He was right. Again. With a sigh, she handed him back the map and they continued on.

Soon the sun sank beyond the horizon and it was almost too dark to continue. She peered into the deepening shadows. Was that another creek? She leaned forward in the saddle. It was!

She scanned the surrounding hillsides. Still nothing that matched the dots on the map. Oh well. Eliza directed her horse toward the new creek. "Let's follow this. See where it leads."

"But there isn't anything that makes sense of the dots."

"So what? Are you going to continue passing creek after creek until you reach the river's source and finally have to admit those dots are just dots?" She crossed her arms. "I'm telling you, this is the creek. It must be. Even the map says to follow the second creek."

Daniel's jaw flexed.

Was she being too harsh? He *was* trying to help. No. He wasn't being reasonable. She lifted her chin.

He sighed. "All right. We'll follow the creek, but not now. It's too dark."

She suppressed a victorious grin and forced herself to sound calm. "Of course. We can start in the morning."

Joy zinged through her as she prepared for bed that night. She didn't even care that they ate fish again. Tomorrow they would start on a new path. The creek didn't seem long on the map. She might be with Pa by day's end.

She lay on her bedroll, staring at the stars. What *were* those three dots on the map? Could Daniel be correct? Was following this creek a mistake? How much time would they lose if they had to turn around and come back to the very spot where they camped tonight?

As far as she could tell, the map, simple as it was, had aligned with each landmark they'd come to. Still, no map was perfect. Certainly not a map drawn in such haste. Those dots were no more than a penmanship error. A few accidental splotches causing them so much confusion.

CHAPTER 24

September, 1853 (4 months before)
Roxbury, Massachusetts

*A*lice held her breath as she stepped down from the hired carriage. The humiliation of sleeping on pallets like servants was at an end, thanks to Richard's friend, Mr. Middleton, losing his job at the mill, but how would the Clarkes react to Alice and Richard's unannounced arrival?

Her gaze locked on the dark windows of the quiet farmhouse. "I told you we ought to have sent word. They're not at home."

"There wasn't time." Richard paid the driver and bid him good-day. "The Middletons will need every morsel and penny they can scrape together until Reuben attains new employment. We couldn't impose any longer." Richard set her carpetbag atop the trunks the driver had left on the Clarkes' front porch.

Her nose wrinkled. "It seems to me Mrs. Middleton's cooking already required quite a bit of scraping."

"Hush, Alice. Do not be so ungrateful." Richard knocked thrice on the front door.

She rolled her eyes. "What are you doing?"

He shrugged. "You're not always right, you know. Perhaps they're at the back of the house and did not hear our approach."

They waited several seconds but no sounds of life came from inside.

Alice stuck her tongue at Richard. "Told you."

He made a face in return. "They're probably in their wood-shop. Wait here, your highness, and I'll go check."

"Yes, sir." She gave him a mock salute, then followed him off the porch. "You're probably right. I'm sure Mrs. Clarke is just inside sawing a table leg."

"Har. Har."

The door to the woodshop opened just before they reached it and Benjamin emerged.

His eyes widened, then scanned the area behind Alice as if seeking escape. It was the same reaction he'd had the last time she saw him. Apparently, he'd been unaware that his mother had invited Alice to dine with his family. Within seconds of seeing her, Benjamin had developed a sudden headache and disappeared for the night. What excuse would he contrive this time?

"Benjamin." Richard offered his hand.

Benjamin shook it. "Richard." Benjamin acknowledged Alice with a stiff nod. "Miss Stevens." He turned back to Richard. "I wasn't expecting you."

"Yes, sorry. This visit is a bit of a surprise to us as well." Richard scratched the back of his neck. "It's something of a long story, I'm afraid."

Alice stepped forward. "We knocked at the door, but no one answered."

Benjamin kept his gaze fixed on Richard. "Father took Mother to the city. He had a delivery to make and they were invited to dine with friends. I suppose you'll have to visit another time. Sorry." He turned toward the woodshop.

Alice took another step forward. "We need somewhere to stay."

Benjamin whirled around, his dark brown eyes narrowed at her.

She swallowed.

Richard cleared his throat. "We didn't mean to spring it on you like that." He cast Alice a disapproving glance. "I know it's an inexcusable imposition and completely boorish of us to arrive unannounced, but—"

"I heard about Caroline's elopement and your mother's"— Benjamin cleared his throat—"accident. Is she still in the hospital?"

Alice nodded. "And she insists on returning to Father as soon as she's recovered."

Benjamin looked at Richard. "I thought you were staying with a friend."

"We were, but that option is no longer viable. I was hoping you're family would take Alice in until Daniel's return."

Benjamin was shaking his head before Richard finished speaking. "She can't stay here."

Richard straightened. "Whyever not?"

Benjamin crossed his arms, avoiding eye contact. "She just can't. You'll need to find somewhere else. Perhaps—"

"That's it?" Alice stepped toward him. "We tell you of the danger our father has become, and you turn your back on us?"

Benjamin's arms fell. "I'm not telling you to go home."

"Good." Richard nodded. "Because that's not an option." He faced the farmhouse and started back toward the porch. "I think we'll just wait and see what Mrs. Clarke has to say."

"Wait!" Benjamin chased Richard across the yard. "I may have another solution."

～

JANUARY 1854 (Present Day)
CALIFORNIA WILDERNESS

When Daniel and Eliza mounted up the next morning, the sky was a bright blue speckled with clouds, though the mountains still cast their little camp in shadow. Despite his conviction that it was a waste of time, Daniel led the way along the banks of the narrow, winding creek. The shade of the trees in the gorge turned the day's cold winds frigid, stinging his face and causing his nose to run. He sniffed and tugged his wool scarf higher.

He glanced at Eliza and pulled his scarf down again. "Are you doing all right?"

She drew her own scarf down. "F-fine, thank you." She flashed him a smile before replacing the garment over her face. He returned his attention to the trail ahead.

About two hours later, they came to a third split in the creek, where the map indicated they should turn. According to the map, however, this split should resemble a *T*—a dead end with a choice to go north or south. Instead, it looked very much like a *Y*.

Daniel checked the sun's position in the sky. One branch appeared to be heading more easterly than it should, though the other pointed directly south. He rubbed his neck through his scarf.

Eliza leaned from her horse to peer over his shoulder at the map. Her nearness made it difficult to concentrate.

"May I see that?" She snatched the map from his stiff fingers. She had changed since entering the mountains. The higher they climbed, the more impatient she became. Now she jabbed at the map. "South. See? It says we should go south." She crammed the map back into his hands. He managed to wrap his fingers around it before the wind swept it away.

She reined her horse toward the southern fork and spurred it forward.

"Wait."

She didn't respond. Had she heard him?

He urged his horse after her. "Eliza, wait."

She pulled to a stop and twisted to face him. "Did you say something?"

"I don't think this is right. I think we should go back to the main river."

"Of course it's right. The map said south and we're headed south." She spurred her horse to continue.

~

*A*lmost three hours later, Eliza reined her horse to a stop at the end of the gorge where the creek disappeared. The mountains sloped sharply upward in every direction except the way that they had come. There were no signs of anyone having been there in the recent past.

She sagged like the sails on the ship when there were no winds to hold them up. *He isn't here.* Tears welled and a lump formed in her throat. She'd failed again. *I'm sorry, Mama.*

The clop of Daniel's horse grew louder.

She swallowed the lump and swiped at the icy trails left by the escaping tears as he pulled up beside her. She glanced at him, then dropped her head. "He's not here."

"I tried to tell you. It's the wrong creek." His tone was a mix of compassion and frustration.

She searched his face. "But the map…?"

"We never found those dots, remember? They must be more important than however many creeks are between where your father might be and the last northward bend." He shrugged. "Perhaps Farley wasn't inclined to draw the extra lines to show the other creeks, or maybe he couldn't remember exactly how many there were."

Eliza ran a hand over the long braid she'd fashioned that morning, then tossed it over her shoulder. She should have listened to Daniel sooner. She was too anxious to reach that *X* on the map—to find Pa. Bits of a childhood memory verse floated to her from some long ago night spent at Mama's knee by the fire, learning to read from God's Word as they made their way across the prairies. `A fool's way is right to him, but he that listens to counsel is wise`.

She grimaced. "Back to the river?"

He clamped a hand on his hat as a gust of wind threatened to sweep it from his head. "Let's eat first." He pointed to a cluster of low-growing trees. "They might provide some shelter from this wind."

After dismounting, they walked into the trees where the wind was gentled by the thick branches. They sat side by side on the ground eating a dinner of salted beef and hard tack that they soaked with their water. Clouds rolled in as they ate, blocking the warmth of the sun.

They'd been eating for several minutes in silence when a gust of wind caused Eliza to shiver. Shoving the last bite of soppy hard tack into her mouth, she shrank into her coat. Drowsiness lulled her.

"I think you're right."

She jumped at the sound of his voice. She was right? About what? Another gust of frigid air snaked down her collar.

He tipped toward her and tugged the collar of her coat closed. "This is nothing compared to the winter winds we have back home. There isn't even any snow." His eyes sparkled as he leaned back and pointed to her quivering fingers. "You never would have made it if you'd come home with me."

He meant to tease her, but for some reason an ache squeezed

her chest. Under the guise of adjusting her coat, she turned her face from him. Why should it matter that he believed she would not do well where his fiancée thrived—where he planned to spend the rest of his life?

CHAPTER 25

*F*requent wind gusts blurred Eliza's vision as they rode back to the river. Then the gusts merged into a continuous strong wind.

She reined her horse to a stop. "I can't see." She wiped at her eyes, but the tears kept coming. The world around her was nothing but blotches of color.

"I'm having trouble, too." Daniel's voice carried on the wind. A tan blur that might have been a tumbleweed blew past and Daniel's horse danced sideways. "We'd better dismount and walk the horses. This wind is making them nervous."

Eliza gritted her teeth as she slid to the ground. It would take them forever to lead the horses out of this place.

The temperature plummeted.

Twilight gave way to the black of night before they reached the river. Large clouds blocked the moon and stars. Daniel's horse, three feet ahead of her, was no more than an inky shape, moving through the dark.

The frigid air slapped the exposed parts of her face and pushed its way through her layers of clothing. It sank through her skin, deep into her aching bones.

Where was the river? It was too cold, too far. The world, these mountains, were too big. How would she ever find Pa? She wouldn't. He was gone. Lost.

No! I promised Mama.

She pressed her lips together. This was just wind. And cold. She'd dealt with both before. She could do it again.

She forced her feet forward, stumbling over the rocks and small plants littering the banks of the creek.

A burning cold grew in her lungs.

Walking against the powerful gusts became too much. Her legs trembled beneath her, threatening to give way. The wind kept her from falling forward. She sank to her knees on the rocks.

Still clutching her mare's reins, shivers racked her body.

The click of Daniel's horse's hooves continued across the rocky terrain, fading away.

Then the sound stopped.

The crunch of boots grew louder.

Daniel's coming.

He dropped to his knees in front of her. "Are you all right? Are you hurt?"

She shook her head. "N-not hurt. Just cold and t-tired."

He wrapped one arm behind her and stuck another beneath her legs. Then he lifted her, cradling her close, turning first one way then another.

She hugged his neck. His arms were warm. Safe. Like coming home.

No. He wasn't her home. He belonged to Alice. She had no right to enjoy being held by him.

She searched for the strength to push away—to lift her head from his chest.

His neck and shoulder muscles stretched as if his face was tipping upward. His groan rumbled against her cheek.

She relaxed. She was safe here.

"You're going to have to walk, Eliza. It's too dark…"

He kept talking, but she quit listening. He was right. She needed to walk. He didn't belong to her.

She leaned away from him as he tilted her to a standing position. Her feet touched the rocky ground. She kept sinking until she'd curled into a ball, her arms pressed between her thighs and her chest. She tucked her chin.

He crouched beside her and spoke near her ear. "Did you hear me?"

She pulled back to examine him. *Had he said something?* Her eyelids grew heavy. She let them close.

The warmth of his breath tickled her ear. "I said, it's too dark to keep going, but we can't camp here in the gorge. It isn't safe. It's too steep here for me to carry you. I need you to walk on your own. Can you do that?"

Eliza didn't bother raising her face. She simply nodded. She'd crawl if she had to.

"Look at me." He took her face in his hands, tipping it up. "Open your eyes!"

She wrenched her eyelids open.

"Good. I'm going to find a place to get the horses out of the gorge. Wait here." Warmth faded as he strode away. "I'll be right back to help you. Stay awake."

Something shifted in her mind. Sure, he would come back to help her, but the second she didn't need his help, he'd be gone. Gone to his Alice.

Pa was gone. Daniel was going to leave. *It isn't fair.*

It's what you deserve.

She let her head tilt forward, her eyes slamming shut.

∾

*L*oud boot steps crunched across the rocks, keeping Eliza from sleep.

Strong hands pulled her to her feet.

Daniel.

Why wouldn't he leave her alone? If he did, blessed sleep would save her from this misery. Despite sitting on the coldest, hardest, lumpiest ground in the world, the warm fingers of sleep pulled on her mind, a soothing promise just out of reach.

"Eliza!" Daniel shook her once. Then harder. "Eliza, look at me." His fingers dug into her upper arms.

She groaned. Her legs wobbled like noodles. She'd collapse if he released her.

"Eliza."

She squinted at him, her vision blurry. "What?"

"You've got to stay awake."

"Mmmm." Her eyelids drifted shut again.

He set her on the ground.

She pulled her knees close and buried her face.

Something warm wrapped around her. Then strong arms scooped her up and carried her somewhere. Couldn't he leave her be? He stopped and lowered himself to the ground, settling her in his lap. She pressed into his warmth. His arms cinched around her. He rotated them both, and the wind lessened.

After a while, the chill left her skin, but she started shaking. Something scratched her neck. Her fingers sought the annoyance and found the coarse fabric of a man's wool collar. She was wearing his coat.

Wait. I'm not shaking.

Through the coat, she felt it. *Daniel's shivering!*

"Daniel!" She leaned back to see his face. His eyes were closed. "You have to take your coat. You're freezing."

"I'm f-fine. You need it more." His arms tightened around her.

Where were they? Moonlight peeked between clouds, illuminating their surroundings. He had tucked them into a crevice in the side of the gorge. His back was to the opening. She peered past him for anything they might use to block the gap.

A solid wall of water rushed toward them.

She screamed.

Daniel's eyes flew open and followed her gaze.

Rumbling filled her ears.

He leaped to his feet, pulling her up with him. Grabbing her waist, he hoisted her against the cliff. Her torso crested the ridge of the crevice. She caught hold of the nearest bush. Hauled herself onto the hillside. Rolled onto her belly. Reached for Daniel.

They clasped arms at the elbows.

Water thundered into the crevice. It soaked Daniel to his thighs. Plants and other debris slammed against him before being washed away with the surging torrent.

"Daniel!" The current threatened to rip him away from her. *Please God, help me!*

Daniel's fingers squeezed her arms. His legs thrashed in the water. Then he shoved himself upward. He must have found a foothold.

He grabbed the same branch she had used.

She let go and he tried to pull himself out.

The branch snapped. He slipped backward. She caught his arms as his feet smacked the water. Her muscles screamed.

He regained his footing and, straining farther, he reached the trunk of the small, thick shrub.

Eliza kept hold of his other arm.

Working together, they pulled him onto the hillside.

He lay on the ground and she sat beside him. The roaring water drowned out the sounds of their panting.

Dizziness overcame her…and Eliza collapsed against the hill beside Daniel.

CHAPTER 26

Several minutes passed before Eliza's breathing slowed and she ventured to sit up.

Daniel's entire body trembled, his teeth clattering.

"Daniel?" She rotated onto her hands and knees, leaning close to his face. "Daniel?"

He didn't open his eyes or answer her.

She shook him hard. "Daniel!"

He blinked and stared at her, eyes glazed. "Eliza?"

She shrugged out of his coat and laid it over him. He needed her coat, too. Her gloved hands shook so hard, her fingers kept slipping from the buttons. She ripped the gloves off. Her bare fingers made quick work of undoing the rest of the buttons. Yanking her arms from the sleeves, she ignored the frigid air that replaced the coat's warmth as she laid it on his torso.

His eyes had closed again.

She shook him. "Daniel, wake up." Her whole body shook as she leaned over him. "L-Look at me." She fought back the drowsiness trying to reclaim her.

He opened his glazed eyes again. "Eliza." He blinked and his gaze grew a bit clearer. He gaped at her. "W-where's your c-coat?" He looked down, grabbed the garment and started to lift it off.

She pressed it down. "You n-need it more than I d-do, now." He was well enough to protest. That was good. But his legs were still soaked. He needed to get out of his wet clothes and into something warm and dry.

She considered the dark, cloudy sky. Would it rain?

Judging by the flooding gorge, it was raining higher in the mountains. If it rained here, they would need their tent. None of the nearby bush-like trees would provide them much cover with their thin, widespread limbs.

Daniel's teeth chattered, his eyes still open.

"Daniel, w-where are the horses?"

He rolled his head and she followed his gaze. Their mounts were not too far away on the same side of the creek as they were. *Praise the Lord!* She patted Daniel's shaking hand where he clutched her coat. "S-stay here. I'll be right b-back."

She forced her shivering muscles to obey her commands as she stumbled to the horses, pulled the bedrolls free, and returned to Daniel's side. She threw both bedrolls across Daniel's legs before shuffling back to the saddlebags to retrieve the heavy canvas tent.

Thank you, Lord, that my time in the mining fields made setting this up second nature.

After checking the direction of the wind, she angled the canvas to release smoke but not let rain in, should it come. She staked the back wall to the ground, blocking the chilling winds. Her stiff fingers, relentless shivering, and groggy mind, reduced her usual efficiency, but she managed to rig the canvas in a roughly triangular formation large enough to shelter her and Daniel.

At Daniel's side once more, she helped him to a sitting position. "We n-need to get you ins-side the t-tent."

He rolled his head toward their tent and gave a small nod.

She grabbed the blankets and stuffed them under her arm. Then she pulled his arm across her shoulders and, together, they staggered to shelter. They crawled inside and as soon as he lay down, she spread the blankets across his legs again. She tugged off his wet boots and socks.

"N-now remove your t-trousers."

"No."

"D-don't be stubborn. You are perfectly covered by t-two blankets, and if you d-don't get warm, you might d-die. Are you going to leave me alone in this wilderness for the s-sake of modesty?" She pivoted away from him. "Here, now I can't even s-see you."

He made an unhappy noise with his throat.

Was that agreement?

The jingle of his suspenders followed by the rustle of fabric sent her thoughts wandering where they shouldn't. *Oh no. Think of something else.* What did she need to do next?

Fire. They needed to get warm. She needed to collect kindling and tinder. Then they'd need dry clothes and warm food. Did they have any potable soup left?

He grunted and there was a soft thump. "Done."

She faced him.

He lay beneath the blankets, still shaking from head to toe.

"I'm going to gather wood for a f-fire." Her body begged her to rest, but she pressed on. Daniel's life was at stake.

Plenty of dry branches and a small patch of dead grass lay beneath a large bush near their makeshift camp. *Thank you, Lord.*

She retrieved the tinderbox from the saddlebags and got a good-size fire going. As the temperature rose inside the tent, Daniel's shivering slowed, as did hers.

He smiled, his eyes no longer glazed. "Thank you."

Thank you, Lord. She smiled. "You're welcome."

A minute later, it began to pour.

$\sim$

*D*aniel awoke to near silence. The howling winds and rumbling waters were no more. A soft crackling of fire and the twittering of morning birds were all that broke the stillness. The sun crested the mountain peaks, casting warm rays of gold and orange into a pale blue sky still mottled with rainclouds. Rolling over, he found Eliza curled beside him, her serene face close enough to reach out and touch. His fingers moved of their own accord. Could her skin feel as soft as it appeared?

Her eyes popped open and she flew to a sitting position.

He jerked his hand back.

"Oh!" Her fingers pressed her lips with a gasp. "I fell asleep."

"What do you mean?"

"I meant to stay awake and…and…well, watch you, but I…" She gnawed her lip as tears filled her eyes.

His own eyes stung. "Eliza. Of course you slept. You were exhausted. And in any case, look at me." He spread his arms above the blanket. "I'm all right. You saved my life."

She blushed, pulling her bottom lip between her teeth. "You need to dress." She pulled his clothes from a makeshift drying rack assembled from branches.

She must have built it while he slept. The woman was incredible.

"Here." Handing him his dry clothes, she crawled toward the tent opening. "I'll be outside."

Daniel finished dressing and they ate a simple breakfast of hard tack. Then they dowsed the fire, packed their belongings, and led the horses down the slope. The creek, already returned to its previous size, trickled through the narrow gorge with no hint of the roaring monster it had become the evening before. Only the wet walls of the gorge and the debris scattered about hinted at the truth.

They reached the river an hour later and he exhaled a long breath as they turned north. After the narrow confines of the creek's gorge, the ravine through which the river ran seemed spacious. Now if the rain would just hold off. He checked the sky again. A scattering of small white clouds remained, but the strong winds had pushed the heavier rainclouds over the mountain tops.

Still weary from their previous night's ordeal, they stopped to rest two hours later.

Taking a long swig from his canteen, Daniel glanced downriver and nearly choked.

A small group of Indians walked south along the riverbank Daniel and Eliza had just traveled. They weren't more than a hundred feet away. Where had they come from? Were they peaceful? Farley had said the townsfolk'd hung two of them for murder. Had anyone else mentioned the local tribes while he was in town? He couldn't recall. The Indians didn't seem to have noticed Eliza and him. Yet.

Forcing the water down his throat, Daniel tapped Eliza's shoulder.

She set her canteen down. "Wha—"

Daniel raised a finger to his lips. He pointed toward the Indians and took her hand. Slowly rising to his feet, he pulled her up with him. The Indians may not be dangerous, but better not to take a chance. Daniel and Eliza led their horses behind a group of large bushes, wincing with every clop of hooves on packed dirt.

Watching through the branches, they waited as the strangers continued downriver. Daniel prayed the Indians wouldn't look back before reaching the next bend.

CHAPTER 27

*D*aniel slumped in his saddle, fatigue urging him to stop for dinner. He scanned the riverbank, the slopes of the ravine, the mountain crests surrounding them. No sign of human life. The Indians didn't seem to be following them.

Daniel and Eliza had spent what seemed like an eternity, peeking between the branches of those bushes, waiting for the Indians to disappear around a bend in the river. The small group showed no sign of having noticed Daniel and Eliza. But Daniel couldn't be sure. Why hadn't he asked more questions about the native peoples in this area? He ran a hand through his hair.

Fool.

He scanned the area again, this time searching for a place to rest.

The glint of sunlight on water drew his attention to the right of the river. He straightened. Another bend in its course? He urged the horse to walk a bit faster. No. Another creek feeding it from the east. This one appeared wider than the last and was full of large rocks. To the western side of the river was a line of boulders in the side of the hill. They sat almost perfectly opposite the mouth of the creek.

"Woo-ha!" He swiveled to share the good news.

Eliza was hanging sideways in her saddle and struggled to right herself.

He tipped his head. "What happened?"

She regained her seat and shot him an accusing glare.

Oh. He must have startled her. She'd been almost asleep in the saddle the last time he'd checked on her.

"Sorry, but look." Keeping his focus on her, he pointed to the creek and then across to the line of boulders.

Slowly, her scowl changed to a grin. Her beautiful brown eyes sparkled. She sat taller in her saddle. "You found it!"

Her eyes locked on his. There was such joy there, such gratitude, such...his chest constricted. Was that...?

She looked away.

Urging her horse closer, she leaned forward and squinted up the creek.

Forget the creek. Look at me. He tilted sideways in his saddle, trying to catch her attention. *I couldn't have seen what I thought I saw.* He cleared his throat. He needed to be sure.

She continued staring at the creek.

He tapped a finger on his thigh. "We should eat before we go any farther."

Finally, she faced him, but her gaze flitted about before settling on the reins in her hands. "Of course."

He rubbed the back of his neck. Why was he torturing himself? He was promised to Alice. Whatever Eliza felt...

He was better off not knowing.

❧

*E*liza excused herself for privacy while Daniel prepared their meal.

She walked uphill until she reached a bush dense enough to hide her from view. Moving to the side opposite from Daniel, she sat on the ground and buried her face in her hands.

I love him? When had she let her guard down? How had she let this happen? She shook her head. *No. I can't be in love with him. He's leaving. He's engaged.* Yet there'd been something the moment her eyes met his. Try as she might to deny it now, the truth had struck her.

She loved him.

She rubbed her arms against a sudden chill. She loved him, and he was taken. He was leaving. As soon as they found Pa.

Which would be soon. Her lips tugged up on one side. Soon she would be with Pa.

And she'd lose Daniel.

Her head sank into her hands. He wasn't hers to lose. Not truly. He was a good man doing the right thing.

This can't be love. It's something else. Loneliness, perhaps? Gratitude? *Yes, that's it.* She was grateful, and she'd let it go to her head.

She pushed herself to her feet and brushed the dust from her skirt. She was being silly. She was overtired from their ordeal and letting her emotions confuse her. Now that she'd recognized it, she could control it. She nodded. It wouldn't happen again.

∾

*E*liza pulled her mare to a stop, considering the narrow stretch of land they would have to follow alongside the creek that ran between the steep walls of the gorge. "I don't see how we'll get the horses through."

"We won't. We'll have to continue on foot, but not now. Let's camp for the night. I saw a plateau a few yards back that seemed big enough for us and the horses."

The next morning, they rose while the sun still hid behind the mountains, but enough light escaped to turn the black sky to gray. After a quick breakfast, they fed and watered the horses before tethering them to trees on the plateau.

Daniel removed the saddles and hid them beneath some nearby shrubs, then shouldered his satchel and led the way up the creek. There was a knife sheathed at his hip and a coil of rope about his torso.

Eliza lifted her carpet bag and followed him. "What's the rope for?"

"In case we need it."

What could they possibly need such a long rope for? Before she could inquire further, her full attention was needed to scramble over a waist-high boulder.

Keeping her balance on the uneven and unstable rocks that covered the bottom of the gorge was challenging, but she managed, thanks to Daniel. He was quick to point out any loose rocks. When they needed to scale large boulders, he would scale them first, then help her up. Still, it wasn't long before her muscles ached and sweat trickled down her back.

"Let's rest here." Daniel sat and leaned against a large rock.

She sank to the earth beside him with a loud sigh.

Their shoulders touched as they chewed their salted beef and sipped from their canteens.

She shook her foot, dislodging a large ant scaling her boot. "Do you think we're following the right creek this time?"

"I certainly hope so." He shooed a gnat from the mouth of his canteen and took another swig. "That line of boulders must be what Farley was indicating with his little row of dots."

She took another sip of water. Pa would be so happy to see her. Assuming he was still here. Was he well or suffering? Why had he not written her? Her throat tightened and she cleared it. She needed to think about something else. "Tell me how you came to be traveling first-class on the *Virginia*."

Daniel blinked at her. "Well...that really has to do with my trip to San Francisco in '49."

"Oh?"

"When I first decided to come to California in search of gold, my cousin Johnny—my best friend in all the world—insisted on coming with me. My father made us wait six months before giving his permission. Looking back, I realize he taught me many things in those six months, which have served me well."

Daniel's face lifted toward the sky and several seconds passed in silence.

He shook his head. "We were just apprentices at the time and barely scraped together the funds for steerage tickets on the cheapest, shoddiest vessel there ever was. Captained by the meanest man ever to captain a ship." Daniel shuddered. "By the time we got to Panama, we were both weak from lack of food, and Johnny had acquired a cough that wouldn't quit. We both caught the yellow fever, but Johnny..." Daniel's voice cracked, and the tears gathering in his eyes reflected those in her own. A muscle in his jaw flexed. "When I got to California, I swore the only way I'd ever board a ship again was as a first-class passenger under a captain with an unimpeachable reputation." He tossed another small rock. "I got it half right, at least."

"Oh, Daniel, I'm so sorry for your loss." Without thinking, she took his hand in hers.

He jerked away and jumped to his feet. "Thank you, but we'd better get moving." He lifted the saddlebags and set off up the creek.

wo hours later, Eliza dropped her bag to the ground. She shifted to stand with one foot on a rock the height of a footstool, considering the giant boulder in their way. "However will we get past it?"

Wedged between the sloped walls of the surrounding mountains—so steep they may as well have been cliffs—the large boulder left no way around.

"We'll climb it like we did the others."

She stared at the giant rock that rose a good five feet taller than Daniel. "But it's so much bigger and looks so smooth."

"There are handholds here and here." Daniel pointed at small divots and cracks in the rock. "I'll use those to climb up first. Then I'll find some way to secure the rope and throw an end down for you to climb up." He studied her booted foot resting on the rock. "It's a good thing you don't go for those prissy little things your aunt wears."

"Are you sure this is a good idea? What if you fall?"

"I won't fall. My brothers and I used to dare each other to climb things all the time back home. I got quite good at it." Daniel grinned.

She crossed her arms. "What kinds of *things* did you climb?"

He dropped his satchel on the ground, wedged the toe of his boot into a crack, and jumped for the first handhold before answering. "Trees. Mostly."

"Trees!" She threw her arms up as he continued to climb. "That's hardly the same."

He moved his foot to the next crevice and stretched for the next handhold. "Sure it is." He sounded winded.

"It most certainly is not." She gasped as he made a small lunge for the next handhold and missed. "Daniel!"

His hands scrambled for a hold on the rock a moment before finding it. He barely managed to stop himself from plummeting to the ground.

"What are you thinking? Get back down here this minute, before you get yourself killed."

Daniel ignored her, climbing higher still.

She clutched her hands together. *Please, Lord. Please get him safely to the top. Don't let him die for my folly.* Would everything she did bring harm to someone she cared about?

Her breath lodged in her throat until, at last, he crawled onto the top of the rock. Standing, he grinned down at her, hands on his hips and cocky as a rooster in a hen house.

She chuckled and crossed her arms. "Proud of yourself?"

He nodded, then pulled the rope from his shoulder and surveyed his surroundings. "Now to find a place to secure this." He disappeared for a few minutes before returning. "Stand back!" He tossed the end of the rope down the rock face.

The sun emerged from a cloud, blinding her. She stumbled back as the tail of the heavy rope whooshed passed her cheek. *That was close.* Lifting her hand to shade her face, she squinted up at Daniel. "What am I to do?"

"First, tie the satchel and your bag to the rope and I'll hoist them up."

She did as he said and in minutes he tossed the empty rope back down the rock face.

She set her hand on her hip. "Now what?"

"Now tie the rope around your waist. Be certain it's secure but won't cinch too tight."

After wrapping the rope around her waist and tying the figure-eight knot Pa had taught her, she gave each strand a few good tugs to check that her knot wouldn't come undone. "It's secure. Now what?" Did he intend to hoist her up? He *was* strong, but she didn't relish the idea of being scraped along the surface of the boulder as her bag had been.

He wrapped his end of the rope behind him and held it in his hands on either side of his waist. "Grab the rope in front of you with both hands."

She did and he pulled the rope through his hands till it grew taut between them.

"Place one foot against the rock and pull on the rope as you walk up its side."

He wanted her to walk up the side of this behemoth? Walk? That made no sense. She examined the rock. Where was she to put her foot?

"Start by putting one foot against the rock."

She considered her booted feet hidden beneath her skirts. "Which foot?"

"Doesn't matter. Just pick one."

Just pick one. Of course. She lifted her right foot and pressed the sole of her boot against the rock. *What am I doing?*

"A little higher." He took up the slack in the rope. "And make sure your heel is pressed firm against the rock. Lean back so you can get your foot flat."

The rope tugged at her waist.

"I've got you."

Lord, help me. She raised her foot to about knee height, but her heel was still off the rock. She pressed her heel down and wobbled sideways. *"Ah!"*

"Use the rope!"

She righted herself and walked her hands higher up the rope. She pressed her heel down and leaned away from the rock. The action caused her skirts to lift well past her ankles. She giggled. Her aunt's face would turn positively scarlet if she could see her now.

"Perfect, now use the rope and your feet against the rock to begin lifting yourself up. You're going to kind of walk your way up."

There he went, talking about walking up this rock again. She gave him a look that let him know exactly how crazy he sounded.

He laughed. "Just trust me."

Trust him. He'd asked her to do that in one way or another from the moment she'd boarded the *Virginia*. And she did. Now. She trusted him.

Pressing her lips together, she pulled herself up until her left boot left the ground and joined the right one against the rock. She kept both legs straight and didn't fall. *I'm doing it!* Walking her hands one over the other, she shuffled her feet up the side of the rock. Then something stopped her. She tried again to step upward, but something held her foot in place. "I'm stuck!"

"It's all right. It's just your skirts, don't panic." Pebbles cascaded over the boulder, dislodged by Daniel shifting his stance. "If you can, slide your left foot back just an inch."

She did as he instructed.

"Good, you're off the skirt. Now this time when you bring your foot forward, slide it a little to the outside."

Again, she did as he said. There was no resistance. She exhaled.

"Perfect. Now, um…" He grimaced, his cheeks pinking. "Shake a little."

Her arms were beginning to shake with the effort of climbing. "What?"

"Shake your...body. I think it will help move your skirts out of the way."

"Oh." She shook her hips and the fabric fell behind her. Her legs were exposed almost to the knee. Her face heated. At least she could move more freely.

Following Daniel's advice, she resisted the urge to glance down and kept her focus on him as she continued shuffling upward. Her palms grew sweaty. She squeezed the rope. Every muscle cried for rest. *Please God, give me strength!* The rock seemed to grow taller beneath her feet.

She focused on Daniel's voice.

"That's it. Just keep looking at me. You're almost there."

At last, she made it to the top. Daniel grabbed her hand and drew her toward him. His arms wrapped around her as she caught her balance. Her muscles trembling, she leaned against him and peeked back. *Thank you, Lord, for the strength to make it to the top.*

Daniel drew her another step from the edge, continuing to support her as her legs shook.

She buried her face in his shirt and drew several deep breaths. He smelled of pine and sweat and horseflesh. Eventually, her legs quit shaking.

He lowered her to a sitting position and handed her the canteen. Ten minutes later she was rested enough to continue the trek.

A little farther along stood another boulder where Daniel had to climb up and throw a rope down to her. Instead of tying her bag to the rope, she retrieved the men's clothes she'd purchased in town. She would not get tangled in her skirts again.

She peered up at Daniel. "Turn your back."

He opened his mouth, then closed it and whirled away.

When she made it to the top a few minutes later, Daniel would not meet her gaze. Nor did he pull her close as he'd done before. Instead, he drew her from the edge, released her hands, and began retrieving their rope.

With a heaviness that had nothing to do with the climb, she plopped beside a nearby pine.

A mountain range surrounded them. The slopes tapered into wide valleys and narrow canyons that led to the ocean somewhere beyond the wall of clouds hovering over the distant horizon. Every shade of green, yellow, and brown painted the landscape before her. Tall pines, red-bark mesquite, and wild oak trees mixed with prickly paw cactus, speckled boulders, and tumbleweeds. It was a strange mixture of desert and mountain, dry and wet. Natural elements that shouldn't belong together somehow lived in beautiful harmony, emanating a peace God alone could create.

A red-tailed hawk soared through the golden rays of the late afternoon sun. *"Everything that has breath praise the Lord."* Still panting from her climb, she snorted. *I wonder what the Good Book says about people who are out of breath?* Chuckling, she glanced over and found Daniel watching her.

She raised her brows. "What?"

"You seem happy."

"Just considering God's creation." She waved her hand to indicate the view.

Daniel studied the landscape. "It is impressive to consider that the God who made all of this made us, loves us, and watches over us every moment of every day."

Had He been watching the day Mama died? How ashamed of Eliza He must have been. She bit her lip and averted her face.

"What?" Daniel dropped the coiled rope and came to kneel in front of her. "What's wrong?" His palm cradled her cheek, urging her to face him. When she met his gaze, his eyes begged her to trust him.

Her secret filled her lungs, threatening to burst from her chest if she didn't set it free. But she'd never told anyone. Not even Pa. She picked at a snag in her clothing. She couldn't tell this man she'd known only weeks, even if he had captured her heart.

Could she?

"God shouldn't love me." She lifted her gaze to Daniel's as the words poured from her mouth like the flood gushing through the gorge. "It's my fault Mama's dead. It's my fault Pa is missing. I try and try to make up for my mistakes, but it seems like everything I do is wrong. Every time I try to fix things, it turns out worse somehow."

Daniel frowned. "Bu—"

"No. He shouldn't love me. I don't deserve it."

Daniel pressed his palm to her cheek. "But He does."

She drew away from his touch. "If He loves me, then why did He take Mama away? Why did He let Pa leave? Why…" She almost asked why God allowed her to fall in love with Daniel when he could never be hers, but she caught herself and turned away. "I don't deserve it."

He placed a hand on her shoulder and gently rotated her to face him. "Whoa. That's a lot of guilt you're carrying around."

She ducked her chin.

He placed a hand under it, urging her to look at him. "Let's start at the beginning. Why do you think you're responsible for your mother's death?"

Eliza hesitated, but now that she'd begun she didn't want to stop. "I knew the wagon was falling. Mama pulled me out of the way, but I fought her and ran back to save Cookie, my dog. Mama chased after me. She pushed me and Cookie out of the way, but she didn't have time to get out of the way." Warm tears streamed down her face.

The image of her mother's crushed body flashed through her mind. Why couldn't she erase that sight from her memory?

Cookie. Think about Cookie. The beautiful golden dog had been her constant companion for the first seven years of her life.

"When I was a baby, Pa found Cookie shivering in the snow outside of town. He was just a puppy, too young to be on his own, so Pa brought him home. Pa said Ma named him Cookie because he was the color of her sugar cookies."

She took a deep breath, but her voice still warbled as she continued. "Two days after Ma died, Cookie took off after a rabbit and never came back. God was punishing me for disobeying and getting Mama killed. I tried to be so good for Pa. I did everything Mama used to do to help him, but it wasn't enough. Pa was never happy. Not after Mama died. And now he's gone and I...I have to find him. I have to fix it. It's my fault."

〜

*D*aniel pulled Eliza close as she broke into sobs. Her bonnet bumped against his cheek. His throat tight, he rubbed her back. "Shh. It's all right." He continued to murmur reassurances until the worst of her crying had passed. Then he pushed her back enough to see her face.

"Listen to me. Your mother's death is not your fault. You were a child trying to save your pet. That is not a bad thing. Your mother made a choice to save you just as you made a choice to save your dog. Would it have been Cookie's fault if you'd died that day instead of your mother?"

She shook her head.

"Of course not. He didn't ask you to save him. You did it because you loved him just as your mother loved you, and just as God loves you. Eliza, God sent his Son to die for you before you were even born, knowing full well every sin you would ever commit. Even if your choice to save Cookie was a wrong one—and I don't think that it was—but even if it was, God still loves you. And as far as you deserving His love? No one deserves

218

God's love. That's what's so amazing about it. God loves us unconditionally, and what's more, He forgives you."

She gnawed her lower lip, wide eyes shimmering.

Please, Lord, let her hear Your Truth.

"Eliza, you need to forgive yourself. You can't keep trying to make up for past mistakes—if that's what you think they were— by trying to control everything and everyone around you." He tilted his head, offering a small smile. "That's God's job, and my guess is He's better at it than you."

"You may be right." Tears still danced on her lashes, but her lips tipped up. "Thank you." Her gaze held a depth of emotion he didn't dare identify.

Her tongue darted out to lick a tear from her lips.

He leaned forward.

Her eyelids fluttered shut. A tiny drop traced a path down her smooth cheek to her pink mouth.

Her warm breath brushed against his lips, jarring him to his senses. What was he doing? He straightened and released her from his embrace.

Stepping back, he cleared his throat. "I, uh, think you should change. We need to get going. It shouldn't be too much farther now." He turned his back to her.

"I'll only have to change again if we come to another climb like this."

"Then you'll just have to change again."

~

*E*liza struggled to catch her breath as Daniel rushed away. He had almost kissed her! He stopped because he didn't love her. He loved Alice. It was good that he'd stopped. He would already take her heart when he left. She shouldn't give him her first kiss, too.

Still, what might it be like to be kissed by him? Was one kiss too much to ask? She squeezed her eyes shut. *I will not cry again.* She'd done enough of that for today.

She straightened her shoulders. It was time to find Pa. Taking a deep breath, she opened her bag and retrieved her dress.

When she finished changing, she called out, and Daniel emerged from behind a large rock. He barely glanced at her as he snatched up the satchel and rope before continuing up the gorge. She hurried to follow.

A few minutes later, she halted, her breath catching. *Could it be?* Through some trees and a little up the hill to the right, she could see a small log cabin in a clearing. Smoke drifted from the chimney.

"Daniel, look."

Ahead of her, Daniel stopped and glanced back.

She pointed to the cabin.

He closed the space between them and reached for her hand but stopped before taking it. "Come on." He led the way up the hillside through the trees and large shrubs.

Halfway between the front door and the edge of the clearing, a large fire pit smoldered.

About ten feet from the yard, Daniel stopped. "Wait there." He pointed to a thick bush.

She raised her brows.

"Please. Just until I'm sure it's safe." His pleading tone undid her resistance.

"Oh, all right." She stepped behind the bush.

"Thank you."

She held her breath as he stepped into the small clearing.

A shot bounced off the ground, scattering the dirt a foot to his right.

CHAPTER 29

*A*lice Stevens clutched the ship's railing as she leaned over its smooth surface to heave the contents of her stomach into the restless waves of the Pacific Ocean. As she straightened, Richard offered his kerchief. She accepted it and wiped her mouth.

Her brother smirked, his golden blonde curls glinting in the afternoon sun. "I told you that bread wasn't worth it."

"I was hungry."

"We're all hungry. We've been hungry for weeks, but you don't see me shoving moldy bread down my throat like a half-crazed mongrel."

"Hungry for *months*." She scowled at him. "And I did *not* shove it down. Your analogy doesn't even make sense."

"Look." He placed a hand on her shoulder and pointed to the smudged line on the horizon that they had been told was the western coast of Mexico. "We're nearly there. A few more days and we'll be free to eat like kings"—he winked at her—"and queens again."

She shrugged out of his grasp. "After five months aboard this rotting woodpile, I'd settle for eating like a human again. The pigs back home are eating better than we are." Why had she ever agreed to embark on this miserable voyage?

Daniel better appreciate the sacrifice she was making. Her conscience nipped, but she ignored it. The past was the past. She'd boarded this awful ship, hadn't she?

"Tsk-tsk. Dear sister, you are never happy. First you complain that the captain never allows us steerage folk above deck. Then we are allowed above deck, and you complain that we aren't being properly fed." He spread his arms wide, sucking in a deep breath. "Look around you. Nothing but beautiful azure sky and clean, ocean air. Can't you enjoy it for even a moment?"

She *had* enjoyed it. At the start of their journey, the wide expanse of sparkling cerulean had seemed like a shimmering blanket of sapphires. But after months of nothing but the endless blue, she was sick of the sight. And when they reached the Cape's riotous waves?

Everything sickened her.

Thankfully, those monstrous swells hadn't lasted, but each day their meager food rations grew more wretched. She could not gain shore soon enough.

Frowning, she held out Richard's kerchief, but he waved her off. She checked that no one else was watching before holding it out again. "Take it, please. If I put it in my pocket I'll reek for the remainder of the trip."

"And I won't?"

Her lips curled. "No one cares if you stink."

He laid his hand against his chest as his eyes widened. "I care."

She giggled and jiggled the kerchief again, but he ignored it.

He pointed at her. "And you smell already."

She gasped and lifted her foot to stomp, but caught herself. She returned it to the deck. They may be in the middle of the Pacific with no one but strangers to see, but she was still a lady.

His nose scrunched. "We all smell. We've just grown so used to our own stench, we don't notice it anymore." He lifted a brow. "Besides, who is there on this ship for you to impress?"

She shook the slip of fabric one last time. "Will you take it back or not?"

"Not until you wash it." He folded his arms.

"Very well." After a quick check that no one was watching, she swung her arm over the rail and tossed the offensive fabric into the sea.

It was Richard's turn to gasp as he watched his kerchief disappear. "Alice!" He threw his arms out, gaping at her. "I cannot believe you did that."

She tipped her nose up and flounced away from him to the opposite end of the deck. Mirth tickled her as she peeked over her shoulder. He hadn't followed. Instead, he'd wandered over to speak with the only other young woman aboard the ship. He'd been infatuated with the redheaded girl from the moment she'd boarded with her family in Boston.

Richard hadn't hesitated to make his admiration known. If only all men were as transparent.

She trained her focus on the hazy strip of Mexican shoreline, following it north to where it disappeared from sight. What was Daniel doing at this moment? Was he carving another piece of furniture like the ones in the set he'd described making for the Davidsons, or was he hammering a nail into the trim on another fancy house? Did he think of her as he worked, planning the future they would have together?

He'd described San Francisco as a contrast of hard, dirty labor and resplendent luxury. An image of the little house he'd been living in popped into her mind. In his letters, he'd detailed its strong construction and firm foundation but left the finer elements to her imagination. Undoubtedly, he'd adorned it with the same trim and decorative work he'd added to the Davidsons' home. After all, the home of a skilled craftsman ought to be a showpiece, declaring to all the world the services he offered.

She imagined herself living in the small, one-room home he was so proud of. Her shoulders sank a little at the prospect of cooking, eating, sewing, and sleeping all in the same room. Hadn't Daniel written that he often worked at home as well? The dirty, sawdust-covered floor of the Clarkes' woodshop in Massachusetts came to mind. Surely, it wouldn't be that bad. She tugged at her glove. What if it was? How would he react to her asking him not to work at home anymore? Where would they go when they were cross with one another?

She patted her curls. She was getting ahead of herself. They weren't even married yet. Would the pastor of the church Daniel attended be available to marry them straight away?

She tried to picture the smile on Daniel's face when he first saw her after all the years that had passed. The image was blurry. He would be happy to see her, wouldn't he? For that matter, how would she feel when she saw him? Would her heart ache any less?

∼

"*D*aniel!"

Why are they shooting at us? Eliza held her breath as Daniel spun and raced back to the her. Grabbing her arms, he tugged her behind him, placing himself between her and the cabin.

"*Vete!*" A female voice yelled from inside the cabin.

Was that Spanish?

"Are you all right?" Daniel whispered over his shoulder.

"Yes, I'm fine." She peered around him. There was no sign of the weapon that had fired at them or of the person holding it.

Daniel faced the cabin. "I mean you no harm! I seek—"

A second shot fired into the dirt near the bush.

Eliza glimpsed the flash of a muzzle as it disappeared through a hole in the cabin wall.

This time the voice shouted in heavily accented English. "Go away!"

Daniel cupped his mouth. "Jim Brooks!"

Several seconds passed in silence.

He tried again. "I'm looking for Jim Brooks!"

As the silence grew, tension built in Eliza's muscles. Who was in that cabin? Was Pa in there? Why weren't they answering? "Pa!"

Daniel startled.

Still no answer came.

Daniel began backing them away. "I'm sorry, Eliza. I…"

He continued talking, but shuffling and scraping sounds from the cabin caught Eliza's attention. She stepped around Daniel as the cabin door creaked open.

An older Indian woman poked her head out the door.

Daniel grabbed Eliza's arm.

The woman's dark eyes scanned the hillside before coming to rest on Eliza.

"Jim Brooks?" The woman pointed at Eliza. "Pa?"

Eliza stepped forward, but Daniel's hold tightened. Casting him a pointed glance, she tugged free.

"Jim Brooks is my pa." Eliza stopped at the edge of the clearing so as not to frighten the woman. "Please. Do you know where he is?"

The woman smiled and opened the door wider, inviting her inside. "You come. You come."

Eliza sucked in a breath. Pa was inside? Why was he not at

the door? Was he ill? Why had he not answered her? She started forward, but the woman stepped out and raised her rifle.

Eliza froze.

"No." Scowling, the woman pointed the weapon past Eliza.

Eliza peeked back.

Daniel was following her.

"You no come." The woman kept her weapon pointed at Daniel but smiled at Eliza again. "You come." She stepped back and beckoned with a tilt of her head. "Come."

Eliza took a step forward.

"Eliza, wait." Daniel's voice stopped her.

She looked back at him.

"I don't like this. We have no idea who's in there."

He had a point. She had no idea what or who waited for her inside that cabin. She searched the yard for any sign that Pa had been there.

Nothing. This cabin could belong to anyone.

She studied the Indian woman, who still waited. Eliza searched her eyes. There was fear and determination in their depths. But no deception. Her expression asked Eliza to trust her.

Just as Daniel had asked her to trust him so many times.

Lord, please give me wisdom. I know I can trust Daniel and that he is only asking me to wait for my own protection. But something is telling me to go with this Indian woman. Is it You, Lord? Please show me what to do.

Walking unprotected into a stranger's cabin in the middle of nowhere had never been part of her plan, but following this Indian woman felt right. Perhaps it was God's way of asking her to trust—not this Indian woman or Daniel—but to trust Him. She took a deep breath. It was time to stop trying to control her fate and, for once, trust in God's control.

She checked over her shoulder. Daniel held his hand out for her. The concern in his gaze tugged at her heart. "I'm sorry,

Daniel. I have to do this." Without waiting for his reply, she strode to the armed woman, who ushered her inside and shut the door.

～

*D*aniel took a step forward as the door closed. He clenched and released his fists, taking deep breaths to calm himself. Why had she gone in there? Should he follow her? Somehow force his way into the cabin? No. Eliza could get shot should the Indian woman start shooting.

He waited.

And listened.

Rifle or no rifle, if he heard the slightest indication that Eliza was in distress, he was charging in there. He slipped his knife from its sheath.

～

*T*he smell of hot, unfamiliar food tickled Eliza's nose as she waited for her vision to adjust to the dim interior. When she could see, she surveyed the single-room cabin.

They were alone.

Her shoulders slumped. *Where are you, Pa?*

The woman motioned for Eliza to sit in a chair near a small table pushed against the wall.

"Pa? Jim?" Eliza asked the questions as she sank onto the rustic chair.

The woman nodded. "He come."

He come. Energy surged through her with the woman's words. Pa was coming? Did he live here? Who was this woman?

Eliza inspected the cabin. It was small. The floor was compact dirt, and the few rough furnishings were handmade, but there was a hominess to it that appealed to her. The unfamiliar scent drifted from a simmering pot set over a fire in the large stone fireplace. Plants she didn't recognize hung from the beams, woven baskets were scattered throughout, and colorful rugs decorated the walls. Again she searched for signs of Pa and came up empty.

Nothing in here looked like something Pa would make.

As the woman stirred the contents of the pot, Eliza shifted in her chair. Was the woman lying?

*D*aniel paced the clearing outside the house. A branch snapped behind him. He spun around.

A deep voice came from Daniel's left. "Don't move!"

Daniel searched the forest. A man stood in the shadow of a clump of trees. Eliza's pa?

His rifle was aimed at Daniel.

Daniel slowly sheathed his knife and lifted his hands to show he meant no harm.

The man's weapon didn't budge. "Who are you? What are you doing on my land?"

It was doubtful the man held any legal claim to the land, but seeing as he had a rifle, Daniel wasn't about to argue the point. "We mean you no harm. We're seeking Jim Brooks. We were told he may have come out this way."

The man stepped forward, his red hair catching the sunlight shining between the branches. "Who's we? What do you want with Jim?"

Daniel hesitated. With the man's red hair and his height about the same as Daniel's, this man didn't fit Eliza's description of her pa. He hadn't wanted her seen by anyone until they'd found Jim, but there was no way to hide Eliza's presence with her already inside the cabin. They were at the mercy of this man and the Indian woman. He sent up a silent prayer for protection. "I've brought—"

The door behind Daniel creaked open. He chanced a peek over his shoulder.

"Daniel?" Eliza stepped outside.

The stranger's rifle turned on her.

CHAPTER 30

"Oh!" Eliza's breath left her. Standing before Daniel was a stranger, who stared at her with wide and wild eyes. And aimed a rifle at her.

She gasped as he stormed across the clearing.

A fierce growl emitted from his throat. "Maria!"

Eliza backed against the open door behind her, a scream in her throat. Did he intend to shoot her? Why was he shouting?

Daniel raced after the man, but he was several steps behind and the stranger was fast.

Her fingers clawed into the rough wood at her back. *Please, Lord.* She closed her eyes, bracing for whatever was about to happen.

"*Sí!*" The Indian woman's voice rose from inside. "*Sí! Estoy bien! Estoy bien!*"

Eliza popped one eye open as the woman exited the cabin. A rapid stream of words flowed between her and the man who skidded to a stop two steps before plowing into Eliza.

Daniel stood at Eliza's side, panting. His brows furrowed as his gaze swiveled between the couple.

Eliza's heart rate began to slow. When she'd heard voices

outside the cabin, she hoped Pa had returned. She hadn't been prepared for this red-headed mountain man. Who was he?

Most of what the couple said seemed to be in Spanish, though Eliza caught a few English words here and there. Despite having no idea what they were saying, she could guess the gist of their conversation from the multiple glances they cast between her and Daniel.

Did the red-haired man say the name, Ysabel? Who was Ysabel?

A moment later, they mentioned Pa.

The Indian woman kept glancing uphill, then at Daniel, and repeating something that made the red-haired man shake his head and point north as he spoke. Were they discussing where Pa was? Did they know where he had gone?

They both paused to study her for a moment, then resumed speaking.

Were they arguing about whether or not to tell her?

"Please." She took a deep breath and stepped forward. "If you know where Pa is, please tell me."

The Indian woman faced the red-haired man, spouted off a few more heated words, cast a glare at Daniel, then stormed back into the cabin and slammed the door.

Eliza flinched.

The red-haired man leaned his rifle against the cabin. "Sorry about that. My wife is very protective of Ysabel."

Daniel cocked his head. "Who's Ysabel?"

The man crossed his arms. "Why don't we begin with who you are?"

Eliza stepped forward. "I am Eliza Brooks, and this is Mr. Daniel Clarke. We're looking for my pa, Jim Brooks. If you know where he is, you need to tell me."

The man guffawed. "I'd ask how you got here, but you father warned me you're as headstrong as you are beautiful."

Pa's alive! She stepped forward. "Then you know him. Is he well? Where is he?" She was beginning to feel like Mrs. Prichard's parrot, repeating the same question over and over again.

"I'll tell you." He retrieved his rifle. "But I think, first, I'd better explain a few things." He opened the door and held it for them.

Her fists tightened as she stepped back inside with Daniel on her heels. *What's to explain? Just tell me where Pa is and I'll be on my way.* She pressed her lips against the impatient words.

At their host's insistence, Eliza sat beside Daniel at the small table. The red-haired man hung his rifle over the door, then took a seat opposite Daniel and motioned for the Indian woman to sit opposite Eliza.

The stranger placed an arm around the Indian woman. "Forgive me for not introducing myself sooner, but we've learned to be careful in these parts. I'm Andrew Cooper, a friend of your father's. This is my wife, Maria." He exchanged an affectionate look with the woman beside him.

Eliza relaxed a little, their loving connection warming her. "A pleasure to meet you, Mr. and Mrs. Cooper."

Daniel shook Andrew's hand. He nodded to Maria. "Pleased to meet you both."

The woman's smile stiffened when Daniel spoke. She said something in Spanish to her husband before standing and walking outside.

Andrew grinned as he rubbed his beard. "My wife wants me to invite you both to stay for dinner."

"Thank you, that's most kind, but…" Eliza glanced at Daniel, then back at Andrew. "If you'll tell me where Pa is, I'd like to get going. I'm anxious to find him."

"Why?"

She straightened her shoulders. "Because he needs me."

"What makes you say that?"

"He hasn't written in months, and I…" She cleared her throat and lifted her chin, schooling her expression into her best impression of Cecilia. "I fail to see how that is any concern of yours."

"I understand his silence may have caused you concern, but..." Andrew narrowed one eye. "Seems to me, the care of a man belongs to God first and his wife second. You're his daughter."

"He's a widower."

"I understand your mother passed on when you were a girl, and I am sorry for your loss, but that still leaves God to care for your father. Do you not trust Him?"

His words echoed Daniel's. Conviction cinched her gut. Hadn't she just decided to trust in God's control? Then what was she to do with this powerful urge to find Pa and assure herself of his well-being? Did God expect her to blindly trust Him to take care of Pa? Putting her own life in His hands by entering this cabin alone was one thing. Trusting Him with Pa's life was infinitely more difficult. What about all those deaths she'd read about in the papers? Was God not in control of those lives as well?

She lifted her chin. "God let my Mama die and I have no reason to believe He'll keep Pa from harm. Sometimes it's up to the people He puts in our lives to watch out for us."

"It's true that God does not promise us a life without grief, or even that we'll live to see tomorrow. But His Word does tell us that He loves us and He promises to be with us through each of the trials we face. It also promises that all things work together for good to them that love God." He leaned forward. "It's true that God often guides His children to accomplish His purposes, but can you honestly say God has sent you in search of your father, or is it fear that drives you? The Bible teaches us that God has not given us a spirit of fear but of power, love, and self-control."

She glared at him. How *dare* he lecture her? She could quote

Scripture as well. "Was He not speaking to us when He instructed, 'Be sober, be vigilant; because your adversary the devil, as a roaring lion, walketh about, seeking whom he may devour'?"

"You are forgetting the words that come before that"—His voice was gentle yet firm as he leaned back—"reminding us to humble ourselves under the mighty hand of God and to cast our cares on Him because He cares for us."

She relaxed her fingers, smoothing her palms over her skirt. She didn't come here for a lecture on trusting God. "Are you going to tell me where Pa is, or not?"

Again, he fell into aggravating silence, one eye squinting at her, his lips pursed to one side.

She squeezed the folds of her skirt beneath the table.

Another minute passed in silence.

Enough! Pa was here somewhere. She'd just have to find him herself. She stood to go.

"Jim's remarried."

She plopped back into her chair. All the air whooshed from her lungs. Pa remarried? When...? How...? Why...? Her mouth hung open.

Daniel placed a steadying hand on her shoulder and squeezed.

Andrew's expression softened. "You have his eyes, you know."

Oh! This man was going to drive her loony! "Will you please just tell me where I can find him?"

"He's gone and not expected back for several days, possibly a week or more."

She sagged.

Daniel leaned forward. "What about his wife?"

Andrew's focus drifted to the closed door, then back to them. "What do you think of Maria?"

Eliza blinked. "She seems...passionate."

Andrew guffawed. "She is that." Sobering, his gaze probed hers as though discerning her soul. "She is also *mestizo*."

So she was part Mexican and part Indian. That explained her tawny complexion and wavy, dark brown hair. So what? Eliza cocked her head, waiting for him to get to the point. Instead of continuing, he shifted his attention to Daniel.

Daniel crossed his arms, regarding Andrew with a hard expression. "Are you truly married?"

Andrew's nostrils flared. "Of course. One of the missionaries who worked with the Indians married us."

"And you intend to honor those vows as you would be expected to do with any other woman?"

A spark lit Andrew's gaze as his lips tipped up. "I do."

Daniel uncrossed his arms. "Then we have no problem here." He quirked a brow, then glanced at Eliza before continuing. "Am I correct in guessing that Jim's new wife is also mestizo?"

Eliza's mouth fell open. Was that what this was about? Andrew was afraid they'd reject Pa's new wife because she was mestizo?

"Not mestizo. Ysabel is Indian. Ipai."

She gripped the edge of the table. Why hadn't Pa written to her of his new wife? He knew Eliza better than to suspect Ysabel's ancestry would matter to her. So why? What wasn't Andrew telling her? "Does he love her? Is he happy?" Her fingers pressed into the smooth boards. "Oh, why won't you tell me where he's gone so I can go and ask him myself?"

"I'm sorry. I can't tell you where's he's gone, because I don't know exactly. A small group of Indians from Santa Ysabel passed through yesterday with information that Ysabel's brothers had been captured again and were on their way to auction in Los Angeles. Jim left this morning to see what he could do for them."

He'd left that morning? She'd been so close.

"I can tell you, however, that your pa loves Ysabel, and I believe he is happy here."

"He's happy?"

"Yes."

"He smiles?"

Andrew's expression softened. "Even laughs."

Awe filled her. Pa was happy. He was in love. And she'd had nothing to do with it. Daniel was right. Restoring Pa's joy had never been her responsibility. *Thank you, Lord.*

Maria returned carrying a clay pot.

Daniel cleared his throat. "You said Maria is very protective of Ysabel." He held Eliza's gaze, his expression seeming to seek her permission to speak on her behalf to reassure the women.

Eliza nodded.

He turned back to Andrew. "Please let Maria know that we would never do anything to harm her or Ysabel, and that we would be honored to accept your invitation to dinner."

Andrew rubbed his hands together. "That's wonderful. Now tell me, how long have the two of you been married? Jim never mentioned a husband."

"What?" Eliza reared back.

Daniel straightened in his chair. "No, sir. I'm sorry, but there's been a misunderstanding. Eliza and I are not married."

Andrew's grin vanished. "You're not?"

"No, sir."

Andrew gaped at Eliza. "I assumed when you introduced yourself as 'Eliza Brooks' you were trying to convince me that you were Jim's daughter. I never imagined—"

"No. Mr. Clarke is engaged"—Eliza dipped her chin—"to Alice Stevens."

Daniel's eyes questioned her. Outside of introducing him, she hadn't used his surname in days.

"But you've been alone together since leaving San Diego? Unmarried and unchaperoned?"

Daniel shifted in his chair. "Yes, sir, but—"

"He's been nothing but a gentleman the entire time." Eliza squared her shoulders. "We slept in bed rolls several feet apart and observed propriety as much as was practicable under the circumstances." Eliza sighed. "You have nothing to be concerned about."

Andrew leaned back as Maria brought four steaming bowls to the table. He scratched his head and rubbed his neck before finally puffing out a long breath. "I suppose I'll let Jim decide that, seeing as I'm not your father. But until he returns, Mr. Clarke, you'll sleep in our lean-to." He held Daniel's gaze. "The door to it groans—loudly—and I'm a light sleeper."

Daniel nodded. "Understood. What about Eliza—er, Miss Brooks?"

Andrew chuckled. "No point in returning to formalities of address at this point, young man. Eliza can stay with Ysabel." His wife took her seat beside him. "It'll give Maria a chance to rest."

Eliza's lips parted.

Daniel stilled. "Ysabel is here?"

"She's up the hill in the cabin Jim built for her." Andrew jerked his thumb over his shoulder, indicating the direction Maria kept glancing toward during the couple's disagreement. "She's been ill for several months now and in no condition to travel. So Jim had to leave her behind when he left to find her brothers. He knows we'll take care of her, but it still killed him to do it."

Cold washed over Eliza. Pa's new wife had been sick for months? That must be why he hadn't written to her. "But you said Pa was happy."

"He is."

Daniel frowned at Andrew. "Is it contagious?"

Andrew chuckled and said something to his wife in that language Eliza couldn't follow. Maria gasped and swatted his shoulder, but there was a twinkle in her eye. Cecilia would be appalled by the exchange.

Andrew faced Daniel. "You've no need to worry. Eliza will be quite safe with Ysabel." He folded his hands above the table. "Now, let's pray."

Eliza bowed her head. There was an Indian woman up the hill in a cabin Pa had built. *I have a stepmother. Is she kind? Does she love Pa? How serious is her illness?* It couldn't be that serious or Pa wouldn't have left her for so long. Not if he loved her as his friend claimed. Yet, what kind of illness dragged on for months?

She swallowed. Pa couldn't lose another wife, another woman he loved. Even if Andrew spoke the truth and Pa was happy despite his wife's illness, that happiness wouldn't survive another loss.

Weight settled on her shoulders. He'd barely survived the loss of her mother. *Thank you, Lord for bringing me to Pa so that I can...*

No. It wasn't her job to make Pa happy, to fix his sorrows. That was God's job. Daniel said God loved her and forgave her. She needed to accept that forgiveness. The weight lessened.

Yet, what was she to do? Did trusting in God mean standing by while Pa suffered? Andrew's lecture had irritated her. He'd only just met her and had no right to question her motives or her trust in God. Yet, if she were honest with herself, there was truth in what he'd said. Fear for Pa's safety *had* spurred her into taking this journey. And she still hadn't figured out how to completely trust God's plans for those she loved.

A throat cleared.

She looked up to find three sets of eyes on her. Had she missed the prayer? Her focus settled on Andrew. "How sick is Ysabel?"

"She's doing better now, thanks to Maria. She tried many different plants—some roots, some leaves, some powdered I-don't-know-what. I'm not sure what ended up helping"—he took a spoonful of the hot stew and swallowed before continuing—"but she's been able to keep her food down for several days now. Thank the Lord. A good thing, too, or Jim wouldn't have left to search for Ysabel's brothers, and she was adamant that he go." He swallowed another spoonful.

Oh! Eliza was being rude, allowing her meal to sit untouched. She picked up her spoon and inspected the contents of her small bowl. There were bits of meat and what resembled the diced parts of different plants, but the only one she could identify with any certainty was the wild celery. From the corner of her eye, she saw Daniel devouring his meal. She dipped her spoon and took a tentative sip. *Mmm.* It was quite good.

Daniel set his spoon in his empty bowl. "Then she's improving?"

Andrew nodded as he turned his attention to Eliza. "I hope you don't mind—Jim shared your letters with us. The ones he received before he met Ysabel and couldn't make it to town." Andrew wiped his mouth on his sleeve. "I almost feel as though I know you. I'm sure Ysabel feels the same. She'll be quite pleased to meet you."

~

The walk through the sparse trees and chaparral to Pa and Ysabel's home wasn't long. If it weren't situated on the other side of a wrinkle in the mountain, Eliza would have seen it from the Cooper's yard.

As they walked, Andrew pointed out the start of a narrow footpath that he'd told Daniel they could take to retrieve their horses later.

Before she could gather her thoughts and courage, Eliza found herself following Maria through the door of yet another one-room cabin. Andrew and Daniel followed her inside.

Across from Eliza, a young woman rose from the lone cot

pushed against the far wall. She didn't appear more than a decade older than Eliza and stood a hair shorter, but there was a proud air to her posture that commanded respect. Her long, dark-brown hair draped down her back and beneath her thick bangs her deep brown eyes examined Eliza.

She was unmistakably Indian like Maria, though paler, significantly thinner, and there were dark smudges beneath her eyes bearing testimony to her extended illness. The most remarkable thing about the woman, however, was the protruding round belly that stretched against the confines of her deerskin dress.

She was in the family way.

CHAPTER 31

*E*liza's knees grew weak. Daniel's hand pressed against her back, steadying her.

She glanced at Maria, who had placed herself at Ysabel's side, the message in her expression clear. *Do not dare to hurt my friend.*

"Ysabel"—Andrew gestured to Daniel and Eliza—"this is Mr. Daniel Clarke, a special friend of Miss Eliza Brooks, your stepdaughter."

Ysabel's eyes widened. "Eliza?"

Eliza shuffled forward, fiddling with the folds of her skirt. "Yes."

Ysabel's eyes brimmed with tears that spilled over and ran down her olive cheeks.

Why is she crying? Did I do something wrong? Eliza glanced at Andrew.

His smile had grown to a grin.

Eliza exhaled and considered her new stepmother. Were those happy tears?

As if reading Eliza's mind, Ysabel smiled. Her accented voice was soft, almost melodic as she spoke. "I am so glad to meet you.

Jim talks much of you. He be so glad you have come. Oh!" The woman wobbled and fell backward onto the cot.

~

$\mathcal{T}$he next morning, the scrape of the cabin door woke Eliza.

Maria stepped inside carrying two bowls, which she set on the small table before exiting the cabin.

Eliza stretched on the pile of furs Andrew had laid out for her the night before. Covered with her bed roll, they made a respectable sleeping surface. Blessedly, no rocks had jabbed her side in the middle of the night.

She rubbed her face and gazed up at the wood-shingled roof above her head. How strange not to see the blue sky.

A picture of Andrew and Maria's lean-to popped into her mind. Had Daniel slept as well as she, or did he shiver with no fire to warm him?

She'd missed his nearness in the night.

Coral and orange embers winked between the ashes in the fireplace. *I must grow accustomed to not seeing his face every morning. He'll leave the moment Pa returns, and rightfully so.* His fiancée had awaited his return long enough. What must it be like for Alice to have waited so many years to become Daniel's wife?

Daniel's wife. The thought pierced her like a cactus needle.

A rustle of blankets drew her attention.

Ysabel propped herself on her thin elbows in bed. She sniffed the air and eyed the bowls across the room. Her mouth quirked to the side.

A grin stretched Eliza's cheeks. It appeared her new step-mother was debating the value of hefting her cumbersome frame from the bed to retrieve her breakfast. Eliza couldn't imagine how awkward it must be to carry so much weight in one place on your body.

After falling onto the cot last night, Ysabel had not risen again. Instead, she remained sitting as they discussed Eliza and Daniel's temporary living arrangements. Andrew dismissed the pregnant woman's behavior as fatigue combined with shock and had assured Eliza that Ysabel was in no danger. Yet even now Ysabel shook from the effort of holding herself up. Eliza's smile vanished.

She pushed aside the blankets. She couldn't let Ysabel fend for herself. What if she fell? Didn't Andrew say Maria had been taking care of Ysabel? Now that Eliza was here, it was her responsibility to care for Pa's fragile new wife.

She would not let him down again.

She shivered as the cold morning air penetrated the thin fabric of her chemise. Ignoring her stiff muscles, still sore from their days of travel, Eliza pressed to her feet. The frozen dirt floor curled her toes as she scurried to the table. She scrunched her nose. The bowls held something that resembled porridge. Forcing her lips upward, she scooped up the bowl and a spoon, then faced Ysabel. "Are you hungry?"

Ysabel nodded, so Eliza scampered across the small room and handed her the bowl and spoon.

"Thank you."

"You're welcome."

Eliza retrieved her own breakfast from the table before retreating to the warmth of her pallet. She settled the blankets over her legs. Then she scooped a spoonful of the mystery food and stuck it in her mouth. The texture of porridge had never pleased her, but the warm meal proved no worse than any other porridge she'd eaten and it filled her belly.

When they'd both finished, Eliza took the bowls outside to scrub. A moment later, Ysabel bolted from the cabin and rushed around the corner.

Eliza sprinted after her. "Ysabel? What's wrong?"

She rounded the cabin to find Ysabel on her hands and knees

retching into a hole in the ground. From the smell, it wasn't the first time she'd done this.

Didn't Andrew say Maria gave Ysabel something that helped keep the food down? Did she need another dose, or had the treatment stopped working? *Lord, don't let this be a sign she's growing worse again.* Drawing in a breath and holding it, Eliza stepped forward. She pulled Ysabel's beautiful hair away from danger and waited for the woman's heaving to stop.

A few minutes later, Ysabel's ragged breathing slowed. Eliza helped her to her feet. With her arm wrapped beneath Ysabel's shoulders, she led them slowly toward the front of the cabin.

Back inside, Ysabel sank onto her bed.

Eliza found a cloth that she dampened and handed to her stepmother.

After wiping her face, Ysabel pushed herself to a sitting position and pointed to a simple cotton dress hanging from a nail in the wall.

Eliza plucked it off and held it out.

Ysabel took it, but then held it in her lap.

Eliza searched the room for a chemise, drawers and petticoats, but saw only her own. Her stepmother must not own any. She appraised Ysabel, who continued to stare at the dress in her lap. Was she too tired to dress herself? Would an offer of help offend her? Only one way to find out.

"May I?" Eliza held her hand out for the dress.

Ysabel handed it to her and lifted the hem of her nightdress. Eliza tugged the garment free, then helped her stepmother into the dress. A pair of soft, deerskin shoes sat beside the bed. Ysabel reached for them, but Eliza nudged her hands away. "Please, let me." She knelt and slid the shoes onto Ysabel's feet.

Ysabel gripped the edge of the bed and struggled to rise.

Eliza held her palms out, motioning for Ysabel to remain sitting. "What do you need? I can get it."

Ysabel shook her head and pushed upward. Heaving a sigh,

Eliza clasped her arms and pulled her up. Her stepmother waddled to a small shelf, where she picked up a comb and lifted it to her hair. The movement threw off her balance and she wobbled. Eliza rushed to steady her, then took the comb and led Ysabel to a seat beside the table.

Standing behind the chair, Eliza combed through the silky, dark-brown strands until all the tangles were removed. The task took little time. Nevertheless, by the time Eliza finished, Ysabel appeared still more tired and returned to bed. Within minutes, the gentle sounds of her rhythmic breathing filled the small, quiet space.

Eliza settled on one of the chairs, watching the rise and fall of Ysabel's breathing. Eliza's foot jiggled. What else could she do? She couldn't just sit here waiting. She must not let anything happen to her new stepmother. Should she find Maria and tell her about Ysabel losing her breakfast? Yes. That was what she would do. Perhaps Maria had another treatment for Ysabel to try.

Eliza stood.

What if something happened to Ysabel while she was gone?

Eliza sat.

She shouldn't leave Ysabel alone. Yet Ysabel had been alone when they arrived yesterday. Still, that was yesterday. Maria was in charge then. Ysabel was Eliza's responsibility now. It was up to her to keep her stepmother alive.

Like you kept Ma alive?

Eliza sucked in a sharp breath. Where had that thought come from? It wasn't her fault Ma had died. Daniel said so. He said God forgave her, that she... How had he put it? Oh, right. She needed to stop trying to control everyone and everything around her, because that was God's job.

She hung her head. Not even a whole day later and she was trying to take God's job again.

Eliza gnawed her lip as she considered Ysabel's sleeping form.

She could help her stepmother, fetch her things, feed her. But keeping Ysabel alive was God's job.

Lord, protect her and Pa. Because I cannot.

~

*E*liza stepped up to the Coopers' front door.

Then she stepped back.

She peered around the far side of the cabin, at the lean-to. Not tall enough to stand in, and barely long enough for a man of Daniel's height to lie down in, it at least appeared well-built and chinked. Was Daniel still in there, or had he joined Andrew in the main cabin?

The cabin door creaked open and Maria stepped outside. "Good morning."

"Good morning." Eliza stepped aside to let Maria pass. "I was looking for Da—uh, Mr. Clarke." Despite Andrew's admonition not to worry about formal address, his negative reaction to her and Daniel not being married was clear. How would Pa react? Returning to formal address might help convince Pa that nothing untoward had occurred. Breaking the habit of addressing Daniel by his Christian name would take practice. She might as well start now.

Maria pointed into the cabin, just as Daniel stepped out.

The morning sunlight glinted off his thick brown hair. "Good morning, Eliza." His breath fogged the air as his warm smile tugged her a step closer.

She curled her fingers against the desire to thread them through his glossy waves. "Good morning, Mr. Clarke."

His smile wilted and his brows pinched.

She stiffened her resolve. The privacy of their journey had drawn them too close, made them too familiar with one another. She focused her gaze on his forehead. "How are you this morning?"

His mouth fell open.

Andrew's voice boomed through the open door. "Don't stand there letting all the heat out. Come in and close the door."

Eliza tried to hurry past Daniel, but he stopped her with a hand on her shoulder.

"Is everything all right?" His low voice tickled her ear.

She kept her gaze focused on the cabin. "Of course." She broke free and rushed to take a seat across from Andrew at the table.

A moment later, Daniel sat beside her. His leg pressed against hers beneath the small table. She scooted to the opposite edge of her chair, creating a tiny gap between them.

Andrew set aside the Bible he must have been reading. "Did you sleep well?"

"Yes, thank you." She smiled. "The furs and blankets you provided were quite comfortable."

"Good. And how is Ysabel this morning?"

"She was sick, but I helped her."

Maria reached for one of the hanging plants. "I make tea."

Was the tea the remedy that kept Ysabel's food down? Why hadn't Maria brought it with breakfast? "She's napping now."

Maria nodded as she set a pot of water over the fire. "Make now. Bring later."

"Ysabel usually sleeps the morning away." Andrew shrugged. "It seems to help. She'll be up and wanting to move shortly before lunch, I expect. Then she'll lie down again in the afternoon."

If Ysabel slept that much, it was a good thing Pa hadn't taken her with him. *Wait.* "Yesterday you said her brothers had been captured *again*. What did you mean by that? Who has captured them, and what did you mean about them being auctioned?"

"I'm not sure about this time. Last time, some rancher

looking for cheap labor snuck in at night with a few of his friends and tied up Ysabel and her brothers. Ysabel's family had just lost their home and employment because the rancher who'd owned the place where they'd grown up had died and his son sold out to a man who didn't trust Indians. So they were camping out, trying to decide where to go when those varmints attacked them, claiming they were being arrested for vagrancy."

Andrew took a swig from his cup and slammed it on the table. "Jim crossed paths with the group as the Indians were being marched at gunpoint to the jail in San Diego."

His expression softened. "Jim told me he took one look at Ysabel and knew he couldn't let her be sold—which is what happens at all of those kangaroo trials. They claim the Indians can gain their freedom by proving employment or they can pay a fee to be set free. But how're they supposed to do that when they can barely speak the language—if it all—and rarely have a cent to their names? Then those same varmints that arrested them pay the fee and get free labor in return." He spit on the floor. "It's disgusting."

Eliza shuddered. How could God allow such injustice?

Andrew took another sip from his mug. "So, Jim bribed the ranchers to let him have Ysabel. They probably thought he wanted her for himself, but he just wanted to set her free. He'd wanted to free her brothers as well, but it took everything he had to buy Ysabel's freedom."

Eliza cocked her head. "But they're married now."

"Jim told Ysabel she was free to go, but..." Andrew flapped both hands. "Well, I'll wait and let him tell you the rest of the story when he gets back."

Daniel leaned forward. "So what's Jim's plan?"

"Her brothers escaped from the jail before the trial last time, but this time Jim's hoping he can buy their freedom before they even reach the jail."

"Does he have enough money?"

"We're not sure. He hasn't been able to work with Ysabel being sick, so I gave him what I could. Won't know if it's enough until he finds them."

Daniel scowled. "Doesn't seem right paying kidnappers to free their victims."

"Unfortunately, it's the only way without bloodshed."

Eliza fell back in her chair. Imagine being arrested for not having a job and then being auctioned like cattle. Her stomach rolled. She'd never understood slavery—how one person could claim to own another. Some even tried to justify their beliefs by twisting Scripture, but God had created them all. He didn't send His Son to die for only the whites or the wealthy, but for all of His children. She shook her head. Enslaving people was the work of the devil and his demons. How could anyone claim God approved of it?

"What will he do if whoever has Ysabel's brothers won't sell them to him?"

"I'm not sure." Andrew's expression grew grim. "I warned him not to try anything foolish, but Ysabel is desperate to have her brothers back, and Jim'll do anything for that woman."

Eliza shivered as cold slithered down her spine. What if something happened to Pa? Was waiting for him here any better than waiting for his letters in San Francisco? How could she help him if she couldn't even find him? She glared at Andrew. "Why didn't you stop him?"

Andrew leaned back, one brow arched. "Has anyone been able to stop your father from doing what he's set his mind on?"

"You could have at least gone with him in case something went wrong. He could be attacked or even killed while you're waiting here in your comfortable cabin."

Daniel's face whipped toward hers. "Eliza!"

Andrew set his mug down. "Would you have had me leave

Ysabel and Maria on their own?" He waved to encompass the cabin. "We live in this place for a reason. Few people come through here since the main trails run north and east of us. But some still do. How do you think Maria and Ysabel would defend themselves should someone come looking to arrest them?"

Eliza sniffed. "Maria seems a good shot."

"She is, but if an Indian can be sold into slavery for no reason at all, what do you think they'd do to one who killed a white man?"

Eliza dropped her gaze. Andrew was right. She squeezed the folds of her skirt. But Pa might be facing down a group of armed men all on his own. "And you have no idea where he is?" If Andrew would give her some direction, perhaps she could go after Pa. Help him somehow. "You said they were being taken to Los Angeles. Do you know which route they took?"

"The Indians who visited us weren't sure. All they knew was that the men were captured somewhere west of Temecula and those who witnessed it believed the men who'd captured them were from ranches nearer to Los Angeles. So it stands to reason they would take the Indians there."

"How did they even know these men were Ysabel's brothers?"

"Ysabel's brothers had been searching for her and were asking about her before they were captured." He shook his head. "There are too many ways to reach Los Angeles from Temecula. As much as I pray for his success, it's unlikely Jim will even find them. If you set out after him, you'd have more chance of finding trouble than finding your father."

She opened her mouth to argue, but Andrew wasn't finished.

"Either way, Jim would have my hide if I let you take off alone with Mr. Clarke again, and taking you myself wouldn't be much better for your reputation. Not to mention that if word reached the men holding Ysabel's brothers that I've been asking around after Jim, it'd cause trouble for sure. Jim's new and mostly unknown around these parts. The Indians who came by yesterday only knew where to find Ysabel because I'd taken Maria to their rancheria to trade for some plants she wanted for Ysabel. They knew nothing about Jim. But I'm a well known *Squaw Man,* as they call it. If Jim's association with me got around, the men holding Ysabel's brothers would know exactly what he was after." He jabbed a finger on the table. "Those kind of men don't take kindly to those of us who treat the Indians with the dignity and respect they deserve."

"But I..."...*could go after Pa myself.* The words died on her tongue. She'd tried that before, and look where it got her. But for Daniel and God's grace, she wouldn't have survived the journey here. She clasped her hands on the table. Still, Pa was traveling alone. If anything happened, there would be no one to help him.

As if reading her mind, Andrew laid his hand over hers. "God is with your father."

An ache built in her throat. She was back to where she'd started—wondering how to trust God with Pa's life. Dipping her head, she squeezed her eyes shut. *God, please keep him safe.*

When she lifted her head, Andrew and Daniel's expressions were somber as they sipped their drinks.

She searched the cabin for a topic of conversation to distract herself from the danger Pa might be facing. The dried plants hanging from the rafters caught her attention. "How long have you and Maria lived here?" The cabin appeared tidy but well lived-in. Its wood siding was seasoned—as opposed to freshly cut—and there was dust in those crevices every house had—the ones that tended to fill over time but refused to be cleaned by anything larger than a toothpick. "How did the two of you meet?"

"Well, I'm originally from Massachusetts."

Daniel leaned forward, his eyes lighting. "Are you really? So am I."

Andrew slapped the table. "I knew I recognized your accent."

"What did you do there?"

"I was the pastor for a small church in a little town in the middle of nowhere."

Eliza smothered a snort. That explained yesterday's lecture.

Daniel straightened. "Why'd you leave?"

"I felt God calling me to serve our men in the army. And there was a new young pastor, fresh from seminary, who was eager to take my place."

As they listened to Andrew talk about his time in the army—ultimately serving in the war against Mexico—Daniel shifted beside her. His leg pressed against hers. With the wall against her opposite side, she had nowhere to go. She inspected him from the corner of her eye. His expression gave no hint as to whether he was aware of the contact or not. Though, surely he was unaware. This was Daniel, after all. He'd never be so forward—even if he weren't engaged.

She returned her attention to Andrew but struggled to focus as he explained that after the war he'd left the army and wandered north, alone. His horse threw him, breaking several of his bones. He was unable to move from the spot where he fell and lay there for three days, nearly dying of thirst, before Maria found him. She nursed him back to health, and they were married shortly thereafter. Two years ago, they'd built this cabin.

Daniel leaned back in his seat, his leg rubbing against hers.

She shot to her feet, covering her reaction with an exaggerated stretch that would have elicited an hour-long lecture from her aunt. "Oh goodness, I think I'm still recovering from our journey. If you'll excuse me, I think I need a walk."

Andrew nodded, though his brows drew together. "Of course."

"I'll join you." Daniel stood.

"No!" She cleared her throat as she walked toward the door. "Er—No, thank you. I...so much has happened, I just need some time...to think it all over. Alone."

Not waiting for his reply, she yanked open the door and rushed outside.

CHAPTER 32

*E*liza wandered the hillside for two hours. She needed to distance herself from Daniel, and he might seek her out if she returned to Pa and Ysabel's cabin too soon. Daniel probably hadn't even realized their legs brushed, so her abrupt departure had surely stirred questions she wasn't prepared to answer.

As she neared Ysabel's cabin, her stomach rumbled its desire for dinner. Inside, she found Ysabel sitting cross-legged on the floor. Beside her lay a pile of long, skinny reeds. On her belly, she held a beautiful woven disk displaying an intricate pattern in various shades of brown. Reed tails stuck out from the edge of the disk closest to Ysabel's face. She held one reed tail between her teeth, while her left hand gripped the disc and her right hand wiggled a thin bone tool between the woven strands. Ysabel removed the bone tool, then threaded the tail she'd been holding with her teeth through the tiny gap she'd created. She pulled the reed tight, creating a loop that secured the loose tails to the disk. Finally, she lifted her face to Eliza.

"Hello." Her wide smile revealed a missing tooth on the right side of her mouth. As if remembering this, Ysabel's lips snapped closed, though they remained tipped up. Eliza's favorite baker in San Francisco—also missing a few teeth—had hid her smile as well. It took more than a year for the woman to relax enough to smile naturally around Eliza.

Please don't let it take Ysabel as long to grow comfortable around me. She has a beautiful smile.

Hoping to set Ysabel at ease, Eliza grinned and sat on the floor in front of her. "Hello. What are you making?"

Ysabel's brow creased so Eliza pointed to the beautiful woven disk. "Is this going to be a basket?"

Ysabel lifted the woven piece. *"Sa weel."*

"Saw wheel?"

Ysabel nodded, then returned to her weaving.

What's a saw wheel? Whatever it was, it was fascinating watching Ysabel work.

Sometime later, there was a knock at the door.

Eliza stiffened. Had Daniel come to check on her?

Without pausing her work, Ysabel called out in that odd language Eliza didn't recognize. It must be Ysabel's native tongue.

Eliza relaxed when Maria entered with two bowls and strode to the small table. She said something that Eliza couldn't understand as she set down the food. Again, Ysabel spoke without lifting her gaze from her work. Maria turned to go.

Steam rose from the bowls on the table. Maria seemed to be constantly preparing for their next meal. Even Ysabel was working, despite her condition. And here Eliza sat. Accomplishing nothing.

She jumped to her feet. "Wait."

Maria paused to regard Eliza.

"Can I help you?"

Maria tilted her head, her brows furrowing.

Eliza pointed to the bowls. "You shouldn't have to wait on everyone. Let me help you cook." She considered the intricate basket taking shape in Ysabel's capable hands. "I'm sure I don't know how you do things here, but I'm willing to learn."

Maria still appeared confused, so Eliza crossed to the bowls, lifted one, and brought it to the fireplace. She pointed to herself. "I"—she held the bowl over the fire and made a stirring motion —"make"—she pretended to scoop the mush from the bowl and eat—"food. All right?"

Maria's furrowed brow eased. "Ahh. *Quieres cocinar!*"

Eliza squinted at Maria. What did 'key-air-ess koh-see-nar' mean?

"You, uh…" Maria's eyes tilted up and to the right. Then she shrugged. "Tomorrow. You come. Yes?"

Did Maria understand what Eliza had asked? Maybe Eliza should go find Andrew to translate. Then again, Maria seemed confident. Eliza smiled. *"Sí.* Tomorrow."

Maria left the cabin.

Tomorrow would be interesting.

∼

*D*aniel adjusted his grip on the heavy buckets of water. Dead leaves crunched beneath his boots as he tromped through the forest. The sound was oddly satisfying. He veered toward a large pile of the fallen foliage and stomped it down. Water sloshed against the wooden sides of the buckets, threatening to escape. He paused to let it settle.

Where is she? He'd exited the Coopers' cabin mere moments after Eliza, but she was nowhere in sight. He checked for her at the Brookses' cabin, but when he peeked inside, Ysabel was alone. The pregnant woman smiled at him from where she sat on the floor weaving something with reeds, but didn't seem to understand his questions about Eliza. The sight of Eliza's belongings at the foot of her pallet assured him that she hadn't left to find Jim.

He waited outside the Brookses' cabin for an hour, but Eliza hadn't returned.

Now he scanned the landscape surrounding him as if she might appear between the bushes. Where did she go? Why had she rushed out the way she had?

Her behavior had been odd from the moment she arrived in the yard that morning. Gone was the warm and open friendship they had developed over the last few days. In its place was the cold, stand-offish woman she'd been in San Francisco. Then she tried to put Andrew in his place, sounding like her aunt. Daniel wrinkled his nose. What was she thinking?

He slowed his pace and took a breath as he neared the rope enclosure they'd penned the horses in the night before. It took Andrew and him hours to lead the horses along the slender footpath that bypassed the gorge he and Eliza had navigated. He and Andrew hadn't returned until long after the stars glowed bright in the dark sky and the moon hung high overhead. The last thing Daniel needed was to spook the tired creatures and have them bust through a rope.

He set down one bucket and poured the other into a large metal tub. Had he done something to offend her? If so, why didn't she tell him what he'd done so they could discuss it? He set aside the empty bucket and poured the second into the trough. They only had a few days until her pa returned and Daniel would need to leave. He didn't want to spend the little time they had left at odds with each other.

~

*L*ate the following morning, Eliza struggled to keep her gaze on Maria and ignore Daniel's attempts to snag her attention. He and Andrew sat at the Coopers' small table swapping stories from their home state, but any time Eliza turned their way, Daniel found some excuse to involve her in the conversation. She kept her answers short, but avoiding his eyes was growing increasingly difficult.

Maria's preparation of their noon meal was fascinating, but now that Eliza had resolved to distance herself from Daniel, his presence seemed to shout at her. *Ignore him.* She shifted so that Daniel was blocked from even her peripheral vision.

Reaching into a large basket, Maria withdrew several handfuls of acorns before spreading them on a large flat stone near the fire. Then she picked up a smaller rock and cracked the shells open. With the shells removed, Maria rubbed each nut between her fingers before placing them all in a shallow basket and carrying it outside.

Eliza followed her.

Maria stood in the part of the clearing where the breeze was the strongest, gently swirling the shallow basket in circles as the wind picked up the nut skins and carried them away. After a few minutes, the nuts were bare and Maria returned to the cabin. Again, Eliza followed.

Andrew paused in his story when they entered.

Daniel looked at Eliza and gestured toward Maria. "What are you doing?"

Eliza's steps faltered. "Maria is teaching me to prepare acorns."

"That's wonderful." He smiled.

Something fluttered inside her and she spun away. *He's leaving, Eliza.*

She hurried to where Maria set the basket on the floor beside the fire. From a nearby shelf, Maria fetched two mortar bowls with pestles sitting inside. She handed one to Eliza, then gestured for Eliza to join her on the floor. Once they were seated, Maria scooped a handful of nuts and poured them into each bowl. They set to work.

Soon the last of Maria's acorns were ground into meal and

she set her bowl aside. *"Gracias.* Thank you." She reached for Eliza's bowl, which still held several larger pieces.

Eliza chuckled as she handed over her mortar and pestle. She had tried. "Thank *you."* Eliza stood to stretch her legs. She'd have to practice grinding acorns when their meal didn't depend on her speed.

She caught Daniel watching her. The look of admiration in his eyes took her breath. She turned away.

It didn't take long for Maria to finish grinding the acorns Eliza had started. Maria poured the meal into a tightly woven basket and carried it outside.

Following Maria down the hill, Eliza scanned their surroundings. Perhaps Pa would return today. If he did, would Daniel leave right away or wait and leave in the morning? She sucked in a deep breath and blew it out, bringing her mind back to the present.

Maria stopped by a creek at a point where the water rushed from one short drop to another. She tied one end of a small rope to the basket and secured the other end around a nearby branch before dropping the basket into the stream.

She faced Eliza. "We go. Come back, two nights."

"But I thought this was for our dinner."

Maria chortled. "Come."

They walked upstream a few feet to where it was easier to cross and then walked downstream until they were opposite the spot where they'd tied the basket of acorn meal. Maria reached into a clump of weeds and withdrew another rope.

Another basket? It was impossible to tell. One end of the rope was tied to a bush beside Maria and the other disappeared into the rushing water.

Maria began pulling and a moment later, a basket emerged from the water. She untied it and removed the lid.

Inside was a clump of mush.

"Acorn?"

"Sí."

Back in the Coopers' yard, Maria poured some of the acorn mush into a basket along with a little water. She set the basket on a rock that was surely extremely hot, as it had been sitting over the fire since earlier that morning. A short time later, the mush was cooked through, and Maria poured it into five bowls.

Daniel patted the seat Eliza had sat in the day before. "Have a seat and we'll pray."

"No, thank you." Eliza lifted two of the warm bowls. "I'm going to eat with Ysabel. I'll pray with her." Her step faltered as she strode toward the door. She hadn't thanked Maria for teaching her about the acorns.

Eliza's gaze flicked toward Daniel of its own volition.

His shoulders were hunched, head drooping.

She hastened her steps.

She would thank Maria this evening.

⁓

*T*wo days later, Eliza paused her stitch in the hem she was mending. "I'm sorry, Maria. What did you say?" She'd been so focused on the stroke of Daniel's wet stone across his knife, she'd pricked herself three times with the needle and had missed Maria's question.

"You go get basket. Yes?"

"One of the baskets with the acorn flour in the creek?"

Maria nodded.

Eliza set aside her sewing. "Of course."

Daniel rose from where he'd been sitting beside the fire, sharpening a knife. "I'll come with you."

"That's not necessary. I'm sure I can manage on my own." She hurried outside, but he followed her.

"Eliza." He caught her shoulder. "I thought we established

that you don't have to do everything on your own." His teasing expression set off the fluttering inside her.

Stop it! Pain sliced her chest. She shouldn't feel this way. He wasn't hers. Could never be hers. She turned her face from him. "I'm all right. I *want* to do this alone."

His hold wasn't tight, but it held firm against her tugging. He rotated her to face him. "Please, tell me what's wrong." The ache in his voice brought her eyes up and the pleading in his gaze nearly undid her resolve. "Or at least, let me come with you. I'll be leaving soon, and—"

"Don't you think I know that?" The words burst from her lips before she could stop them. She wrenched her shoulder free and spun away. "Just lea"—her voice cracked—"leave me alone, Daniel." Tears blurring her vision, she raced up the hill.

~

She'd used his Christian name. Daniel took a step to follow her, then stopped—the agonized expression on her face before she'd run from him halting him in his tracks.

He had known for a while now that she, too, fought the attraction between them. They had come too close to kissing to deny there was something there. Still, what he'd seen in her eyes just now was more than attraction. It confirmed what he'd suspected since the day after the flood—she cared deeply for him.

His heart wanted to soar, but he reined it in. He had promised his heart and his future to Alice. He had no right to feel joy at the thought that Eliza might love him—especially when it was clear that his presence, while knowing he intended to leave, was hurting her.

~

*A*lice held a gloved hand over her nose as the gangplank was lowered. San Francisco at last! Though her heart and mind rejoiced, her stomach rebelled. The stench of the filthy wharf was nearly as bad as the stench in steerage.

She ran her free hand over her curls, checking that they were in order as she and Richard waited for the upper-class passengers to disembark first.

Richard stood beside her, two of their bags in hand. "Isn't it marvelous?"

She surveyed the rambling city before them. What did her brother see that so impressed him? A haphazard assemblage of ramshackle structures, middle-class storefronts, and a handful of mansions met her gaze. Set in neat, crisscrossing rows, the streets appeared muddy, even from this distance. The hem of her skirt would be ruined if they did not hire a carriage to carry them to Daniel's place of residence.

Draymen scurried about the docks collecting passengers from the boats. Perhaps they could hire one of them.

Spending any of our precious-little funds on transportation when we are perfectly capable of walking may not be the wisest of choices.

Nonsense. Consider the cost of repairing a ruined hem.

As if to make her point, a wagon raced past, splattering a man below with mud to the waist.

You see? She lifted her chin. *I* will *convince Richard to hire a drayman.* She couldn't afford to replace an entire dress and she certainly wouldn't walk about in a stained one.

At last, it was their turn to disembark and she followed her brother to the top of the gangplank. Her legs wobbled as she stepped down the boards. Her grip on the left railing tightened. If only her other hand were not required to carry her carpetbag so that she might clasp both rope railings. By the time she'd reached the dock, her left palm burned.

She paused to check her glove. It had worn clean through in one spot.

Richard bumped into her as an eager passenger shoved passed him. "Will you move?" Richard's exasperated tone caught the attention of a passing drayman.

The filthy man faced them as sweat dripped into his smile. "Need a lift?"

She opened her mouth to negotiate a fee, but her brother waved the man away.

"No, thank you. We'll walk."

The man hesitated, his attention shifting to Alice.

She affected her best pout. "My legs are all wobbly, Richard."

"All the more reason to walk. We need to reacquaint ourselves with a surface that doesn't dip and sway, but remains firm beneath our feet." He stomped one foot for emphasis and a loose board shifted beneath him. He teetered precariously near the edge of the planks.

She resisted the urge to shove him into the water.

Once he'd righted himself, he tugged down his vest, adjusted his cravat, and lifted his chin. "Come." He marched off down the dock without so much as glancing back to see whether she followed.

She should have shoved him.

Better yet, she ought to hire the drayman just to see the expression on Richard's face as she passed him.

She pivoted toward the drayman.

He was already speaking with another man disembarking behind her.

She huffed and hurried after her brother.

*D*espite Alice's pleas, Richard refused to hire a carriage. He would have also denied her a place to freshen up if she hadn't refused to budge until he agreed to find her a bathing saloon. She would *not* show up on Daniel's doorstep filthy and reeking of bilge water.

Several wrong turns and hours later, she picked her way down another muddy street, careful to avoid the worst of the puddles. Despite the cool weather, sweat trickled down her back, soaking her chemise and causing her to shiver with each gust of wind off the bay. So much for feeling clean. At least the stench of steerage was banished from her body.

The time her bath had taken and their slow progress through the bustling city meant the sun hung low in the sky by the time they neared the address Daniel had given them. Her steps slowed. It had taken months to get here, but now that they were, she wasn't ready. What would she say to Daniel? She'd sworn her silence, but could she keep it? Was it right to keep secrets from one's husband? It wasn't as if Daniel were anything like Father, but—

She faltered before the squat little building as Richard stepped up to its gloomy, unpainted door. "Wait."

Richard froze, his hand poised to knock. "What?"

"Are you certain this is it?" She checked Daniel's letter, then appraised the structure before her. Although it appeared to be in better shape than the rest of the buildings on this block, its plain, unfinished walls were washed gray by the sun and were topped with dull, gray shingles. Not one bit of trim adorned its eaves or windows. There was nothing to indicate that a skilled craftsmen lived here.

In her mind, she saw the beautiful two-story home Daniel's brother, Benjamin, was building on his family's land. There was a wide porch along the front, with turned spindles in the railing, and Benjamin had been adding eave brackets and decorative window trim when she left. It would be finished by now—painted and papered for whomever he chose as his wife. Her hands fisted. How could Benjamin have done this to her?

Richard's voice brought her back to the present. "Only one way to find out." He knocked.

Several minutes passed with no response.

Richard knocked louder.

The thud of boots stomping across floorboards reached them through the walls. A moment later, the door flung open to reveal a slovenly attired man with a paunch that hung over his trousers and a balding patch of brown hair. He glared at Richard. "What do you want?"

"Where is Daniel?" She hadn't intended to voice the question, but both men turned to her, so she must have.

"Well, now. Who are you?" The man's leer made her shudder.

Richard moved to block the man's view. "We're looking for Daniel Clarke. We were told he lived here."

"Clarke moved on. He ain't here no more."

Her mouth dropped open. Daniel *must* be here. He'd lived at this address for more than two years. Where would he have gone?

Richard craned his neck, seeming to peer over the man's shoulder. "Do you happen to know where he's gone?"

"'Fraid not. Sorry." The man shut the door in Richard's face.

Stepping back, Alice scanned up and down the street again. There were at least two dozen other buildings on this block alone—more than half of which appeared to be housing of some kind, and they had passed dozens of streets before reaching this one. There were so many places Daniel might be. She wrung her hands. "What are we to do now?"

"Do you know where he works?"

She shook her head. "He's always moving from one project to the next. Wherever Mr. Davidson has need of him."

"What about Mr. Davidson? He must have an office of some kind? Do you know its location?"

"I don't remember Daniel mentioning an office, but…" Her gaze drifted to the dismal gray sky. What had Daniel written about Mr. Davidson? "He owns a shop, I believe. Near the wharf."

He took her elbow. "Then we'd best walk quickly. It'll be dark soon and I want you settled." He glanced at her. "I know you hoped to marry today, but with the hour so late, I doubt we'll be able to find a clergyman once we find Daniel."

"But if we're not married, I can't stay in his house." What if the boarding house rates were still as high as Daniel had written? Were there any decent enough for a lady to set foot in? She'd read horrid stories in the papers of men being bitten to death by fleas and robbed in their sleep. She stared down the mud marring her pale blue dress. Why had she wasted her money on a bathing saloon?

Did she have enough left to rent a decent room for the night?

CHAPTER 33

*E*liza slouched in the small chair, shredding a discarded piece of reed.

Across the cabin, Ysabel's chest rose and fell in peaceful slumber. Her stepmother was gaining in strength with each passing day. Despite Eliza's fears that first morning, Ysabel's body had rejected her meals only twice in the past three days—a vast improvement from how Andrew had described the previous months. Ysabel still napped each morning and afternoon, but in between she was able to assist Maria with meal preparations, making Eliza's fumbling efforts less necessary. Still, Eliza had promised Maria her help.

Eliza eyeballed the door. Should she leave?

All morning, she'd kept busy boiling water and washing their laundry that now hung drying on the line. At noon, Maria brought them dinner and admired Ysabel's basketry, then went back to her own cabin. After Maria left, Eliza had checked the laundry, fetched fresh water, and helped Ysabel retrieve more reeds from the bundle outside.

Now her stepmother slept.

There was nothing to keep Eliza from seeking out Maria and offering her assistance.

Eliza didn't budge.

Helping Maria meant facing Daniel, and there could be no doubt he'd discerned her feelings for him. Facing him would be humiliating. Not that he would be unkind. Daniel was too noble to take pride in her broken heart. Instead, he would pity her, avoid her gaze, and guard his every word and action, fearful of encouraging her inappropriate feelings for him. She couldn't bear that.

Yet Daniel would be leaving as soon as Pa returned and she'd never see him again. As painful as it may be, should she give up the little time she had left with him? He may not love her, but he had proven himself a true friend. Was it wrong to want to keep that friendship for as long as she could?

She imagined herself in Alice's place. *Would I want my fiancé spending time with a woman who coveted him for herself?*

Eliza's head dropped. *I'm coveting Daniel's heart.*

Though she hadn't memorized any particular Scripture verses on the matter, she'd heard enough sermons to know that coveting something was a sin. *Please, God, help me let Daniel go. Help me stop loving him this way. Help me desire his friendship and nothing more. I cannot do it on my own.*

An odd scratching sound penetrated the walls of the cabin. She tilted her head, listening. Boots crunched across the dirt outside. She rose and cracked open the door.

Daniel stood in the trees past the clearing, taking her laundry from the line, one item at a time. He folded each piece and set it in the basket at his feet. The basket scratched across the ground as he nudged it along. When he reached her unmentionables, he hesitated. His face grew red. He turned his back to the garments and surveyed the yard, his gaze halting on hers. She resisted the urge to close the door.

Then his shoulders sagged and his lips turned down.

She spun away before his sorrow could become pity.

She checked that Ysabel was still sleeping, then slipped outside and shut the door. She traced the outline of a boot print in the dirt with the tip of her shoe. What would she say to him?

He walked toward her.

She hurried away from the house. They mustn't wake Ysabel. She met him at the edge of the clearing.

He stopped one step away and glanced back at the laundry. "I thought I'd lend a hand, but..." He rubbed the back of his neck.

"I understand. Thank you. It was a kind thought." Stepping around him, she yanked her unmentionables from the line and dropped them into the basket. She tugged a blanket from the bottom of the pile and set it on top. Lifting the basket, she straightened and settled it on one hip. She paid inordinate attention to where she placed each footstep as she passed him.

"Eliza."

She paused, taking a long, steadying breath.

He was silent for so long.

Her muscles tensed, preparing to face him.

Then he spoke in a voice so quiet she nearly missed it. "I'm sorry."

Covering her mouth, she sprinted into the cabin.

~

*T*wilight blanketed the city in shadow by the time Alice and Richard found the address that Mr. Davidson's shop clerk had given them. Alice inspected her dress and smiled. She'd managed to keep it free of mud on their trek uphill.

The narrow, four-story home before them was topped with

elaborate roof cresting and adorned with fish-scale shingles. Gingerbread scrollwork hung from its eaves, and an intricately carved balustrade enclosed its second-story balcony. A stained-glass transom above the front door drew the eye. In short, it was a house that commanded attention and respect.

She lifted her chin. Her fiancé had built this. And he'd rebuilt it after each of the great fires. He'd written to her of his employer's insistence that Daniel be the one to oversee the building project and personally complete all the unique design elements that made this house a masterpiece. Mr. Davidson's steadfast faith in the quality of Daniel's work, and his reliance on Daniel to take on his unending list of projects, was one of the reasons Daniel had given for his delayed return to her.

Richard knocked and, moments later, a negro man in a servants' uniform opened the door. "May I help you?"

"My name is Richard Stevens and this is my sister, Miss Alice Stevens. We'd like an audience with Mr. Davidson if it's not too much trouble."

"I'm sorry to inform you that Mr. Davidson is not at home."

Richard frowned. "May we wait on him? We're searching for an employee of his, Mr. Daniel Clarke." Richard gestured to Alice. "This is his fiancée. We've been to Mr. Clarke's home, but the gentleman there told us he'd moved on. We're hoping, as his employer, Mr. Davidson might know where he's gone."

The servant's eyes grew wide as Richard spoke.

Alice's breath caught. He knew something. She leaned forward. "We won't be any trouble, I promise. It's important that we find Daniel as soon as possible. Please, may we wait?"

The servant stepped back. "Please, come in."

Alice exhaled and followed Richard into the elegant foyer.

The servant closed the door before taking their bags and setting them to the side. He opened another door and motioned for them to enter a parlor that could have held its own among the best homes in Boston. "Please wait here while I see if Mrs. Davidson is available."

Alice paused beside a tufted, velvet settee. "There's no need to trouble her. We don't mind waiting on our own." She cocked her head. "Or perhaps *you* have information you might share with us?"

The man backed away. "If you'll excuse me. Mrs. Davidson will want to be informed of your presence. Please, wait here."

"Certainly." Richard nodded and the servant disappeared down the hall. Richard waved at the door. "What was that about?"

She shrugged. "I thought he knew something. He wore such an odd expression when you mentioned Daniel." She surveyed the furniture. Which of these beautiful pieces could be attributed to Daniel's skill?

Richard strode to the window, where he stared out at the fading light. "If Davidson doesn't return soon, perhaps we can prevail upon his wife to keep you while I find us suitable accommodations for the night."

"That's rather presumptuous, Richard."

"It is, but I'm hoping she'll be sympathetic to our situation and understand why I'm reluctant to have you wandering the streets with me after dark."

Alice stomped her foot. "You promised that if I came to California, I'd be through with begging for a place to stay. Was Benjamin's rejection not enough humiliation for you? What happened to a fresh start? No more scandals, no more feeling like parasites?"

Richard spread his arms. "What would you like me to say? It never occurred to me that we wouldn't be able to find Daniel when we arrived. You told me he'd been living at the same address for years."

She sniffed. "Well, he had."

"Well, all right." Richard spun toward the window. "I'm

271

doing the best I can. I'm sorry if it isn't enough for your highness."

Alice flinched. He was right. She wasn't being fair. But this whole situation wasn't fair. Why must she constantly be at the mercy of other people's decisions? First Father and Mother, then Richard, then Benjamin, and now Daniel. When would *she* get a say in her life?

Several minutes later, an elegantly coiffed woman entered wearing a pale blue dress patterned with delicate pink roses. She paused in the open doorway, inspecting them from head to toe.

This must be Mrs. Davidson. Alice held her breath. Thank goodness she'd convinced that clerk to let them freshen up. But was it enough? She resisted the urge to recheck her skirts.

Their hostess stepped forward with a warm smile. "Hello. I understand you wish to speak with my husband."

"Yes, ma'am. I'm Richard Stevens." He bowed and then motioned Alice forward. "And may I present my sister, Miss Alice Stevens?"

Alice bobbed a curtsy.

Mrs. Davidson dipped her chin. "Pleased to meet you."

"We're terribly sorry to arrive unannounced like this." Alice suppressed the urge to tug at her glove. "I hope it isn't too inconvenient, our waiting here for your husband."

"It's no inconvenience at all." She motioned to the settee. "Please do be seated. I'm sorry to have kept you waiting. May I offer you some refreshments?"

They sat where indicated.

Richard spoke at the same moment as Alice.

"No, thank you—"

"Yes, if it's not too much trouble." No doubt the tea in such a fine home would banish all memory of the retched hot water they'd called 'tea' aboard the ship.

"No trouble at all." Mrs. Davidson pulled a cord before

lowering herself to one of the matching chairs. A moment later, a flushed maid appeared in the open doorway. Mrs. Davidson instructed her to bring tea and a tray, then regarded Alice and Richard. "Now, tell me. What brings you to San Francisco? You are newly arrived, are you not?"

Alice nodded. "We arrived this afternoon."

"And have you found a place to stay?"

"Well—"

The front door opened.

A tall man shuffled inside. His shoulders were hunched, his brown hair mussed. His glasses were perched cockeyed on his nose, and he appeared to have encountered the same careless wagon that marred Alice's dress earlier.

The servant appeared and took the man's outer coat. "You have guests, sir."

Alice's nose wrinkled. *This* was Mr. Davidson?

The bedraggled man turned toward them. "Oh!" He straightened and strode into the parlor. "Have you come about my niece? Do you know where she is?"

Alice blinked and exchanged a confused glance with Richard as they all rose and stepped forward to greet their host.

"Henry, this is Mr. Richard Stevens and his sister, Miss Alice Stevens." She glanced down at the muddy boot prints her husband had tracked across the floor, then back to her weary husband. "They've been waiting to speak with you, but I'm certain they won't mind waiting a bit longer while you freshen up. You have had a long and trying day."

"Nonsense. I'm perfectly well." His eager gaze hopped from Richard to Alice and back again. "What do you know of my niece's whereabouts?"

"Nothing, I'm afraid." Richard shrugged. "We've come about a different matter."

Alice cringed as Mr. Davidson plopped onto the settee in the spot Richard had vacated. She gathered her skirt away from his mud-splattered trousers. Would the maid be able to remove the mud being pressed into the velvet?

Mr. Davidson raked his hands through his hair. "It's hopeless. I've looked everywhere. I've even searched the brothels and cribs in case she'd been kidnapped"—Mrs. Davidson gasped and sank onto her chair as he continued, tears welling his bloodshot eyes—"but there's no trace of her. It's like she's vanished into thin air."

Alice sat on a chair opposite the settee. How should she respond to such an uncouth display of emotion?

Richard took Alice's former position on the settee.

Mrs. Davidson straightened. "My dear, if you would but listen to me, there would be no need to overextend yourself like this."

"I *have* listened to you, and I refuse to believe Eliza ran off with some delivery boy. Especially without leaving me word. She wouldn't do that."

Mrs. Davidson's spine straightened and her hard gaze darted to Richard and then Alice. Her silent message was clear—this conversation was to remain private.

Mrs. Davidson regarded her husband. "I know how much you hoped for your niece's future, Henry. Heaven knows I did my best for her while she was here, but some people simply cannot be made fit for society. We must learn to accept this and move on." She shifted toward Richard. "Now, Mr. Stevens, what was it you wished to speak with my husband about?"

Alice shifted in her seat. It seemed their arrival could not have come at a more inopportune time for the Davidsons. How humiliating to have a relation with such low morals.

"My sister and I are looking for a man we understand to be in your employ. Mr. Daniel Clarke."

Mr. Davidson removed his spectacles and cleaned them with the hem of his shirt, then replaced them. "What business have you with Mr. Clarke?"

"My sister is his fiancée."

It seemed impossible, but Mr. Davidson's expression grew even more distressed with this revelation.

"But he's gone."

Alice leaned forward. "That's what the man at his address said. We were hoping, as his employer, you might know where he's moved to."

"No. I mean, he's gone. Sailed back to The States. He told us he was returning to you."

Cold washed over her. "But he can't have gone. He never said..." *Or had he?* The bundle of unopened letters in her carpetbag convicted her.

She'd assumed his recent missives were filled with the same message they held the last three years. *"I miss you. I love you. As soon as this new project is complete, I'll pack my bags and return to you."* Yet he never did, and after the events of last summer, she was unable to bring herself to read his loving words and empty promises. Particularly as they must now be accompanied by questions regarding her lengthy silence.

Even after she boarded the ship to California with Richard, there seemed no point in opening the letters. She would see Daniel soon enough. He could tell her whatever she needed to know in person.

Her gaze traveled to their bags in the foyer. Had Daniel written of his plans to return in one of those letters? Surely not. He would have written to his mother as well and she would have wanted to discuss wedding plans with Alice. No. Mrs. Clarke hadn't mentioned a thing, so he must not have written.

Mrs. Davidson leaned forward. "I'm sorry, but my husband is correct. Mr. Clarke departed on the *Virginia* more than two weeks ago."

Richard frowned at Mrs. Davidson. "But I read that the *Virginia* wrecked off the coast of San Diego."

Alice's vision blurred. *No.*

Mr. Davidson waved a hand. "It did, but few lives were lost, and Mr. Clarke's name was not listed among them."

She sucked in air. *Daniel's alive.*

Richard's expression smoothed. "Then he continued on to Massachusetts with those who survived?"

"I presume." Mr. Davidson shrugged. "We've not received word either way."

The maid returned with the requested refreshments, set them on a small table near their hostess, and left again.

Mrs. Davidson poured four cups of tea. "What a terribly long way to come, only to have to turn back again." She tried to give the first cup to her husband, but he waved it away and snagged a slice of bread from the tray. So she handed the cup to Richard and then offered one to Alice.

"But we can't go back." Alice accepted the offered cup. She'd counted her money while they were at the store. She might have enough funds to secure a single-night's accommodation—if the rates were the same as what Daniel had written they were. And Richard needed every cent he'd saved to sustain him until he found employment with one of the mining companies farther inland. Even if she could somehow come up with the exorbitant sum the shipping companies required for passage to the east, who would be her chaperone?

Mr. and Mrs. Davidson exchanged a glance.

Their hostess set her cup in its saucer on the table and folded her hands in her lap. "I don't mean to be indelicate, but is it the trial of the journey or the expense of it that makes you speak so?"

Richard lowered his cup. "It's true we lack the funds to purchase a return ticket, but it wouldn't matter if we did. I mean to remain in California." He cast a grimace toward Alice. "Alice would have no escort."

"I see." Mrs. Davidson appeared thoughtful as she appraised Alice's appearance once more.

Mr. Davidson stood and ran a hand down his face. "I'm sorry, but might we continue this conversation at a later time? I do need to eat something more than bread before I resume my search."

Mrs. Davidson reared back. "You're going back out? At this hour?"

"I told you. I'll not rest until I know what's become of her." He bowed to Alice and Richard. "If you'll excuse me." He strode from the room.

Mrs. Davidson's mouth hung open a moment as she stared after her husband. Then she closed it and turned their direction. "Please forgive him. As you can see, he is not himself."

"Of course."

Mrs. Davidson returned to studying Alice in a way that made her sit straight and smooth her skirts. Their hostess glanced at Richard and then out the window to where night had engulfed the city. "Am I correct in assuming you have not secured accommodations for the evening?"

Richard blew out a breath. "I'm afraid we've been too busy searching for Mr. Clarke."

"Well, we can't have a lady like your sister wandering the streets at this hour." She stood, causing Richard and Alice to rise as well. "You're both welcome to stay for the evening, and if the situation proves mutually agreeable, we may discuss the possibility of an extended stay to-morrow. How does that sound?"

~

*E*liza burst into the cabin and slammed the door behind her, waking poor Ysabel.

"Sorry." Eliza dropped the basket to the floor and flung herself face down on the pallet, sobbing into the blankets.

Instead of lecturing her on decorum as Cecilia would have,

Ysabel crossed the cabin and sat beside Eliza. She stroked Eliza's hair.

Several minutes later, Eliza's breathing was still ragged, but the raw agony of Daniel's rejection was fading to a dull ache. She'd expected it, deserved it even. What kind of woman falls in love with another woman's fiancée? There was no denying the attraction between them, but Daniel was far too good to let his feelings develop beyond that.

If only she had been as strong.

Her stuffy nose made it difficult to continue breathing with her face pressed into the blankets. She pushed herself to a sitting position and her stepmother's hand fell away. Eliza kept her chin down. She couldn't face Ysabel's pity.

After a moment, the woman patted Eliza's back and returned to her own bed. Seconds later, Ysabel's soft breathing resumed. She'd fallen asleep again.

Eliza lay back on her pallet and stared at the ceiling.

What was she to do?

~

A knock on the cabin door roused her. When had she fallen asleep? No light pierced the cracks in the walls and the temperature had lowered several degrees while she'd been sleeping.

Ysabel's bed was empty. When had she left? Was it supper-time? Maria must have come to fetch her for the meal.

Sliding to her feet, Eliza hurried to the door. Her hand on the latch, she paused. Why would Maria knock and not enter? It had to be one of the men. Had Andrew come to fetch her? What if they'd sent Daniel? The stirrings of hunger vanished.

She leaned toward the closed door. "Who's there?"

"It's Daniel. May I speak with you?"

She drew back. What was there left to say? His pity for her

had been clear enough this afternoon. She didn't need another apology. It wasn't his fault she let her emotions get away from her.

She should tell him to leave. The sooner he returned to Alice, the sooner she could forget him. No, that wasn't right. She could never forget Daniel. But perhaps if he left, this ache in her chest might begin to dull. Eventually.

His voice came through the door again. "I wanted you to know that I'm leaving tomorrow."

"What?" She pressed her palm against the door. "Where are you going?"

"Back to San Diego. Back to Boston."

What? Her knees weakened. She opened her mouth but couldn't speak.

"I know I promised to see you safely reunited with your Pa, but I think you're safe here with Andrew and Maria and Ysabel. I'm going to speak with Andrew. I'm certain he'll agree to look out for you until your Pa returns."

~

*D*aniel leaned his forehead against the door. *Say something, Eliza. Anything. Argue with me if you want to. Yes, please argue with me. Convince me to stay. And not because you need my assistance, but because you want me.*

He straightened. What was he thinking?

This was exactly why he needed to go. He needed to leave before he did something to dishonor himself. God expected a man to keep his word. He'd promised Alice his heart, but if he remained with this incredible woman any longer, he'd be in serious danger of breaking that promise.

He stepped away, but Eliza's soft voice stopped him.

"What time will you leave?"

He faced the closed door, imagining her on the other side.

Were there tears in her eyes as there had been this afternoon? He wanted to punch himself for hurting her. "As soon as there's light enough to see the trail."

She didn't respond.

When another minute passed in silence, he whispered, "God bless you, Eliza." Then he trudged to the Coopers' lean-to for the last time.

CHAPTER 34

The familiar *thwack* of an axe biting into a distant log lured Eliza outside. The sun was kissing the tops of the trees. Another thwack cut the silence. It was coming from the Coopers' yard. She peered toward the rise separating the two cabins. Daniel had been adding to the couple's woodpile every morning. Were those his blows striking wood? Had he changed his mind?

She hurried back inside and spent a few extra minutes twisting the sides of her hair so that they swooped over her ears and tucked into a twisted bun, low on her neck. After a quick check in her small hand-mirror, she left Ysabel still sleeping in her bed and hurried toward the Coopers' Cabin.

She crested the rise and wove through the trees.

Andrew stood at the back of the clearing, chopping a tree.

Her steps slowed.

Daniel was nowhere in sight.

She stopped. Then she forced herself to take another step and another until she reached the far side of the cabin and could see the rope enclosure for the horses. The crackling of a tree crashing to the ground destroyed the quiet of the morning.

A single horse remained.

~

*A*lice let the book fall from her hands to the carpet in the upstairs drawing room. She'd always despised reading, but there was little else to do while their hosts were out and Richard was off in search of long-term accommodations.

Below, the front door squeaked opened and thudded closed. Had Richard returned? She retrieved the book and tossed it onto the table before scurrying from the room.

Had he found them accommodations? Her steps slowed. The Davidsons' home was lovely, and she'd slept quite well last night. Waking to a maid preparing a fire to warm her room before she had to emerge from the cozy bed was a luxury she had missed. And they hadn't even needed to ask. Mrs. Davidson had generously invited them to stay.

Still, they couldn't impose on the Davidsons forever. Their invitation to stay had officially been for a single night. But Mrs. Davidson *had* promised to discuss extending their stay at some point today. Alice wrinkled her nose as she descended the stairs. That had been several hours ago and their hostess had yet to raise the issue. Should Alice bring it up herself? No. That would be indelicate.

She reached the bottom stair and was about to head toward the foyer when tense voices caught her attention. She crept toward the back of the house instead.

A door hung ajar near the end of the hall. As Alice neared it, the voices became discernible.

"It ain't right." The voice sounded like that of the servant who showed them inside the evening before. "That's his letter, not yours."

"Of course it's right. I'm looking out for Henry's best interests. And I'll thank you to keep your nose out of affairs that are of no concern to you."

Alice almost didn't recognize Mrs. Davidson's voice. Its warmth had been replaced by an icy tone that sent shivers down Alice's spine. She shouldn't be listening to this. She pivoted to creep away, but the servant's next words stopped her in her tracks.

"I care about Mr. Henry, and he done worn himself ragged looking for that girl."

"He'll give up soon enough, and I suggest you do the same before you find yourself without employment."

"You go on and fire me, then. I kept quiet the last two times, but I can't do it no more. Mr. Henry's got a right to know."

She couldn't help the gasp that escaped her lips. Every muscle in her body tensed. What was happening in the room beyond the open door? Had they heard her? Were they even now coming out to see who was foolish enough to eavesdrop on their conversation? Was that a floorboard creaking?

Mrs. Davidson's quiet words did nothing to ease Alice's tension. "Now, you listen to me, Frank. I know exactly where Mr. Davidson keeps your freedom papers, and I've got a case full of matches. Do I make myself clear?"

"Yes, ma'am." Frank's voice had lost its bluster.

"Good. You're dismissed."

Before Alice could move, the door flew open and Frank came storming out of what appeared to be a study. His gaze flickered to her, then past her, as he stomped right on by and out the front door. The bang of the door slamming shut rattled the hall mirror.

Wow. Patting her curls, Alice pivoted and froze.

Mrs. Davidson stood in the doorway examining her through narrowed eyes. "Alice. Do come in, won't you?"

~

283

*T*he thwack of Andrew's lone axe reverberated as blows to Eliza's heart. Daniel was gone, and he hadn't said good-bye. She ran from the yard into the wild chaparral, where she wandered until she could no longer hear Andrew's strikes.

Plopping onto a small boulder, she wrenched the pins from her hair, undoing the beautiful twists she'd created.

She swiped the tears from her cheeks. *Stop crying! You're being foolish. He told you he was leaving. Why would he change his mind?* Still, the tears did not stop. Pressing her face into her palms, she gave in to the ache inside and sobbed.

When her tears finally subsided, she straightened. Tangled strands clung to the dampness of her cheeks and she brushed them back. Her fingers threaded through her long hair. The familiar motion soothed her. She continued to finger-comb her hair as her mind tortured her with memories of Daniel, from that humiliating supper in her uncle's home, to the moment he'd almost kissed her, to the low rumble of his voice through the door, telling her he was leaving.

From habit, she divided her hair into sections and plaited it into various styles. She retrieved her hair pins from the ground and blew them clean. Then she pressed them into her hair. Eventually, her arms grew tired and she left her hair styled in a large braided bun as she stood and plodded back to the cabins.

With no mirror, she had no way of judging the results of her efforts—and little care—but when she entered Pa's cabin a few minutes later, Ysabel cooed over her. She pointed back and forth from Eliza's hair to her own until Eliza understood. Ysabel wanted Eliza to fix her hair the same way. Eliza forced a smile and nodded.

Several minutes later, she finished braiding the center section of hair at the back of Ysabel's head. She wound it into a low bun that she pinned in place. Moving to the smaller section of hair on the right, she began braiding again. Ysabel's hair was thicker and more slippery than Eliza's, which made braiding it more difficult, but Eliza didn't mind. She had a task to focus on, and that kept her mind from wandering to other things. As she worked, the scrape and rumble of a shovel moving earth came through the walls of Ysabel's cabin.

She asked Ysabel about the sound.

"Andrew make fence. Horses stay. He..." She moved her hand in a plucking motion, then mimicked tossing something away. "Make room."

"I see." Eliza wrapped the smaller braid around the bun. She tucked the ends in with her extra hair pins. Taking the left section of hair into her hands, she split it into three parts and began braiding them together. When she reached the end of the strands, she wrapped the left braid around the bun and pinned it to hide the end.

Andrew's shoveling stopped. "You're back!" His voice was muffled by distance and walls, but seemed happy.

She caught her breath as Ysabel tilted her ear toward the voices. Daniel had returned? Why? Why would he come back unless...

She jumped up, charged toward the door, and flung it open. Her feet fluttered across the ground as she crested the rise and wove through the trees and shrubs until the Coopers' cabin came into sight.

She skidded to a halt.

Andrew stood at the opposite end of the yard giving someone a hardy hug and slap on the back, but it wasn't Daniel. This man was too tall, too broad.

"Pa?" Her voice came out as a whisper. Was it truly him?

Andrew stepped back, giving her a clear view.

She sucked in a breath. *It is him.* He was weary and dirty, but grinning at the man before him.

Andrew chuckled. "Have I got a surprise for you!"

"Do tell!" Pa rotated as if he'd sensed her gaze on him. His jaw fell. "Eliza?"

"You're alive!" Her feet ate up the distance separating her from him. "You're safe!" She crashed into his open arms and his embrace squeezed the air from her. Tears spilled down her face.

He pressed a kiss to the top of her head. His breath stirred her hair. "Is it really you, Angel?" He held her out, scanning her head to toe. "Are you all right? What're you doing here?"

She laughed. "Am I all right? I've been worried sick about you!" She examined him. His eyes were clear, not red-rimmed or glassy with illness. His skin bore a healthy glow, no sheen of fever, nor pallor of starvation. His posture was strong, not slack, and his muscles had filled out almost to the size they'd been back in Oregon. He appeared healthy and well fed. "Why haven't you written me?"

"Well, I—" His gaze flashed to something behind her. "Whoa! What're you doing out of bed?" He released Eliza and rushed to Ysabel, who had followed Eliza to the Coopers' yard.

Ysabel said something in her native language and Pa responded in kind. His words were slower and more wooden, but it was clear he was speaking Ysabel's language and she understood him. When had Pa learned to speak another language?

Eliza stilled. The love in Pa's eyes as he gazed at his wife... It was the way he'd looked at her mother.

Pa put his arm around Ysabel and they crossed the clearing to stand before her.

He cocked his head, his forehead puckered. "Then, you've met my new wife?"

Eliza beamed. "She's been kind enough to share her cabin with me while you've been away."

Maria stepped out of the cabin. "Welcome back, Señior Jim." She scanned the clearing.

Oh, right. Where were Ysabel's brothers?

Andrew gestured toward the open door. "Let's go inside."

Chili spices filled the air inside the cabin. A pan of venison simmered over the fire, an enormous metal dish warming beside it. Maria must be preparing to cook that thin corn bread she called *tortillas*.

Pa helped Ysabel into a seat, then wrapped his arms around Eliza before she could sit.

When he pulled back, tears shimmered in his eyes. "It's so good to see you."

She tugged him in for another squeeze. "I've missed you, too." She wiped the tears from her cheeks.

"Look at you!" He laughed as they all took a seat at the table, except for Maria who served them coffee from the pot she kept warming at the back of the fire. "So grown up and still with dirt beneath your nails."

She inspected her fingers. He was right. She tucked her hands beneath her legs.

Andrew's eyes sparkled with mischief, though his expression was sober. "Are you certain this young woman is your daughter, Jim?"

Pa glared, but his lips twitched. "Of course. You think I don't know my own child?"

"Sure. Sure. I just don't see how any child of yours could turn out to be so beautiful."

Pa barked a laugh. "I told you she took after her mama."

"Thank you, Andrew." Eliza's face warmed.

Pa sobered. "Where's Henry?"

She swallowed. Where was Daniel? He should be here to help explain. She pictured him riding back the way they'd come. *No, he's gone a different way. Andrew told him about a quicker route back to San Diego.* The easier terrain and well-traveled trail meant he'd be there in under three days instead of the almost six it took them to reach the cabins.

"Eliza?"

She refocused on Pa. "Uncle Henry is in San Francisco."

Pa's fists landed on his hips. "Don't tell me you come all the way from San Francisco by yourself."

She lifted her chin. "You know I'm perfectly capable—"

"That's not the point and you know it." Pa scowled at her. "I thought you had better sense than to do something as foolish as coming here on your own."

Andrew cleared his throat. "She wasn't entirely alone, Jim."

"What do you mean, she wasn't alone?" Before Andrew could answer, Pa whirled on her. "What's he mean you wasn't alone? If you're uncle isn't with you, who is?" He glanced around as if expecting another person to magically appear in the tiny cabin.

She squeezed her hands in her lap as her throat constricted. She wasn't ready to speak about Daniel.

Maria's rhythmic slapping on the corn dough filled the awkward silence.

Andrew opened his mouth to speak, but Eliza cast Ysabel a beseeching glance.

Ysabel laid a hand on Pa's arm. "Where my brothers?"

Pa took his wife's hands in his. "I'm sorry." His words switched to her native language for several minutes before she nodded, and he faced Andrew. "I couldn't find them. When I finally found the wastrels who'd captured them, they told me her brothers got loose the night before."

Pa blew out a breath. "Not hard to figure. I came on them kidnappers just past dawn and they was *still* pickled. Seems like her brothers hightailed it out of the area. Asked the few folks I felt were trustworthy. But if anyone knew the brothers' where-abouts, they wasn't saying. I kept looking for a couple days more, but there weren't any sign of them, and I was worried about Ysabel. So I came home."

Ysabel closed her eyes and her lips trembled for a moment. When she opened her eyes a moment later, they shimmered with tears that overflowed and traced shiny paths down her tan cheeks. She cupped Pa's chin. "Thank you."

Sincere gratitude and love shown in Ysabel's gaze. She truly cared for Pa.

He said something in Ysabel's language and Ysabel responded.

"How do you know what she's saying, Pa?"

"I didn't at first." He glanced at Andrew. "How much have you told her?"

"Only about Ysabel being arrested with her brothers for no good reason and how you bought her freedom but couldn't afford to free her brothers."

"That's right. I'd been heading up to see you when I saw them. Took a while before we understood each other enough for me to know those men who'd been with her were her brothers. Not to mention her only living relatives. I tried to find them soon as I knew, but they'd disappeared. Vanished like dust in the stream. Sickness took the rest of her family years ago."

Ysabel patted Pa's cheek. "You told me go."

He wrapped an arm around his wife and squeezed her shoulders. "But you, stubborn woman, wouldn't go." His grin faded and he glanced at Eliza. "I didn't realize at the time she had nowhere to go."

"So you got married?" Ysabel was so tiny and delicate, her bump seemed to pull her around the more than she carried it. Yet there must be a hidden strength in her, to have endured the life she'd lived. If Eliza could speak Ysabel's language, she'd ask her how she endured losing so many loved ones.

"First, I took her 'round some of the rancherias I knew of, but she didn't want to stay at any of them. So we headed up here to see Andrew and Maria. I thought maybe the two women might hit it off and she'd want to stay with them." He smoothed his hand over Ysabel's cheek, wiping away her tears. "By then, though, my heart was hooked. So I stayed on—"

Andrew pointed at Pa. "You put on that you were just visiting me, but I wasn't fooled."

"That's the truth of it, I admit." Pa's face was flushed as he turned back to Eliza. "After a bit, I worked up my nerve and she was kind enough to accept my proposal. Andrew, here, married us, and God has blessed us." Pa placed a gentle hand on Ysabel's belly. "You know there hasn't been anyone since your mama. I know this may be hard for you, but I love Ysabel. I hope…"

Eliza raised a hand to silence him. "Pa"—her voice caught —"Ysabel is lovely. I'm so happy for you."

Pa leaned back in his chair. "Thank you."

Eliza cleared her throat. "But I still don't understand. Why didn't you write? I was worried sick."

"Didn't you get my letter? How'd you know where to find me?"

"What letter? The last letter I received said you were going to look into work on that dike."

"But I wrote you that I'd be staying in the mountains a while. Told you not to worry if you didn't hear from me." Pa glared at Andrew. "You said you mailed it."

Andrew held his palms up. "I did."

"I knew your letters must have gotten lost." She gritted her teeth. She had a few choice words for that postmaster if she ever saw him again.

"I'm sorry, Angel. I should have written you again. But Ysabel wasn't keeping a thing down and she kept getting skinnier. Her skin was so pale I thought…" His words trailed off and he swallowed hard. "Been all I could do to keep her on this earth." He squeezed Ysabel's hand. "Andrew offered to post another letter for me, but truth be told, I couldn't hold my mind to the task long enough to put words to paper. The one time I tried, didn't know what to say. I wasn't sure what you'd think of my remarrying, 'specially with her being Ipai and all. I wanted to word it just right, so you'd understand how special she is, and that I wasn't replacing your ma. But the words wouldn't come. So I guess I gave up. I meant to try again, but with Ysabel so sick, months passed in a blink. I'm sorry I worried you."

His eyes met hers in shared understanding.

Andrew swiveled to say something in Spanish to Maria, who was busy cooking tortillas on the hot plate over the fire. She answered him as she pulled the last tortilla from the plate and added it to a cloth-lined basket, folding the corners of the cloth over the top to keep them warm.

Andrew turned back to them. "Maria says dinner is nearly ready."

Maria pulled the pan of sizzling meat from the fire.

Eliza stood. "Can I help?"

Maria used her free hand to wave away Eliza's offer. "Gracias, no."

A continuous scraping noise caught her attention. It was coming through the cabin walls and growing louder. Snapping and rustling joined the ruckus. *What in the world?*

Andrew stood. "That must be Daniel."

CHAPTER 35

*a*lice tried to swallow as she stepped into the study, but her throat was dry.

Mrs. Davidson motioned to the small chair facing the desk. "Please, have a seat."

Alice forced herself to lower to the edge of the cushion instead of bolting for her chamber, where she could pretend none of this had ever happened.

Mrs. Davidson took the large, leather chair behind her husband's desk. "I apologize for keeping you waiting, but I had several matters to attend to this morning that could not be put off."

Alice folded her hands in her lap. "Of course. I understand. You've been very gracious to allow me the use of your drawing room while I await my brother's return." Smoothing her skirts, she relaxed her posture a touch. She mustn't appear nervous. She needed to remain in the woman's good graces. Where would she go if Mrs. Davidson put her out before Richard returned? "I'm sure a lady in your position has a good many important tasks that require her personal attention. If there's any way that I can be of assistance, please do let me know."

Mrs. Davidson's shoulders relaxed. "Actually, Miss Stevens, I believe *I* may be able to help *you*."

Alice's breath caught.

"I've just had word from a dear friend that she is still in need of a tutor for her young daughters. Their last tutor left over a week ago and they've had a dreadful time finding a suitable replacement." She paused and tipped her head forward. "You have had educational training?"

"Yes, ma'am." She nodded so fast her curls flapped against her cheeks. A tutor was a far cry from the position of esteemed craftsman's wife in San Francisco's society, but what did it matter if she was going home? No one back east need know the details of her time here. "My family employed an excellent governess, who instructed us in reading and mathematics, as well as the arts, music, and the social graces."

"Excellent. I thought as much after our conversation at supper last night, which is why I sent a note to my friend this morning inquiring as to whether the position had been filled. I didn't mention anything to you earlier, as I didn't want to get your hopes up if the position had, indeed, been filled."

Were there people who became excited about such menial positions? "That was very considerate of you."

"The position comes with room and board along with a salary that should earn you sufficient means to return to your beau in three months time, should you still wish to go."

Now *that* was something to get excited about! Alice suppressed a squeal. She'd never dreamed it was possible to earn so much in so short a time. "That sounds wonderful."

Mrs. Davidson lifted a quill from the desk top. "Shall I inform her of your desire for an interview?"

~

*D*aniel had let the horse set its own pace down the hill, but as he came in sight of the Coopers' cabin, he pulled on the reins. Eliza was likely inside helping Maria prepare their dinner. Had Andrew shared Daniel's change in plans? How had she reacted?

When he'd spoken with Andrew the night before, the man was adamant that Daniel remain until Jim returned. Andrew claimed Jim would be livid if he allowed Daniel to leave without explaining his actions regarding Eliza. Daniel protested that nothing untoward occurred and therefore nothing needed explaining, but Andrew refused to budge. So, Daniel agreed to remain an additional two days, but no more.

He couldn't wait indefinitely. It wouldn't be fair to either Alice or Eliza. With that in mind, he'd requested to be the one to head uphill this morning and fell some trees for the corral Andrew wanted to build. It might have made more sense for Andrew to go, as the one more familiar with the area, but the tree line was only a few miles away and Andrew hadn't questioned Daniel's request. Daniel suspected the man understood more than he was letting on.

Daniel managed to down three large trees and remove their branches in the space of the morning. The branches he bundled and tied to the horse's saddle easily enough. However, he was unused to hauling his own timber, so it took some trial and error to get the trunks attached in a way that didn't interfere with the horse's gait. He'd had to stop whenever a trunk snagged on a bush or small rock. Thankfully, that didn't occur too often. The logs were heavy enough, and the slope gentle enough, that there was no risk of them picking up speed and outrunning the horse.

He was almost to the Coopers' clearing when Andrew stepped out to greet him.

"Any trouble finding the spot I told you about?"

Daniel shook his head. "Your directions were clear enough."

The door creaked open a second time. Was Eliza behind him, or had Maria come out after Andrew? Daniel resisted the urge to glance back as he led the horse to the edge of the space where Andrew had decided to build the new corral. If Daniel went inside for lunch, he'd see Eliza for sure. "I'll head back up as soon as I refill my canteen. Figured I'd grab a little of that dried beef you've got in the lean-to and eat it on my way up, if you don't mind."

Andrew helped him relieve the horse of its burden. "I think it'd be best if you joined us inside."

Daniel gritted his teeth as he added the bundle of branches to their woodpile. Didn't Andrew understand his need to avoid Eliza? "I appreciate the invitation, but I'd rather..." Eliza *had* come outside. She stood near the door, a large man at her side.

The older man's feet were spread wide, his arms crossed. He appraised Daniel with eyes the same shade of brown as Eliza's.

Jim.

Daniel ran a hand through his sweaty hair, then wiped it against his thigh. *Lord, please let him understand our choices.*

∽

*E*liza blinked. *Daniel's here.* Why didn't he leave?

Andrew led Daniel across the yard to the cabin. "Mr. Clarke, may I present the man you've been anxiously waiting to meet? This is Eliza's Pa, Jim Brooks."

"It's a pleasure to meet you at last, Mr. Brooks." Daniel offered his hand to Pa.

Pa slowly accepted, his gaze hopping from Daniel to Andrew to Eliza, then back to Daniel. "And what brings you way out here, young man?"

Daniel shifted his feet and squared his shoulders. "I escorted your daughter, sir."

"Escorted her where?" Pa's brows pinched, then lifted. "Here? You brought her *here*? *Alone*?" He spun toward Eliza. "You forget to tell me something, Angel? Like 'bout you getting married?"

"No, Pa. He's engaged to someone else."

Pa's face grew red as he leaned to within inches of Daniel's face. "You mean to say you been frolicking about the mountains, alone with my daughter for days, not married, and haven't any intention of marrying her?"

Ysabel slipped outside to stand beside Pa. She rubbed her belly, a frown marring her face as she took in the scene.

Pa's hands clenched into fists.

"Pa, wait." Oh, this was ridiculous! Eliza gripped Pa's shoulder, but he shook her off.

"Sir…" Daniel's face grew pale as he took a step back.

Andrew stepped between the two men. "Jim, hold on. Give them a chance to explain."

"What's to explain? He's ruined my daughter! Either he's going to marry her or I'm—"

"Pa!" Eliza thrust herself in front of Andrew to face Pa. Her hands clamped on her hips. "Enough! I am not ruined and Daniel has done nothing but protect me since—"

"*Daniel*, is it?" Pa raised his fists and sidestepped to go around her, but Andrew held him back.

"Jim, calm down now. I know it looks bad, and if it is, I promise I'll help you see it set right, but first let's let them talk. I can attest that he's been a true gentleman since they arrived here."

Pa spit in the dirt. "As if he'd dare act different with others watching. That don't account for how he's acted when no one was looking."

"*Pa!*" Did he think she had no morals?

Andrew caught Pa's eye and lowered his voice. "Remember what we've been talking about—'in your anger do not sin.'"

Pa glowered at Andrew for a tense moment. Then he drew a deep breath, held it, and slowly released it as he relaxed his fists. He stared daggers at Daniel over Andrew's shoulder. "So talk."

Ysabel placed a hand on Pa's arm. "Eat first?" She placed her other hand on her belly and looked at her husband with doe eyes.

Pa melted. "Of course, dear." He took his wife's hand and led her into the Coopers' cabin.

Following Pa, Eliza preceded Daniel and Andrew into the cabin.

Pa helped his wife take a seat at the table. Then he disappeared outside for a moment and returned with two chairs and two plates. Where had those come from? He placed the chairs at the end of the small table and set the plates before them as Maria put the basket of tortillas and a heaping plate of meat in the center of the table.

Daniel held Eliza's usual seat, but Pa pulled out the chair beside Ysabel and insisted Eliza sit there instead. She hesitated, then gave Daniel an apologetic shrug before moving to sit where Pa wanted her. After pushing her in, Pa walked around the table to sit beside Daniel, across from his wife. Andrew and Maria occupied the seats Pa had placed at the end.

Andrew said grace. Then they each took a tortilla, onto which Maria scooped a small pile of meat.

They ate in silence for a few minutes before Ysabel spoke again. She waved a hand between Pa and Eliza. "He miss you very much, I think."

Eliza peeked at Pa, who was glaring at Daniel as he chewed. She smiled at Ysabel. "I've missed him as well."

"Must be hard. Apart so long."

"Yes." She considered Pa's filled-out face. He was truly healthy. "I was worried he'd forget to eat again."

Andrew guffawed. "That doesn't seem likely. I've never known a man who can eat like your father."

"You didn't know him in the gold fields. I couldn't get him out of the water. If I hadn't brought him his meals, he'd have keeled over with that pan still in his hands."

"Not sure how dumping our last beans in the river was supposed to keep me from keeling over." The mischievous glint in Pa's eyes, along with his chuckle, removed any sting from the memory.

"It's not as if I dumped them on purpose." She crossed her arms in mock offense. "It was that Morgan Channing's fault. He was always pulling some prank. I don't think his father ever got a lick of work out of him."

Pa laughed. "Ain't that the truth."

Although the rest of the meal passed in lighthearted conversation filled with anecdotes from Eliza's childhood and their escapades in the mining camps, there was an underlying tension. Soon, everyone's plate had been emptied, and Eliza breathed a sigh of thanks when Maria handed her a warm mug of coffee. The hot liquid slid down her throat to her belly, banishing the chill of the cold mountain air. *Lord, please help Pa understand our choices.*

Pa tipped back his chair, his mug cradled between his hands. He took a long sip then focused on Daniel. "So."

It was the cue they'd been waiting for. Daniel began by explaining how he'd officially been introduced to Eliza at the Davidsons' home. Then Eliza pointed out how Daniel had warned her and protected her on the ship when nothing had gone as planned.

Eliza fidgeted as Daniel described the shipwreck and her near drowning.

Pa took her hand. "Thank the Lord you were saved."

By unspoken agreement, she and Daniel skipped over the steward's frightening behavior.

Daniel explained searching for Pa in San Diego and how he came to the decision to accompany Eliza into the mountains.

"You've raised a very independent-minded daughter and she was determined to come to you with or without me."

Pa lifted a brow at Daniel. "And you decided with you was better."

"I decided that her safety was more important than her reputation, though I did what I could to protect that as well."

Daniel explained the precautions they had taken against being seen traveling alone together, and how they'd slept several feet apart each night. He left out the part where they'd nearly been killed in a flash flood, and Eliza didn't see the point in sharing that part of their journey, either.

Eliza held her breath through the long silence that followed the close of their story.

Pa sat in his chair, sipping his now-cold coffee, staring first at Daniel, and then at Eliza. Finally, he squinted at Daniel. "You say you have a fiancée waiting back east?"

"Yes, sir."

"What do you think she'll think of"—he waved his hand in Eliza's direction—"this?"

"I'm not sure."

Pa raised one eyebrow.

"Truthfully, I believe she'll be angry, but I'm hopeful she'll forgive me."

"She may not." Pa took another sip of his coffee. "What you've done is hard enough for me to accept and I know how things are here. I know my daughter. Back east, they're rarely as understanding."

"True, but—"

"But you chose to stay here and help my daughter."

"Yes, sir." Daniel met her gaze across the table.

Her heart leaped to her throat. What was that look in his eyes? Could it be? Was it...?

Daniel lowered his face to his hands. "I couldn't leave her."

No. It can't be love. He doesn't love me. He loves Alice. He'd intended to leave. Why hadn't he left? She stared at the top of his head. *Look at me. What are you thinking?*

He didn't move.

She squeezed her eyes shut. *Care. Concern. The love of a dear friend. That's all you saw, Eliza. He loves* Alice. *He is engaged to* Alice.

Why wouldn't her heart listen?

Pa rubbed his chin, drawing her attention. "I see."

He was silent for another long moment as he studied them. Then he settled all four legs of his chair on the floor and looked Daniel in the eye. "I appreciate your honorable intention to protect my daughter and I'm sorry about your fiancée, but the two of you have still got to marry." He smacked a hand on the table. "At once."

Daniel gaped at him. "But sir, I—"

Enough! Eliza slammed both hands onto the table. "How can you ask this? After everything we've just told you. After everything Daniel has already sacrificed to protect me, how can you demand that he sacrifice the rest of his life as well?"

Pa held out his hands. "Eliza—"

"No!" Eliza jumped to her feet. Pa didn't understand. Daniel's conscience wouldn't allow him to break his promise to Alice. No matter how it shattered Eliza, he must leave. Why was Pa making it so much worse by teasing her with the thought of keeping him? "No! We have done nothing wrong and I refuse to marry him." She whirled toward Daniel. "You need to go." She dug her fingernails into her palms. She would not cry. "Now. This very minute."

Pa stood, warning in his tone. "Eliza—"

"No!" She shook her head as she backed toward the door. "I won't do it. I won't take his life from him."

Daniel's face was pale. His mouth opened, but he made no sound.

"I'm sorry." Wretched tears blurred Daniel's image. "Thank

you for everything you've done. I hope—" Her voice cracked as her hand fumbled for the latch behind her. She had to get out of here before she lost control. "I hope you and Alice have a wonderful life together." Her fingers caught on the latch and she lifted it, then shoved through the door and dashed away from the cabin.

Pa called after her, but she lifted her skirts and increased her speed, heedless of the fabric catching and tearing on the scrub brush. If Pa chose to chase her, she'd never be able to outrun his long stride, but she wasn't going to make it easy for him.

∾

*D*arkness masked the mountains by the time Eliza returned to the cabins. She needed to go straight to Pa and Ysabel's cabin and sleep.

Her feet took her to the Coopers' yard.

Again, one horse stood in the rope corral. Had Daniel left as she'd told him to, or was he out searching for her?

Pa exited the Coopers' cabin.

She gestured to the lone horse. "Is he gone?"

"Yes, Angel. I'm so sorry. I thought—"

"I know, Pa." She held up her hand to stop his apology. He'd meant well. "I forgive you. You were trying to protect me. I know that, I just…I need some time to myself. Is it still all right for me to sleep in your cabin?"

"Of course. Ysabel and I will be along shortly."

∾

*A*lice leaned away from Richard's horrified stare. She lifted her chin. "What?"

"And you said nothing to Mr. Davidson when he returned for supper this evening? Just let him hurry through his meal and dash back out the door again in search of a niece whose where-abouts are clearly well-known by his own wife?" Richard's increasing volume made her flinch. "You heard her threaten a man's freedom because he'd dared to speak up for what was right, and you did *nothing* to stop her?"

Alice glanced toward the open door of the drawing room. "Hush!" she whispered. "Do you want her to overhear us?"

"Yes! I do." If anything, Alice's obstinate brother raised his voice still further.

"What would you have had me do?" Why couldn't he be sensible? But no. It fell to her, as it always did, to be the sensible one. "You said yourself the position you acquired as a day laborer will only pay you enough to afford us accommodations in a seedy section of the city."

"I said the neighborhood wasn't as nice as here. It isn't seedy. I promise you, you'll be perfectly—"

"Well, I don't want to just be safe and scraping by. If I'd wanted to live a simple life, I could have married Johnny when he asked me."

"You were already engaged to Daniel."

"Exactly. Daniel, whose skills as a craftsmen can provide me with a house I can be proud of and whose natural connections to the wealthiest of clientele might allow me, or at least our children, to move up in this world. I am not interested in settling, Richard."

She sniffed and brushed imaginary dust from her skirt. "I must return to The States as soon as possible and marry Daniel. Mrs. Davidson's offer to recommend me as a tutor for her friend's children is my only hope of earning my fare quickly." She shook her head. "Mr. and Mrs. Davidson's private affairs are simply not my concern, and I won't risk her good opinion of me by interfering where I am neither needed nor wanted."

Richard stood and glowered down at her. "I doubt Mr.

Davidson would see it that way. I should think he would be grateful for your interference."

"What's this?" Mr. Davidson stood in the drawing room door. "Did I hear my name? I should be grateful for what?"

Alice jumped and cold washed down her body. "Mr. Davidson." He appeared as disheveled as the first time she'd seen him.

Richard bowed. "Good evening, sir." He glared at Alice. "I believe my sister has something to tell you."

CHAPTER 36

The ache in Daniel's back after nearly three days in the saddle was nothing compared to the ache in his chest. He'd left without saying good-bye. *Why?*

Because there was nothing left to say.

He shook his head as he reined his horse to a stop in front of the Exchange.

No, that wasn't true. There were three very important words he yearned to speak to Eliza. *But I can't. I shouldn't even think them.* Yet the moment she'd dashed from the cabin, he knew them to be undeniably true.

I love her. With a depth and a breadth that seemed impossible.

He had glimpsed her physical beauty many times from afar, but the day he spotted her on the Davidsons' balcony, he saw her soul. It was a rare, vulnerable moment when she allowed her true heart to show through the tough exterior she'd developed to survive the upper social circles of San Francisco.

He hadn't recognized it right away, but he could see it now. As she grew to trust him, she opened her true self to him. The more he learned of her heart, the more he lost his own. Who could help falling in love with such a loyal, loving, courageous, and beautiful woman?

He slid from the horse and leaned his forehead against its side, his eyes closed. *Lord, how do I forget her?*

～

*A*lice glowered at Richard as Mr. Davidson stuck his head into the hall and bellowed for his wife.

Richard had left her no choice but to tell Mr. Davidson what she'd overheard. The longer she talked, the redder Mr. Davidson's face had become. Far from appearing grateful, the man seemed ready to spit nails. Why hadn't her brother listened to her and kept his voice down? There would be no chance of her attaining that position as a governess once Mrs. Davidson obeyed her husband's summons and learned of Alice's betrayal.

"Cecilia!" Mr. Davidson pivoted and paced the room. Hurried footsteps drew nearer.

Mrs. Davidson appeared in the doorway, short of breath. "Henry? What is it? My goodness, is everything all right?"

Mr. Davidson paced away from his wife.

She glanced at Alice and Richard. "Is this something we should discuss in private?"

Mr. Davidson spun toward her. "Yes. I do believe this is something we ought to have discussed in private, but it seems you have chosen not to discuss it at all."

Mrs. Davidson's face screwed up. "I don't understand what you're talking about."

"My *niece*, Cecilia." Mr. Davidson stepped toward his wife. "*Where* is my niece?"

All color drained from Mrs. Davidson's face. She stiffened. "H-how should I know?"

Alice sat frozen beside her brother as Mr. Davidson leaned forward, towering over his wife. A vein pulsed in his forehead.

"Will you stop lying and tell me where she is?" His eyes narrowed. "Or should I ask Frank?"

"F-Frank?"

Mr. Davidson stepped around his wife and leaned into the hallway once more. "Frank!"

Footsteps pounded up the hallway. A moment later, Mr. Davidson stepped back to allow Frank into the room.

Frank's gaze moved from face to face, his expression inscrutable.

Mr. Davidson took a deep breath. He opened his mouth to speak, but Mrs. Davidson stepped forward.

"My dear, why trouble Frank about this? Surely if he knew Eliza's whereabouts he'd have said so instead of driving you all over town to search for her." She sniffed. "After all, what kind of loyal servant would hide such information from the man who's been a more-than-generous employer?"

"Well, let's see." Mr. Davidson tapped his lips. "Perhaps one who's had his freedom threatened, hmm?"

Mrs. Davidson whirled on Alice. "Well! What lies have you been feeding my husband? Is this the thanks I get for taking you into my home and—"

"Enough!" Mr. Davidson's roar brought his wife's rant to a halt. He spread his hands and focused on the servant. "Tell me, Frank. I promise you, nothing bad will happen to you or your papers. You have become more than a servant to me. You have become my friend. I am unspeakably sorry that my wife ever made you question your place here or feel that you needed to worry for your freedom. Please. Tell me what you know of my niece."

Frank eyed Mrs. Davidson, who slumped on the settee, staring at the ceiling. He raised his chin and reached into his pocket. He withdrew a singed piece of paper, which he handed to Mr. Davidson. "Mrs. Davidson tried to burn it, sir, but I done saved it when she left the room. Somes the words are gone, but most seems all right."

"It was mailed from Monterey." Mr. Davidson unfolded the paper and squinted at the top. "This is dated two days after Eliza disappeared." He scanned the contents. "She departed with the *Virginia*...and is headed to San Diego. Of course." He regarded Frank. "You know I suspected as much, but none of the ticketing agents or seamen I spoke with could remember seeing her." He scanned the letter again. "Foolish girl! Why did you not wait?"

"Sir, there's another one come this morning, but Mrs. Davidson kept it."

Mr. Davidson faced his wife.

She heaved a sigh and twisted so that her back was to the room. Despite her attempt at discretion, it was clear she withdrew the missive from her bosom. She pivoted and held the letter out.

Mr. Davidson snatched it and checked the address. "She made it to San Diego." He opened the letter and read in silence for several moments. When he lifted his head again, he focused on Alice. "It would seem your Mr. Clarke has not returned to Boston after all."

Alice sucked in a breath. "What?"

"My niece writes that he has offered to assist her in her search for Jim, my brother." His gaze returned to the letter. "Someone has told them Jim is in the mountains, and she intends to search for him there."

Their hostess emitted a humorless laugh. "So she's gallivanting about the wilderness unchaperoned and with another woman's fiancé. I told you, Henry, the girl has absolutely no sense. She—"

"That's *enough!*" Mr. Davidson waved the letter in his wife's face. "I'll not hear one more word against Eliza."

Mrs. Davidson pressed her lips together and lifted her chin, but Alice detected a tinge of fear in the woman's eyes.

Alice regarded Richard. "Would Daniel truly do such a thing?"

Richard eyed the ceiling for a moment. "If he felt Mr. Davidson's niece would be in danger traveling on her own and could not dissuade her from going, I think he might."

"And Eliza is not easily dissuaded of anything, especially when it comes to her father." Mr. Davidson folded both letters and tucked them into his coat pocket. He shook his finger at Mrs. Davidson. "You've gone too far this time, Cecilia. I've put up with your behavior because I know how difficult your childhood was and how much gaining acceptance in society means to you."

Mrs. Davidson straightened and cast a glance at Alice and Richard, but said nothing as Mr. Davidson continued.

"Not being female myself, you know I leaned on your judgment of how best to prepare Eliza for womanhood. I excused your coldness toward her as a way of buffeting yourself from her resemblance to your painful younger years. Each time Eliza complained to me of your actions, I defended you. I *trusted* you." He cut his hand through the air. "No longer. You are forbidden to attend any more of the social gatherings you care so much about."

Alice cringed at the thud of a coffin closing on her chance of attaining that position as a tutor.

Mrs. Davidson opened her mouth, but Mr. Davidson held up his hand as he continued. "Whatever engagements you have on your calendar must be cancelled. For the next two years, you will devote yourself to assisting and socializing with those of our city who are in need. You will also find somewhere that you may be of use. Be it in a baker's shop, a dressmaker's store, or even one of my own storefronts, you must find a position and earn every cent that you wish to spend on dresses, shoes, hats, or the like, because beginning this minute, your allowance is no more."

Mrs. Davidson surged to her feet. "You can't be serious."

He tipped his chin down to peer at her over his spectacles. "I have never been more serious in my life. You clearly need reminding what it is to be in need. I only hope it isn't too late for you to learn some compassion and humility."

"But I'll be a laughingstock." Her hands clutched at her neck. "I won't ever be able to show my face again in good society." Her creamy complexion turned sickly gray. "My friends will disown me."

"Then they were never your friends to begin with."

Mrs. Davidson stepped forward and caught her husband's arm in her hands. "Henry, think of your own reputation. If I go out and find a"—she shuddered—"position. The men you do business with are sure to hear of it. Why, they'll believe your businesses must be on the verge of collapse for you to send your own wife out to earn a wage. They'll be afraid to do business with you. You'll be ruined!"

"Nonsense. The men I deal with have far more common sense than you give them credit for. One frank conversation will set them right. So that's the end of it. I will not be dissuaded." He broke free of his wife and turned toward Alice. "Now then, Miss Stevens, can you be packed by tomorrow?"

He was throwing her out. Alice tugged on a curl and wrapped it around her finger. "To-tomorrow?"

"There's a ship that departs tomorrow and will set in at San Diego on its way farther south. I don't believe another ship will do so for more than a week. I'm determined to reach my niece as soon as possible, and I assumed you would feel the same about Daniel."

Did she? No thrill seized her at the idea that Daniel might be closer than they had believed. Until this moment, it had not even occurred to her to join him in San Diego. She had somewhat formed the notion of sending him a letter and awaiting his return to this city. Although, where would she send the letter? Also, now that her welcome in this home seemed at an end, what return address could she give? "Didn't you say they'd left San Diego?"

"Yes, but only to the mountains east of there. I'm certain we'll be able to find them without too much trouble. In any case, I'm determined to try and I'm more than happy to pay your fare so that you may reunite with Daniel. He was as fine an employee as I've ever had, and after his loyalty all these years, it would please me to return his fiancée to him."

Richard shifted in his seat. "I hadn't planned on leaving San Francisco, but I suppose—"

"Oh. No, your escort would not be necessary, Mr. Stevens." He waved to his wife still gaping at her husband from the settee. "My wife and I will be more than happy to act as your sister's chaperones so that you may retain your job here or else venture off into the gold fields, as I know you had planned to do."

Richard clapped Alice on the back. "It's all settled then."

Was it? She did not remember agreeing to go.

Then again, no one had asked her whether she wanted to go to California either.

～

Stirring across the tiny cabin woke Eliza the next morning.

Daniel's gone. I'll never see him again.

She pulled the blanket over her head.

"Eliza? Are you awake?"

Burying her face in the furs, she pretended not to hear Pa's whisper.

"Let her sleep. I sleep, too."

Bless you, Ysabel.

Eliza spent the entire first day crying into her pallet.

The next day, even Ysabel was dressed and prepared to head out before Eliza.

Then Pa came and shook her.

"All right." She pushed his hand away. "I'll get up."

He left and she got dressed. She skipped the bowl of meal he'd left for her and wandered down to the gorge. Memories of Daniel assisting her over the giant boulders played in her mind. She lingered at the spot where they'd almost kissed.

Thankfully, no one came searching for her.

By the end of the third day, though, she needed something to occupy her time, or she would go mad dwelling on how much she'd lost.

Convincing Pa and Andrew to let her help them build the corral didn't take long. Pa never tried to stop her doing anything that wasn't dangerous, and hacking off the extra branches before guiding the horse downhill with the felled trees could hardly be considered that.

The bigger problem was controlling her thoughts on those solitary trips up and down the hill. No matter how she tried, her heart kept pulling her mind back to the man she'd lost.

In the yard behind the Coopers' cabin, she untied the last tree trunk and led her horse to the metal tub they used as a trough. As she waited for the animal to drink its fill, her face lifted to the cloud-covered sky. *Lord, I don't understand why you brought Daniel into my life only to rip him away again, but Andrew says You work all things for good for those who love You. I do love You, God. Help me to trust in You as well. I don't want to carry this pain alone. Please, Lord. Take it from me.*

The mare lifted her head, and Eliza led her back up the hillside. As she threaded her way through the sparse trees and shrubs, her heart still ached for the man she loved, but somehow, pressed in beside the pain, was an inexplicable peace. She didn't understand God's ways and probably never would, this side of heaven, but He did love her. He loved Daniel as well. She could cling to her disappointments and let the fear of more pain control her future, or she could choose to give her worries to God and trust that the One in control was more loving and wise than she could ever comprehend. It wouldn't be easy, but for the first time in her life…

She was ready to let go.

~

*P*uffy gray clouds muted the morning sun and dulled the sparkle of San Diego's bay. A ship sat anchored in the calm water. Daniel stood on shore, his carpetbag in hand and his trunk beside him. He awaited the first small boat of arriving passengers. Once they were deposited, Daniel and the one other man waiting nearby would be taken aboard.

His gaze fixed on the gentle waves lapping against the ship's hull.

He had been made to wait four days for the next southbound ship to set in at San Diego. It took him less than a half day to stroll the town's plaza and browse its few shops and businesses. Visiting the river to the north brought back painful memories of the night he found Eliza casting rocks into its shallow waters.

He needed distraction.

So he wandered south of the plaza toward Davis's New Town, which Daniel had read about in the *Alta California* some years back. Seeing what remained of the businessman's specula-tion was nothing short of depressing. The majority of the build-ings were gone, their wood presumably scavenged. Of the few buildings left, most appeared unoccupied and dismal—their interiors hollow. What remained of the wharf poked through the surface of the bay like the rotted teeth of a mouth screaming at the sky.

What had Davis been thinking?

In the end, Daniel abandoned his pursuit of external diversion and spent the majority of his days and every evening reading his Bible, searching in vain for the peace that had disappeared the hour he left the mountains.

It was the right thing to do. Scripture could not be more clear in its admonition that a man must be true to his word. Yet, a sense of unease filled him as he'd departed the mountains, and he had yet to shake it. Mourning the loss of such an amazing woman was understandable. Expected, even. But why did he have this inexplicable feeling that something more was wrong?

"Mr. Clarke!"

Daniel's head whipped up. His mouth dropped open. Mr. Davidson waved at him from the approaching boat. Beside him sat Mrs. Davidson—a wilted version of her former haughty self, with her shoulders curled inward and her skin even paler than when he'd last seen her. Perhaps she was among those whose constitution could not tolerate the rocking of the ocean.

What were they doing here? Had they come to see Eliza?

Daniel turned to contemplate the distant mountains as passengers disembarked behind him. If the Davidsons *had* come to visit Eliza, he must draw them a map of the way he came down. Mrs. Davidson wouldn't be able to endure the route he and Eliza had taken into the mountains.

"Daniel?"

That voice. His heart raced. It couldn't be.

He whipped around, then staggered backward. The curves of her dress were fuller, and her youthful glow had begun to fade, reflecting a maturity she'd not had when he last saw her. Still...

It *was* his fiancée standing before him.

*A*lice stretched her lips in a soft smile. "Hello." A strong breeze tossed a strand of her hair into her face. She tucked it behind her ear.

Daniel gaped at her. "What are you doing here?"

What kind of welcome was that? Alice's smile stiffened. "I've come to be with you, of course."

"But why? How?"

She let her smile fall. Daniel did not seem happy to see her. Her breath caught. Had he changed his mind about marrying her? What would she do if he had?

Benjamin's handsome visage flashed through her mind.

Mr. Davidson joined Alice and Daniel, Mrs. Davidson behind him.

Daniel offered his hand. "Mr. Davidson. A pleasure to see you again, sir. Have you come to visit your niece? I want to assure you that she has found her father and is doing well."

"That is so good to hear." Mr. Davidson's posture relaxed. "We've also brought you your fiancée, as you can see. She was keenly disappointed to arrive in San Francisco last week and find you gone."

Alice pressed her fingertips against her cheek, considering her fiancé's former employer. Mr. Davidson seemed to be a sympathetic man, and he was fond of Daniel. If Daniel rejected her, could she prevail upon his kindness to loan her the fare for a return ticket to Boston? Surely Benjamin would admit his love for her once he knew Daniel no longer wanted her. That kiss had to mean something to him as well. For her part, she'd not been able to forget it.

She resisted the urge to stomp her foot. Why must the Stevens brothers be such a noble lot?

Daniel ran a hand through his hair. "Of course, I'm delighted to see you, Alice. I'm surprised, is all." He shifted his stance and raised the carpetbag, then gestured toward the trunk waiting beside him. "I was on my way to be with you."

She dropped her chin. A tiny crab burrowed into the wet sand. Had she truly bemoaned his nobility? Daniel was too good for her.

Mr. Davidson stepped forward. "Then it's a very good thing we arrived when we did." He surveyed the area. "Now, tell me. Where is my niece?"

Daniel squared his shoulders. "She's in the mountains, sir. With her father and his new wife."

Mr. Davidson blinked, his eyes wide. "New wife? Jim has remarried then, has he?"

Daniel nodded. "His new wife is"—he lowered his voice—"in the family way, and I understand she's had a very difficult time of it the past few months."

Mr. Davidson rubbed his chin. "Well, I guess that explains it then. How does she fair now? Better, I hope?"

"Yes. She's much improved, even in the few days since Eliza and I arrived."

"Good for him." Mr. Davidson clapped his hands together. "He was happy to see his daughter, I trust?"

"Extremely."

Mrs. Davidson faced her husband. "You see, I told you there was no need to worry. Absolutely no need to place your businesses in the hands of managers and come all the way down here."

A seaman stepped closer and pointed at Daniel's trunk. "This going on board?"

CHAPTER 37

aniel rubbed the back of his neck. How should he answer?

He tried to catch Alice's gaze, but it seemed fixed to the sand. "What do you think, Alice? Are you prepared to board the ship and continue the journey…"

He'd intended to say *home.* But the word stuck in his throat.

Alice peered over her shoulder to the ship. "I suppose the captain could marry us." Her fingers fluttered at her collar. She flicked a glance at Daniel before returning her gaze to the sand.

Her tone was not that of an excited bride eagerly anticipating her union with the man she loved. Nor did she seem delighted to see him, despite having braved an ocean voyage to join him. Was it possible…?

Had she changed her mind?

In spite of himself, his heart lifted. If Alice no longer wished to marry him…

He'd be free to return to Eliza.

Daniel cleared his throat. Why wouldn't Alice look at him? "Would you prefer to remain here for a few days, Alice? I'm not sure whether the priest will marry us, since we're not Catholic, but I believe someone mentioned an army chaplain who holds services in the courthouse. Perhaps we can prevail upon him to perform the ceremony."

"Yes. I'd like to stay." Still scrutinizing the sand, Alice wrinkled her nose. "Are there proper accommodations to be had in this place?"

"It may not equal what you're used to, but I've been staying at a nice hotel." He gestured to where the seamen were stacking several bags and trunks on the shore. The one who'd inquired about Daniel's trunk had moved on to other tasks. "Let's gather your things and I'll show you to it."

Mrs. Davidson's face twisted as she lifted her skirt to step over a clump of kelp. "Do you mean to say we must walk to town?" The rich brown fringe dangling from the bottom of the woman's tan skirt was coated in wet sand. No doubt the impractical garment hid useless, expensive shoes.

Alice's wide gray skirt was equally sand-caked, though it at least lacked the silly fringe. What sort of footwear did it conceal? Had she come in the fancy things he'd seen her wear in Boston, or did she consider his descriptions of California and make a more practical choice? Was there any chance she'd chosen sturdy boots?

He counted the number of layers on Alice's skirt. Four. And in place of Mrs. Davidson's fringe was a white stripe with delicate flowers trimming each layer. Not exactly practical travel wear.

Probably no boots, then.

He ran a hand through his hair. "I apologize. I was not thinking. You must be tired after your journey. If you'll wait here, I shall return to town and see about hiring a wagon to come and fetch you."

*E*liza's breath fogged the crisp afternoon air as she held the second post upright in her gloved hands. Pa swung his sledgehammer to sink it into the hole in the bunk. The short length of log would keep the posts upright without the hard labor of digging into the hard-packed hillside. They had already sunk one post into the other end of the bunk. The side-by-side vertical posts created a slot into which they would slide their fence rails.

Across the yard, Andrew pulled another log from the pile. Straddling it, he hammered a wedge into its chopped end. When he had a long split running into the log, he took a second wedge and placed it where the split stopped. He exchanged his hammer for a sledgehammer, which he swung in a high arc over his head and brought down to slam the second wedge into the wood. With each swing and hit, the split grew. He moved his wedges along with it.

The loud hammering echoed over the hills. Could the echoes be heard in the valleys below?

Seven days had passed since Daniel left. By now he was aboard a ship bound for Boston. She dipped her head so Pa wouldn't notice her tears. She blinked to keep them from falling down her cheeks.

Pa finished pounding the post into the bunk and set his sledgehammer aside. She released the post.

Maria rounded the cabin carrying a stack of cups and the coffee pot.

Eliza hurried to relieve her of the stacked cups. She handed one to Andrew and one to Pa, keeping one for herself. Maria poured them coffee and their breath fogged the air between sips.

The temperature had dropped several degrees overnight, and Eliza awoke to a dull gray sky that grew darker as the day wore on. Despite the chill, Pa and Andrew both wiped sweat from their foreheads.

Pa squinted at the clouds, which sank lower with each passing hour. "What do you think Andrew? Think we'll see snow tonight?"

Andrew considered the sky. "Certainly looks that way."

"Does it snow as much here as up north, Pa?"

Pa cocked his head at Andrew.

Andrew scratched his beard. "I haven't been up north in the winter, but from what I've heard it's much milder here. Still, it'll get mighty chilly and I wouldn't advise walking around in the thick of it."

A wind gust sailed through the yard and snaked down her neck into her coat. She shivered. The last time she'd been this cold, Daniel was with her.

"This is nothing compared to the winter winds we have back home. There isn't even any snow. You never would have made it if you'd come home with me."

Now he was going home without her. She'd never know what it was like to waltz with the man she loved.

Had she made the right decision?

Another shiver slid down her body and she clenched her jaw. It didn't matter. He was gone now. *Lord, help me to accept the consequences of my actions and to trust you to use them for good.*

Andrew handed his empty cup to Maria and returned to his log pile.

Pa and Eliza followed suit.

An hour later, Pa tapped the first blow on the last post as tiny white flakes began drifting down from the sky.

She adjusted her grasp on the post. "I'm glad we're not planning to go anywhere right now."

Pa grunted as he took another swing. "I'd hate to be caught out in a snowstorm. Let's finish and get inside."

~

*A*fter seeing Alice and the Davidsons settled at the Exchange, Daniel bought back the same horse he'd sold four days ago. Then he rode to the mission.

He spoke with the chaplain, who agreed to perform the ceremony that afternoon.

As he rode back to town, the feeling that something was wrong grew until he could no longer ignore it. He reined his horse to a stop and scanned the gloomy sky above. "What am I missing, Lord? What is it that You want me to see? I'm trying to obey Your Word, so why does it feel like I'm doing something wrong?"

He waited, but no answer came.

After several minutes of silence, he nudged his horse forward.

~

*D*aniel found Alice sitting in the front room of the hotel, staring into the fire.

Mr. Davidson sat on a nearby bench reading a copy of the *San Diego Herald*. He lowered the paper. "Ah, Mr. Clarke. Were you successful in your endeavor?"

"I was, sir." He pivoted to Alice. "Things are all set."

She made an ambiguous sound, her stoic expression unchanging as she continued regarding the flames.

He ran a hand through his hair. Things had not been this awkward between them when he left Massachusetts. Was she upset that he had escorted Eliza?

He sat on the chair across from her and checked that the three of them were alone in the room. They were. Nevertheless, he dragged the chair forward until their knees were inches apart and kept his voice low. "I can understand how my decision to aid Miss Brooks in her search for her father might be concerning to you. But please trust my honesty when I tell you absolutely nothing untoward occurred."

A near-kiss did not count, no matter how many times he'd remembered it.

She twisted the glove in her hands. "I have never doubted your loyalty, Daniel."

Yet she still didn't look at him. How could he set her at ease? Perhaps if he shared the details of their plans... "The army chaplain has agreed to marry us this afternoon."

At last she regarded him, her hand fluttering to her collar. "So soon?"

Mr. Davidson shook his newspaper and lifted it close to his face, despite wearing his glasses. Did he need a new set of lenses?

Daniel shifted in his chair, refocusing on Alice. "I thought you'd be pleased."

"I am. Of course. But I..." She watched the fire again. "I need time to prepare."

"The chaplain won't be here for a few hours yet. I'm sure there's plenty of time to change and do whatever else you'd like to do beforehand."

"Yes. I'm sure you're right. Only..." She wrung the glove in her hands.

Daniel leaned forward. "Only...?"

"Nothing." She thrust the mangled glove into her lap. "Forget it."

Perhaps if he waited, she would elaborate.

Three minutes ticked by.

Or not.

Clearing his throat, he mentioned the idea that had occurred to him as he'd ridden past the restaurant. "I know you have a lot you want to accomplish between now and when the chaplain arrives, but I thought it might be nice to enjoy a meal together. I'm sure you're hungry and—"

"Actually, I'm still quite tired from the journey." She stood and backed out the door toward the stairs. "I think I'll go to my room and rest."

Before he could reply, she hitched up her skirt and sprinted up the stairs.

A rest? Hadn't she complained of not having enough time to prepare?

Something was not right.

～

*D*aniel drummed his fingers against his thigh.

She's hiding something.

When he left Alice in Massachusetts four years ago, she had been a confident, outgoing young woman, who adored being the center of attention. Her letters to him were filled with words of love and her eagerness to become his bride. Yet in the several hours since her arrival, she'd wrung the life out of her glove, avoided eye contact, and seemed to have no interest in spending time with him.

He checked the mantle clock again. Two hours had passed since his fiancée's odd departure. The chaplain would be here soon.

He must speak with Alice before the chaplain arrived. He strode across the room.

At the foot of the stairs, he paused. What if he was wrong? What if everything he was seeing was a young woman nervous about marrying a man she hadn't seen in four years. Much could change in such a long period of time. It didn't explain her reluctance to dine with him, but perhaps he'd suggested the wrong activity. If she were as nervous as she seemed, her stomach may be unwell.

He swiveled away from the stairs and crossed to the front door.

"Daniel?"

He pivoted.

Alice dashed down the stairs. A telltale puffiness surrounded her red-rimmed eyes.

Did nervous brides cry? He took her hand, giving it a gentle squeeze. "Alice, what is it?"

For the first time since her arrival, her gaze held his. "Is there somewhere we may speak in private?"

Should he take her to the river? No. Too many memories. Another idea came to mind. He placed her hand on his arm. "Come."

∾

*A*lice allowed Daniel to guide her out of the hotel and through the plaza toward the south. Once she and Daniel passed the half dozen or so houses situated south of the plaza, the wide, undulated land stood empty. A few abandoned buildings stood—apparently on the verge of collapse—down by the south end of the bay, but not a single person could be seen on the road between.

The silence was suffocating.

This is madness. Confessing risks everything I've planned and hoped for. It was one kiss. Daniel doesn't need to know.

He was everything she wanted in a husband. Not only could he give her the life she dreamed of, but he was certain to treat her and their children with kindness and respect. He would never leave her to pretend all was well while he disappeared for days at a time with whatever strumpet caught his attention. The idea that his actions with Mr. Davidsons' niece were anything but honorable was ludicrous. Daniel was nothing like her father. Daniel was everything true and good and noble. Why should she risk losing him?

Tell him.

No! Go away!

Her conscience had been driving her mad since she stepped off the boat this morning. Why must she tell Daniel? It would hurt him to know his brother and fiancée had betrayed him and what good would it do? She'd witnessed enough of Mother's crying spells to know the damage truth could cause. Some things were better left unsaid.

She swallowed the bile in her throat. Was that why her father had stopped explaining his absences? Did he tell himself what mother didn't know couldn't hurt her? It made her sick to think she was anything like him. Yet confessing the truth to Daniel might end their engagement and damage his relationship with Benjamin.

No, the kiss did the damage. Confession means accepting the consequences.

But would Benjamin forgive her for revealing their secret? What if, by telling the truth, she lost them both?

She tripped over a small rock in the road, but Daniel caught her and kept her from falling. "Thank you."

"Of course."

As he drew his hands away, they were shaking. His attention was fixed on the vacant road ahead of them. What was he thinking?

Tell him.

She ignored the voice and studied Daniel. His lips were pressed together as he rubbed his palms against one another. Why was he so nervous? "What aren't you telling me?" The question popped from her lips without forethought. Did she just insinuate that he was being less than open with her? How ironic. Daniel was the most honest person she knew. It was she who could not be trusted.

Something flickered in Daniel's eyes before he spoke. "Me? You're the one who asked to speak in private. You're the one who's been avoiding looking at me. What is it *you* aren't telling *me?*"

Wait a moment... Had that been guilt in his eyes? Surely not. What could Daniel have to feel guilty about? Unless he'd lied about Miss Brooks.

No. This is Daniel. He would never—

There it is again. "Daniel, what did you do?"

He whirled away from her and silence reined for several tense seconds.

He is *hiding something.*

Then he turned, his face crumpled and his shoulders hunched. "I'm so sorry. I never meant for it to happen. I—"

"How *could* you?" Her hand flew to her mouth. *This isn't happening. Not with Daniel. He's different. Except he isn't. Is every man like Father?* "I trusted you."

"I know. I'm so sorry." He held his hands out to her. "Please let me explain."

She stepped back. "To think I was feeling guilty about one little kiss, and the whole time you were... You're exactly like him."

Daniel's eyes grew to the size of Mr. Davidson's spectacles. "What? No! That's not what I meant. I give you my word, nothing like that happened. I— Wait, what kiss?"

"Don't you try to turn this around, Daniel Clarke. You know my family's secrets. I know guilt when I see it. How can you expect me to believe you when I can see the guilt written all over your face? What else *could* you have done?"

His mouth opened and closed several times. Then he shrugged. "I fell in love with Eliza."

Oh. "You fell in love with her?"

He raised his hands to squeeze his head. "I tried not to, but I couldn't help myself."

"But you didn't kiss her or…?"

He waved his arms in front of him "No! I couldn't—wouldn't—do that to you."

She studied him, waiting for his gaze to falter, his hands to fidget the way her father's did when he was lying. Daniel held her gaze, his hands limp at his sides.

He's telling the truth.

She grabbed her skirts, whirled, and ran.

Daniel blinked. *Where is she going?* He sprinted after her.

She stopped and he caught up to her.

Clutching at her bodice, she gasped for air. Her face was an alarming shade of red for such a short run. She pulled at the collar of her dress and undid the top button.

He whipped his head away as her fingers moved to the next button.

He scanned the area for other people. No one was close enough to discern what Alice was doing. *Thank you, Lord.*

He scrutinized the bay while listening to her continued struggle for air. Gulls soared over the brilliant water. "Is there anything I can do to help?"

From the corner of his eye, he saw her shake her head. She laced her fingers behind her head and took long, deep breaths. After a few seconds, her breathing returned to normal.

"I kissed him."

He whipped toward her, glimpsed her skin revealed by the four undone buttons, and spun away again. "Who?"

In his periphery vision, he saw her button her dress. When she was finished, he faced her.

She bit the finger of her glove. "Benjamin."

Daniel waited for shock to set in.

It didn't come.

Not anger, either. Not even a speck.

Why am I not angry? My brother kissed my fiancée. I should be angry. Instead, he felt strangely calm. As though he had expected it. But it was unlike either Benjamin or Alice to betray his trust. *So why doesn't it feel like betrayal? Why does it feel...right? As if this is the way it's supposed to be?* A light dawned inside him. "Do you love him?"

She nodded as tears spilled down her cheeks. "But I don't think he loves me. Not enough, anyway, or he wouldn't have purchased my ticket and talked Richard into bringing me here."

Daniel grinned. That is *exactly* what his honorable big brother would have done. The stronger the temptation, the farther he would have wanted Alice from him.

She frowned at him. "Why are you grinning? Don't you understand? I betrayed your trust while you held yourself true. Aren't you angry with me?"

He chuckled. "I should be. But I'm not. Actually, I'm relieved."

A tentative smile lifted her trembling lips. "I think you just insulted me."

"Never. But I think we both know this"—he wagged his finger between them—"isn't meant to be."

"I would've made you a good wife, Daniel. I know I made a horrible mistake, but I never would have..." Her throat bobbed. "I'm not my father."

"Oh, my dear, I know that." Daniel withdrew his kerchief and handed it to her. "Remember that time, just before I left, when you helped that nervous young singer... What was her name?"

Alice's voice steadied as she patted her face. "Miss

Humphrey. Mother had her brought up all the way from Washington to perform for our party."

"And she was so nervous you feared she would lose her accounts, so you took her out to stroll the garden until it was time for her performance." Daniel clasped his hands together. "You missed half the party just to cheer up an eleven-year-old girl."

Alice sniffed. "I suppose that was nice of me."

"It was extremely kind and it is something a selfish man like your father would never do." He held out his arm. "Now, shall we go tell the chaplain his services are no longer needed?"

She tucked away his kerchief before accepting his offer, and they started their walk back to the hotel. "Oh, Daniel. What are we going to do?"

He smiled down at her. "I do still have that ticket back to Boston."

"But you aren't going back now, are you? I assumed now that you were free..." She gasped, coming to a halt. "Oh, but I never asked. How does Miss Brooks feel about you?"

Daniel tipped his head. His leaving made Eliza cry, and she'd been vehement about not allowing him to sacrifice his future for her. Then there was that near kiss. He stood taller. "I believe she cares for me."

"Does she love you?"

He set his jaw. "I intend to find out."

"What are you going to do?" She tugged at one of her blonde curls. "You can't just ask a person if they love you. What if they say no, or"—she pulled her hand from his arm, her chin lowering—"refuse to answer you at all."

Daniel dipped his chin to catch her eye. "Sounds like you're speaking from experience."

Her cheeks pinked as she studied the ground.

He nudged her with his shoulder. "Do you want to tell me what happened?"

She peered up at him through her lashes. "Are you sure you want to know?"

"If it will help you to talk about it."

She pulled her glove free and twisted it for a minute before speaking. "All right, but remember, Benjamin's been my escort for social events for years now. And *you're* the one who asked him to fill that role. It isn't like we planned for—"

Daniel held up his hand. "I remember. It was my idea for Benjamin to escort you. In fact, it took me three letters and an ounce of gold to convince him to take you to that first dance."

Alice staggered back a step. "You *paid* him!"

Daniel restrained a smile. "Mm-hm. But only for the first few months. After that, you started writing that he had offered to escort you to events before I even knew to ask him." Daniel clasped his hands behind his back.

"But...he always said you'd asked him. Or did he? Now I can't remember. Maybe I just assumed..." Alice tapped her chin.

"For my part, since he said that taking you convinced Mother to quit nagging him about finding a wife, I assumed Benjamin was enjoying socializing with the other single ladies at the events you two attended." He tilted his head. "Why did my mother think you and Richard were visiting a friend? She couldn't have known you were coming to California, or she'd have said so in her letters."

"She didn't know. Benjamin swore us to secrecy when he purchased our tickets. I think he worried she'd stop us from leaving."

Yes, Mother probably would have done just that. "But why *did* you come to California? You've already admitted you love my brother."

Alice told him how her father's behavior had spiraled out of control and that Richard had convinced her to flee.

He'd known her father was a scoundrel, but to strike his own daughter? The man was a cad! "Good for Richard. I'm glad he got you out of there." Daniel held his hands out and she accepted them. "Why didn't you write me that things had gotten so bad? I'd have come for you sooner, savings or no."

She squeezed his hands. "I know you would have, but by that time…" She pulled away and shrugged.

Aha. He crossed his arms. "By then you'd fallen for my brother and didn't *want* me to come for you."

She nodded.

"So what happened? You mentioned a kiss?"

She swung her skirt side to side, like a bell. "It happened at the Summer Ball."

Daniel couldn't restrain the smile this time. "So *that's* why you stopped writing." Her last letter had been all about preparing for the ball.

She quit moving and clasped her hands together. "At first, I didn't know how to tell you I couldn't marry you because I'd fallen for your brother. Then Benjamin started avoiding me, and I didn't know *what* to think. I'd promised to marry you and I was convinced your mother would hate me if I broke your heart. And I was so desperate to escape my father's house and behavior…I didn't know what to do." She stepped forward, lifting her clasped hands. "I'm so sorry. I never meant to hurt you."

Daniel laid his hand over hers. "You didn't. Remember?" He cupped her cheek. "Everything's all right. I love Eliza and you love Benjamin. It's clear God didn't intend for you and me to marry. It just took *us* some time to realize that." He tweaked her nose. "And now, you are free to return home and tell that brother of mine how foolish he was to let you go."

She swatted his hand away, frowning at him. "But how? I've no money and no chaperone."

"Use my ticket to Boston." He took her hand and returned it to his arm. "It's all paid for. And I'll speak to Mr. Davidson about a chaperone. Surely he can recommend someone."

"Thank you." She didn't resist when he resumed their walk back to town. "But what if Benjamin doesn't want me?"

"Oh, he wants you. Trust me." He grinned at her. "And when you see him, tell him I want my ounce of gold back."

CHAPTER 38

he chaplain didn't seem to mind their change of plans. When they announced their ended engagement to the Davidsons, Mr. Davidson grilled Daniel anew on the details of his trip with Eliza before granting his blessing for Daniel's pursuit of his niece. Mrs. Davidson remained silent and glared out the window. Giving Alice Daniel's ticket was a simple matter, but the next ship bound for Boston wouldn't arrive for another week, and finding a suitable escort—something Mr. Davidson promised to arrange—could take even longer. So they all agreed that Alice would travel with the rest of them to the mountains.

If all went according to plan, the Davidsons would return with Alice to San Francisco in one week.

By the time everyone was prepared to leave, the sun hung low in the sky, but Daniel talked them out of delaying their departure. As they rode out of San Diego, he nearly urged his horse into a gallop, but out of respect for his horse and the fact that none of the others knew the way, he kept to a brisk trot.

When it grew dark, Mr. Davidson called for them to make camp. Had Daniel been on his own, he'd have continued. As it was, he heeded Mr. Davidson's decision to let the women rest and settled in for what promised to be a restless night.

~

$\mathcal{E}$liza pressed her boot down as hard as she could but only managed to sink it an inch or two into the snow. Andrew was right. This snowstorm was nothing like what they experienced up north. It had been snowing for three straight days, yet the amount that fluttered from the heavens barely covered the ground.

She leaned back in the little chair she had brought outside before Pa and Ysabel retired for the evening. Pa didn't like the idea of Eliza sitting alone in the growing dark and had given her his Colt, just in case. His concern hadn't disturbed her sense of peace, though. God was watching her. She sensed His presence.

Wrapped in a thick pelt, she wasn't bothered by the cold, and the sight of the flakes drifting through the twilight was breathtaking.

When it grew too dark to see God's artwork, she stood to go inside. Holding Pa's pistol in one hand, she grasped the pelt with her other to keep it from slipping as she approached the door of the cabin.

A branch snapped behind her.

The rhythmic crunch of boots plodding through snow disturbed the quiet. Someone was approaching from the west, opposite the Coopers' cabin.

The back of her neck tingled.

She adjusted her grip on the pistol so that her finger lay over the trigger.

Who would be out on a night like this?

She strained to discern movement among the sparse trees. Clouds blocked the glow of the moon and stars, leaving the hillside in shades of black.

Should she wake Pa? No. She couldn't wake him without waking Ysabel, and her stepmother had been worn through by mysterious cramps that came and went all day. Maria—who birthed and raised two sons only to watch them die of smallpox before reaching adulthood—assured everyone that Ysabel's pains were normal and nothing to be concerned about. Pa didn't seem convinced and hovered at Ysabel's side, making sure she rested as much as possible. He'd exhausted himself with worry. They both needed their rest.

Lord, please don't make me have to shoot. That would wake everyone in a hurry.

The crunching of snow grew louder as the intruder approached.

There. A darker shade of black moved among the trees.

She let the pelt fall and cocked the gun.

The click echoed as she took aim.

～

*D*aniel froze. Was that a gun cocking? Jim or Andrew must have heard him approaching. He should have listened to Mr. Davidson when he'd argued that approaching the cabins in the dark was foolhardy. But they were so close. He couldn't bear waiting until morning to see Eliza again.

Now he raised his hands slowly. "Jim? Andrew? It's Daniel Clarke."

"Daniel?"

"Eliza?" What was she doing outside in the dark? With a gun?

Snow crunched beneath boots.

"Ah—!" *Thud.*

"Eliza!" He sprinted in the direction of her voice.

A second later, he found her sprawled in the snow at the

edge of her pa's yard. He knelt beside her. "What happened? Are you hurt?"

She lifted a gloved hand to the back of her head.

"Eliza!" Jim's voice came from the cabin as Eliza sucked in a loud breath. She must have had the wind knocked out of her.

Gunfire shattered the night. "That's a warning shot and it's the only one you're gonna get. Now speak up! Who's out there, and where's my daughter?"

"It's Daniel Clarke, sir. Eliza's with me. I think she fell."

Eliza's head tilted up, the whites of her eyes barely visible. Were they glazed or clear? Was she happy to see him? It was impossible to tell.

"Do you think you can stand?"

She lifted a hand. He took it and helped her to her feet. She slipped a little and his arm went around her. He pulled her close.

Jim skidded to a stop behind her, his gun lowered.

Thank you, Lord.

Still, it was probably wise to loosen his hold on the man's daughter.

The second Daniel eased back, she stepped away.

He pressed his empty hands against his thighs, resisting the urge to pull her back.

Jim wrapped a thick pelt around Eliza.

"I'm all right, Pa. Daniel's right, I fell. Slipped on a patch of ice."

"Well, why didn't you answer me when I called?"

"I couldn't breathe and—"

Boot steps pounded over the rise between the cabins.

"Everything all right, Jim?"

Andrew. Probably toting his rifle.

Daniel couldn't see Jim, but somehow he sensed the man's narrowed eyes on him.

Jim turned his head toward the rise. "Think so. Know for sure soon enough."

A line of yellow light crossed the snow as the cabin door cracked open. "Jim?"

Jim said something in Ysabel's native language and the door closed again.

Andrew stomped across to them. "Why'd you fire your gun?"

Daniel cringed. "That would be my fault. Mr. Davidson warned me to wait until morning, but I was too impatient to see Eliza."

"To see me?" Was that hope in her voice?

"Mr. Davidson?" Jim spoke over his daughter. "You've seen my brother?"

"Yes, sir." Daniel pointed the way he'd come. "They're all camped about four miles back. They set up tents and I made sure they had a warm fire going. I told them I'd go back for them in the morning."

Jim shifted toward Andrew. "You think Maria'll mind if we come and set at your place? I don't like to keep Ysabel up and I got a feeling I'm gonna need to look this young man in the eye."

"I don't think she'll mind. I'll run ahead and let her know you're coming."

Andrew jogged off and Jim followed at a brisk walk.

Eliza started to follow Jim.

Daniel caught her hand where it poked from beneath the pelt. Her step faltered, but she didn't pull away.

～

*D*espite Eliza's thick gloves, Daniel's warmth radiated through her fingertips all the way to her toes. *Lord, what is he doing here?* He should be halfway down the Pacific coast by now. He'd never held her hand like this before. Had he changed his mind? But why? What about Alice?

Eliza yanked her hand away. *Don't forget about Alice.*

"Eliza?" His voice was too low for Pa to hear.

She ignored him and hurried ahead.

He couldn't have broken his engagement with Alice yet. It took far more than a week's time for a letter to even reach The States, let alone receive a reply. He must have come as a guide for her aunt and uncle. Then why did he take her hand like that?

She followed Pa into the Coopers' cabin.

Maria set the coffee pot on the fire as Andrew waved them over to the table.

Eliza set her pelt aside and sank into the chair Daniel held out for her.

The moment everyone was seated, Pa eyed Daniel. "So, young man? What's your excuse for coming at this hour and scaring us all half to death?"

"I'm sorry, sir." Daniel craned his neck to catch Eliza's eye.

She ducked her chin. Still, she sensed his gaze on her.

His hand nudged hers under the table. "I'm especially sorry to have scared you, Eliza."

She clasped her hands together. The warmth of his nearness drew her. *Don't look at him.* Every beat of her heart shouted for her to turn and claim him. *He isn't mine to claim.* Why was he torturing her like this?

"What is it you've come back for, son? And what's my brother doing here?"

"Mr. Davidson and his wife received Eliza's letter, but they wanted to see for themselves that she was well and safe."

Eliza snorted. If Cecilia was here, it wasn't out of concern for Eliza's well-being.

"Seems like you could've drawn them a map. Henry's not bad with direction. I think he could've found us without you coming along." Pa tilted his head toward her. "Might've been better that way."

She flushed. Did Pa have to speak so plainly?

"You're right. I could have drawn a map, but..." Daniel cleared his throat. "Well, the truth is, I came back for a different reason."

Eliza tensed. *Why is he here? Why would a carpenter come to the mountains? Maybe he wants Andrew to harvest wood for him. Daniel's a carpenter. Carpenters need wood. That makes sense. Somewhat.*

"I've had a lot of time to think over what you said, sir, and I believe you're right. Eliza and I should marry."

She whirled toward him. "What are you *saying?* What about Alice?"

"Eliza, may I speak with you, please?" Daniel stood and pulled her chair back. Her legs wobbled as she rose.

He lifted a candle from the mantle. "In private, sir?"

Pa nodded and Daniel placed her hand on his arm.

Eliza took a deep breath...and let him lead her out of the cabin.

CHAPTER 39

*T*he cold winter breeze slapped Eliza's cheeks, causing her to shiver as they stepped outside. She could see her breath in the air. Daniel set the candle on a nearby stump and went back inside the cabin. Then he reappeared with two fur coats he must have borrowed from Andrew and Maria.

He helped her into the smaller coat, then slid his arms into the larger one.

She crossed her arms, trying to smother the ache inside her. Rather than meet his gaze, she settled her focus on the gloomy forest behind him. "Daniel, I appreciate what you're trying to do, but you can't sacrifice your life for me. I'll be all right."

Daniel stepped closer.

She shook her head and stepped away. "You shouldn't marry someone to save their reputation. You're a good man. You deserve to marry the woman you love."

He took another step and his hands clasped her arms, drawing her close. "What if I told you the woman I love is standing right here?"

She sucked in a breath and searched his eyes. *Is it true? Do you truly love me or are you only trying to protect me again?* "What about Alice?"

He held her gaze with a look of peaceful reassurance. "I've been fooling myself. I was homesick, and she represented everything I'd left behind. Proposing to her was like promising myself that I'd return someday, but it wouldn't be right to keep my promise to her, because I never truly loved her the way a man is meant to love his wife. And Alice deserves to be loved that way." His smile tilted. "Besides, she's in love with my brother."

"What?" Eliza froze. Could it be true? "How do you know?"

"She arrived with the Davidsons and—"

"She's here?" Eliza peeked in the direction he'd come from. "But how? Why?" If Alice was here, she must have come to marry Daniel. So why was he standing here, saying these things? It didn't make any sense.

He chuckled and slid his hands up and down her arms. "It's a long story. I'll explain it all later. Right now, you need to know that Alice and I have agreed to call off our engagement, and Alice is going to be all right."

Lord, is it true? She placed her hands on his chest. "Are you sure, Daniel?"

He nodded, covering her hands with his. "Trust me."

She peered up at him through her lashes as peace settled over her. "I do."

"Eliza," he whispered. "I love you. Will you waltz with me?" He stepped back and lifted his arms into place.

Pure joy bubbled up her throat and erupted in laughter as she stepped into his arms. "Yes, Daniel. I will waltz with you."

As they danced slow circles around the clearing, snow fluttered from the sky, coating his dark hair in white. She imagined him old and gray. She would love him even then. With one hand on the small of her back and the other gripping her fingers, he held her with a strength that promised never to let go. His eyes caressed her face with such love, she could scarcely breathe. She'd never felt so cherished.

Warmth swelled her chest. "I love you."

"And I love you." He paused their dancing and knelt before her. "Will you do me the great honor of becoming my wife?"

She laughed again. "Yes."

"Good." He grinned as he jumped to his feet and grabbed her hand. He pulled her back toward the cabin, and they burst inside. "She said yes!"

"Of course she did." Pa waved at Andrew to stand. "Well? What're you waiting for? Go on and marry them."

Eliza's mouth fell open.

Maria said something in her language to Andrew and he responded.

Eliza peered down at the fur coat hiding the smelly, dirty dress she'd been working in all day, then up at Daniel. *Is this what you want?* She'd marry him right now if it was what he wanted, but...

Daniel's expression softened. "Sir." He kept hold of her hand as he stepped toward Pa. "I want to marry your daughter." He beamed back at her, his eyes glowing. "I love her. And I think she's beautiful as she is, but I know your daughter." He shook his head. "She'll not be happy marrying this way."

"There's no need for that fancy party nonsense, son—"

"No, sir, but I think we ought to allow Eliza a chance to rest and refresh herself. After all"—he squeezed her hand and pulled her forward—"we're only doing this once. I want to make sure it's something she'll remember with joy. The others will be here in the morning and I know she'd like her uncle to be here for the ceremony."

He knows me so well. She squeezed his hand. "Thank you."

Pa grunted. "I suppose you're right."

Maria cocked her head at Andrew. He said something to her and she jumped to her feet.

"I help Eliza." Maria took Eliza by the elbow. "Ysabel help, too. In morning."

Eliza stared at Daniel with wide eyes. All she needed was some sleep and a bath. It wasn't as though she had a fancy gown to stuff herself into or a tong to curl her hair. *What were these women planning?*

Andrew guffawed. "Maria loves weddings."

Well, that explained nothing.

Maria pulled Eliza toward the door and gestured for Pa to follow. "Jim go too. Sleep now. Daniel stay here. Marry in morning."

Whatever Maria had planned, she seemed determined. Eliza shrugged. "I guess I'm leaving now. Good night!"

"Good night." Daniel's deep, warm voice followed her as Maria dragged her out the door. "I love you!"

~

A knock jarred Eliza from slumber the next morning. She rubbed her face. What time was it?

It had taken hours for sleep to claim her. She'd been too busy imagining her future with Daniel to give in to fatigue.

She bolted upright. *I'm marrying Daniel today.* She pressed a fist to her mouth to muffle her squeal.

Ysabel sat up.

Pa's side of the bed was empty. He must have snuck out while she slept.

Maria entered carrying a large metal tub and spoke rapidly in her native language.

Ysabel beamed at Eliza, then spoke to Maria. The older woman set the metal tub in the center of the room and hurried back outside.

Eliza surveyed the one-room cabin with fresh eyes. Where were she and Daniel going to sleep tonight? Let alone the rest of their lives? Images of them pitching a tent in the bitter cold flashed through her mind. Or what if he still wanted to return to his family in Massachusetts? How would she face his parents? They surely adored Alice. Would they like Eliza? Boston was even more civilized than San Francisco. Could she ever learn to follow all those rules? She gnawed her lip. Would she ever see Pa again?

She reached for the Bible Andrew had loaned her and flipped it open to the verse she'd been working to memorize.

"Be careful for nothing; but in every thing by prayer and supplication with thanksgiving, let your requests be made known to God."

She closed the book. "I'll be right back."

Ysabel nodded and Eliza stepped outside for a moment alone with God.

As she prayed, she pictured Pa's expression as he gazed at Ysabel. He had never truly needed Eliza. God had been with him all along. Then she'd told Daniel to go, but God sent him back to her.

Peace settled over her.

Things might not always work out the way she wished them too, but as long as she kept her trust in God, she could face the future without fear. With a contented sigh, she closed her prayer.

When she opened her eyes, Maria was walking toward the cabin with two steaming buckets of water. Eliza opened the door and held it for Maria to step through. Maria poured the hot water into the tub. Then Ysabel added cold water from the bucket they kept in the cabin.

"You wash." Maria pointed to the tub and handed Eliza a bar of soap before she and Ysabel left.

I'm getting married today! I wonder what Daniel is doing right now. Eliza made quick work of her bath. She was almost finished drying herself when there was a knock at the door.

"Just a moment!" She quickly tied her drawers and slipped

on her chemise, then wrapped herself in a blanket. She approached the closed door. "Who's there?"

"It's Uncle Henry, Eliza. May I come in?"

"Uncle Henry! Oh, I'm sorry. You can't come in right now, but I'll be out shortly."

"That's all right. I understand, but your aunt has something to give to you that I think will please you. May she come in?"

Eliza stifled a groan lest her uncle hear it through the door. The last person she wanted to speak to right now was her sanctimonious aunt. Eliza didn't even have a proper dressing gown to put on. What would Cecilia think?

Eliza made a rude noise with her tongue.

Who cared what her aunt thought?

"Yes. She may come in." *But if she doesn't mind her tongue, I'll kick her right out again.* They weren't in Cecilia's home anymore.

Eliza opened the door, keeping well behind it.

Cecilia entered carrying a large wrapped parcel and surveyed the room. Her attention landed on Eliza as the latch fell over the door. Her lips pinched. "Hello, Eliza."

"Aunt Cecilia." Eliza gaped at her aunt.

She had never seen her aunt so undone. Cecilia was coated in trail dust, there was a tear in her skirt, and strands of tangled hair poked out from the bonnet that sat askew on her head. Cecilia scowled as she handed Eliza a note.

The note stated that while Uncle Henry had scoured San Francisco for Eliza, her aunt had attempted to destroy or hide all of Eliza's letters. Uncle Henry forced Cecilia to write this apology and deliver it in person. There were no expressions of remorse, only a simple accounting of the facts followed by an obligatory apologetic phrase.

Well, at least Eliza could be certain her aunt had written the letter herself.

Eliza crushed the paper in her hands. How could Cecilia be so cruel to her own husband? To let him scour all of San Francisco—frantic with worry—when she had the answers all along? *Yet, if I'd remained, none of this would have happened.*

Eliza's fingers relaxed. God had forgiven her much and He expected her to forgive in return.

She looked up.

Her aunt appraised the tub, her nose wrinkled.

Maria and Ysabel had honored and blessed Eliza with all the hard work they'd put into helping her prepare for her special day, but undoubtedly all Cecilia saw was dirty bath water.

Her aunt caught her staring.

Eliza pressed her lips into a smile. Today was her wedding day. She refused to allow negative emotions a place in it. "I accept your apology."

Cecilia sniffed as she held out the package. "Your uncle insisted I bring this to you." She cast a scathing glance around the cabin. "Though I can't imagine what you'll do with it here."

Eliza peeled back the brown paper and gasped. It was an evening gown made from the rich blue silk her aunt purchased for her to wear to the charity ball. The fabric was even more exquisite than she remembered. *Thank you, Lord.*

She dropped the blanket.

Cecilia whirled around. "What are you doing?"

"Putting it on." She dashed to her pallet, where she'd left her stockings.

"Excuse me." Her aunt bolted out the door, slamming it behind her.

Eliza paid her no mind as she slipped her stockings on before pulling on her boots. It seemed a shame to wear scuffed boots with such an exquisite dress, but they were all she had. Her petticoats weren't in much better shape, but they would have to do. Hopefully Daniel wouldn't mind. Her cheeks flamed. *He'll see them tonight. Will he expect...?* She slipped on the undergarments. *Worry about that later.*

She soon had her corset on and her chemise adjusted so that the thin sleeves fell over her shoulders.

It was time for the dress.

First, she pulled on the skirt. She adored how the dress-maker had cut the fabric so that the gorgeous white flowers ran in wide vertical stripes along the dark blue silk. So many women wore horizontal stripes these days. This was something unique.

The bodice was next. Its small, off-the-shoulder, puff-sleeves were trimmed with tulle and the pointed front of the bodice was well-tailored. For the first time, she missed the mirror that stood in her room in San Francisco. She ran her hands down the smooth silk. Would Daniel like it?

She took extra care braiding her hair into a fancy twisted bun and pinning it in place.

Another knock sounded as she settled the last pin. Before she could reply, Maria and Ysabel entered. They both gasped and rambled in their native language as their hands skimmed over the dress.

Eliza bit her lip. "Do you like it?"

Ysabel beamed at her. "You beautiful."

Maria sighed and clasped her hands together. *"Si."*

Someone pounded the door. "Angel? You 'bout ready?"

She opened the door wide.

Pa whistled. "Well, now. You look right pretty. Just like your mama." He offered her his arm. "Shall we?"

She grinned as she placed her hand on his sleeve. Maria and Ysabel followed them back to the Coopers' Cabin.

Just outside their door, stood a petite blond woman Eliza had never seen before. *Alice.*

The young woman offered a small smile as she crossed the yard to meet them. She bobbed a curtsy. "You must be Eliza. I'm Alice Stevens. Daniel has told me so much about you."

As Maria and Ysabel continued to the cabin, Eliza dipped

her chin. A curtsy might soil her hem and, for once, she cared. She considered the woman whose former fiancé Eliza was about to marry. What should she say?

Alice waved a hand. "Please don't be embarrassed. Daniel told me how you sent him away to keep his promise to me. Thank you for that, but the truth is, Daniel and I were never in love." She shrugged. "I actually think you'll be perfect for him, and I'm happy for you both."

"Thank you." Eliza tipped her head to the side. "Daniel tells me you'll be returning to Boston. I hope you'll be happy as well."

Pa patted Eliza's hand. "That is very kind of you, Miss Stevens. Now, let's not keep Daniel waiting."

Pa led her around Alice to the cabin door. Inside, Andrew, Uncle Henry, and Daniel chatted by the fireplace while Aunt Cecilia perched on a chair at the table with Ysabel and Maria. The tiny cabin was crowded with everyone inside, but as Eliza surveyed the faces of those who loved her, she wouldn't have it any other way.

Daniel's hair was damp, his jaw was shaved, and he was wearing a new suit he must have purchased in San Diego. He swiveled toward Eliza and his jaw dropped.

She bit her lip. "It's a present from my uncle. Do you like it?"

Daniel crossed the room and took her hand. He held her gaze as he pressed a kiss to the back of her fingers. "You are enchanting."

Uncle Henry stepped forward. "It looks lovely on you, Eliza."

She pulled her hand from Daniel and gave her uncle a hug. "Thank you." She whispered in his ear. "For everything."

"You're welcome." He gave her a squeeze, then set her back.

Daniel snatched her hand again and led her to where Andrew waited by the fire.

CHAPTER 40

A few moments later Eliza had pledged to love, honor, and cherish Daniel, for better or worse, till death did they part, and he had done the same for her.

Andrew's voice boomed in the tiny cabin. "I now pronounce you, husband and wife!"

Cheers erupted as Daniel's head lowered to hers. Their breaths mingled and then his lips were on hers. Warm and sweet and full of promise.

Pa clapped a hand on Daniel's shoulder, jarring their lips apart, though Daniel kept hold of her hand. "Congratulations, Son. Welcome to the family." Pa offered Daniel a hand.

Daniel swapped Eliza's hand to his left and accepted Pa's shake. "Thank you, sir."

Pa clasped her shoulders. "Your ma would be so proud of you." He wiped a tear away and cleared his throat. "I'm proud of you too."

"Thank you, Pa." She hugged him with her free arm and blinked back tears. She would not have red, puffy eyes on her wedding day.

Uncle Henry offered his congratulations next, shaking Daniel's hand and pecking Eliza's cheek.

Her uncle moved to the side and Andrew stepped forward with his hand extended. "Congratulations, Daniel. You've got yourself a true lady."

"Thank you, I know." Daniel shook his hand, then stepped back, put an arm around Eliza and regarded the men and women before them. "I'm very grateful to call this woman my wife. I promise I'll take good care of her."

"I know you will, Son. I can tell." Pa cocked an eyebrow. "Else I never woulda let you marry her. Reputation or no."

Eliza gaped at Pa and he laughed.

"Angel, any fool could see this boy was in love with you and you was in love with him. I wasn't about to let some promise he'd made to a gal he hadn't seen in years—no offense, Miss Stevens—get in the way of my Angel's happiness."

"Pa!" She bit her lip, but Daniel and Alice laughed.

Then Daniel hugged her close and gave her a kiss that lingered and grew until Pa cleared his throat.

Daniel pulled back and Eliza blinked. She'd forgotten there were others in the room. Her face flamed and she buried it in Daniel's shirt.

"Jim?" Ysabel's quiet voice drew Eliza's attention.

Pa faced his wife. "What?"

Ysabel stretched to her tiptoes and Pa bent sideways so his wife could whisper in his ear. Then he straightened and stared down at Ysabel as if she were crazy. "Why would I—?"

Ysabel glared at him with pursed lips and a head shake that said he was clueless.

Pa's lips formed a silent *o.* He cleared his throat. "Right." He trained his focus to some point on the wall behind Daniel. "Ysabel and I will bunk with Andrew and Maria tonight so you and Eliza can…uh…sleep in our cabin."

Was Pa's face turning red? She tried to catch his eye, but he coughed and rubbed a hand over his face. What had he said? *So you and Eliza can sleep in our cabin. Oh!* Her own face flared again.

Daniel squeezed her gently and nodded to Pa. "Thank you, sir."

Uncle Henry cleared his throat. "Speaking of sleeping arrangements, Alice and my wife are anxious to return to civilization, and I can't say I relish the idea of spending another night camping in the snow. I think we'd better head out now so we can get far enough down the mountain to leave the snow behind before nightfall."

Eliza leaned against Daniel. "But you've only just arrived. Must you leave so soon?"

"I'm afraid so, but there is one thing I'd like to discuss with Daniel before we go."

Daniel straightened beside her. "Yes, sir?"

"I've recently purchased a hotel in San Francisco that needs a lot of polish to bring it up to my standards. The building itself needs trim work and there isn't a stick of furniture left in the place. I need someone I trust to oversee the project and make sure everything runs smoothly. I want this to be a place people go home and talk about and then come back and stay again."

Daniel shifted to face her. "What do you think? I know you were thinking of moving back to Oregon."

She shook her head. She'd had a lot of time to think after Daniel left, and God helped her see that her dream of returning to Oregon had been about reclaiming the familiar to maintain her illusion of control. She didn't need that anymore. She had God.

And He'd given her Daniel.

"Oregon's a beautiful place, but anywhere you are, I can be happy." She laid a hand on his chest. "What about your family? Doesn't your father need your help?"

Alice cleared her throat. "If you'll forgive my saying so, I believe your mother has been exaggerating the situation, Daniel."

Daniel sighed. "I suspected she might be."

"I'm sure once Benjamin finishes his house, he'll be able to handle whatever your father can't take on."

"And perhaps someday we can visit." He brushed a loose strand from Eliza's face, tucking it behind her ear. "Still, I know you weren't fond of San Francisco."

"That's true." She faced her uncle. "Would we need to live in the city?"

"Not necessarily. I have some property on the edge of town you might like. A real pretty spot that wouldn't leave you with too far of a ride into the city every day." He widened his stance "Some days—like when he's working on the furniture—Daniel could even work at home, if he likes."

Pa's shoulders sagged, then he shrugged. "There's not much work for a carpenter out here. It'd be a shame to waste talent like you and Henry say Daniel has."

Daniel stroked her arm. "We can come back and visit every Christmas, but it's up to you. I don't want to live anywhere you aren't happy."

She surveyed the people watching her, then faced her uncle. "We'll come, but not until after Ysabel has her baby. I want to be here for that."

Her uncle threw his hands up. "I suppose I can find another project to keep me busy in the meantime."

She let go of Daniel and hugged her uncle again. "Thank you."

"Anything for my favorite niece."

After her aunt and uncle left with Alice, everyone sat around the table, drinking coffee and discussing plans for improvements to the cabins and the property around them. Among other things, it was agreed that a room would be added to Pa and Ysabel's cabin as soon as possible.

After a hearty dinner, they moved to the yard and Pa got out his harmonica. Andrew tapped a beat on the base of a bucket and Daniel asked Eliza to dance. She readily agreed. As the afternoon passed, the men took turns playing and whirling their wives about the yard.

Eventually, the setting sun urged them back inside where Maria served everyone a stew that had been simmering all day. When everyone had finished, Daniel stood and took her hand. "Come on." He lifted a candle from the mantle and led her outside.

As they walked toward Pa's cabin, her stomach somersaulted. She loved Daniel with all her heart, but everything had happened so fast. Was she ready for this? What did she know about being a bride? Pa never spoke of such things and she'd never braved asking Cecilia. All she knew were the bits and pieces she'd overheard while living in the mine camps. It seemed a very pleasurable thing for men. Plenty of them shelled out their last dime to spend time at the brothels, but she'd never seen a woman from there who seemed truly happy. The few wives she'd seen in the camps had seemed miserable—though that could have been a result of the mining conditions and have nothing to do with the matrimonial bed.

Eliza blinked. Ready or not, they were at Pa's cabin. *Lord, help me.*

Daniel opened the door and held it for her.

She peered at her skirt as she entered. She stopped next to the table, staring at the wall. Behind her, the door scraped closed. Daniel's boots thumped across the floor. Shadows flickered across the woven rug as he set the candle on the table beside her. He grasped her arms gently and turned her to face him.

"Don't worry, darling." He whispered though they were alone. "I love you and want to make you my wife in every sense, but I know this has happened fast. We don't have to do anything you don't want to do."

Her muscles unfurled like sails caught in the wind. "Thank you."

He rubbed her arms, smiling down at her. She rested her cheek on his shoulder, wrapping her arms around his waist. Incredible peace filled her. They stood holding each other for a long while as he rubbed her back. She listened to his heartbeat.

Thank you, Lord, for this wonderful man. Daniel would love and protect her and always consider her needs and wants. Lifting her face, she held his gaze. "I love you." The words felt so inadequate.

"I love you, too."

Though they stood wrapped in each other's arms, she wanted to be closer. Needed to be closer. She raised her lips and he lowered his head to meet her. Their breath mingled and she melted into him. The kiss continued and her hands roved across his back, pressing him closer still. His arms tightened around her as she moved her own to circle his neck and run her fingers through his hair.

I can't believe this wonderful man is my husband. And I'm free to love him, deeply, openly, for the rest of my life. How am I so blessed?

His lips left hers and trailed kisses along her jawline and down her neck.

"Daniel." Heat raced through her.

He tensed and pulled back, "I'm sorry. I—"

"No." She placed her palms on either side of his head, pulling his lips back to hers.

He combed his fingers through her hair.

Her hands slid down his chest and slipped around to his back. She pressed her body against his. Suddenly she understood what the Bible meant when it spoke of husbands and wives becoming one. She wanted to be one with Daniel.

She pulled back to hold his gaze. "Daniel, make me your wife."

His gaze searched hers. "Are you sure?"

She took his face in her hands. "Yes."

He stooped to lift her into his arms. Then he carried her to bed.

*E*liza surveyed the sprawling city of San Francisco from the deck of the *Goliah* as it dropped anchor in the bay. It was incredible how much the city had grown in just the short time she and Daniel had been away.

Living in such close quarters with Pa and Ysabel these past four months while sharing a bed with Daniel had been awkward, to say the least. Thankfully, they worked it out so that each couple had enjoyed time alone.

Noisy shouts from sailors as they secured ships, the rumble of drays running along the docks, and the chatter of busy people hustling to and fro, reminded her of how different their life would be from now on. She'd forever cherish the time she and Daniel had spent living in those peaceful mountains. Her bond with Ysabel had deepened, while Pa and Daniel grew to be great friends as they built the addition to the cabin.

A month ago, Ysabel delivered a healthy baby boy, whom Pa joyfully named Ashur. Eliza praised God for the love and happiness He had brought into their lives.

It had been difficult saying good-bye, but as the *Goliah's* gangplank lowered, she found herself raising onto her toes.

Daniel chuckled beside her. "I thought you weren't fond of this city."

"I'm not, but since it's to be your place of business, I've decided to at least *try* to like it." She squeezed the handle of her carpetbag. "But that's not why I'm excited."

"No?" The twinkle in his eye told her that he knew exactly what made her so eager to disembark.

She looked back toward the end of the dock. "Do you think he's arrived yet?"

"He's probably been waiting for hours."

"I hope you're right. I can't wait to see him."

Seconds later, the gangplank was in place and Eliza hurried down its rickety boards, Daniel on her heels.

As Eliza and Daniel reached the end of the wharf, her uncle hailed them from his carriage. She waved back as he jumped down and rushed to embrace her.

Uncle Henry offered Daniel a hand. "So glad to have you back, Daniel."

"Thank you, sir."

"The drayman's already loaded your things in the wagon and I've sent it ahead to the house." Henry gestured toward the carriage where Cecilia waited. "Shall we?"

Eliza turned to Daniel, but he was staring at the post office. He'd not received a single letter in San Diego. Might there be any waiting here? She nudged him. "Go on and check. I want to say hello to Frank."

Uncle Henry regarded the post office, then waved Daniel on. "Certainly. Go. We'll wait for you."

Eliza hurried toward Frank as Daniel strode toward the post office.

Heedless of the onlookers, Eliza threw her arms about Frank in a quick hug. "It's so good to see you again."

"Good to see you, Miss Brooks."

"It's Mrs. Clarke, now. Remember?"

"Mm-hm. I still think you done lost your senses in that ship-wreck." Frank assisted her into the carriage. "You was fit to spit spark that night he come to dinner. How'd you wind up married to him?"

Eliza laughed. "God, Frank. It was all God's doing."

"Well, so long as you're happy, I guess."

Daniel strode up to the carriage, a stack of letters tucked under his arm and one already open in his hands.

He climbed onto the bench beside her.

She pointed to the letter. "Good news?"

He grinned. "It's from Alice."

"How is she?" Eliza rubbed her dress where it pulled tight over her swollen belly. If she didn't let out the waist soon, she risked popping a seam.

"She's married." He skimmed the letter, then slapped his leg. "I knew it. Benjamin proposed the second she stepped on shore. But they waited a month to give the families time to prepare for the ceremony." He laughed. "She says there's an ounce of gold in my name waiting at the Wells Fargo Office."

Eliza chuckled. "Does she sound happy?"

"Very."

Thank you, Lord.

Frank clicked to the horses and they set off down the muddy streets, leaving the stench of the wharf behind.

Daniel folded the letter. "What about you, Mrs. Clarke? Are you happy?"

The carriage jerked to a halt and Frank clambered down to dig their wheel from the mud.

Her aunt scowled at her uncle. "I told you we should have taken the other route. This one always turns impassable after a storm."

Eliza tipped her head onto Daniel's shoulder. Her aunt may not have changed and there was no guarantee Eliza wouldn't face loss in the future, but she was forgiven, she was loved, and she was in the hands of her Heavenly Father.

She stretched up and pressed a kiss to her husband's lips. "I couldn't be happier."

Did you enjoy this book? We hope so!
Would you take a quick minute to leave a review where you purchased the book?
It doesn't have to be long. Just a sentence or two telling what you liked about the story!

Receive a FREE ebook and get updates when new Wild Heart books release: https://www.subscribepage.com/whbebook

FROM THE AUTHOR

Dear Reader,

Waltz in the Wilderness is a work of fiction, and any names, characters, businesses, places, events, locales, and incidents are either the products of the author's imagination or used in a fictitious manner. However, there are bits of history sprinkled throughout the story which many readers will find interesting.

The Ladies Protection and Relief Society was and *is* a real organization, established in 1853 by wives of influential citizens, that really did (among other things) aid women in distress by arranging comfortable homes and work situations with respectable families. I love that this organization is still around and doing good today. Please note: the names, personalities and motivations of those associated with The Ladies Protection and Relief Society as portrayed in *Waltz in the Wilderness* are entirely fictional.

The scene at the San Francisco Post Office was based on true accounts of its operations during the 1850s. Accounts such as an 1858 Hutchings' California Magazine article (https://www.s-fgenealogy.org/sf/history/hgpoh.htm) and a USPS document describing the history of the ladies' delivery windows (https://about.usps.com/who-we-are/postal-history/ladies-delivery-windows.pdf) that were in use from about 1830 to the early twentieth century were especially inspirational. While the San Francisco Post Office at this time had many windows for men, women were given a special window from which to retrieve their mail. If a woman was unable to retrieve her own mail, a designated male could stand in the women's line and retrieve the mail for her. However, the etiquette rules that I have Eliza taking advantage of in chapter two were based on actual expectations: any gentleman standing in the women's line was expected to give his place to any woman that arrived after him. So I have to imagine it would take a male *much* longer to retrieve a woman's correspondence than if she fetched it herself! In any case, it was very common for a person to wait hours in line at the post office.

One of my favorite people to include in this story was Lieutenant George Horatio Derby, a soldier, cartographer, cartoonist and humorist. Derby went by many pen names, including Squibob, which Uncle Henry mentioned in his conversation with Daniel in chapter three. While Lieutenant Derby was officially stationed in San Diego to head the project for diverting the San Diego River by building a dike, he also spent some time running the San Diego Herald in the temporary absence of the paper's owner. This term as editor of the local paper caused quite an uproar in the small town since his political views didn't exactly match those of the owner, but my favorite story is of the time he sent several tongue-in-cheek suggestions regarding the new design of the army's uniform to Secretary Jefferson. Unfortunately, Jefferson did not share Derby's sense of humor. To learn how things turned out and see images of Derby's uniform illustrations, you can visit my blog post at https://kathleendenly.com/2017/01/20/did-you-know-lt-george-horatio-derby/. And in case you are wondering, yes,

Derby really did rent that two-story white house from Don Bandini (also a real historical person).

While the *Virginia* was not the name of a ship which sailed the California coast during this time period, the steamship, *Goliah* (not a typo), which was mentioned near the end of chapter thirteen and again in the final chapter, was a real ship which serviced the California Coast in various capacities from 1851 to 1898. Of particular relevance to *Waltz in the Wilderness* is that the Goliah aided in the recovery of passengers and cargo following the wreck of the *Yankee Blade* off the Santa Barbara coast in the spring of 1854. At least one account tells of crewmembers becoming confused, resulting in the loss of a lifeboat filled with 21 passengers, 17 of whom perished. The *Goliah* took as many of the wreck's survivors as it could hold to San Diego before returning to retrieve the rest who had been left on shore.

In contemporary accounts, the captain of the *Yankee Blade* was painted in a very unflattering light which helped to inspire my unethical (fictional) Captain Swenson. (You can read more about the wreck of the *Yankee Blade* at https://tinyurl.com/y3s-nq3ms and https://tinyurl.com/y6ov6b5z.) The events of the shipwreck in *Waltz in the Wilderness* were inspired by the events of the *Yankee Blade's* wreck, combined with the events of another wreck involving a ship (one of many) stranded on the Zuniga Shoal near the mouth of the San Diego Bay and Point Loma. At least one of these San Diego wrecks was also aided by the *Goliah*. In case you were wondering, the Zuniga Shoal is located near the mouth of San Diego Bay, and is a natural bar of land, which is sometimes below and sometimes just above the surface of the water. It acts as an obstacle which makes navigating the mouth of the bay tricky enough to have required detailed instructions during the nineteenth century. You can see a map of the shoal's exact position at https://mapcarta.com/23168150.

The novel Eliza reads while waiting for Mrs. Swenson, *Woman in the Nineteenth Century*, is a real book. It was written by American journalist, editor and women's right advocate Margaret Fuller. Along with some ideas about the origins of depravity, the book presents ahead-of-her-time views on the treatment of Native and African Americans as well as the equality of men and women. While Fuller's ideas may not fully align with a Christian worldview, the tones of cultural defiance and female independence would have appealed to Eliza. You can read the full text of the book at http://www.gutenberg.org/files/8642/8642-h/8642-h.htm.

The *Playa* mentioned in the novel, is also known as *La Playa*. It was a collection of ramshackle buildings that primarily served as storage sheds for the cowhides awaiting export. Although there were a *very* few other businesses there, they often sat abandoned for lack of customers to sustain them.

George Tebbetts was a real man who actually ran The Exchange Hotel in San Diego in 1854. However, my portrayal of him and his wife are entirely fictional. Also, it is interesting to note that there is some debate regarding the correct spelling of his last name due to inconsistent spelling in local historical records.

With one minor exception, all of the buildings mentioned as being in San Diego, *were* in San Diego in 1854. I have described them as historically accurate as possible. The one exception is the store where Eliza and Daniel purchase their supplies. While there were stores in San Diego, this particular store (while based on the true stores there at the time) is entirely fictional and is run by the family of my heroine in *Sing in the Sunlight*. *Sing in the Sunlight* will be the second novel in the *Chaparral Hearts* series. (BTW—I can't wait for you to see how Richard Stevens meets his match!)

There is far more fascinating history to the San Diego Mission de Alcala than I can relate in this brief note, but I want to confirm that the United States Army truly did occupy the mission beginning after the Mexican-American War (1848) and ending in 1858. For photographs and details on how they used the sanctuary and treated the grounds in general, read my blog post at https://kathleendenly.com/2018/10/08/did-you-know-mission-basilica-san-diego-de-alcala-2/.

As you can see, I tried to remain as true to history as possible while maneuvering my characters through nineteenth century California. However, I did take a bit of artistic license during Eliza and Daniel's journey into the mountains. Two years prior to the start of this novel, certain clans of the Kumeyaay Nation were forced to relocate their village to a spot on the San Diego River which Eliza and Daniel would have walked straight through as they followed the river. Ultimately, I decided that including these Kumeyaay settlements would have slowed the story too much with details that didn't affect the overall plot. My nod to this decision is the moment when Eliza and Daniel spot the traveling group of "Indians" in chapter twenty-six. I hope it is clear that no offense was intended by this omission. I'm looking forward to sharing more about these unique First Peoples in *Sing in the Sunlight.*

Blessings,

Kathleen

ABOUT THE AUTHOR

Kathleen Denly lives in sunny Southern California with her loving husband, four young children, and two cats. As a member of the adoption and foster community, children in need are a cause dear to her heart and she finds they make frequent appearances in her stories. When she isn't writing, researching, or caring for children, Kathleen spends her time reading, visiting historical sites, hiking, and crafting.

If you enjoyed *Waltz in the Wilderness*, be sure to sign up for Kathleen's Readers' Club! KRC Members will be the first to know when *Sing in the Sunlight*, the second book in the *Chaparral Hearts* series, is scheduled to be released!

QUESTIONS FOR DISCUSSION

At the beginning of the novel, Jim Brooks is suffering from chronic depression due to the loss of his beloved wife and mother of his child. He is seeking happiness through staying busy and has become obsessed with finding enough gold to build the house he once promised Eliza's mother. Eliza is obsessed with restoring Jim's joy.

- Have you or anyone you know, ever experienced clinical depression? How did you/they handle it?
- What does the Bible say about grief, depression, and heavy hearts?
- What does the Bible say about joy?
- Have you ever struggled with witnessing a loved-one's suffering? How did you handle it?
- What does the Bible say about comfort?

At the end of chapter one, Jim Brooks leaves his daughter in the care of relatives whom she has just met because he believes they can do a better job of raising her than he is doing. Eliza vehemently disagrees with his decision.

- What do you think of Jim's decision and how he chose to leave?
- Have you ever had someone with good intentions make a decision on your behalf that you vehemently disagreed with?
- If you're a parent, what decisions have you made that you knew your child would strongly disagree with, but which you felt was in his/her best interests?

At this point in California's history, long distance communication was extremely unreliable and when a letter *was* successfully delivered, it was weeks or months after the sender sent it. The sole telegraph line in California at the time ran only from San Francisco to Marysville, California—a distance of approximately 130 miles. The connection to the rest of the country would not be completed until October 1861. Today, we have reliable postal service, emails, cell phones, and even video chatting which can make it seem that your relative living on the opposite side of the globe is standing in your living room.

- How do you think you would respond if our modern communication methods suddenly disappeared and you were left with only the communication methods available in 1854 California?
- How do you think the lack of efficient and reliable communication methods affected the characters in *Waltz in the Wilderness*?

As a result of Eliza's decision to take matters into her own hands, against the advice of her uncle, Eliza finds herself in a very vulnerable position. Her determination to solve her pa's problem of depression only creates more problems.

- Have you ever made a decision that left you unexpectedly vulnerable?
- Do you struggle with issues of control?
- Have you ever tried to fix someone else's problems?
- Have you ever prayed about something for so long that you wondered whether God was even listening?
- What does the Bible say about control?
- What does the Bible say about godly counsel?
- What does the Bible say about patience?

When the *Virginia* wrecks and Eliza's lifeboat capsizes, Eliza clings to the bag holding Mama's Bible—despite its weight threatening to drown her—until Daniel forces her to release it. The loss of Mama's Bible in exchange for Eliza's life triggers a panic attack brought on by the parallel of how, years prior, Mama exchanged her life for Eliza's during the wagon accident.

- Have you or anyone you know ever experienced a panic attack? What was it like and how did you/they manage it?
- What does the Bible say about fear and anxiety?

After the wreck, Daniel and Eliza have an illogical argument brought on by stress and adrenalin. The tension ends in hysterical laughter.

- Have you ever argued with someone over something that you both later agreed was a ridiculous thing to argue about?
- Have you ever experienced tension-releasing laughter?
- What does the Bible say about laughter?

The moment Eliza's carpet bag hit the ocean, Mama's Bible was ruined, but given the chance, Eliza would have kept the water-damaged book. For her, the importance of that Bible wasn't in its words (though those were clearly important), but in the person who'd once cherished it.

- Are you more likely to hold on to sentimental objects or toss aside anything damaged or nonfunctional?
- Is there anything you own that you wouldn't give up even though it was damaged or quit working?

Eliza's refusal to release the bag with Mama's Bible symbolized her refusal to release the guilt she carried regarding her role in Mama's death. This guilt affects every decision she makes, many of which go horribly awry.

- Have you ever carried guilt in a way that affected the decisions you made?
- Have you ever tried to make amends only to have your efforts backfire?
- What does the Bible say about guilt/shame and how is it different from conviction?
- What do you think helped Eliza eventually learn to release her guilt?

Today women travel alone on a regular basis, but Daniel and Eliza were raised to believe that women traveling alone are not only vulnerable, but their morality is subject to public suspicion and even condemnation. Thus, they go to great lengths in San Diego to conceal the fact that Eliza is traveling unescorted. Later, this extends to concealing that Daniel—an unmarried non-relative—is traveling with Eliza, unchaperoned.

In chapter nineteen, Daniel and Eliza have an open discussion regarding lies and deception, during which Daniel justifies not correcting Tebbetts's assumption about their travel plans, by paraphrasing, in part, the King James translation of 1 Thessalonians 5:22 "Abstain from all appearance of evil."

- How does the King James translation of 1 Thess. 5:22 differ from more modern translations, such as the ESV, NIV, or NASB?
- What do you think of Daniel's application of this verse and do you think he might have acted differently had he had one of our more modern translations?
- What do you think of the methods Daniel and Eliza employed to pull off the concealment of their traveling plans?
- What is the difference between deception and secrecy?
- How do you think you would handle the social expectations and pressures of this time period?

Which characters in *Waltz in the Wilderness* did you empathize with and which characters did you dislike?

Did your feelings about any of the characters change over the course of the story?

How does this book compare to other historical Christian romance novels you've read?

Which parts of this story did you find fresh or unique?

Did the story take you anywhere you haven't been before or portray an issue in a new light?

Were there any parts of history or culture included that were new to you?

Did this story challenge you or your perceptions in any way?

Did reading this story help you understand someone better, or even yourself?

What do you think happens when Alice returns to Benjamin in Massachusetts?

What did you think of Richard Stevens? Would you like to read how he meets his match in *Sing in the Sunlight*? Who do you think would make a good match for Richard?

If you love historical romance, check out the other Wild Heart books!

Marisol ~ Spanish Rose by Elva Cobb Martin

Escaping to the New World is her only option...Rescuing her will wrap the chains of the Inquisition around his neck.

Marisol Valentin flees Spain after murdering the nobleman who molested her. She ends up for sale on the indentured servants' block at Charles Town harbor—dirty, angry, and with child. Her hopes are shattered, but she must find a refuge for herself and the child she carries. Can this new land offer her the grace, love, and security she craves? Or must she escape again to her only living relative in Cartagena?

Captain Ethan Becket, once a Charles Town minister, now sails the seas as a privateer, grieving his deceased wife. But when he takes captive a ship full of indentured servants, he's intrigued by the woman whose manners seem much more refined than the average Spanish serving girl. Perfect to become governess for his young son. But when he sets out on a quest to find his captured sister, said to be in Cartagena, little does he expect his new Spanish governess to stow away on his ship with her six-month-old son. Yet her offer of help to free his sister is too tempting to pass up. And her beauty, both inside and out, is too attractive for his heart to protect itself against—until he learns she is a wanted murderess.

As their paths intertwine on a journey filled with danger, intrigue, and romance, only love and the grace of God can overcome the past and ignite a new beginning for Marisol and Ethan.

~

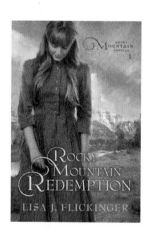

Rocky Mountain Redemption by Lisa J. Flickinger

A Rocky Mountain logging camp may be just the place to find herself.

To escape the devastation caused by the breaking of her wedding engagement, Isabelle Franklin joins her aunt in the Rocky Mountains to feed a camp of lumberjacks cutting on the slopes of Cougar Ridge. If only she could out run the lingering nightmares.

Charles Bailey, camp foreman and Stony Creek's itinerant pastor, develops a reputation to match his new nickname — Preach. However, an inner battle ensues when the details of his rough history threaten to overcome the beliefs of his young faith.

Amid the hazards of camp life, the unlikely friendship growing between the two surprises Isabelle. She's drawn to Preach's brute strength and gentle nature as he leads the ragtag crew toiling for Pollitt's Lumber. But when the ghosts from her past return to haunt her, the choices she will make change the course of her life forever—and that of the man she's come to love.

Made in the USA
Columbia, SC
08 February 2020